The Godell Prism

RAYMOND HAN

Little Rocket Books

Web site: www.raymondhan.net
Email: raymond@raymondhan.net

Little Rocket Books, Singapore

**National Library Board, Singapore
Cataloguing-in-Publication Data**
Han, Raymond, 1958-
The Godell Prism / Raymond Han. –
Singapore : Little Rocket Books, 2014.
pages cm
ISBN : 978-981-09-0369-5 (paperback)
1. Treasure troves – Fiction. 2. Teenagers –
Fiction. I. Title.
PR9570.S53
S823 -- dc23   OCN879146468

DEDICATION

To my dearest Cindy, who has been my guiding light in life. Her selfless love and encouragement have given me the inspiration to complete this my first novel.

VISIT THE AUTHOR'S WEB SITE

Find out more about Raymond Han on his Web site
at www.raymondhan.net

CONTENTS

ABOUT THE AUTHOR

Raymond Han is a late baby boomer in Singapore. He has worked as a banker, an editor and a teacher. After he left the banking sector, he found a second career teaching English Language to upper and lower secondary students in Victoria School, Montfort Secondary School, Greendale Secondary School and Hougang Secondary School.

Raymond also taught English at 'O' Level and General Paper to students in a private school for several years. He has a Specialist Diploma in Psychology (Counselling Psychology).

Besides teaching, Raymond has written two books for young adults. The first, a short-story compilation entitled 'Spice of Life: Singapore Short Stories', traces the trials and tribulations of some ordinary youngsters living in different periods of time in Singapore's modern history, from the late sixties and early seventies, through to the eighties and nineties. The second, 'Essential Guide to O-level English Composition', aims to help students build a systematic approach to tackling essay writing for the GCE O-level English Language paper. It incorporates a step-by-step method to teach students to write better paragraphs and essays.

Two of his short stories appear in Life Accents, an English Language textbook for upper secondary, in Singapore.

1 *GETTING ALONG*

Just one more round to go and he could stop, Jing Yang thought to himself as he panted along the pavement. Jing Yang hated these morning runs around the perimeter of his school. It had been seven months since he stepped foot into this school and he had been hating every moment. He hated just about everything to do with the school. First and foremost, he hated the fact that the school did not allow the use of mobile phones. Why, it even banned the possession of mobile phones. He was completely lost without his trusty Nokia N1800. Montfort Secondary School – the school he had been transferred from – was loads better. At least, he could bring his Nokia N1800 to school, though he was not allowed to use it in class.

It was Jing Yang's mother's idea for him to change schools so he could be in the same school as his cousin, Tim, who had just relocated to Singapore. Jing Yang's mother wanted him to get along with his cousin and also help keep an eye on him as he was two years older than Tim. But the two of them were perfect strangers. How could his mother expect him to treat his cousin as a buddy? What made things worse was that Tim was an *Angmoh* – well, at least half-an-*Angmoh* anyway. Tim was his mother's older sister's son. Aunt Dorothy had married an Englishman hailing from Norfolk in the East of England, he was told by his mother. Tim was the couple's only child. Tim had spent many of his growing years in England, and received his education in a comprehensive state school. Norfolk was a predominantly rural county in England so Tim was not used to city living. It would take him some months to settle in here in Singapore.

Jing Yang's mother's instructions were very clear. Both boys had to go to school together and keep each other company. Period. No buts about it. Now, to Jing Yang, that was no mean task!

A loud honk jolted Jing Yang out of his thoughts. Jing Yang turned the corner of the road. Finally, the school gate was in sight. He jogged past a big sign reading 'Greendale Secondary School'. A security guard was on hand to help stop traffic as Jing Yang and other students streamed through the gates. Jing Yang heaved a sigh of relief as he trudged into the driveway. One quick turn, and he was already in the quadrangle. There were no signs of his classmates among the runners fanning out into the quadrangle. Gee! Was he really the first from 3E3 to finish the run? He had been too engrossed in his thoughts earlier to take any notice.

Jing Yang threw himself onto the floor adjacent to the canteen. He rolled over, wiped his sweat with the sleeves of his T-shirt and propped his back against a pillar. Soon, he was staring into space. He was now totally exhausted.

'Jing Yang. Jing Yang.'

'Jing Yang, don't dream. Gosh! It's only 7.55am, for goodness' sake,' exclaimed Angelina.

Angelina Goh was Jing Yang's classmate. A sweet-looking girl with shoulder-long hair which she would invariably tie into a neat bundle on the back of her head, allowing it to bob along as she moved around during school hours, Angelina was the centre of attraction both in class and at school.

'Don't forget my birthday this Sunday,' Angelina said.

'I won't – not with you reminding me every other day,' quipped Jing Yang.

'Aw! Don't be like that! I was merely afraid that you would not turn up.'

'It's only a joke! Don't be upset. You won't look pretty any more wearing that sulky look.'

Jing Yang had a way with words. He could hurt people one moment and then make them smile the next. But, as an intelligent boy, surely, he could not have missed sensing this girl had a crush on him. She would always speak up for him when their classmates poked fun at him for being dreamy and not paying attention in class. They also took issue with what they perceived to be his lofty attitude. Only Angelina knew it was because he was a loner, preferring to be left alone to his thoughts. It was not that he was autistic and therefore withdrawn from the world. It was just that with his parents away from home much of the time, he had gotten used to being by himself – to the extent that he was not at ease with company. Sure, he was living with his grandma, but other than accompanying her at meals, he would be holed up in his bedroom. His room pretty much had everything a boy his age would fancy – a mini-fridge stocked with his favourite Coca-Cola and Mars bars; a personal computer and a notebook computer; a hi-fi system; and more!

The last remark made Angelina's face light up. She was temperamental, but easily pleased. She had no airs about her though she was easily the prettiest girl in secondary three in school.

Their form teacher, Miss Lee, was standing in front of them now. She was taking a headcount of her students before they headed for the classroom. Miss Lee's eyes met Jing Yang's.

'The principal wants to see you in her office now,' she said, 'Leave your bag with Angelina. She will take it to class for you. Go quickly now. And tuck in your shirt.'

Jing Yang walked the length of the quadrangle, at times pausing to give way to the snaking columns of students heading for their classrooms. Outside the general office, it was a hive of activity. There were students seated at three evenly spaced desks placed alongside the entrance to the office. These were the ones being punished. Jing Yang had done duty behind one of these desks quite a few times and he did not quite relish the idea. Suddenly, it struck him that he might be spending that morning at one of these desks.

'Here you are, Jing Yang,' a voice rang out from behind him.

It was Mrs Tan, the principal.

'Come along. I don't have much time to spare but talk to you I must,' said she.

The principal's office was tucked away in a quiet corner, two rooms away from the general office. From her desk, she had an uncluttered view of the quadrangle and the canteen.

'Take a seat.'

'Now, I am sure you know why I have asked for you. Tell me why you did what you did yesterday afternoon.'

'I…I.'

'I really have no time for your mutterings.'

'Er... It was afternoon time, ma'am.'

'So?'

'It was after school hours and I was in Punggol Plaza taking my lunch. That's when Mr Lau caught me using my mobile phone, ma'am.'

'You are not answering my question, Jing Yang.'

'I mean, I was not using the mobile phone in school. I know it's banned in school so I didn't use it in school.'

'So you used your mobile phone in a shopping centre after school hours, and you really think in all honesty that you did not break the school rules. Am I right, Jing Yang?'

'Er… Yes! Ma'am.'

'Jing Yang. You are a bright boy. I am sure you know what you did was wrong and why as well.'

There was silence in the room.

'Well. Don't keep me waiting. I haven't got all day you know.'

'Ma'am, I…'

'For goodness' sake, stop sputtering. There's nothing wrong with you. Just own up and I will let it go at that. Just this once.'

'Ma'am. I know I was wrong in bringing my mobile phone to school yesterday morning, and hiding it from my teachers.'

'That's the way to behave – like a man, Jing Yang.'

'Yes. Ma'am.'

'Are you going to do it again?'

'No. Ma'am.'

'All right! This time, I will let you off. Don't let me see another report like this – or else.'

'Yes. Ma'am.'

'Good! Now, go back to your class – and when you are free today, write an essay reflecting on what you did wrong yesterday. Give it to your form teacher tomorrow. Now leave the room.'

'Thank you. Ma'am.'

Mrs Tan had been using this approach for several years now. Rather than punish her students for doing wrong things, she made them come out front and confess their misdeeds. This method, she thought, was good in that it made her students realise that owning up was not a bad thing to do. In fact, it was the right thing to do. It was far better than letting them lie their way out of their wrong doings and then thinking they could wriggle out of all their problems just by lying. That would not be a good solution for problems they would meet once they left school and entered society. In school, they always had second chances, but not so in society. So she saw it as her duty to imbue in her students the right attitude, even if it meant that she had to spend quality time with each and every offending student of hers. To her, it was well worth the effort and the time spent.

In her heart, she empathised with Jing Yang for carrying his mobile phone to school. Her own daughter carried a mobile phone to school and it was this useful device that enabled her to track her daughter's movements throughout the day. She felt safe knowing that her daughter was just a phone call away. Even if she was busy running the school, she could always spare some time SMSing her daughter to keep in touch. This, she thought, in a small way made up for her lack of quality time with her daughter. Being a principal was a tough vocation and it was certainly not easy being a parent and a school principal at the same time.

But she could not rescind the rule banning mobile phones in school out of deference to her predecessor who had started the rule in 2005. Her predecessor had been her mentor at one time and she was thankful for his guidance. She had experienced some tough times as a novice vice-principal at another school and it was he who had got her out of some pricky situations. She did not want to be seen as being an ungrateful person who had no qualms about tearing down rules laid down by her mentor.

To Mrs Tan, Jing Yang was not a bad boy. He just needed some nudging occasionally to steer him back on track. Today's meeting with him was sort of a pep talk to remind this boy that there was someone in school who was concerned about him and what he was doing. Jing Yang's parents could not be around to keep an eye on him so Mrs Tan was acting on their behalf. This boy could go far, Mrs Tan thought to herself. She had a special file which she kept on several students whom she needed to keep tabs on. Jing Yang's cousin, Tim, was the latest addition to the list. It was she who had agreed to Tim's admission to her school. Having worked as a volunteer for the Singapore

International Foundation some years back, Mrs Tan was supportive of the reintegration of foreign-born Singaporeans in local schools.

There was a knock on her door. She glanced at the doorway. Standing there was a lanky boy with curly hair tucked neatly behind the ears.

'Yes, Tim, come in and take a seat,' she said. 'So, how are you adapting to the school?'

'Okay, I guess,' he replied.

'Do you have any problems with your teachers?'

'No, ma'am.'

'Do you have any problems with your classmates?'

'No, ma'am.'

'I don't seem to be getting anywhere with this line of questioning.' Mrs Tan paused for a moment to gather her thoughts.

'Tim, your form teacher has been telling me you keep to yourself in class. Your subject teachers say you keep a straight face during lessons so much so they do not know whether you are not paying attention or do not understand their lessons.'

The young boy was now fidgeting in his seat. He had begun to slide his fingers along his hips. There was a silence in the room.

'Tim, I am not reprimanding you now. I merely want to find out what's wrong so that I can help you.'

'Say something.'

'Were you also like this in school back in England?'

'Looks like you do not like to talk, Tim.'

'Who are you living with now, Tim?' Mrs Tan had changed the subject matter. She thought that if she could not get the boy to contribute feedback this way, she had to change tack.

'My mum, ma'am.'

'Are both of you staying by yourselves?'

'No. With my grandma, cousin and aunt.'

'You mean – Jing Yang?'

'Yes, ma'am.'

'I see. So both of you must be getting along well, I guess.'

'Sort of, ma'am.'

'There is no need to keep addressing me as ma'am now. It gets in the way of our conversation.'

'Yes, ma'am.'

'Do you come to school together?'

'Yes.'

'And go home together?'

'Yes.'

'Now, we are getting somewhere.'

'But, both of you are in different standards, with lessons ending at different times – so how do you get to go back together?'

'It's my mum's instructions. We have to come to school together and go home together.'

'Is Jing Yang easy to get along with?'

'We do our own things.'

'What do you mean by that?'

'Well, he minds his own business and I mind mine.'

'So that's how you get along?'

'Yes.'

'I see. Do you miss England? Do you miss your friends there?'

'Yes, I reckon I do.'

'You do know why your parents want you to come over to Singapore, don't you?'

'Sort of.'

'Sort of?'

'I mean they want me to get used to this place so it will be easier when I do national service.'

'I see.'

'Did they tell you this?'

'Nope. I sort of guess so.'

'Well. I think your parents didn't want you to forget that you are a Singaporean – that you belong in this land.

They didn't want you to spend too much time in England in case you liked it so much you would rather remain there for the rest of your life.'

'Do you understand what I am saying, Tim?'

'Yes.'

'Good.'

'So in order to belong in this land, you need to adapt to the surroundings.'

'Yes.'

'And the people around you.'

'Yes.'

'I am glad you now understand, Tim. That's why your teachers –and I too – hope you can get along with your classmates.'

'Yes.'

'Can you give it a try, Tim?'

'Yes.'

'Good. Now, for a start, just smile a little more often in class. When people around you see you smiling, they will respond warmly. Can you do this for me, Tim?'

'Yes.'

'I am not asking you to jump in and start a party with your classmates. Just be natural. Be yourself.'

'Sure.'

'That's better.'

'Was Jing Yang here just now, ma'am?'

'Yes,' said Mrs Tan. 'Come to think of it, I seem to have forgotten to do something.'

'Oh! That's it! I knew there was something I had forgotten to do.'

Mrs Tan pulled out a drawer at her desk and retrieved a mobile phone which she then passed to Tim.

'Tim, on your way back to class, please stop by Jing Yang's class and return this to him for me. Tell him next time he won't be so lucky.'

With that, she dismissed Tim and got on with her work. She had already spent an hour mentoring two young men and the pile of paperwork on her desk had yet to be dealt with.

Tim walked out of the room, and made for the next block. He did not like having to sit in the principal's office and listen to her dishing out all that advice. He had no need for such advice. In England, he never once had the dubious honour of stepping into the principal's office. He had never given anyone any trouble whether in England or in Singapore and was surprised at the way things were handled here. Over in Norfolk Junior, he would have been cited for exemplary behaviour.

Was it anybody's business that he preferred to keep to himself? Had he not done the work given by his teachers? Why were they such busybodies? He was simply puzzled by the culture of this new school.

Tim thought to himself it would take him forever to get used to school life in Singapore. He still had a long way to go – he was now only in secondary one.

'Oh drat!' he said under his breath, 'I just went past his class.'

Tim was now on the third level. He turned around and walked towards the main doorway to 3E3. There seemed to be a teacher in the class as Tim could hear a woman's voice. The double-leaved doors to the classroom were open and as soon as Tim stepped up to the doorway, Miss Shih came into view. He knocked on the door. Miss Shih turned her head to take a quick glance but she did not stop talking to the class. She was ignoring this visitor to the classroom. Tim knocked again. This time, Miss Shih appeared a little annoyed.

'Can't you see I am addressing the class?'

'Couldn't you have come back later?'

'Sorry, Miss Shih – I need to see Jing Yang.'

Miss Shih put down the book she was holding and, with a quick flicking of an index finger and then a thumb gesture, motioned to Jing Yang to go to the doorway to see the visitor. She then continued with her lesson.

Tim handed to Jing Yang the mobile phone which he had been holding, said a quick thank you to Miss Shih and dashed down the corridor. He did not even bother to check whether Miss Shih was listening. He had heard about this fierce teacher and did not want to stay long enough to incur her wrath for whatever reason she might come up with.

'Jing Yang, what's that in your hand?' asked Miss Shih. She had caught sight of the mobile phone Jing Yang was slipping into a pocket.

'Don't you know mobile phones are banned in school? How dare you bring your mobile phone to school!'

Miss Shih was now glaring at Jing Yang.

'Give me the mobile phone,' she ordered.

Jing Yang, who had not been given any opportunity to utter a reply, glared back at her. This teacher liked to pick on her students and they were all afraid of getting into her bad books. But he was not going to let her bully him. After all, he was not in the wrong.

'How dare you glare at me like that,' said Miss Shih.

Though Jing Yang's face was contorted in anger, he resisted the urge to shout at the teacher. That would earn him some time in detention class and he did not want to stay back in school longer than necessary. He bit his lips and looked away. He was no longer glaring at her. He had shut off his mind.

'I said – give me the mobile phone.'

Miss Shih's voice had become louder. But Jing Yang was ignoring her altogether.

The entire class was quiet as every student was watching to see who would win the faceoff. This was not the first time Jing Yang was behaving like this. When he stood his ground, it was almost always because he had a valid argument and he would pursue it to the very end regardless of the consequences. To him right was right and wrong was wrong, and the difference was as clear as the colours black and white. Some would misconstrue this as stubbornness – a flaw in his character. But, he did not care a hoot whether the teacher blacklisted him, and other teachers caught in this situation with him would invariably back down, not wanting to appear unreasonable in class. They knew too well that it was difficult to win an argument with Jing Yang. This boy was no pushover. Moreover, he had brilliant parents who were scientists. They did not want to risk entanglement with his parents who, though out-stationed most of the time, had in the recent past written to the school to protest against some teachers who they claimed were biased against their son. Jing Yang liked to blog about his 'mis-adventures' in school and his parents were faithful readers of his blog. It was through this blog that they got wind of their son's problems at school and elsewhere.

But, Miss Shih was different. She was not bothered about public opinion, least of all the opinions of her students. To her, in class she was the authority and she always flaunted this perception. She also did not want to lose. Today, she thought she could not lose. After all, it was a school rule that mobile phones were not allowed in school. Period. There was no way this boy could wriggle out of the situation. She did not like it that Jing Yang had the audacity to stare at her. To her, this was total disrespect. She was determined to have this boy punished this time. She was not going to back down. She already had a bad impression of Jing Yang who she thought did not hold her in high regard. She did not like the way he glared at her when she was in his class. This was a deadly sin in her eyes. Now was a perfect opportunity to bring him down a few pegs.

'You have disobeyed my order, Jing Yang. This is a serious offence which merits caning.'

'Class chairman – please keep the class quiet while I take this boy to see the principal.'

'Jing Yang, come with me.'

Miss Shih picked up her things and stomped out of the

classroom. With every few steps, she paused to see that Jing Yang was following her. She was fuming mad. This boy had challenged her orders in front of her class and she was determined to seek caning for what she deemed to be gross disrespect. By now, students in 3E3 were craning their necks out of the two classroom doorways to peek at the two of them as they straggled to the staircase at the end of the block.

At the bottom of the block, Miss Shih saw the principal walking past the classrooms across the courtyard. She quickened her steps and finally caught up with the principal.

'Mrs Tan. Mrs Tan.'

Mrs Tan stopped and turned around.

'Yes, Miss Shih?'

'Mrs Tan, I want to talk to you about Jing Yang.'

Miss Shih pointed at Jing Yang who was now standing next to them.

'What have you done now, Jing Yang? Haven't you learnt anything from our meeting earlier this morning?'

Jing Yang was silent. He held his head down.

'Mrs Tan, this boy brought his mobile phone to school today. When I asked him to hand over the mobile phone to me, he refused to do so. He even glared at me!'

'That was rude of you, Jing Yang. I do not tolerate rudeness in my school. Now, apologise to your teacher.'

'Sorry, Miss Shih.'

'See? All settled. Actually, Miss Shih, I was the one who asked his cousin to hand the mobile phone to him just now. I wasn't free to return it to him personally. He isn't totally at fault.'

Mrs Tan knew that Miss Shih liked to talk down to her students and though she disagreed with the way Miss Shih handled her charges, she could not embarrass her in front of them. With just a few sentences, she had diffused the situation without any loss of face to both parties. Many years of experience and lessons learnt from earlier mistakes in handling teachers and students went into forging this set of people management skills.

Mrs Tan remembered early in her career as a teacher she had the misfortune to meet with some really bad students who were bent on defying her just for kicks. Why, one of them – a secondary four express student – mocked every sentence she made when she first came into his class. He seemed to be enjoying making fun of her – using her as a tool to entertain his classmates. Not being able to rein in the boy, she told him to follow her to the vice-principal's office and this boy, instead of tagging along with a subdued look, was happily sauntering along the corridors of the school ahead of her. When he saw the vice-principal making his rounds, he ran over to him and spoke to him like a friend, complaining about her. By the time she approached the two of them, the vice-principal was reprimanding the boy for being disrespectful. The boy was standing there wearing a forlorn look. Then the vice-principal led the boy to his office for caning. She just stood alongside them, enjoying the free show, not needing to utter a single word. Now that sort of student deserved to be caned, not Jing Yang! How could Miss Shih, who had more than ten years of experience, place Jing Yang in the same category as those audaciously rude students who regularly defied authority for the thrill of it.

'Go back to class, Jing Yang.'

'Thank you, ma'am,' said Jing Yang.

Mrs Tan turned to Miss Shih.

'Miss Shih, how's the preparation for national day celebrations getting on?'

Seeing Jing Yang still standing with them, Mrs Tan waved him off.

Jing Yang entered the toilet next to the language labs on the second level. It was a place where he would find refuge in whenever he encountered a problem which needed a quick fix. He shut the door in a corner cubicle adjacent to the standing urinals. He could think clearly in this – his favourite – cubicle in the toilet. Overhead, through a casement window, he could hear the traffic moving along the street. He leaned against a partition wall. He had to think of a way out. Though Mrs Tan had apparently settled the problem for him today, he somehow felt that Miss Shih would be declaring an all-out war against him. He could no longer be safe in her geography class. He had gotten away safely today. But, there were still one and a half years to go in her class. He was sure he would not be as lucky the next time – not if she was determined to find fault with him. He had to switch to another elective subject.

At the beginning of the school year, he had chosen geography as he hated history – the only other elective subject available in this school. He had had two years of history in secondary one and two. He found it a boring subject, studying about dead old people. Alexander the Great, Pu Yi, the silk route and World War Two were all too distant to him. They were long gone from this earth. What use had he of the knowledge gained? But now, he realised he was beginning to hate geography even more than history and it did not even have anything to do with the subject. Somehow, he had to get his parents to agree to a change of subject late that night. It would be early morning in New York. He could sleep late that night. Nothing else was more important. He would work on his argument for the proposed change in subject that evening. He was sure he could convince his parents.

Besides geography, Miss Shih also taught English – but in the lower secondary levels. There was no way their paths would meet for the remainder of his stay at Greendale Secondary. He marvelled at the thought that he would soon be free of Miss Shih's grasps. Jing Yang had heard stories of other students in secondary four who had suffered under Miss Shih. He did not fancy being enlisted by her as her next victim – not if he could help it.

'Ring...Ring.' The bell for the next period had rung.

Two periods of geography had ended. It was now one period of English, after which it would be recess time.

Jing Yang was at home with English. He did not have to lift a finger to ace the subject. He had gotten straight As since primary school. The boy hurried to his classroom for the lesson.

Angelina who was attending history elective class had returned to 3E3. She had heard from her classmates what had happened when she was away. She was worried for Jing Yang.

'Why is he always so stubborn?' Angelina thought to herself as she got behind her desk.

'Poor Jing Yang! Miss Shih is going to make mince meat out of him this time,' she mumbled. She decided that she would meet him after school to talk about this incident.

The remainder of the school day was a breeze to Jing Yang. Soon it was the end of the last period. It was Monday so all classes ended at 1.35pm today. When the bell rang for dismissal, the whole school became noisy. It was mayhem now as students emptied into the corridors and made their way down the stairs. They were all in a hurry. It was as if they had not left the school building in a month.

The two cousins had agreed to meet at the open area next to the staircase, in front of the art and music rooms. When Jing Yang reached the place, Tim was already at a study table – one of several lined up along the walkway. He was resting his head on his bag, waiting for him.

'Wait for me, Jing Yang,' cried Angelina who was a few steps behind Jing Yang. Apparently, she had followed him all the way from 3E3.

'Not again!' Jing Yang said.

'Well, we live just two blocks away from each other. I don't see why we can't go home together. You are a gentleman, aren't you, Jing Yang? Surely you are not going to let this girl go home all by herself, right?'

'You can tag along – if you want to. But, let's get this clear – I am not going to entertain you all the way home.'

'Sure!'

'Can we move off now? I am hungry already,' said Tim. His mum would prepare lunch for both of them every Monday, knowing that they would be back early. Tim was anxious to return home early today as every Monday was pork chops day. His mum cooked the most delicious pork chops with apple sauce. Just thinking about it was causing his stomach to rumble.

'Can't we go now?' Tim was getting impatient.

'Okay. Okay. Let's go.'

The threesome walked out of the side gate, and headed for the bus-stop along the main road. It was searing hot here in Punggol. Hougang was much cooler. They had reached a bend in the road when Angelina saw their bus approaching the bus-stop.

'The bus is here! Quick! Let's make a run for it.'

All three dashed towards bus service number 136 which would take them to Upper Serangoon Road, near where they lived.

'Phew! It certainly is hot!'

'Yeah! I am sweating all over.'

'Tim, come sit with us in the back seat.'

'You two lovebirds can sit there. I will sit here by myself.'

'Tim, we are not lovebirds, okay?'

'Oh Jing Yang. Be a sport! Tim was just joking with you. Can't you see that?'

'I know. I know. I just want all of us to know that.'

'Oh, look! Jing Yang. There's a *pasar malam* along the road.' Angelina was pointing to a row of make-shift stalls being set up along the roadside pavement.

'Shall we go there this evening?' she continued.

There was no answer from Jing Yang. But, he would surely go along with her – as sure as night followed day.

The rest of the journey on the bus was a quiet affair.

Tim had propped his legs up against the backrest of the seat in front of him. His legs were too long to fit in the space between the seats. He was enjoying a little shuteye. Jing Yang and Angelina were two seats behind, in the end row. With Angelina next to him, Jing Yang was feeling a little uncomfortable. He had long been accustomed to being by himself and this girl was now intruding into his private space. But, he could not tell her to leave him alone. He did not want to hurt her. Though Angelina was a happy-go-lucky type of person, she was prone to breaking into tears – especially when she thought she had been ignored. Jing Yang pretended to be asleep. This way, he did not have to make conversation with her. Angelina was enjoying herself. She was one who was easy to please. As long as someone she cared much about was with her, it did not matter to her whether he kept quiet throughout the journey. She had plenty of time to change him, she thought to herself.

Let us be clear – Angelina was not one who would throw herself at a boy. Angelina was not the type of girl who routinely went beyond platonic relationships with members of the opposite sex. Although it was now a trend for teenagers her age to go steady with boys and oftentimes be into an intimate relationship – and girls were under peer pressure to be in a boy-girl relationship by the age of fifteen or be a square, Angelina was not one of these teenagers and neither was Jing Yang. These two could be described as a rare breed indeed – teenagers who valued friendship more than sexual relationships. Granted, both of them were at the peak of pubescence and thus susceptible to peer influences – yet, they remained grounded to the realities of life; both were too young and immature to be in a sexual relationship. Also, they were wary of becoming teenage parents. A nearby school last year had seen two secondary four students become young parents after engaging in unprotected sex at each other's homes. They had no wish to be in this year's statistics.

But, in the first place, Angelina and Jing Yang had not yet started a platonic relationship, let alone indulge in an intimate one. There was no physical desire between them at this early stage, for they were not in love – yet – so it was really premature to talk about affairs of the heart. Today, Angelina was merely interested in getting to know Jing Yang better. She felt that he was one who could be trusted – he was honest and harboured no ill intentions when they were together, unlike some of the other boys in school who had arms like an octopus, ever ready to wrap her around them. These boys were up to no good. They were more interested in adding her to their list of conquests than striking up an intelligent conversation with her. She felt at ease when she was with Jing Yang.

As for Jing Yang, having come from a boys' school, he was wary of relationships with girls. He was ill at ease with girls. Here at Greendale Secondary, he just thought of them as fellow students who happened to wear skirts. He never thought of them as young attractive girls wearing uniforms. Actually, Jing Yang was insecure when dealing with any type of relationship. He tended to be detached and withdrawn from others – in short, he valued his privacy. It would take some doing for Angelina to break the ice with Jing Yang. But the effort would be worth it – both complemented each other in character and would make a compatible couple when they were older. They were about to start on a course of action which would bring them closer and help them find direction in life. For now, the twosome were just content with being classmates.

'Jing Yang, do you think I can join you guys for lunch?'

'I love to eat pork chops. Can I? Can I, please?'

'I don't know. I don't know whether there is enough food to go around. Ask Tim! His mum is doing the cooking.'

'Tim! Tim!'

Angelina went to sit next to Tim.

'Please ask your mother whether I can come for lunch.'

Without as much as a reply, Tim dug out his mobile phone and dialled home. Students at Greendale Secondary were not supposed to bring their mobile phones to school, yet these three students chose to ignore the rule and preferred to take their chances. It was difficult for them to live without their mobile phones. Of course, it helped that the school would only do a check for mobile phones once every two weeks so they could get away with bringing their mobile phones to school much of the time. The next check for mobile phones would most likely take place next Monday – a week away from today. The school rarely strayed from this arrangement. It was as if the school was clandestinely condoning the possession of mobile phones at school.

'Mum, Jing Yang's classmate wants to have lunch at our place. Can she?'

'Did you say she?'

'Yes, Mum. Her name is Angelina.'

'Is she the girl living near us?'

'Yes.'

'Okay, Tim. I cooked extra today. She can come. Are you on the way back now?'

'Yes, Mum. Bye Mum.'

'My mum says you can come.'

'Thanks, Tim.'

Angelina returned to the rear seat.

'Okay. Settled. I can come.'

Jing Yang did not reply. He appeared nonchalant. He was busy tapping his bag with an index finger. That was his style. He would pretend not to care a hoot. He did not want anyone to come away with the impression that he was happy with company. Secretly, he thought that having company was not a bad thing. Being a detached teenager sometimes left him feeling isolated. His peers thought he was aloof. Some even thought that he looked down on them. So they left him alone to his thoughts. This was sometimes a blessing in disguise. They would not ask him to join their gang or take up smoking. He would be free of such bad peer influences and his parents never needed to worry about him. But, when he was alone, he sometimes felt the pain of feeling lonely and longed for someone to reach out to him. Being the type of person he was, he would never open his mouth to ask for company. He was too proud to admit he needed friends. So, having a classmate such as Angelina surely helped him become comfortable with having people around him. He could not be alone forever.

Although he and Tim were now living under the same roof, they seldom connected with each other. Perhaps, it was because both were similar in character. Was it a hereditary trait? Both boys' mothers were sisters! It did not help matters that they were living in a big house so they seldom saw each other, except at mealtime.

To get these two boys to open up and become bosom friends, it would take an outsider such as Angelina – someone who gave warmth without any ulterior motive, someone the boys needed not be wary of, and someone who could act as a go-between.

Bus service 136 arrived at the bus-stop in front of the Nativity Church in Upper Serangoon Road. The three schoolmates alighted the bus and walked up Lorong Low Koon and then turned into Hai Sing Close. The boys' home was the first house in the street – a three-storey semi-detached house. From where they were standing, they could see the block of flats Angelina was living in. It was only two blocks away.

'Is this where you live? *Wah*! It sure is big!'

It was Angelina's first visit to the place. She knew Jing Yang lived near her, but she did not know that he was living on landed property.

'Boy! You sure are rich! *Wah*!'

'As if everyone living in landed property is rich. Young lady, it belongs to my parents, not me.'

'Mum. We are back!' Tim had already opened the front

door and entered the living room.

Angelina and Jing Yang were still in the porch. Angelina had not gotten over being impressed with the size of the house. She walked around the open area, looking up at the balconies and bay windows on the upper levels.

'*Wah*! You have four balconies! What's that up there?'

'Where?'

'That thing up there – on the top!'

'It's a pergola. There is a roof terrace on the top level of the house.'

'Didn't you say you wanted to eat pork chops? Can we go in now? It's hot out here, you know?'

'*Wah*! You sure are a lucky boy!'

'Come in.'

'Aunt Dorothy! We are back!'

Aunt Dorothy was at the dining table in the living room. She had finished laying the table for lunch and was now placing plates of pork chops on the table.

'Wow! This place is huge! And the floor is marble!' said Angelina as she glided through the living room towards Tim's mother.

'Hi. Aunt Dorothy!'

'Oh! Hello, you must be Angelina. Come sit down for lunch. Jing Yang, where's your manners? Take her bag for her.'

'Thanks, Aunt Dorothy.' She handed her bag to Jing Yang who placed it on an armchair.

'Where's your grandma? I thought you live with your grandma.'

'She's visiting her sister in Malacca. She'll be back next month.'

Angelina was now looking at the table, admiring the layout.

'*Wah*! You even have placemats below the plates and cutlery – and napkins as well.'

'For goodness' sake, stop all that *wah*-ing and wow-ing,'

snapped Jing Yang. He was getting flustered.

'I can't help it. This place is so nice. You are really lucky, Jing Yang.'

'Come, dig in. It's already past two. All of you must be famished.'

The three teenagers ate noisily. They were enjoying lunch. Angelina sat next to Jing Yang – she always made sure she sat next to him, not across the table, at school. Aunt Dorothy and Tim were on the other side of the table. There was a bouquet of pink roses in a glass bowl in the middle of the table.

'Aunt Dorothy, why did you marry an *Angmoh*?' This girl sure was blunt.

'Don't call my father an *Angmoh*, okay?'

'Tim. Don't be rude.'

'She's the one who's rude.'

'Sorry, Aunt Dorothy, I didn't mean to be rude.'

'It's alright, Angelina.'

'Well, I didn't set out to marry an *Angmoh*. I never thought I would marry outside my race. You see, it was fate that brought us together. I met Tim's father at university. I had just stepped into the place barely two weeks and I noticed this tall gentleman following me around. He wasn't terribly handsome but he was neat and presentable. When I visited the library, he would be sitting at the next table. It seemed that everywhere I went on campus, he was there too.'

'Sounds familiar to me. Reminds me of someone I know,' Jing Yang interjected, looking across the table at Angelina. Angelina blushed.

'One day, he summoned the courage to come over and sit next to me. When I didn't look cross, he would come sit next to me when I visited the library. Then he passed me a little slip of paper, asking me whether we could have lunch. He wasn't the typical English gentleman, you know – he was too meek!'

'So Aunt Dorothy, that's how the two of you got

together?' Jing Yang asked. He was curious. His mother had not talked about this aspect of her sister's life.

'So, finally, we had our first date – a lunch date.'

'Was it love at first sight?' asked Angelina.

'Well, I was hesitant. I mean, he was likeable but I was afraid. I didn't know whether it was right for me to be close with an Englishman. I feared the consequences of marrying someone other than a Chinese. So, in that way, it wasn't love at first sight. It took some prodding from Tim's father before I agreed to more dates.'

'Gee, you are brave, Aunt Dorothy. I don't think I can ever marry an *Angmoh*.'

'There you go again – using that derogatory word!'

'Tim. Stop it.'

'Mum! She's such a racist!'

'Tim. She's using the term affectionately. It wasn't intentionally rude.' Dorothy had herself been guilty of using this word to describe Caucasians all her life – till she married Tim's father. Even when she was studying in London, she would be calling the English *Angmoh* in her thoughts. It was simply one of those *Singlish* slang words. There was no need to get hot and bothered over its use. She had to get Tim to accept this and other slang words commonly used in Singapore. She had better start now. He would likely be living here for many, many years and he should not get angry every time someone uttered the word *Angmoh*. It was a common word among the locals here.

'Dear, I used to call your father an *Angmoh*.'

'Really?'

'Yes, dear. I have been guilty of using that term to describe Caucasians for as long as I can remember. Since primary school, really. But I meant no harm. It's a neutral word – no offence intended by the speaker, usually.'

'Gosh! Mum.'

'Angelina, don't mind Tim. It's just that the Caucasian community here doesn't quite like that word. Can you use Caucasian or Englishman instead?'

'Yes, Aunt Dorothy. Sorry Aunt Dorothy.'

'Now, where was I?'

'You were saying Uncle Peter was too meek,' volunteered Jing Yang.

'Oh yes. Soon I came around to accepting his requests for dates. Then I got hooked. I realised I couldn't live without him. From then on, there was no return – we were in love.'

'Gosh! So it wasn't love at first sight!'

'How's the apple sauce?'

'It's great. You make great pork chops, Aunt Dorothy. Can I come next time you have pork chops for lunch?

'Thank you for the compliment. Sure, you are very welcome to join us for lunch anytime.'

'Can I see your room, Jing Yang?'

'Aunt Dorothy, can she?'

'Why, yes, of course.'

'Tim, help me with the plates. You two run along. Angelina, you are a guest here. Put down the cutlery. Tim and I can manage.'

Jing Yang and Angelina clambered up the stairs. Jing Yang's room was on the second level, on the left.

Mother and son were left in the living room. They carried the plates and cutlery into the kitchen.

'Mum.'

'Yes, Tim.'

'Was it a difficult decision to marry Dad?'

Dorothy paused for a moment.

'Well, how should I put it?' She thought now was the right time to talk frankly with Tim. He would be thirteen in two months' time. He should know.

'Well. It wasn't as difficult as deciding to have you, dear.'

'What do you mean?'

'Dear, I am Chinese. Your father is English. I spent many nights pondering over whether to marry your father. Then when we were married, I spent many more nights worrying about what would happen if we were to have children.'

'Why, Mum?'

'Because..,' Dorothy paused. Then she continued, 'Because I didn't know whether you would come out looking like your father or me.'

'What do you mean?'

'I mean,' she paused again.

'Er… I mean. I didn't know whether you would turn out looking Chinese or *Angmoh*, dear.'

'Mum, you are using that word, too,' said Tim.

It was intentional of her. He had better get used to being called an *Angmoh* or half-an-*Angmoh*, she thought to herself.

'Tim,' she continued.

'I was worried for you. If you came out looking like your father, you would have a hard time adapting to life in Singapore. I really wanted you to live in Singapore after you were born. And if you came out looking Chinese, then you would have an equally difficult time living in England.'

'Do you understand what I just said, dear?'

Tim understood this part clearly. He had had trouble getting his schoolmates to accept him at Norfolk Junior. So he kept pretty much to himself and had few friends. He looked English to Singaporeans here. But, over in England, he was not treated as a native. His schoolmates could make out the physical differences between him and them. He was more of a hybrid – a mix of Caucasian and Chinese races.

Here in Singapore, he had also been keeping to himself. He stood out in class. He was the only white boy in class. He was also the only white boy in Greendale Secondary! At least, in Norfolk Junior, he looked more or less Caucasian and could easily blend in with the other students in the class.

'Mum.'

'Yes, dear.'

'Will I ever be able to fit in here in Singapore? And will I ever be able to be one of the guys in England?'

Dorothy took a deep breath. She had seen this day coming. Her boy was now old enough to feel hurt over such issues. He was no longer the innocent little boy who flitted through childhood.

'Mum, why did you decide to have me?'

'It was an accident, dear. I had not planned to have children yet so we practised safe sex for several years.' She paused for a while.

'Your father was eager to have children. But I wasn't ready.'

'Why not?'

'You see, I foresaw this day happening. That you might have trouble fitting in, wherever we lived.'

Dorothy was tearing at the corner of her eyes as she gazed at Tim.

'Aw! It's alright, Mum. I can handle it,'

Tim did not want his mother to be sad. He thought he was too old to hug her so he did the next best thing – he grabbed a box of tissue paper from the counter-top and put it in front of her. Dorothy dapped away the tears. Tim kept silent. He did not want his mum to be upset – not now, not ever.

'It was an accident really, but I am glad it happened. Your father and I did want so much to have you. You were a sum total of our love, so to speak.'

'Mum, you don't have to talk about it if you don't want to.'

'Let me continue.'

'Anyway, we have been much happier having you around. It was a good accident.'

'Mum.'

'Yes, dear.'

'Why can't Dad stay in Singapore? I miss him.'

'Dear, your father needs to look after his business. He can't just drop everything and come join us here. He's spent many years building the business, you know.'

'Yes, but... but, can't he transfer everything here?'

'Dear, how do you think he can transfer his customers, the location and the goodwill – the good name – of the company just like that?'

'He would have to start all over again. He's too old for that,' she went on.

'Do you want to be a businessman like your dad?'

'Oh no, not if it means I will be away from you and Dad.'

'I see. I see. Thank you for thinking of us, Tim.'

'Of course! Who else is there for me to think about, Mum?'

Tim was indeed too young to think about the birds and the bees. Dorothy worried about the years ahead – when Tim would be old enough to date girls, when he would have to find a partner. He would have trouble finding a suitable partner, one who could accept that he was half-English, half-Chinese. And even if she liked him, her parents might not welcome him. Indeed, Dorothy's worries would be compounded in the years to come – all because she had chosen an Englishman for a husband. Sometimes, she would wonder how different her life might have been if she and Peter had not met.

Tim was not a Chinese or an Englishman. He was a Eurasian – a European Asian. His descendants would also follow his roots. She was perhaps the last Chinese in the Street family. Then it dawned on her that her future daughter-in-law might be a Chinese.

Up on the second level, in Jing Yang's room, he and Angelina were busy taking turns to explore the Internet. They were now on a popular community portal, singhosts.com, visiting Jing Yang's blog which was hosted free on the Web site.

'Jing Yang, can I upload my picture onto your blog?'

'Ha? What for?'

'Just to show we are friends. Can I, please?'

Jing Yang did not know how to say no to her. The last time that he turned down a request of hers, she bawled non-stop. This girl could not handle rejection. And she cried easily. She did not seem to realise she was fifteen this year.

As Jing Yang did not give Angelina an answer, she took his silence to mean a yes. Angelina inserted a thumb-drive into the computer. Jing Yang had already logged into the control panel of the blog, so she clicked the Edit Profile button, entered this section of the blog, deleted a handsome-looking cartoon caricature which Jing Yang had placed there and uploaded a picture of her and Jing Yang – one which she had taken in class using her mobile phone when there was no teacher in. She inserted the following text caption:

Angelina and Jing Yang Forever

Then she clicked on the publish button and visited the blog to view the change. She was pleased to see the photograph of her and Jing Yang in the right column of the blog.

Angelina elbowed Jing Yang who was seated next to her at the desk, SMSing on his mobile phone.

'Take a look at your blog now. Don't you think it looks better now?'

'*Aiyah*! Why did you put that picture on my blog?' Angelina was intruding into his personal space. In fact, she was moving in and taking over!

Then he backed down. He had sensed an outpouring of emotions happening soon and moved quickly to save the situation.

'Oh alright! Leave it there.'

Angelina's face lit up. The looming storm in her face had dissipated.

She remembered that they were going to the *pasar malam* that evening.

'What time are we going to the *pasar malam*?'

'I can't go, not today anyway.'

'Why? Didn't we agree earlier?'

This time, Jing Yang had to stand firm. He could not let her win every argument.

'I need to do something important tonight.'

'What?'

'I need to prepare an argument to use in convincing my mother to let me switch elective subjects.'

'Oh that! I see. I think Miss Shih is going to pick on you when she comes into the class on Thursday.'

'Exactly! She will never let me off. She will likely tear me apart – like this and this!' He raised his hands in the air, stretched his fingers and pretended to claw the air animatedly. Angelina broke into giggles immediately. She seldom saw this funny side of Jing Yang. He was pretty serious most of the time. It was so unlike him. This boy had a lighter side to him after all! She had to have broken the ice between them.

'That's why I have to act fast. I am going to call my mother late tonight. I must get her to agree tonight.'

'I don't think you can get a transfer so fast. How are you going to avoid Miss Shih on Thursday?'

'Yes, that seems to be a problem that needs fixing. I will have to think of something tonight.'

'Aren't you going home now? I need some time alone to think.'

'It's only 3.30pm.'

'Doesn't your mother miss you when you don't come home straight after school? I haven't heard your mobile phone ringing the whole afternoon.'

'My mother trusts me. She won't worry about me.'

'I really need to think about this geography thing.'

'Oh alright.'

Jing Yang led her down the stairs to the kitchen. Aunt Dorothy was preparing some scones for tea. Tim was with her.

'Time for tea soon,' Dorothy said.

'Aunt Dorothy, Angelina's going home now.'

'Aunt Dorothy, thanks very much for lunch. The pork chops were delicious.'

'Aren't you staying for tea?'

Before Angelina could get a chance to reply, Jing Yang had already cut in.

'No, she can't. Her mother is waiting for her. Isn't she, Angelina?'

'Er...yes. See you, Aunt Dorothy. Bye, Tim.'

'Bye bye,' said Dorothy.

'Ta-ra,' said Tim.

'Bye, Aunt Dorothy.'

'What's ta-ra?' Angelina asked Jing Yang as they were walking into the living room.

'Search me!' he replied.

'That's British English slang for goodbye,' Tim called out from the kitchen. He had overheard their conversation.

'Hey! You seem to be wrong. Your cousin is not really unfriendly.'

Once Angelina had left, Jing Yang zipped up the stairs to start work on ways to convince his mother to let him change subjects.

By the time Jing Yang finished rehearsing what he would be saying to his mother when they were on video chat that evening, it was almost half past eight in the evening. New York was twelve hours behind Singapore. It was almost half past eight in the morning in New York now. Jing Yang went online to connect with his mother who he figured would have had breakfast by now. He put on a headset, opened the video chat program in his computer and adjusted the Web camera sitting on top of the LCD monitor. Then he waited for his mother to connect to the video chat.

'Hi Mother!'

'Oh! Hello Son. Aren't you supposed to be in bed?'

'Mother, it's only half past eight.'

'Oh, is it now? I didn't look at the clock. Still, it is a good idea to sleep early. By the time you finish washing up, it will have been nine o'clock.'

'Mother, I have got something I want to talk to you and Father about.'

'Your father has left the house. He has an early morning meeting today. Can this wait? You have got school tomorrow. You should be getting ready for bed right now.'

'It won't take long. I am going to bed right after this. I promise.'

'Okay. Don't tell me you have gotten into trouble at school again.'

'Sort of, Mother.' Jing Yang was not one to hide things from his mother. He had learnt from young that his mother would indulge him, unlike his father, and he knew the best way to get her to do things for him was to talk straight to the point and not keep things from her. He was more comfortable discussing things with his mother than with his father who would tolerate no nonsense – not from him or anybody, except, of course, his mother.

'I have told you many times already, don't be stubborn when in school. Your teachers won't like it. Just do what they tell you to and things will turn out fine.'

'Mother. I was not being stubborn. This Miss Shih likes to pick on me for no rhyme or reason. I can't take it anymore!'

'Miss Shih? Isn't she your geography teacher? The one who had taught overseas?'

'Yes, Mother.'

'What's wrong now?'

'This Miss Shih embarrassed me in front of class today. She accused me of bringing my mobile phone today but I did not.'

'Son, if you did not have the mobile phone with you, how could she have caught you?'

'Mother!'

'I have told you many, many times not to bring your mobile phone to school, but you wouldn't listen. I can't interfere in this. You know that it's wrong for me to intercede for you, don't you?'

'Mother, it's not that. Listen!'

'I haven't got much time this morning. Can't this wait till tonight?'

'I only need five minutes – just five minutes.'

'Okay. Make it fast.'

'The principal had asked Tim to pass the mobile phone to me in class. Miss Shih saw me taking the mobile phone from him and confronted me in front of my class.'

'Now, why would the principal be doing that? Why did she have your mobile phone?'

'I was caught using the mobile phone in Punggol Plaza in the afternoon, after school the previous day.'

'So that's it. So how do you want me to help you? Talk to your principal?'

'No, Mother. The principal saved me from Miss Shih today.'

'She saved you? Now, that's news.'

'Yes, she did, Mother. If you don't believe me, go ask Mrs Tan.'

'Alright, son. I believe you. So the matter is settled. What is it you want me to do?'

'Mother, I want to change elective subjects. I want to give up geography and take up history instead.'

'I see. Now I know what you really want. You want me to get you out of Miss Shih's class, right?'

'Mother! You are so smart!'

'Your father won't like it one bit, you know.'

'Mother, help me, please…please.'

'Let me think about it. I have to go now. I need to pick someone up.'

'Mother, I need an answer now. I have got geography class on Thursday. Miss Shih will slaughter me when she

33

comes into my class on Thursday.'

'Dear boy, you are always like that – running away from situations. How will you learn to handle matters when you grow up?'

'Mother, please…please.'

'Okay. Let me deal with this. I have got to go now, son.'

'Okay Mother.'

'Okay. Bye bye. Say hello to Aunt Dorothy for me, will you?'

'Right, Mother. Bye Mother.'

Jing Yang took off the headset and closed the video chat on the computer.

Jing Yang knew his mother would act quickly. She might nag at him but she would almost always give in to his requests. It was the only thing she could do to indulge him – she was always thousands of miles away when she should have been at his side when he was growing up. It was a difficult decision leaving Jing Yang to the care of her mother. His parents originally wanted to place him in boarding school in New York but later thought it best that he should remain in Singapore in his formative years. They did not want to alienate him from his native Singapore.

Jing Yang went online to surf his favourite Web sites.

2 *PROJECT BATTLE BOX*

When Thursday came, and it was almost time for geography lesson, Jing Yang was fidgety. He was still attending Miss Shih's lesson. He had hoped to get transferred out of her class but, alas, things were not moving as fast as he wished they would. As promised, his mother had spoken to his principal on Tuesday to request a switch in subject for him but it would take at least a few days for that to come about.

Jing Yang hoped Miss Shih would not come in the next period. Otherwise, he would have to endure two periods of geography and he would be her target – he was sure.

The atmosphere was tense. Miss Shih was nitpicking from the moment she stepped into the classroom. She was allowing her pettiness to get in the way of her teaching. The students were wary of getting into her bad books that morning and were unusually quiet and reticent. But it was of no use. Miss Shih embarked on a fault-finding frenzy, requiring those whom she called by name to stand up and answer questions she put forward to them. She quizzed them on chapter six of the geography textbook covering the topic of rivers – from river basin and watershed to erosion and transportation, even going as far as river channelisation.

Actually, Miss Shih was not gunning for Jing Yang. It was several of his classmates who were at the receiving end of her fury. All could not answer her questions in a way that satisfied her. She even stumped them with some of her questions. What the students did not know was that she was in class seeking revenge. The night before, Miss Shih had browsed through all their personal blogs. Innocently enough, she had started with a visit to Jing Yang's blog to find out what he would be writing about her after the mobile phone incident. But, Jing Yang was not one who would disparage his teachers on his blog on the Internet. So, there was nothing interesting for her to read on his blog. Then out of curiosity, she clicked on the links to his classmates. These links were placed on one side of the blog.

What she read on some of the students' blogs infuriated her. They were mocking her mannerisms and teaching. Why, some even went as far as to call her names.

Miss Shih was adamant to punish these students. She could not let out in class that she had read their blogs. She had to take revenge on them covertly. She could not report her discovery to the principal. Mrs Tan would want to read all these blogs. What if she thought these students' complaints had some merit? She could not take the chance.

By the end of the first period, three students were standing behind their desks. They were looking sombre. They did not know why they were being targeted. Only Miss Shih knew. She had made a mental note of the names of the culprits and was now dealing with them one by one. Beng Huat, who was standing in the third row in front of the teacher's desk, was the one who called her an ugly old hag on his blog. Standing behind him was Johari who did not realise he was being punished for blogging about how he had made fun of her surreptitiously in class the previous week. Teck Lee, standing in the last row, had posted a picture of her with the words 'spinster in menopause' scribbled on it.

The students in this class were incorrigible, Miss Shih thought to herself as she surveyed the classroom. They had no respect for her whatsoever. She would make them pay dearly for their insolence.

Meanwhile, Jing Yang was keeping very quiet, to the extent that he hardly moved an inch. He tried hard to keep from scratching his nose, which was itchy. He was afraid to attract her attention. He only had to keep still for a few minutes more as the bell would be ringing shortly to signal the end of the second period of her lesson. He had thought he would be the focus of her wrath this morning but it turned out otherwise. Some of his classmates who were expecting to enjoy the spectacle had become Miss Shih's prey.

When the bell rang, six students were standing in the classroom.

'Those of you who are standing report to me outside the staff room at two o'clock this afternoon.'

'Thank you, class.'

'Thank you, Miss Shih. Goodbye Miss Shih,' the class chorused in unison.

Noise returned to the classroom.

'*Heng-ah*!' exclaimed Jing Yang.

'Jing Yang, I thought you would be singled out for punishment but it was us instead,' said Beng Huat.

'There goes my afternoon,' said Teck Lee.

'What's wrong with her today? Did she wake up on the wrong side of the bed?' exclaimed Jolene.

'*Wah*! Today is an unlucky day for us,' Su Bing shrieked.

'Luckily, Beng Huat was standing in front of me, blocking her view of me. I tried hard to remain still so she could not see me.'

So the day was uneventful as far as Jing Yang was concerned. The storm he had feared came but it passed him by and instead engulfed several of his classmates.

The next geography lesson would be on next Monday. Jing Yang hoped approval for his change of elective subject to history would be received by then.

Students attending history lesson in the language lab on the second level were now returning to the classroom. Among them was Angelina. Jing Yang would be joining this one-third of the class soon.

It was now a free period as Mr Seng, their English teacher, was on medical leave. Jing Yang was left alone to his thoughts while many of his classmates were debating the happenings in the earlier two periods. They were guessing the reasons for Miss Shih's sudden ferocity today.

Suddenly, the classroom became quiet. Mr Chan, history teacher for 3E3, had appeared at the doorway. He had come to see Jing Yang.

'Jing Yang, can I see you for a while?'

Jing Yang was deep in thought and did not hear him.

'Jing Yang! Mr Chan wants to see you,' said Angelina.

Jing Yang got up and went out of the classroom. Mr Chan was holding on to a pile of books which he had laid on the parapet in the corridor.

'Mrs Tan has spoken to me about your transfer to my history class. Are you sure you want to join my class?'

'Yes, Mr Chan.'

'Okay! You can start attending my lessons from Monday onwards. Remember to buy your history textbook; you will need it next week.'

'And, get your classmates to fill you in on the course work that I have covered with them so far. Read up on the important chapters before you come into class next week.'

'Yes, I understand, Mr Chan.'

'I will inform Miss Shih about the change. You don't have to see her. This is Mrs Tan's instruction. That's it!'

Jing Yang returned to the classroom, feeling elated. He was now safe from Miss Shih. His mother sure worked fast to help him.

'Hey! Did Mr Chan tell you something about your transfer?' Angelina was curious.

'Yes, I am to join your history class next week.'

'Good for you. Don't worry, I will tell you all you need to know.'

Angelina was glad Jing Yang was taking up history. She missed his company during her history periods.

'You are so lucky, you know,' said Angelina. She could not conceal her joy.

Angelina had another reason for being joyful. She was looking forward to her fifteenth birthday party.

That day came quickly. She had invited Jing Yang, his cousin Tim, classmates and schoolmates for the party at home that afternoon. Her mother was busy preparing the food in the kitchen. Home was a three-room flat in Hougang Avenue 5. For the family of five, living in this small room was a bit of a squeeze. Her parents occupied the rear bedroom, while she and her older brothers shared the front bedroom. For a pubescent girl, it was not the best of environment, but she had to make do. The family was not rich. Her father worked as a delivery truck driver while her mother was a full-time housewife. Money was tight most of the time and her eldest brother had dropped out of school to help support the family. It was good that he decided to come out to work – he was not the studying type. Going to school was akin to going to the playground. All he did was play. He was disruptive to lessons and it was only a matter of time before the school expelled him. But, he was not a bad boy. Her eldest brother adhered to his three principles: honesty, loyalty and trust. He could be counted on to help his friends in times of need. But, alas, some of the friends were not equally reciprocative. This brother did not complete normal technical education. He left school in the middle of the third year and since then had been working as a kitchen assistant in a restaurant.

The other brother was in secondary four normal academic stream in Holy Innocents' High School in Upper

Serangoon Road. It was not easy for him to get to secondary four. He fumbled along the way as he was playful and inattentive in class. He was a borderline case. This was a crucial year for him as he would be sitting for the 'N' level examinations in October.

Angelina was the only one in the family to get into the express stream. She was also the youngest in the family. From young, she did not have any problems with getting good grades at school. A happy-go-lucky girl, she never let her parents worry about her school work and the company she kept. She had simple needs and was easily satisfied. Though other girls her age were vying for the latest mobile phones and craving for the latest fashion in the clothes that they wore, Angelina did not follow suit and also could not — not with hand-me-downs for clothes and limited pocket money. She made do with a Nokia 4303 mobile phone. It did not have bells and whistles, but it worked well and let her keep in touch with family and friends. She was satisfied. But Angelina was no plain Jane. From the age of two, when her facial features developed, everyone knew she would grow up into an attractive girl. Whatever she wore did not detract from her beauty — she looked lovely and sweet in all sorts of attire.

Though the family was poor, Angelina had it good at home. She was loved by all. Her parents doted on her and brothers yielded to her so she got to do everything she wanted, so much so she had become sort of an empress dowager at home — she ruled the roost! Just how did she manage this? By crying when she did not get her way. Nobody at home wanted to see her cry so they just let her have her way. Now she was using the same method with Jing Yang, and it was working on him too.

This birthday, her mother had agreed to her holding a party. It would be a simple affair — with some balloons and streamers for decoration, food prepared by her mother, packet drinks and a no-frills birthday cake from a bakery in the next block. But Angelina did not mind. She was easily pleased. Today's birthday party was her first since she stepped into secondary school. Her eldest brother and father were at work so they would not be at her party. This party was held mainly for her friends and schoolmates to celebrate with her.

It was past eleven o'clock. Angelina was busy arranging the food on a rectangular table placed against the wall in the living room. The spread was scrumptious, she thought. There were fried meehoon, fried rice, chicken wings, fish balls, French fries, chicken curry, sausages, and agar-agar. Packets of drinks were stacked neatly on a corner of the table. Next to them were paper plates, plastic cutlery and napkins. Her elder brother appeared at the door. He was carrying her birthday cake. She stopped what she was doing, grabbed the box from him and opened it. She wanted to know what the cake looked like. It was her eldest brother's present to her. It was a round sponge cake, with fresh cream icing all over and beads of chocolate on its rim. Her favourite strawberries and some cherries lined the top of the cake on which were iced the words:

Happy Birthday Angelina

By noon, the work had been done. It was she who put up the streamers and the balloons. It was she who arranged the food on the table and mopped the floor in the living room and bedrooms. Her elder brother merely went down to get the cake for her and promptly disappeared downstairs to be with his friends. He did not want to be around. It was not that he did not want to help out. The truth was – Angelina was a fusspot! It was difficult working with her on anything. She had her own ideas which she would not bulge from easily. Her elder brother knew too well! Her mother knew too! Simple tasks such as helping her tie her hair in the mornings before she went to school were exasperating things to do. She would look in the mirror, and appearing dissatisfied, unknot the ponytail at the back of her head and ask her mother to start all over again.

Angelina went into the bathroom for a shower. Her guests would be arriving soon and she had better shower and get dressed up quickly. In the bathroom, she was scrubbing herself and thinking of what Jing Yang would be getting her for her birthday.

'Horror of Horrors! What if he came empty-handed?' she thought to herself.

'He wouldn't dare! Or would he?'

It was quarter past one and her schoolmates were streaming into the flat. Some were helping themselves to the spread of food laid on the table. Others were engaging in small talk. The party was actually an opportunity for the boys and girls to show off. They would not miss it for the world. It was also a time for them to be seen as being oblivious to all notions of school rules and other restrictions – they were blatantly ignoring all these rules, albeit here in Angelina's house and not in school. The boys were in T-shirts and jeans. Their hair were all spiked up. Some of them had outlandish ear, nose and tongue studs. None wore Bermudas! This was a formal occasion and they wanted to impress their host and the other girls. The girls looked sweet and pretty in their dresses and costume jewellery – some were wearing faux pearl necklaces; others were decked out in big pendants and sported multi-coloured bangles on their arms. Everyone was wearing a big watch. There was one girl with a large faux precious stone ring on a finger. Another had an oversized ring with the word 'ROCK' on it while the one sitting next to her had a similar ring, but with the word 'ROLL' on it. These girls were all trendy and they outclassed simple Angelina who wore a non-descript pink dress and no accessories – and it was her birthday! But, Angelina did not mind. She knew her station in life. Her mother was already over-budget that month, splurging on her birthday party. She could not complain. The girls were just doing what girls their age did perennially – getting dolled up to impress the boys! There was a good turnout today. Angelina was a popular girl at school.

'Hi Angelina. Happy Birthday!' said Jing Yang, handing to Angelina a small present as he stood at the doorway.

'Hi Jing Yang. Come in.'

Jing Yang was in a tucked-out red T-shirt and blue denim jeans. He stood out from the rest of the boys! He was the only boy who looked decent – no studs or spiky hair!

'Aunty,' Jing Yang called out to Angelina's mother who was in the kitchen washing some vegetables in the sink. She nodded to him.

'Where's your cousin?' Angelina enquired.

'Oh! He should be here anytime. We came separately.'

'Gosh! Both of you live in the same house, you know. Why didn't you come together?'

Jing Yang looked away. He pretended not to hear what she was saying. He was now mingling with his classmates.

'I've got to do something about these two boys,' Angelina thought to herself. Coming from a closely knit family, she could not understand their behaviour. Their problem had to have something to do with the sheer size of the house, which hindered their communication, she decided.

'I still can't understand,' said Jing Yang, pointing at a portrait of the Goh family hanging on the wall behind the television.

'What?' asked Angelina.

'Why are your brothers all so fat and you so thin?' said Jing Yang.

'I don't know. Go ask the factory,' Angelina retorted, pointing to her mother who was in the kitchen. It was not the first time she had been asked this question. She was not offended in the least bit. Secretly, she was glad.

'What if she had been fat like her two brothers? What if?' she almost thought aloud.

The small flat looked uncomfortable with so many teenagers in it. Some of the guests spilled out into the wide corridor. They made themselves comfortable in chairs and on stools placed alongside the corridor. There was chatter everywhere – these teenagers sure were noisy! All sorts of topics were being discussed – from Lady Gaga to Miss Shih, from homework to grades, and oversized sunglasses to faux baubles.

'Hi Angelina.' Tim had just stepped into the house and was now giving her a present. 'Happy Birthday!'

'Hi Tim. Thanks for coming.'

The girls in the room were now looking at Tim. He looked handsome in a vintage T-shirt and jeans. The curly hair which was tucked neatly behind his ears during schooldays was now covering his ears. His grey eyes, enhanced by double eyelids, looked piercingly inviting. He was thin and tall – standing at five feet nine inches tall – though he was only thirteen years old. And he looked every inch a Caucasian. These local boys certainly could not match that attraction factor the girls in the room yearned for – an *Angmoh* boyfriend.

Angelina made Tim sit next to Jing Yang.

'Come on, you two boys! Say something to each other!' Angelina was trying to help them break the ice between them. She squeezed a stool between their chairs and joined them. These boys needed some help in getting along.

'I hear that British teenagers are pretty materialistic. Is it true?' Angelina asked.

'Nope, not really. We are the same as you guys, interested in the latest gadgets, clothes and computers.'

'How about mobile phones?'

'We are not as crazy about mobile phones as you are.'

'I hear girls there like to appear sexually alluring too.'

'Actually, under-age sex is common there. I mean brief sexual encounters.'

'I thought British kids are level-headed.'

'Well, the girls like to be popular and that means being

amenable to relationships.'

'Oh! I see. I read somewhere on the Internet recently that more girls below fourteen years old are engaging in sex.'

'Wow! I am surprised you can talk to me openly about this topic.' He was amazed that girls in Singapore were not shy about sex.

'We are not a backward country you know so it's no big deal. But, I am not one of those girls who flirt around. I just like to read widely – be in touch with what's happening, you know. And we do receive sexual education in school. You have only been here two months, so you missed the last lecture by one of the teachers.'

'You mean, the teachers here talk about such things?' Tim said in disbelief. He had all along thought Singapore schools were strait-laced in everything.

'They try to,' said Beng Huat. He had overheard their conversation and decided to cut in. 'But we boys give them left, right and centre, till they turn red in the face.'

'What do you mean by that?' asked Tim.

'Well, we embarrass them with lewd jokes. Ha! Ha! Ha!' Beng Huat's voice crackled as he spoke. 'Fancy them teaching us about such things. I think I know more than they do.' Then he guffawed. As the other guests shared anecdotes of their verbal exchanges with their teachers during sexual education period, laughter rocked the small living room.

Noticing that Jing Yang was keeping quiet, Angelina turned to him.

'Wasn't that funny?'

'Er…yeah.'

'Jing Yang, have you been to England? Have you ever visited Tim in England?'

'No. I seldom travel.'

'Do Tim and you go out together – I mean, to the movies, shopping?'

'Er…'

'*Alamak*! You boys don't behave like cousins!'

'Why don't we go out together? I haven't visited VivoCity in ages. Why don't we go there?'

Angelina did not suggest going to the movies, though it was one of her loves. It was a luxury she could not afford. But visiting VivoCity was easy – she only had to pay the MRT fares to and fro. It would be fun – window shopping and taking pictures while they were there.

'Alright,' said Tim.

'Okay,' was the rejoinder from Jing Yang.

'Settled,' Angelina exclaimed. She had at last done something to get these boys closer.

The birthday cake was not big so Angelina had to cut thin slices for her guests. But, they did not complain. They were having fun being with one another, enjoying moments of laughter reminiscing about life at school. Angelina sliced the strawberries on the cake into halves, kept a half for Jing Yang and another half for herself, and offered the rest to her guests. Jing Yang did not take the piece of strawberry. Though she loved strawberries, she did not realise Jing Yang did not like sour stuff. She certainly had a lot to discover about Jing Yang.

When the party was over and the guests had left, Angelina heaved a sigh of relief. It had been a busy day and she had been a good host. Now she had lots of cleaning up to do. But first, she just had to see what Jing Yang had given her for her birthday. She could not resist reaching for a small bright pink wrapped box lying on her bed, among the pile of presents she had received today. She tore the wrapping and opened the box. In it was a set of three plastic heart bangles – in red, yellow and blue. It was just what she wanted. The girls in her house today had showed off their oversized faux pearl, crystal and silver bracelets and bangles earlier. She was secretly envious of them. Now, she had her own set of gorgeous bangles too.

'Jing Yang gave me a set of hearts. I must mean something to him. He must be sending me a message,'

Angelina thought aloud as she mopped the living room. Her mother helped her to keep the leftover food in the kitchen. They could have it for dinner that evening.

It was a cold drizzly Monday morning at school the next day. The bell had rung to signal the end of the maths period. It was now time for two periods of history in the language lab downstairs. Jing Yang and Angelina were among the history students making their way out of 3E3. As Jing Yang passed his classmates, he could sense they envied him for being so lucky to have got out of reach of Miss Shih's claws, while they themselves were resigned to more suffering under her. The mood in the classroom was as bleak as the weather outside. Miss Shih, they reckoned, had not yet finished dealing with them.

In the language lab, Angelina waved Jing Yang to sit next to her. The classroom looked empty as there were only a handful of students taking history. She could not sit next to Jing Yang in class but at least during history periods they could sit side by side.

'Class stand,' the history representative for 3E3 called out. Mr Chan had just entered the classroom.

'Good morning, Mr Chan,' the students chorused.

'Good morning, class,' said Mr Chan.

'Remember, two weeks ago, I spoke about a history project for you to undertake? I have decided on the title. It is 'An Episode in the History of Singapore'. You may choose any period in the history of Singapore and report on a single area of interest,' he said.

'You will be graded as a group. Each group consists of four students. Marks will be awarded as follows: Content 40%, Research 40%, Presentation 20%. Each member of the group will get the same mark awarded to the group,' he continued.

Mr Chan passed a stack of notes to the history representative who distributed them to the students.

'All the details of the project are in the notes. Please look through them carefully. Any questions?'

'What's the format of the report?' asked a student.

Mr Chan proceeded to describe the format to the class, scribbling on the whiteboard as he talked.

'What is the name of the project?' asked another student.

'You may discuss among members of your own group and decide on the name for the project. There is no need to get my concurrence.'

'Mr Chan, can we get schoolmates to help out?' asked Angelina.

There was a pause before their history teacher answered her question.

'As long as you write your own report, I have no objections,' he said. 'But, strictly no plagiarism please. You have to come to your own conclusions. Agreed?'

'Yes! Mr Chan,' the students shouted.

'Now, use the next five minutes to choose your own group – I do not wish to interfere in your arrangements. That way, you get to choose the classmates you work best with.'

The classroom erupted into activity as students moved from one desk to another and negotiated with one another.

'Jing Yang, you and I are in the same group. Mabel and Fanny have agreed to be in our group,' said Angelina.

'Anything,' said Jing Yang. This girl was in the habit of making decisions for him. He could not say no for fear of offending her. At the same time, he secretly longed for her company. He was in two minds. On the one hand, he wanted to withdraw into his private space. On the other hand, he realised that being alone had its painful moments. He was slowly getting used to having this girl around him much of the time. He figured that till he sorted out his thoughts, it was best he did nothing that would provoke any adverse reaction from Miss Cry Baby.

'So, have you guys decided on your own groups?' asked Mr Chan.

'Yes, Mr Chan,' echoed the class.

'Now, please re-arrange the desks so that there are four desks in a group and discuss the project among yourselves. You have half-an-hour for the discussion. Approach me if you have any questions.'

There was the sound of desks and chairs being dragged across the classroom as each group of students moved some desks and chairs together.

The students opened their textbooks to pore over the events in Singapore's history. Then they suggested suitable topics to their group leaders who listed them on paper. Angelina who had appointed herself as their team's group leader was busy writing down suggestions made by Jing Yang, Mabel and Fanny. They narrowed their selection from six topics to two:

1. Fall of Singapore
2. Singapore's separation from Malaysia.

It was difficult deciding on the topic for the project.

'I don't think topic number two is as interesting as topic number one,' said Fanny.

'The second topic is of great importance to us Singaporeans as it focuses on how we gained our independence. The first merely talks about the British,' said Mabel.

'I don't agree with you, Mabel,' said Jing Yang. 'If the British didn't surrender to the Japanese but instead fought on, the Japanese might not have won and we would have remained a free people. Our history would have been different then.'

'It's the same case with topic two. If we did not break away from Malaysia, Singapore would not have progressed this much,' Mabel argued.

'Looks like we have a situation here,' said Angelina. 'Let's vote for it,' she suggested.

'I agree,' said Mabel.

'Me too,' said Fanny.

'Okay with me,' said Jing Yang.

'Show of hands, please. Those for topic number one raise your hands.' Angelina and Jing Yang and Fanny raised their hands.

'It's decided. Fall of Singapore is the chosen topic for the project,' said the group leader.

'Shall we focus on the underground bunker at Fort Canning Park?' asked Jing Yang. 'That was the place where the British made the decision to surrender to the Japanese invading forces.'

'No objections,' said Mabel.

'Sure,' said Fanny.

'Fine with me,' said Angelina.

'What shall we name our project?' Fanny asked.

'It's a battle box and we are doing a project. Why don't we name it Project Battle Box!' exclaimed Angelina.

'Sounds cool!' said Jing Yang.

'Agreed,' said Mabel.

'Okay,' said Fanny.

'It's settled then, Project Battle Box it is,' said Angelina.

3 *THE GODELL PRISM*

'When do we have to submit the project?' asked Jing Yang as he, Angelina and Tim were making their way to the bus-stop outside school.

'Didn't you hear Mr Chan just now?'

'I wasn't paying attention.'

'Dreaming again, right?'

'Don't start again! It's already too hot out here. I don't need more heat from you.'

'Aw! Stop it, you two. Can't you walk to the bus-stop without quarrelling?'

'We aren't quarrelling, Tim. Just talking!'

'Yes. Jing Yang is right. We were just talking loudly. That's all.'

'You haven't told me the dateline for submission of the project.'

'End of the fourth week in the third term, that is 31st July 2009.'

'That means we have got about three weeks.'

'That's right. We need to divide the work so we can make full use of the time we have.'

'Have you decided on the duties for the group members yet?'

'Nope! But I have got a draft of it in my mind already.'

'So, what am I in charge of?'

'The bus is here! Let's talk on the bus.'

The threesome boarded the single-deck bus and headed for the seats in the rear. They sat three abreast. Tim took the window seat as he enjoyed looking out of the window. Angelina sat between the two boys.

'So what is it that I have to do?'

'You will do research on the British side of the surrender story.'

'And you?'

'Me? I will follow you as backup.'

'Ha! Ha! I don't need a backup.'

'You sure do. You need someone to help you keep notes and contribute ideas.'

'How about the other two?'

'Mabel will handle the Japanese side of the surrender story. Fanny will research the aftermath of the British surrender.'

'*Wah*! You sure know how to delegate work.'

'I do?'

'Yeah! You delegated all the work to the rest of us and leave yourself with nothing.'

'That's not a fair thing to say. I am the group leader. I have to keep everything together. Then I have to write the report. I am also helping you with your research.'

'You win! You win!' Actually Jing Yang knew he would be the one writing the report. Angelina's English was barely passable. But he did not want to hurt her.

'What do you mean, I win? Don't be like that. There's nothing to win. I am also helping out.'

'You guys are very quarrelsome people, you know. Can't you just talk nicely to each other? Is it that difficult?'

'I am sorry, Angelina.'

'It's okay, Jing Yang.'

There was silence in the rear of the bus for the rest of their journey. The three teenagers were taking a sorely needed nap after a long hot day in school.

'Can I come to your place?' asked Angelina as the three of them were walking up Lorong Low Koon.

'Why?'

'To help you with your research on Project Battle Box.'

'But I haven't started yet.'

'We can start afterwards.'

'I need a rest. I'm too tired now.'

'But you just had a nap. Can I, please?'

'Just let her come.'

'Does that mean I can get a free lunch too?'

'Ah! You greedy pig! You know my mum is cooking pork chops today, don't you?'

'Something like that.'

'Any objections, Jing Yang?'

'Nope. Okay by me.'

The three schoolmates walked into the house at the corner of Lorong Low Koon and Hai Sing Close.

'Come on in.'

'Aunt Dorothy is in the kitchen.'

The group left their bags on the big sofa in the living room and went into the kitchen.

'Aunt Dorothy, we're back!'

'Mum, we have a guest for lunch.'

'Hi! Aunt Dorothy.'

'Oh! Hi. Young lady. Gosh! I think I have forgotten your name.'

'It's Angelina, Mum.'

'Hope you don't mind me staying for lunch, Aunt Dorothy.'

'Not at all. Not at all, Angelina. Do sit down.'

'Thanks, Aunt Dorothy.'

'Dear, help me lay the table, will you?'

'Yes, Mum.'

'Jing Yang, did you remember to shut the front door?'

'Yes, Aunt Dorothy.'

'Aunt Dorothy, your pork chops are very delicious.

That's why I am coming for another round.'

'Why, thanks for your compliment. It's Tim's favourite. I hear you celebrated your birthday yesterday. Happy belated birthday.'

'Thanks, Aunt Dorothy.'

'Tim tells me you are on quite good terms with Jing Yang.'

'Aunt Dorothy, she and I are classmates only.'

'I know. I know. Angelina, what do you think of my nephew, Jing Yang?'

'He's...he's an altogether nice boy.'

'Ha! Ha! Ha! Fancy you saying that of my cousin.'

'Why are you laughing, Tim? There's nothing funny.'

'I was simply tickled pink. Just now, both of you were quarrelling all the way to the bus-stop and on the bus as well.'

'No, it's not like that. Aunt Dorothy, don't listen to Tim. She and I were talking loudly, that's all.'

'I see. Seems this girl has a good impression of you, Jing Yang. She seems such a sweet young lady. Do be nice to her. Be a gentleman. Can you?'

'Yes, Aunt Dorothy.'

'What my mum really means is this girl likes you, Jing Yang.'

Jing Yang glared at him. He was not ready for a relationship with a girl and did not like Tim pointing a way into a relationship with Angelina.

'Don't be rude, Tim. We have a young lady with us.'

'Sorry, Angelina.'

Angelina was now blushing. Aunt Dorothy had read her mind. She tried to change the subject.

'Aunt Dorothy, Jing Yang says you are sort of a medium, is it true?'

'He said that, didn't he? Well, I am what you might call a psychic medium.'

'What's a psychic medium?'

'Angelina, it means I communicate with things from

another dimension.'

'Things?'

'Yes, things – you know – spirits.'

'Do they really exist?'

'Of course, they do, Jing Yang. There's so much about our world that we have yet to find out about. For thousands of years, people have been dying – of illnesses, of old age, from accidents and suicides. Many have been murdered or killed in battle. Some of these souls do not get a chance to move on. They linger around.'

'You mean that they fly around us?'

'No, not like that, Angelina. The souls of some of these people who died for whatever reasons linger around because these souls are in a confused state.'

'Why should they be confused? Aren't they supposed to be dead – meaning the brain is dead too? How can they think without a brain?'

'Young lady, these are not people anymore. They are what I might call wandering spirits. No body. No brain. Just plain energy. These spirits have an unresolved matter that they need to settle so they cannot move on to the next world as they are supposed to.'

'So where do they go then?'

'Angelina, these wandering spirits never came to terms with something that happened to them when they were alive. So they end up haunting the place where they died.'

'That's rather eerie, Aunt Dorothy. Does it mean these spirits are everywhere?'

'No, Jing Yang. Why do you think that?'

'I mean, people die all the time everywhere throughout the ages. Therefore, these spirits are everywhere.'

'That's not it, Jing Yang. These wandering spirits most likely experienced sudden, very traumatic deaths. They become so shocked that they don't realise they are dead. They think they are still alive and this thought keeps them moving along as spirits in our world.'

'Do they ever get to know the truth – that they are

dead?'

'Yes, of course. That's where I come in. As a psychic medium, I help them to wake their memory. I help them to remember the moment of death. Once they realise they are dead, they will move on to the next world gladly. They know this is no longer their world.'

'Aunt Dorothy, are there spirits in this place?' asked Angelina. She was getting scared.

'Oh, no. Not here, Angelina. There's nothing to be afraid of here.'

'Aunt Dorothy, Have you seen these spirits before? How do you make contact with them?'

'Jing Yang, remember the crystal prism I put on the dining table when I am meditating?'

'You mean the palm-sized multi-faceted thing?'

'Yes. That's the one. I use it to communicate with spirits.'

'Wow! That's cool!'

'Do you want to take a look at it?'

'Yes, please. Can we?'

'Sure. Tim, please go into my room and bring me the prism.'

'Yes, Mum.'

Tim left his seat and returned quickly, holding a twisted piece of crystal in his hands. It was roughly three fingers thick and its height was about the length of an outstretched hand. Its facets were slightly bent in a clockwise direction.

'This is the Godell prism. It's made of smoky quartz. It's quite rare – comes from the Alps in Switzerland.'

'Can I hold it, Aunt Dorothy?'

'Sure, you can, Angelina. Here! Use both hands. Place it in the palms of your hands.'

'It feels cold.'

'Of course, it should feel cold. It's real crystal. This one's been around for millions of years on earth. It takes that long to grow to this size.'

'Really?'

'Really, Angelina.'

'Wow!'

'It is believed that piezoelectricity is responsible for its growth.'

'Pie so what?'

'Piezoelectricity! The ability of some materials to generate an electric charge. In this case, the crystal can generate electric charges. It's been doing so for millions of years, powering its own growth, and causing other things to react with it – for example, move. It can cause magnetic waves to vibrate simultaneously in different spectrums, transferring electrical energy and enhancing contact between spectrums; in other words, it can communicate with another dimension.'

'That sure is dense stuff.'

'What's that, dear?'

'I mean, it's...it's powerful stuff!' Tim could not find a fitting description for the prism.

To put things simply, this Godell prism helps us mortals make contact with people in the other worlds – spirits and souls.'

'Like Tim says, it's powerful stuff, Aunt Dorothy.'

'Yes, Jing Yang. Used properly, it offers hope for our world – helping these wandering spirits find their way to their new home. But, in the wrong hands, it could bring about destruction.'

'Is there a limit to its power?'

'On the contrary, it gets immense power when there is an eclipse of the sun.'

'Really? Mum?'

'Yes. An eclipse of the sun causes *yin* energy on the earth to build up rapidly and it is this energy that concentrates in the Godell prism. But, the prism must be in the path of the eclipse for it to happen.'

'In fact, there's an eclipse of the sun happening soon over our skies.'

'When is it, Aunt Dorothy?'

'The solar eclipse will take place on 22nd July 2009 over Asia Pacific.'

'That's only weeks away.'

'Yes. The heavens will darken for six minutes and thirty-nine seconds during the solar eclipse.'

'That short a time, Mum?'

'Enough time to give tremendous power to the Godell prism. I can't wait for that day.'

'Gosh! Can I come see you work on the Godell prism that day, Aunt Dorothy?'

'Sure, you can, Angelina. I will give you a demonstration of its power then.'

'It will be the last solar eclipse I get to watch in my lifetime. It's the ultimate experience for me.'

'I don't understand.'

'The next eclipse will happen on 13th June 2132. All of us will not be around then.'

'That's…that's one hundred and twenty-three years from now!'

'We will be long gone.'

'*Wah*!' I must not miss this one then.'

'Yeah, we must watch, even if it means waiting till the next morning.'

'Jing Yang, there's no need for you to lose your sleep. This solar eclipse will take place at about seven o'clock in the morning here in Singapore.'

'Don't forget to remind us.'

'Of course, dear. We will all witness the event together.'

'How long have you been a psychic medium, Aunt Dorothy?' Angelina could not resist asking.

'Many years. Let me think. I joined the SAUK in 1979.'

'Goodness! There's even an association for it?' cried Jing Yang.

'Yes.'

'Mum, what does SAUK stand for?'

'Spiritualists Association of United Kingdom. We have

over five thousand members worldwide.'

'Do they all have a Godell prism?'

'No! Goodness gracious me. This prism is extremely rare. There are only a handful around, and this is the largest, I think.'

'How did you get your hands on it, Aunt Dorothy?'

'It was my mentor who gave it to me. No, that's not correct. He passed it to me for safe-keeping.'

'Safe-keeping?'

'Yes, dear. You see, we do not own the Godell prism. We hold it in trust. We are duty bound to protect it and we appoint another to continue our work when we are too old. It has been like that for generations.'

'You mean it has been passed down from generation to generation?'

'Why do you need to protect it? I thought it has tremendous power.'

'Angelina, the Godell prism needs to be protected from people who have no qualms about using it for evil deeds.'

'Aunt Dorothy, you haven't told us yet – whether you have seen these spirits.'

'Jing Yang, spirits cannot be seen in their pure form.'

'Hah?'

'In their original form, they are just energised air particles – sort of like moving air.'

'You mean, wind?'

'Something like that.'

'When can we see them – like in the movies?'

'Ah ha, Jing Yang. You have been watching too many ghost movies, haven't you?'

'Tell us, Mum.'

'Well, spirits do not have form, that is, they have no shape. They need to take over another material to have form.'

'Hah?'

'You mean they need to possess people?'

'Not in that sense, Angelina. But when they acquire

enough energy they can move chairs or stools – something like that.'

'How about people, can they possess people?'

'No, Jing Yang. It's not like what you see in the movies.'

'Have you come across such strange happenings?'

'Yes, of course.'

'How do you deal with these spirits, Aunty?'

'I help them find release.'

'You release them? Do they go around wearing chains?'

'No! Not at all. Not at all. That's not the way it happens.'

'I help release them from their troubles. I help them realise that they are already dead. Once they know this, they will move on to the next world.'

'Don't dead people know they are dead?'

'Sometimes, they don't. That's where I come in – to help them know.'

'Aunty, do you need to chant a spell for the crystal to work?'

'Goodness! It doesn't work like that. Not like black magic.'

'How then, Mum?' Tim had never been interested in the strange things his mum had been accustomed to doing, not till now, that is. Now his curiosity had been aroused.

'I just need to think, to meditate. I concentrate on the prism, and use it to reach out to these wandering spirits. Then I speak with them.'

'Is that so? What if they don't speak English and you don't know their language?'

'Jing Yang, you do ask difficult questions.'

'There are many of us mediums around the world. Those who seek help from us usually will look for mediums in their own country as the spirits are likely to speak their native tongue.'

'Aunty, how do you find work? You are a housewife and do not have an office. How do people know you are available?'

'By word of mouth, dear girl. I have been doing this for more than thirty years, so people will come looking for me.'

'Oh my, it's already three o'clock. We have been chatting for an hour. It's almost time for tea. Are you staying for tea?'

'Yes, Aunt Dorothy, she is. We are going upstairs to do research on a project.'

'Run along now, both of you.'

Once in Jing Yang's room, Angelina plunked her bag onto the floor next to the bed and settled into a chair next to the computer. The computer was sitting on top of a wall-to-wall desk-cum-cabinet resting next to the windows of the bedroom. There were drawer units on castors at the two ends of the desk-cum-cabinet. Jing Yang sat in a chair in front of the computer.

'Don't touch my things.'

Angelina was opening the drawers one by one and rummaging through his things.

'I am just curious. What's in this lower drawer? It's locked.' Angelina was trying in vain to pull open the drawer.

'My personal things. Please stop pulling the drawer. You will spoil it.'

'Can I see what's inside, please?'

'It's men's things. Not for women to poke their noses into.'

'Please…can I see just once?'

'Did you come here to help me with the project or to turn my room upside down?'

Angelina was now frowning. When she was sulking, her face would be contorted, causing her eyes to look very small indeed. This girl's sudden weather changes irritated Jing Yang but he kept his calm.

'Are all girls like this?' he thought to himself, shaking his head.

'Why are you shaking your head?' she asked. 'I don't like you to shake your head. If you have something to say, just say it.'

'Never mind. If you don't want to let me see, I won't force you. I don't like to force people.'

'Good! Come on. Don't let's waste time on these trivial things.'

'Oh! Alright!'

Angelina was obliging just this time. She thought that there were always more opportunities for her to get him to open the drawer. She could try asking the next time she came to his house. She was sure he could not refuse her request forever. On the other hand, Jing Yang thought he was winning the fight over control of his private space. It was the second time that she had backed down from throwing her tantrum when he rejected her request. But what he did not realise was that he was getting comfortable having Angelina around – that it was getting more difficult for him to withdraw from this new relationship with her. They had greatly differing personalities – she gave too much and he valued his private space too much! Yet, somehow, both would find a meeting point where they would compromise, accept their newly defined mutual space, and then become bosom friends.

'So where shall we start? Shall we search the fall of Singapore on a local search engine?'

'Sure. Which search engine do you know of?'

'How about getforme.com? It's been around since 1999.'

'That long? Must have a large database. Let's visit the Web site.'

Jing Yang typed the words Fall of Singapore into a search box on the homepage of getforme.com. On the screen, 488 matches for the search term were displayed. He scrolled down the links on the results page and clicked on a link entitled Remembering the Fall of Singapore. His eyes focused on the following text:

15 Feb 1942 – Singapore surrendered to the Japanese. It was also the first day of the Chinese New Year. British Lt General Percival surrendered to General Yamashita at the Ford Factory's Board Room in Bukit Timah.

'Gosh! I didn't know it was on the first day of the Chinese New Year that Singapore fell to the Japanese. Just imagine! These people had put up banners and decorated their homes for the new year and the Japanese entered Singapore that day. It must have been terrible! The people must have suffered under the Japanese.'

His interest in history had been piqued. It was a good beginning.

'Yes, we are really lucky to be born many, many years after the war ended. Hey, Jing Yang. I thought you didn't like history!'

'Don't put words into my mouth. I never said I didn't like history. I merely said it was a boring subject.'

'So, is it a boring subject to you now?'

'Still early to say, still early to say.'

Jing Yang clicked on more links to articles relating to the search term. They led to uninteresting information. Then a link caught his eye. It had the description 'World War II'. He clicked on this link. This Web page was long. He scrolled down the page. There was information on the Changi Murals and farther down were details of the Japanese assault on Malaya and Singapore. Then there was information on where the prisoners-of-war were housed in Changi.

Right at the bottom of the Web page was the following heading:

A World-War-II underground tunnel was discovered last year.

Jing Yang read the entire paragraph under the heading.

Alas! It was not what he was searching for. This bit of news was about an underground tunnel running under Labrador Park in Pasir Panjang Road.

Just then there was a knock on the door. Tim opened the door and announced that tea was ready.

'Jing Yang, I am hungry.'

'Alright. Let's go down for tea. We'll continue our search later.'

To Aunt Dorothy, tea was an elaborate affair different from what HDB dwellers were accustomed to. Angelina did not have any proper tea or coffee break at home. Whenever she was hungry, she would go into the kitchen and pour herself a cup of coffee from a hot-water flask on the counter-top in the kitchen. Her mother would prepare a pot of coffee at about two o'clock every afternoon. She would then pour this piping hot into a big flask. Those in the family wishing to drink coffee would help themselves to the coffee. There were no designated coffee break times. Angelina would eat a slice of buttered bread by herself while sipping the coffee in front of the television.

Things were way different at Jing Yang's place. Aunt Dorothy had set the table for tea. There was a pot of tea on the table. Next to it were a milk jug, a sugar bowl, and a small plate on which were slices of lemon. There were plates of scones, sandwiches and biscuits. There was also some jam and marmalade. The tea had a strange smell to it.

'What's that smell?' asked Angelina. It was the first time in her life she had smelled such tea.

'It's Earl Grey Tea, Angelina,' said Aunt Dorothy.

'Why does it smell, Aunty?'

'Dear girl, why do you always ask strange questions? It is bergamot – an oil extracted from the rind of the bergamot orange, a fragrant citrus fruit. Earl Grey Tea is extremely popular in England.'

'Is it?' Angelina asked as she sipped the tea. She was not used to the strong taste of bergamot. She could not taste the flavour of tea. This tea sure took some getting used to. She glanced at Jing Yang. From his eyes, she could see that he was not enjoying the tea either. But he was not telling anyone. He sipped his tea in silence.

'Here! Help yourself to the scones and the other stuff,' said Aunt Dorothy.

'Mmm. It's very delicious,' exclaimed Angelina as she bit into a scone.

'Glad you like it. I baked it.'

'You did, Aunty? My, you do know how to cook. I like your pork chops. I like your scones too.'

'Indeed, you do! Have some more.'

Aunt Dorothy was getting to like Angelina more. This girl was sometimes blunt, but she was honest and likeable. She was going to tell her sister about this new lady in her nephew's life.

Back up in Jing Yang's room, Angelina dug into her bag for her water bottle. She sat on the bed and gulped down some water.

'It wasn't easy drinking the tea. Do you drink this every afternoon?'

'Yes. And after two months, I have got used to this strange taste. I don't want Aunt Dorothy to be unhappy.'

'How about Tim?'

'Well. He drinks the tea as if he was drinking water.'

It seemed that Angelina would have no choice but get used to drinking this strange tea. She wanted to visit Jing Yang at his house often. That would invariably mean that she would be invited to afternoon tea.

Jing Yang went online to visit getforme.com again. This time, he perused the menu on the top of the homepage. He clicked on the link to the travel section and scrolled down the page to the part listing local attractions. He clicked on the museum link. He read the page from top to bottom. Half-way down, he saw a listing which attracted his attention. It read:

The Battle Box

Jing Yang nudged Angelina who was flipping through a teen magazine. He clicked on the link which took him to a page with information on an underground bunker belonging to Britain's HQ Malaya Command during World War Two. He gazed at some text which read:

It was the site where General Percival reached the fateful decision to surrender Singapore to the invading Japanese forces.

It was what they were looking for! Below the text was a picture of a wax figure in uniform standing in the corridor of the bunker. The following information was listed:

Opening hours: Daily 10am - 6pm
Admission: Adult $8, Child $5 for guided tour

'We must visit this place.'
'Why don't we go there tomorrow, after school?'
'I'll contact the others.' Angelina SMSed Mabel and Fanny on her mobile phone. While they waited for the replies from the girls, they jotted down the information on a piece of paper. Jing Yang added the Web page to his favourites folder on the Internet browser, just in case he needed to refer to the page again. This way, he did not need to remember the long URL address. Soon, Angelina's mobile phone was beeping away. The girls had replied.

'They can't make it tomorrow. How about Saturday?'
'Too late! We won't have enough time left. Let's go by ourselves tomorrow.'
'Okay. I will let them know. Can you ask Tim to come along?'
'You ask him!' Jing Yang found it difficult to open his mouth for favours. He did not want to impose on others. He had been used to doing things alone, till Angelina intruded into his life.

'Okay. What's his mobile phone number?'

'He's just next door. Can't you pop over and ask him.'

'Give me his number, please. I'll SMS him.' Angelina preferred SMSing her friends to calling them on her mobile phone. Besides, she wanted Tim's number so that she could contact him to arrange outings. She figured that it would be easier for her to ask Tim to come along with them for outings. If she had to rely on Jing Yang to open his mouth, they would never get Tim to go out with them. These cousins certainly were not friendly to each other, she thought. They needed some prodding along, she decided.

Angelina's mobile phone beeped again. Tim had replied to her SMS message.

'Good news, Jing Yang. Tim has agreed to go to the bunker with us.'

'Do they have a discount for students? Can you call them to ask, Jing Yang?'

'Alright.' Jing Yang picked up his mobile phone and dialled the number for The Battle Box's ticketing office. He waited for someone to come to the phone.

'Good afternoon, Battle Box.'

'Hi. Can I know whether students get a discounted price for admission to the Battle Box?'

'Of course. It's five dollars for students.'

'Do we have to be in uniform?'

'You just need to show us your student's concession pass.'

'How long will the tour take?'

'You will first watch a ten-minute video. Then the guide will take you into the Battle Box for a thirty-minute guided tour.'

'Jing Yang, ask the guy whether we can take pictures in the bunker.'

'Can we use our cameras to take pictures in the Battle Box?'

'Sure, you can. But, video-taping is not allowed.'

'I see. Thanks.'

'You are welcome. Hope you will visit us soon.'

'We will. Thank you.' Jing Yang ended the call.

4 *TREASURE IN SINGAPORE?*

Now Angelina had to ask her mother for five dollars for the ticket. She dreaded approaching her mother for money. Her mother already had a difficult time making ends meet in the Goh household and her birthday party the day before had to have cost her mother a bomb. She could not ask Jing Yang for help. She was above that sort of thing. Angelina was what you would describe as a fiercely independent girl. While her peers would get their boyfriends to pay for them when they were out on dates, she preferred to rely on herself. Also, Jing Yang was not her boyfriend – not yet anyway, she thought. She could not impose on him. It was this trait, among others, that made Angelina popular and likeable to many.

When Angelina reached home that afternoon, she changed her mind about asking her mother for money. She decided she would dig out some coins from her piggy bank below her bed. Space was tight in the small room which she shared with her two brothers so she kept her personal things in a plastic container under her bed.

Angelina was given three dollars a day as pocket money. This was hardly enough for a growing girl in secondary school. Food during recess cost two dollars per meal. She brought her own drinking water in a plastic bottle. There was hardly enough money for lunch when she had to stay back for afternoon remedial lessons and co-curricular activities. She had to plan carefully how to spend her money.

Sometimes, she would skip recess meals so she could save her money for other uses. She could not ask her mother for more money. There was none to spare. Her mother had already been generous. It was typical HDB living – trying to make ends meet. But Angelina had few complaints. She thought she was lucky, for she was loved in the family. Her family was complete. Some schoolmates were growing up in broken families. They hung around void decks after school, wasting away their time doing nothing constructive and smoking with their peers. Their parents bothered not what company they kept.

Angelina glanced at the clock on a side cabinet next to her bed. It was past six o'clock. Soon her eldest brother would be back from work. She was hopeful of receiving some pocket money from him. It was that time of the month when her brother would be generous. This brother would give her fifty dollars every month to help her with her expenses. She was not being greedy. It was the way things worked in her family. The eldest child in the family, having worked, would give a portion of his salary to their mother to help with the family expenses. He would also give fifty dollars to each of his two other siblings as long as they were still schooling. Then when her elder brother went to work, he would contribute to the family the same way the eldest brother did. This arrangement was common among poor HDB dwellers. It had been going on in many households since the 1970s. The system worked well. Several generations of students had grown up benefiting from it. Such a thing was alien to well-off teenagers like Jing Yang who never had to worry about lack of money. He was certainly lucky to be born in a rich family.

When Angelina went to bed at ten o'clock, her eldest

brother had yet to return home. She had already used a pair of tweezers to dig out some one-dollar coins from her piggy bank. These were now in her wallet. She only had to skip recess to make her daily allowance of three dollars last till afternoon. Angelina was no stranger to carrying around just a few dollars in her pocket. She was not alone. A number of her school mates were in her situation. Greendale Secondary was located in the heartland, and with the exception of a few students like Jing Yang and Tim, drew its student strength from HDB dwellers. She was now thinking of the next day. Her mind was drifting away fast to what she and Jing Yang would be doing after school.

When Angelina got up the next morning, she was pleasantly surprised to see five ten-dollar notes neatly placed under her alarm clock. Her eldest brother had not forgotten to give her an allowance for the month. She put a ten-dollar note in her wallet and hid the rest in an old diary which she dropped into the container under the bed. Now she did not need to worry about her expenses that afternoon but she knew she had to be frugal in her spending. She would try hard not to use the red note in her wallet today.

Soon it was time for school. Angelina had pestered Jing Yang to let her go to school together with him and Tim. She had argued that since they were living so close to each other, it was only natural for them to go together. Moreover, they were classmates. This arrangement made sense to her and she did not see why it would not make sense to Jing Yang. He caved in to end her nagging. Today was the first time all three would be going to school together. They had agreed to meet at the walkway outside the sub-station between their homes. Angelina was early. She sat on a concrete bollard next to the kerb, munching on a piece of buttered bread. From where she was sitting, she had a clear view of the front of Jing Yang's house.

'Hi boys!'

'Morning, Angelina. You are early.'

'Hi.'

The three of them made their way to the bus-stop along the main road.

'Jing Yang, did you remember to bring along your camera?'

'Yes, it is in my bag but I am worried there may be a spot-check during assembly afterwards.'

'It's Tuesday! They don't carry out spot-checks on Tuesdays.'

'What if?'

'You are such a coward! Here, let me keep it for you.'

'Thanks Tim. You are so brave, unlike your cousin.'

'Different genes, you know,' said Tim, pointing to his skin. He was telling her he was an *Angmoh*.

'Hah! What nonsense!' cried Jing Yang.

'It's true. We British are brave chaps, you know.'

'I thought you are a Singaporean, Tim.'

'Angelina, my father is British so I am British.'

'No, you are not. My mother told me you are a Singapore citizen. That's why you had to come to Singapore – to do your national service.'

Tim glared at Jing Yang. Both boys had trouble getting along. They tried hard to irritate each other. But they did not try hard to be friends.

'Now, it's not you and me quarrelling, Jing Yang. It's you and your cousin quarrelling.'

'We are not quarrelling. We are just arguing. Don't you know the difference between arguing and quarrelling, Angelina?'

'I don't. Please tell me, Jing Yang.'

'Arguing means to put forth reasons for doing something; quarrelling means to find fault.'

'I already told you I am British. See the colour of my skin?'

'Stop it guys! For goodness' sake, it's only quarter to six in the morning. Here comes our bus!'

Angelina was glad that the arrival of the bus had saved them from an ugly situation. She resolved to ask Aunt Dorothy about Tim's nationality; she wanted the matter settled so the two cousins would not have reason to find fault with each other over it.

It was crowded at the bus-stop as students from different schools were waiting to board service number 136. This service plied the Hougang, Sengkang and Punggol public housing routes, along which were more than seven secondary schools nestled in the three housing estates. It was a motley group of students that jam-packed this bus as it cruised along Upper Serangoon Road, heading towards Sengkang housing estate. There was standing room only on the bus for the three friends. By the time the bus arrived in Punggol housing estate, it had already discharged more than half of its load, allowing Jing Yang, Tim and Angelina to find some vacant seats.

Jing Yang and Angelina had a surprise that morning during social studies period. Their teacher, Mr Zee, told the class that 3E3 and 3E4 would be touring Fort Canning the next week and on the itinerary was a guided tour of The Battle Box. The excursion would be paid for using the students' education fund. The students did not need to pay. This was news to Jing Yang and Angelina. They had already planned on visiting The Battle Box that afternoon. Now the trip might not take place after all.

Both students huddled together in a corner of the canteen during recess. Angelina had said she was not hungry. Actually, she wanted to save the money from not taking a meal. Jing Yang had no idea what she was up to. He had no appetite so he joined her in a discussion on the proposed Battle Box visit. Tim was in class.

'Now, what shall we do?'

'Mabel and Fanny are going along with us on the trip next week. Should we cancel today's trip?'

'I reckon so. But I do so much want to go.'

'Make up your mind!' said Angelina. Although she

might save five dollars if they did not make the visit, it was not important to her at the moment. If Jing Yang wanted to visit the place today, she would follow him.

'Let me think.'

'Why don't we postpone the trip? We could instead go to VivoCity today! Since you have brought your camera today, we can always use it to take pictures at VivoCity.'

'Okay. It's settled. Let's go to VivoCity.'

'Good! Let's go tell Tim.'

They walked to the adjoining block where the secondary one classes were. In Greendale Secondary, secondary one and two students had their recess at quarter past ten, a period earlier.

'Let me talk to Tim. You two had a tiff early this morning. I think he is still sore. I don't want him to say no to going to VivoCity.'

'Alright. I will wait for you here.' Jing Yang sat on the steps of the staircase at one end of the block.

Angelina was visibly excited when she returned.

'*Wah*! Luckily, you did not come with me,' she told him. Jing Yang looked puzzled.

'Guess who was in the classroom!'

'The principal?'

'Miss Shih!'

'What's she doing there? She doesn't teach the lower secondary levels.'

'She must be doing relief duty. Mr Fong is not in school today.' Mr Fong was a geography teacher.

'Thank you for asking me to wait for you here.'

'Since you are so grateful, give me a treat then.'

Angelina was not one to ask others for a treat. But this was a different situation for two reasons. First, it was reward for her effort so the treat was earned. Also, that she opened her mouth to suggest one showed the two classmates were drawing closer.

'I will. I will.'

'Don't forget, ah. Let's go back to class.' The bell had

rung for the next period.

'So, did you get to ask Tim?'

'Done!'

It was two periods of English now.

Mr Seng was holding some scripts in his hands.

'Class, I am disappointed in most of you. Only twelve of you handed in the 500-word essay which I asked you to do over the mid-year holidays.'

'Mr Seng, five hundred words is a lot of words you know.'

'If you don't even try to write the essay, how can you complain?'

There was silence in the classroom.

'I am surprised at you, Jing Yang. I thought you knew better. Fancy you not doing my work. It's plain sailing for you. Why did you not do the essay? Don't tell me it's writer's block again.'

'I forgot, Mr Seng. Sorry!'

'Angelina, what's your excuse this time?

'Sorry, Mr Seng.'

'And you, Beng Huat?'

'Mr Seng, it's five hundred words.' Beng Huat gestured with his left hand, spreading five fingers apart to emphasise the number five.

'So? An entire month I have given you guys to do just one essay and you can't even do this simple thing.'

'Ramesh! Wipe that smurk off your face.'

'Sorry, Mr Seng.'

'You have today to finish the assignment. I expect to see you submitting the essay to me by the end of today – or else.'

Then Mr Seng went into length explaining the five basic elements of a short story. He said nothing more about the 500-word essay for the rest of his lesson. The students thought it was just another of his harmless threats, uttered in despair, so they did not take notice.

Unfortunately, an unpleasant surprise awaited 3E3 at

the end of the school day. Five minutes before the end of the last period, Mr Seng appeared at the main doorway to the classroom. He knocked on the door and asked to speak to the class chairman. The students were paying attention to the teacher in the classroom so they did not see Mr Seng taking the keys to the classroom from the class chairman. By the time they realised what was happening, it was too late. The bell for dismissal of school had rung and Mr Seng had locked the rear door to the classroom. He was now standing at the front doorway to the classroom.

Once the teacher had left, Mr Seng walked in. Standing at the doorway, he spoke to the class.

'When I call your names, take your bag and go out of the room.'

He proceeded to read the names, and one by one the students filed out of the room. By the time he got to the last name on the list, twelve students had left the classroom.

Mr Seng locked the door behind him and turned to look at the students seated in the classroom. He was no stranger to neighbourhood schools. He had spent eleven years teaching in such schools so he knew how to handle non-compliant students.

The students were trapped – the doors to the classroom were locked and Mr Seng had placed a desk against the main door. He was now sitting on it, holding the keys to the locked door.

'Relax. Enjoy the afternoon breeze coming in through the windows. When you have finished the 500-word essay, hand it to me and you can leave the room. I have plenty of free time today – in fact the whole afternoon.

The students in 3E3 now realised that Mr Seng was not joking with them. He meant business. Everyone settled down to completing the assignment reluctantly. Their afternoon plans had been quashed. They could not get out of the classroom – not unless they finished the 500-word essay.

Some of the boys grumbled aloud. How could he expect them to finish writing five hundred words that afternoon? How could he? They moaned and groaned, as if in great pain.

Alas, all the moaning and groaning could not save them from having to spend the afternoon in the classroom. Mr Seng was adamant in getting what he wanted from them. He was dead serious this time.

Meanwhile, schoolmates of 3E3 had gathered outside the classroom. They were peeking into the room. Mr Seng made no effort to shoo them off. On the contrary, he wanted them to watch. He knew that news of the incident would spread like wildfire in the school the next day. It was just what he wanted. His students in the other classes would not dare not do his assignments – at least for the next month. These students' memory spans were short. Soon they would forget what had happened and be back to their old ways. He could not use this trick again. He had to think of new ideas. Alas, this was part and parcel of a teacher's work in a neighbourhood school. But he was resourceful so the students were always outwitted.

'*Alamak*! There go my plans for the afternoon.'

'What time are you coming out?'

'No idea. I don't know when I can finish writing.'

Mr Seng did not stop the students from both sides of the windows from conversing with one another. He knew the students in his class had made appointments to spend the afternoon with their friends now loitering outside the classroom. He felt their presence outside the classroom would spur the class on. After all, they knew that they could leave the room when they had completed their work.

Some students had finished writing one page of foolscap paper. Some were staring into space, trying to think of things to write about. More moans punctuated the air.

It was now half past two. Six students had completed

their assignment. They picked up their bags, walked up to Mr Seng and handed him their work. He pushed aside the desk next to him and unlocked the door to let the students out. By then some students had got up from their desks and were walking towards him.

'The rest of you remain where you are. Don't try to be funny with me. There is no need to come up as I won't let you out until you have handed in your work.'

'Why are you like that?' one student cried.

'Teacher, I can't think right now. Can I give you the essay tomorrow? I promise I will finish it by tomorrow,' said another student.

But Mr Seng was not listening. Resigned to spending the afternoon in the classroom, the students of 3E3 groaned as they penned their thoughts on paper.

Some wrote furiously, determined to get out of the room as soon as they could. Their friends out in the corridor were getting impatient. Some were pacing up and now. Some had left. But there were some students who were waiting quietly. Among them was Tim. He sat on the floor outside the classroom, leaned against the wall and closed his eyes. He was taking a nap now.

In the room, Jing Yang had completed his work and was waiting for Angelina to finish hers. Writing an essay of five hundred words was a challenge to her as most of the time she communicated in Mandarin. At home, she used Mandarin with family members. In school, she spoke to her schoolmates and her friends in Mandarin. In supermarkets and food-courts, she also conversed in Mandarin. It was only with Jing Yang and Tim that she spoke English. Occasionally, Jing Yang dropped an idea or two when she encountered the writer's block.

It was now three o'clock. Angelina had at last finished her essay. Both she and Jing Yang packed their things and approached their teacher. As Mr Seng unlocked the front door, he surveyed the room. There were fifteen students left.

Though Tim was left to wait for them in the corridor, he was not annoyed. He had spent the time reminiscing about the good old days in Norfolk, England. He was not used to the weather here – it was too hot. Nor was he used to the people here, they liked to chat in Mandarin, Malay and Tamil – these were all Sanskrit to him. His mother had made a mistake moving them here. Worse, she made him stay with a Chinese cousin whom he had trouble getting along with. Why could they not rent a place while they were house hunting? He just could not fathom this.

'Tim, thanks for waiting for us.'

'My pleasure.'

'So are we still going to VivoCity?'

'I'm very hungry, Tim. Can we go get a bite first?' Angelina had not eaten anything since breakfast. Her stomach was grumbling to her now. She was feeling faint.

'Angelina, what's the time now?'

'A little over three o'clock.'

'Gosh! That late already. Let's hop over to Compasspoint Shopping Centre for a bite,' Jing Yang suggested. 'Angelina, my treat today.'

They took the LRT opposite their school and arrived at Compasspoint some ten minutes later. Jing Yang led them into McDonald's restaurant in the basement. They ordered a complete meal each and ate heartily. For Angelina, it was a treat, not just because Jing Yang was paying, but also because she rarely ventured into a fast-food restaurant. Angelina thoroughly enjoyed the meal. She was too hungry to talk so the three ate in silence as the two boys did not make conversation with each other.

'So are we still going to VivoCity?' Tim was asking again.

'No, it's already almost four o'clock. The journey there takes an hour and by the time we come back it will have been night time. Aunt Dorothy will be worried about us. Angelina, your mother will be worried sick, too, I am sure.'

'Let's stay here. We can walk around and perhaps visit

the library.'

'Why not? What say you, Tim?'

'Alright by me.'

'Yes, we can do some research on the fall of Singapore.'

'Don't you need to call home, Angelina?'

'As long as I am home by seven o'clock, my mother is not worried.'

Tim took out his mobile phone and called his mother to tell her both of them had changed their mind about going to VivoCity. He told her where they were now.

'*Wah*! Tim. You are very obedient.'

'I just do not want my mother to worry about me.'

'Jing Yang, can you come with me to collect my new identity card next week?'

'You are collecting your identity card so soon? I haven't received any notification yet.'

'That's because you were born in December.'

'Oh yeah, I forgot. Silly me.'

'So, is it a yes or a no, Jing Yang?'

'Can do.'

'Don't forget, ah!'

'How can I forget when you are always reminding me – like every other day?'

'Don't be so mean to me, Jing Yang.'

'I was only kidding.'

'Tim, why are you always so quiet?'

'I am like that – a man with few words.'

'You are only thirteen years old; you are not a man yet, dear boy.'

'Don't go disturbing Tim like that, Jing Yang.'

'I just couldn't resist. Besides it's just plain banter.'

'What's that word?'

'You mean banter?'

'Yes. Jing Yang, you are always using big words. Sometimes, I don't know what you are saying.'

'It's not a big word. Humongous is a big word.'

'There you go again. If you carry on like this, I won't talk to you anymore. Tim is so much better than you. He doesn't ever tease me.'

'Alright. Alright. You were asking about the word banter. It means speaking in a playful way. Anyway, don't you think your English has improved since you knew me?'

'So? Does that mean you can tease me?'

'I'm not teasing you – just helping you to learn more English words, that's all.'

'Tim, help me, please.'

'Angelina, I do not want to be involved in your husband-and-wife affairs.'

'Tim, Angelina and I are just classmates.'

'Really? Then why is she blushing? Ha! Ha! Ha!'

'Excuse me. Please keep your voices down. This is a library,' said a uniformed lady. The three students had not noticed they had stepped into a public library in Compasspoint.

'Sorry!' they chorused in unison.

The three students sat on the floor in a corner of the library, poring over several books on World War Two. They lapped up information on the key players in the war – Lieutenant-General Arthur Percival and Lieutenant-General Yamashita. Though it was not their responsibility to do research on this Japanese general, they thought it would help them in understanding why Singapore was lost to the Japanese invading forces.

'It says here in this book that General Yamashita had hidden a cache of treasure in the Philippines,' said Jing Yang.

'Really? Wow! It would be great if we were to stumble onto his treasure,' said Tim.

'Don't dream, boys. Read the text again. The treasure was hidden in the Philippines, not Singapore,' said Angelina. 'Besides, let's not get off-track. We are looking for information on the fall of Singapore, not the Yamashita treasure.'

'No harm looking. Anyway, the treasure is rumoured to be in the Philippines. There is no confirmation, only rumours so the treasure, if it exists, could be hidden anywhere, even in Singapore,' said Jing Yang.

'What if it's in Singapore?' enquired Tim.

'*Wah*! We could go searching for the treasure, instead of finding out about the fall of Singapore,' Angelina said.

'What's in the treasure?' asked Tim.

'It says here: gold bars, golden statues and gold coins,' said Angelina.

'Where?' asked Jing Yang.

'See here! In the second paragraph, under the illustration,' said Angelina.

'Wow! So much gold! Whoever finds the treasure will be super-rich!' exclaimed Tim.

'How did they get their hands on so much gold?' asked Angelina.

'They plundered the lands in Asia. They must have taken all the gold from the governments, banks, temples, businesses and rich people's houses,' said Jing Yang.

'Look! That's a picture of General Percival,' said Angelina, pointing at a distinguished looking man with a moustache in the book she was reading.

'So that's what he looks like,' said Jing Yang.

'Who's he?' asked Tim.

'He's the one who surrendered Singapore to the Japanese during World War Two,' said Jing Yang.

'He is? I thought the Japanese invaded Singapore,' said Tim.

'That's your thought, but it was not what happened,' said Jing Yang.

'So we are going to find out all about him too?' Tim asked.

'Yes. Angelina, jot down this information about General Percival,' said Jing Yang. 'Don't forget to include the information about the Yamashita treasure,' said Jing Yang.

'Why?' asked Angelina.

'You never know whether we would need it. Copy it down, just in case,' said Jing Yang.

'Alright. Tim, help me copy this part, please,' said Angelina. She handed him the book which was on the floor next to her.

'We need to find out what happened to the British soldiers after they surrendered – where they were interned,' added Jing Yang. He stood up and walked towards the shelf displaying the Singapore collection of books. He fingered them. Minutes later, with some books in his hands, he returned to his place on the floor and put them down beside him.

'I've found some more books on World War Two,' Jing Yang said. 'This one is about the battle in Singapore,' he continued.

'What's this about?' asked Angelina, pointing to a picture of some women on the front cover of a book.

'It's about comfort women,' said Jing Yang.

'Comfort women?' asked Angelina. 'Are they supposed to comfort the soldiers whose buddies have died in battle?'

'No, Angelina. It says on the blurb that the Japanese forced women to entertain their soldiers. These women were known as comfort women,' replied Jing Yang.

'Entertain their soldiers? How? They sang and danced for them?' quipped Angelina.

'Open the book and read the preface,' said Jing Yang. He did not want to talk in detail about these comfort women. He was a little embarrassed. He knew these women were forced to have sex with the Japanese soldiers, but having come from a boys' school, he was not used to talking about sex matters, and certainly not with Angelina.

There were some minutes of awkward silence as Angelina read the preface of the book. Then more silence prevailed. Angelina had found the answer to her question. She was now blushing.

'There you go again – red in the face!' cried Tim.

'Really?' asked Angelina. She took a mirror from her bag and surveyed her face. Then she patted her cheeks gently.

'No, *lah*! Tim, you are horrid, teasing me like that,' said Angelina.

'It's true. You were red-faced just now. If you don't believe me, ask Jing Yang,' Tim retorted.

'Was I blushing, Jing Yang?' Angelina asked.

Jing Yang pretended to be absorbed in reading the book that he was holding. He ignored the question.

'Children, please keep quiet in the library,' said a librarian who had appeared in front of them.

'Sorry!' they whispered in unison.

Once the librarian was out of earshot, Tim turned to the other two.

'Children, indeed. Fancy calling us children!' he exclaimed.

'Yeah, we are not children any more. She must be short-sighted!' quipped Jing Yang.

They giggled. Then they covered their mouths, as if to stifle the sounds from it. It was rare for the two cousins to be in agreement about anything. But it was an improvement. Angelina's idea of getting these two boys to go out more often with her was good. It was helping them get along with each other, albeit slowly.

'So, what have we got on the fall of Singapore so far?' asked Jing Yang.

Angelina referred to the slips of foolscap paper in her hands.

'We have got biographies of General Percival and General Yamashita, the Japanese attack on Singapore and some information on the housing of prisoners-of-war in Changi,' said Angelina.

'That's not enough. We need to find out how the Japanese landed in Malaya too,' Jing Yang said.

'But, that's not about Singapore,' said Angelina.

'Still, it is relevant,' replied Jing Yang. 'It shows how

the attack was possible – all the way from Malaya to Singapore. It shows the beginning of the assault.'

'There's nothing here about Malaya,' said Angelina.

'We may need to visit other libraries. How about going to the library in Hougang?' said Jing Yang.

'What's the time now?' asked Angelina.

'Just after six o'clock,' said Tim.

'*Wah*! So late already. I need to be home before seven o'clock,' said Angelina.

'Yes, it's too late today. How about tomorrow afternoon, after school?' asked Jing Yang.

'Can do,' said Angelina.

'I have got to ask Mum. I am supposed to go house-hunting with her tomorrow,' said Tim.

'House-hunting? I thought you are living with Jing Yang,' said Angelina.

'Temporarily only, till we find our own place,' replied Tim.

'Can we come along?' asked Angelina. She had not been house-hunting before and thought it was fun to do.

'Must ask my Mum first,' said Tim. Then he whipped out his mobile phone.

'We are not supposed to use mobile phones in the library,' said Angelina.

'Sh!' replied Tim. Covering his mouth with a hand, he proceeded to call his mother. In the short conversation he had done two things: obtained permission to take Angelina along for the house-hunting trips, and told her where he was. Tim would always keep his mother informed on all matters – big or small. Mother and son were close.

'My mum asked me when we are going home and I told her we would be back by seven o'clock,' said Tim.

'Gosh! It's now half past six. We better get going,' replied Jing Yang.

'Tim, you haven't told me whether I can go along with you,' said Angelina.

'Mum says okay,' replied Tim.

'Surely, you are coming along, Jing Yang,' said Angelina.

'Yeah *lah*!' said Jing Yang. He had no choice. This girl was persistent. She would nag him till he gave in.

Angelina beamed. She was too young to be house-hunting; she was not yet married. But here was a chance to live this experience. Living in a cramped HDB flat, she had no idea what upper-class Singaporeans were privy to in their selection of homes. She already had an eye-opening experience when she first visited Jing Yang's home. There had to be many more such houses in Singapore, she thought. Here was an opportunity to visit some of them and she would not miss it for the world, she concluded.

'Come on, let's go,' said Jing Yang.

They made their way down the shopping complex, heading towards the bus terminal and MRT station, both of which stood side by side.

'Shall we take the train back?' asked Angelina.

The boys nodded in agreement. The bus journey would have taken a half-hour but the journey by train would only be ten minutes long.

'Oh! I have no more trips left,' cried Angelina. 'I need to top up my MRT card.' She could not go through the turnstile at the station.

'No need. Here! Use this card,' said Jing Yang.

He extracted an MRT card from his wallet and handed it to Angelina.

'Don't worry, it's got enough for about forty trips,' he said.

'I can't use your card,' said Angelina. Truly this girl was not proud but she had pride. She would not take charity.

'We are not strangers. We are friends and classmates. Doing this project means we have to take many trips on the bus and MRT. These trips will drain the value in our MRT cards quickly,' Jing Yang said. 'Quick! The train is almost here.'

Jing Yang pointed at a screen above them showing the

arrival times of the trains. Angelina took the card and tapped it on the turnstile sensor. The boys followed. Then they dashed down the escalator to the train which had just arrived at the platform.

Jing Yang was being thoughtful nowadays. He was beginning to think of the people around him, especially Angelina, who was now often by his side. At first, he had found that the more she gave in their friendship, the more he wanted to withdraw from her, for she was intruding into his privacy. But now he realised that the more she gave, the more warmth he discovered in their relationship. It was new to him – this feeling of being close to someone. His parents were always so far away. Although the Internet drew them closer in distance, it did not make their relationship warmer and warmth was what he needed more than anything else. But he understood their jobs were more important. Discovery of new things was in their blood. They just had to be where the centre of pioneering genetic engineering was – at the prestigious Rockford University in New York. He had no inkling what genetic engineering was, but understood its importance for his parents to be involved in it – his parents were the best in the field!

The trio emerged from Hougang MRT station almost fifteen minutes later. They sauntered along the walkway from the station to Upper Serangoon Road, passing through the void decks of some HDB blocks, pondering the next few days' activities.

It was seven o'clock when the boys bade goodbye to Angelina and walked to their house.

There was the usual silence between the boys as they went into the house. Without Angelina around them, the gap between them was obvious.

Both boys made for their bedrooms quietly. There was something Jing Yang wanted to ask his aunt and during dinner he broached the topic which was on his mind.

'Aunt Dorothy, are you a Singapore citizen?'

'Why yes, of course.'

'So is Tim also a Singapore citizen?' Tim was now looking at him.

'Tell him, Mum, that I am British. He keeps telling people I am Singaporean.'

'People? Which people, dear?'

'Angelina, for instance.'

'Aunt Dorothy, I only told Angelina.'

'I guess so, Jing Yang. You don't mix around with other people, so it could only be Angelina.'

'Tell him, Mum.'

'Boys, both of you are correct, to a certain extent.'

'Mum, I don't get it. What do you mean by to a certain extent?'

'Well, you are a British citizen by birth and your father is British.'

'You see, I told you so!'

'But Jing Yang is also right.'

'Mum, you are confusing me.'

'Your mother is a Singapore citizen, you know.'

'So?'

'So you are a Singaporean by descent.'

'What do you mean?'

'Simply this, dear. Because I am a Singapore citizen, you can become one too, easily. When you turn fifteen, you will take up Singapore citizenship.'

'But, Mum, I don't want to.'

'Why not, dear?'

'Because...because I don't like this place. I don't have friends here.'

'You will have plenty of friends. Just give yourself some time.'

'But, why do I have to become a Singapore citizen?'

'Yes, why indeed, dear. Your mother has spent a lifetime here. All my relatives and friends are here. I have been away from Singapore too long. I want to spend the rest of my life here. You are my son. I wish you can be a part of the world I grew up in – the world I truly belong in.'

'But I don't belong here, Mum.'

'Yes, you do, dear.'

'Aunt Dorothy, he doesn't like it here. Why don't you let him stay in England?'

'I am not going back to England, except for visits. Your uncle hardly has any relatives in England. He will be moving here permanently at the end of next year. So we will all be here. Tim will be all alone if he returns to England.'

'Aunt Dorothy, will Tim have to give up being a British citizen when he turns fifteen?'

'Singapore does not accept dual citizenship, that is, it doesn't allow Tim to be a Singapore citizen and a British citizen at the same time. So Tim will have to give up British citizenship.'

'Mum, I don't want to.'

'Tim, you have two more years to get used to life here. We shall wait till you are fifteen before we make a firm decision on your citizenship, so there's no need for you to worry your head over this matter now.'

'But, Mum.'

'Give yourself two years, Tim. That's why we are here now instead of when you are fifteen years old. We want to give you time to adjust to life here.'

'Jing Yang, please don't talk to Tim about his citizenship any more. I don't want him to be unduly worried over this.'

'Yes, Aunt Dorothy.'

'So the matter is settled. I want no more mention of it. Is that clear, Tim?'

'Yes, Mum.'

'Beep! Beep!' Jing Yang's mobile phone had received an SMS message. Jing Yang took out his mobile phone to read the message. It was from Angelina. She wanted him to go online to search for information on the Battle Box.

Angelina did not have a computer at home as the family could not afford to buy one. So whenever she wanted to look up things on the Internet she would visit the school library where access to its five computers was free. She only had to book in advance. Sometimes, she would use the computers in the public libraries at Compasspoint Shopping Centre and Hougang Mall. But tonight, she was counting on Jing Yang to surf for information.

Jing Yang had little success looking up information on the term Battle Box. The search engine threw up all sorts of links, pertaining to games, fun communities, business strategies and solar heaters. He then tried looking up the term Battle Box Singapore. He had some success. There were links to blogs, travel sites and picture galleries. Jing Yang visited all these links. After an hour of surfing, he gave up. The information he had retrieved was the same as what he had found earlier about the Battle Box. He thought that, perhaps, the only way to find out more about the Battle Box was to visit it. The visit was already on the cards. He decided to focus his efforts on other aspects of the fall of Singapore first.

5 *AT THE LIBRARY*

The next day, Jing Yang and Angelina had to stay back after school for remedial class. Their maths teacher had given them no prior notice and insisted that they should stay back for the lesson. Jing Yang told Tim that they could not follow him and Aunt Dorothy on their house-hunting exercise.

Jing Yang remembered what Aunt Dorothy had told him about not discussing Tim's citizenship anymore. He asked Angelina not to bring up the subject with Tim or Aunt Dorothy.

At half past three, the two of them left the school grounds and headed for the bus-stop. They had some free time before dinner and decided to visit the public library in Hougang Mall. They took bus service number 136 and alighted outside Hougang Plaza. Then they walked to Hougang Mall which was about six hundred feet away.

'The information I looked up on the Battle Box wasn't useful. Looks like we can only get what we want from the Battle Box itself.'

'It's only Wednesday. The visit to Fort Canning Park is on Saturday. We won't have much time to prepare our research after the visit.'

'We do what we can. Go to the public libraries first to get whatever information on the fall of Singapore that we can get our hands on. Then we start collating the data and preparing our draft report. After we have visited the Battle Box, we can fit in the Battle Box information. This way, we need not waste our time waiting for the Battle Box visit.'

'Good idea! Jing Yang, are any of the other groups in the class doing the same topic?'

'Not that I know of. No one else is doing a project on World War Two.'

'Good! Then we won't have to worry about competition.'

'By the way, my mother wants to get me a tutor for history.'

'Why?'

'I lost precious time studying geography the last six months. She thought it best that I get some help on the subject to make up for lost time.'

'How is she going to do it? She's thousands of miles away, you know.'

'She has asked Aunt Dorothy to do the work for her. Aunt Dorothy is looking around for a suitable tutor.'

'You are so lucky, you know. You can get everything you need.'

'Don't feel sad. I didn't tell you this to make you envy me.'

'I am not jealous. I just feel that you are lucky to be born rich.'

'I am not rich. My parents are well-off but they don't spoil me. I also am not boastful.'

'I know. I know. How should I put it? It's all fated. Some like you are born in a well-off family. Others like me come from a poor family. I am not complaining. I am happy to be in my family. They all love me. That's all that is important to me, nothing else. I just feel that you are very lucky, that's all.'

'Glad you feel that way. I don't want you to be upset.'

'Don't worry! Besides, when you get a tutor, we can share the notes that the tutor gives you.'

'Yes. I will make sure I make a copy for you every time I get the notes.'

'Thanks, Jing Yang. You are good to me.'

'It's only right that we help each other.'

'Shh! We are now in the library.'

They walked past rows of shelves till they reached the section labeled 'Singapore collection'. There were more books on World War Two in this library than in the one at Compasspoint. Jing Yang browsed through the titles row by row. Each time he found a suitable book, he would take it out and hand it to Angelina. The books he selected were on the British army in Singapore during the war years, critical reflections written by generals and politicians after the end of the war, the battles in Malaya and the defence of Singapore.

'That should be enough to last us the afternoon.'

'Jing Yang, shall we sit there, next to the magazine section?'

'But there's a toilet next to it.'

'It's a staff toilet. It won't smell. Come on.'

They unstrapped their backpacks and sat leaning against the wall next to the racks of magazines. They laid the books they had picked on the floor next to them.

'Here! You handle these three books. I'll take care of the rest.'

'Jing Yang, are you taking down the notes or am I?'

'Both of us will. You write down the information from the books with you and I will do the same for these books here.'

They spent the next two hours poring through the books. It was not easy reading through so much text and deciding what was important and what was not. Both of them had different yardsticks for deciding what they thought was relevant. In the end, the stuff they had written down seemed to resemble a collection of mishmash.

'Let's do a quick assessment of what we have collated. *Wah*! This looks messy.'

Angelina looked disappointed. She had put much effort in sieving the information.

'We need to do some work putting this stuff in order. Don't worry. I am good at doing this.'

'Of course, you are. Your English is so good.'

"I wasn't boasting just now, just telling the facts.'

'I know. I know. But it's already quarter past six.'

'Let me handle this. I will put this together nicely tonight. Happy?'

'That takes a load off my mind. You know my English is so-so. It will take me forever to put this in order.'

'Let's go. It's late!'

The two teenagers retrieved their bags from the floor. They placed the books they had taken on the sorting tray, and walked out of the library. Their homes were a five-minute walk from Hougang Mall – which was nestled in the middle of Hougang housing estate, next to the MRT station, and across from the bus interchange. As they passed Cheers, a 24-hour convenience store, Jing Yang went inside to get them some Coca-Colas. It was his favourite drink and it quickly became Angelina's. By now, both of them had become accustomed to having each other around and Jing Yang had become thoughtful of people around him. He was no longer thinking of himself only. Though Angelina had not said a word about it, he now realised Angelina was not in a position to afford even simple things like soft drinks – she was on a tight budget. He did not tease her about it. Instead, he sought to treat her to these little snacks and beverages whenever they were together. Angelina appreciated his kind gestures and polite manners so she did not refuse his free drinks and food. She was beginning to discover the good in this boy whom she once labelled as uppity – a word her secondary one English teacher used frequently to put down one of her former classmates who was arrogant.

That boy also came from a well-to-do family. Jing Yang was so unlike him, she thought. Jing Yang was reticent and she had mistakenly marked him as being proud and criticised his behaviour when he first came into their class at the beginning of the school year. Now she regretted what she did. She had been too blunt. But it was not too late. Both were still young and growing. They were learning to discern attitudes in people, a skill that would put them in good stead when they went out into working life. After all, this was what school was also about – meeting people and learning to get along.

Though the two classmates were getting closer in their relationship, they were not yet a couple. They did not hold hands. They never thought of holding hands. For Jing Yang, it would be an awkward thing to do – he had never held hands with a girl before. However, he remembered being close to a classmate in primary school. They had gone to school together every school day and it was she who had got Jing Yang interested in reading books. In fact, he took up reading just to get close to her. In the end, his English improved by leaps and bounds. He had her to thank for his current proficiency in English. They were just children so when Jing Yang entered a boys' secondary school, everything changed. They lost touch and he became alone again.

Angelina had never been close to any boy before. Sure she was friendly to everyone but she believed there was a line drawn between friendship and intimate relationship and she never once stepped across that line – that is, till she met Jing Yang. Now, the line between friendship and relationship had become blurred. As they crossed the junction between Upper Serangoon Road and Hougang Avenue 5, Angelina slipped a hand in Jing Yang's. She was now crossing the line between friendship and relationship. Jing Yang was surprised by the sudden gesture. He felt awkward but did not let go of his hand. Indeed, they were now an item. This was good news for both of them. Jing Yang was finally letting go of his need for privacy and Angelina now had a confidant. She squeezed his hand. Jing Yang felt a tingling sensation running through him.

Jing Yang accompanied Angelina to her block and then headed for his house across the carpark. When he entered the front door, he saw Aunt Dorothy and Tim sitting in the living room, watching television.

'Hi Aunt Dorothy.'

'Oh, hi Jing Yang. Dinner is prepared. Come down when you are ready.'

Mother, son and nephew sat down to dinner that evening. It was so unlike that of a typical HDB household where family members were accustomed to having their dinners by themselves in front of the television, whether on a stool, in an armchair or on the floor leaning against the wall – this happening though the entire family was at home as was happening in Angelina's house.

'I have found a history tutor for you, Jing Yang.'

'Gosh, so fast?'

'I ran into our neighbour Mr Wang early this morning when he was walking his dog outside.'

'The one living two houses away? He knows a history teacher?'

'No! He is a history teacher; rather he was a history teacher.'

'Was?'

'Yes, indeed. He taught history in Temasek University till he retired last year.'

'How do you know so much about him, Mum?'

'You know, we women like to get to know our surroundings and the people living around us.'

'Mum, you mean gossip, don't you?'

'Tim, dear, aren't you being rude to your mother?'

'Sorry, Mum. Just kidding you, Mum.'

'Was he a lecturer?'

'He was an associate professor. Now, he's an emeritus

professor.'

'A what?'

'Tim, emeritus means retired.'

'Yes, Jing Yang is right.'

'So has he agreed, Aunt Dorothy?'

'Why, yes, of course. And I will be speaking to your mother afterwards.'

'When will the lessons take place?'

'As soon as possible. You know how your mother is when she wants things done.'

'Why aren't you like that, Mum?'

'Why, your aunt and I may be sisters but we are as different as day and night.'

'What days of the week can you have the lesson, Jing Yang?'

'Let me think. Tuesdays and Thursdays after four o'clock should be fine.'

'How about Fridays, in case he should ask?'

'I need to go out with my friends on Friday. Can we not have lessons on Fridays, please?'

'Alright. Mr Wang says he can spare two hours per week. He says that should be enough for secondary level history.'

'Aunt Dorothy, where will the lessons take place?'

'Why, here of course.'

'Fancy you getting a professor as a tutor.'

'Dear, it just happened that Mr Wang is our neighbour and agreed to help us. It's not that we went out purposely to look for a professor.'

After dinner, Jing Yang retreated to his bedroom while Aunt Dorothy and Tim sat down in the living room to watch television. They were watching a Chinese serial programme on Channel 8. Tim did not understand what the characters were saying. They were talking in Mandarin. He had to read the subtitles on the bottom of the screen to follow the story. But his mother was clearly enjoying herself. It had to be a comedy, Tim thought, for his mother was smiling away as she watched.

Meanwhile, Jing Yang was busy compiling the information that he and Angelina had gleaned from the books they had read.

It was not easy when he had to extract relevant facts from Angelina's datasheets. But he did not grumble. It was work that only he – being good at English – could do. As he worked on the pile of foolscap paper, he conversed with Angelina using SMS. It was too bad that Angelina did not have a computer at home, otherwise he could chat with her using Internet messenger. It would have been fun exchanging pictures and emoticons.

There was a knock on the door. He went to open it.

'Jing Yang, your mother has agreed to hiring Mr Wang. Can he start tomorrow?'

'Sure, Aunt Dorothy.'

'Good! I will let him know. By the way, your mother knows about Angelina. I told her all about this girl. I also told her she's a very nice girl. Your mother doesn't object to her coming over often.'

'Thanks, Aunt Dorothy.'

'Yes. Remember – Angelina is a nice young lady so do mind your manners when you are with her.'

'Yes, Aunt.'

'And, no hanky-panky.'

'Yes, Aunt.' Jing Yang was blushing. He understood at once what his aunt meant.

'Good!' Then she left the room.

'Beep! Beep!'

Jing Yang's mobile phone was beeping again. He grabbed the phone and plunked onto his bed to read the SMS message that had come in. Angelina was bidding him goodnight. She was going to bed. He wanted to tell her about his new tutor but that had to wait till the next day now.

That night, Angelina could not sleep. She tossed and turned in bed. She was thinking about that afternoon at the junction when she held Jing Yang's hand. It was brave of her to have done that. No, it was rash of her to have done that, she thought to herself. It was early days yet in their relationship. What if he had shaken off her hand then? But, she was glad she had done it. And she was happy that Jing Yang had accepted her gesture. She was certainly not one of the hoi polloi in school so Jing Yang was not frightened off. Should she have waited a month or two? Did she do the right thing? How would Jing Yang behave towards her the next day? Would he remove his hand if she grabbed it again? Boy! With such thoughts churning in her mind, it was no surprise that she lay awake till the wee hours of the morning.

6 *THE NEW HISTORY TUTOR*

It was a rainy Thursday morning. The wind was strong and the roads were wet. Angelina met the two boys at their gate. Her umbrella was small and did little to keep her dry. Jing Yang saw this and exchanged umbrellas with her. At least, with the bigger umbrella that she was now holding, she would not be that wet. They walked side by side. As they were walking towards the main road, Jing Yang reached out and grabbed the hand that was nearest him. He held it tight. Then he pulled her against his shoulder. This way, they could keep warm, he thought. Angelina smiled.

Tim, who was a few steps behind them, noticed the hand-holding between them.

'Why so lovey-dovey nowadays?' he remarked.

The couple merely smiled and continued on the way. But they did not hold hands when in school. It was a secret between them and Tim.

That day after school, Tim almost got into a fight with a secondary one normal technical student over name calling. Tim had been sitting at a table outside the art room waiting for Jing Yang and Angelina. The boy had passed by and called him some nasty names and Tim had stared at the boy. The boy then went up to Tim and leaned forward, shaking his chest at Tim. Tim tried hard to restrain himself from lunging at the boy but the two boys were near tipping point.

Just then, Jing Yang and Angelina were arriving at their regular meeting point outside the art room. Angelina was the first to see the quarrelling boys. She pointed at them. Jing Yang ran towards the two boys. He stood between the boys, waving both hands in the air frantically to prevent them from trading blows. It would mean caning and detention if the fight had happened. Jing Yang pushed Tim a few steps away and then turned around to face the other boy. He warned the boy to back off. He was older than the boy and a head taller too. The boy's schoolmates waved him to go off with them. He gesticulated rudely and left with them. Luckily, no teachers were around the area or it would have been serious trouble. Fighting was not tolerated in school and those caught fighting were invariably caned in public during the morning assembly. It would have been a shameful experience for Tim. Luckily, Jing Yang had got between the two boys in time.

'What was this about?'

'He called me names.'

'Did he call you *Angmoh*?'

'No.'

'Just what did he call you?'

'He called me a freak!'

The boy had insulted Tim over his mixed parentage. When Jing Yang heard this, he was furious. He took Tim to see the vice-principal. Angelina tagged along behind. She had not seen Jing Yang this angry.

It was quarter past two when the three of them went out of the school gate. As they walked along the roadside, they discussed the incident.

'Luckily, you stopped them from fighting.'

'I wouldn't have fought with that fellow. It would have been beneath my dignity fighting with such scum.'

'There you go again. These people do not talk reason, you know? They only know how to use their fists.'

'I was minding my own business. He was looking for trouble when he came.'

'Tim, these boys are like that. They just like to irritate people. Just ignore them and things will be okay.'

'But that boy called me names!'

'Go see the discipline master or the vice-principal or the principal. They are only afraid of these three. They are not afraid of teachers.'

'Yes, nip the problem in the bud. That's the only way to deal with these people.'

'Jing Yang, should we talk to the boy who confronted Tim?'

'What for? This is a neighbourhood school, not a premier school. Don't let these people get down to discussing terms with you because once you allow them to start, they will use their gangs to back them up. How are you going to win against a gang?'

'You are right, Jing Yang. Tim, they like to look for trouble. They purposely disturb other students, find some lame excuse to get these students into a fight with them, and then get their gang to bully these students. That way, these students will fear them so they get to step over these students.'

'What if they come making trouble every day?'

'Ignore them totally! They are just spoiling for a fight – that's all they want. They won't dare to make trouble in school.'

'If they persist?'

'As I have said earlier, go and see the discipline master. He's also a volunteer police officer so these students are afraid of him.'

'Yes, Tim. Jing Yang is right.'

'I don't think that boy will look for you again. He's only in secondary one so he's easily frightened.'

They were so engrossed in their conversation that they

forgot to keep a look out for the bus they were taking. By the time they reached Hougang, it was already past three o'clock.

After a bath, Jing Yang got down to preparing his table top for the tuition. After putting his history stuff on the table, he went down to the living room. Aunt Dorothy had told him it was only polite for him to wait for his new tutor.

At four o'clock sharp, the doorbell rang. Aunt Dorothy opened the door. The man who walked into the living room did not look like a retired professor, Jing Yang thought. He was thin, clean-cut and respectable looking. Of course, he was bespectacled. He had a full head of black hair. Surely he looked younger than a retiree would look.

'Mr Wang, come in please.'

'Jing Yang, this is Mr Wang, your new history tutor.'

'Hi Mr Wang.'

'Hello Jing Yang. We have met before, I believe.'

'Yes, along the street outside.'

'A fine young man, indeed. Good!'

'Mr Wang, Jing Yang will show you to his room.'

'Oh, yes please. Yes, please.'

Jing Yang led Mr Wang up to his room. He walked to the table and invited Mr Wang to sit in one of two chairs he had placed there. Then he sat next to him.

'Nice room. Nice room.'

'Yes, Mr Wang.'

'Shall we start? First show me your textbook and workbook. Then tell me what you have been taught so far.'

Jing Yang placed his school books in front of the tutor and waited for instructions.

'Your aunt has told me you just crossed over to history. Did you study history in secondary one and two?'

'Yes, Mr Wang.'

'Good! Then it will be easier for you to catch up with the others.'

'What are the topics you need to study for this term?'

'Here's the list, Mr Wang.'

'Listen, young man. There's no need to keep calling me Mr Wang all the time. It must be tiring for you. It certainly is jarring to my ears. Just omit addressing me, except when we are with your aunt. Clear?'

'Yes.'

'Good! Let's get down to business.'

Just then, there was a knock on the door and Aunt Dorothy entered the room. She had a cup of tea with her.

'Have some tea first, Mr Wang.'

'Thank you very much.'

She placed the tea next to him on the table and retreated from the room, closing the door behind her.

Mr Wang made full use of the next two hours. He plunged into the thick of the topics for the year, enlightening Jing Yang on the salient points for these topics. Occasionally, he stopped to ask Jing Yang questions on what he had taught. He was pleased that Jing Yang was bright and could follow his lesson quickly. Near the end of the lesson, he summarised the points of discussion.

Jing Yang was glad to have Mr Wang as his tutor. This guy certainly knew how to teach. He did not confuse Jing Yang. He did not speak gibberish. His knowledge of history was astounding. He did not even once refer to the textbook and yet spoke accurately about historical events recorded in the textbook.

'Do you have anything else you wish to ask me?'

'Yes, I have a history project on the fall of Singapore. I hope you can help me with it.'

'Sure, no problem. How far have you gone into it?'

'Here are the notes we have compiled. It's a group project.'

'I see. What's this about the Battle Box?'

'I have little information on the Battle Box now. I will be able to get more when we, I mean, the group visits the place next Monday.'

'I see. I see.'

'What is this about?'

'Oh! It's just something we picked up – some information on the Yamashita treasure.'

'Yes, of course, the famed Yamashita treasure.'

'You know about the Yamashita treasure?'

'My dear boy, of course, I know. I am a history teacher.'

'Oh! Sorry!'

'It's alright. Let me see. Not much is known about the treasure. The people involved are long gone – dead!'

'What do you mean?'

'The Japanese soldiers who hid the treasure were executed after the Japanese surrendered. There is no way to find out where the treasure is now – no way at all.'

'Then there's such a treasure?'

'Yes, of course. Many men looked for it in the past. Many are still looking for it now. So much gold in the treasure. Just imagine – they snatched all the gold from the countries they conquered: China, Manchuria, Burma, Thailand, Malaya, Singapore, Indonesia and the Philippines. It's no wonder so many are still searching for the gold.'

'Why did they execute the men before finding out where the treasure was? They should have interrogated the men first, get the information, find the treasure and then execute them.'

'The Allied forces did not know there was treasure hidden away.'

'Just how much treasure was hidden?'

'More than a hundred thousand pounds of gold. At today's high gold prices, worth many billions, maybe.'

'Maybe?'

'Yes. Nobody knows just how much gold was squirrelled away.'

'So it is not just a rumour.'

'No, definitely not! Indeed not.'

'Beep! Beep!' Something was beeping and it was not Jing Yang's mobile phone. It was not his alarm clock either.

'Dear me, how time flies. It's six o'clock already.'

Mr Wang was looking at the time on his mobile phone which was on the table. He pressed a button on the phone and silence prevailed.

Turning to Jing Yang, he said, 'We will discuss your project the next lesson. Remind me, will you?'

'Yes.'

They went down to the living room. Aunt Dorothy was not there. Jing Yang poked his head in the kitchen.

'Aunt Dorothy. Mr Wang is leaving.'

Aunt Dorothy was near finishing preparing dinner. She washed her hands and wiped them with a flannel. Then she went into the living room.

'Thank you, Mr Wang.' She handed him an envelope she had taken from a pocket.'

'Not at all. Not at all. Jing Yang is a bright boy. He will have no trouble catching up.'

Aunt Dorothy showed him to the door. There they chatted some more. Jing Yang excused himself and clambered up the stairs. He checked his mobile phone. There were two SMS messages – both from Angelina. She wanted to know how the lesson went. He wanted to call her as he had lots to say to her but decided otherwise. He remembered that Angelina was using a pre-paid SIM card in her mobile phone and his frequent calls would drain the value in it too quickly. He knew Angelina only called from her phone when really necessary and he knew too that Angelina used SMS sparingly.

Jing Yang sent two long SMS messages to Angelina summarising what had happened. In them, he also told her Mr Wang had agreed to help in Project Battle Box.

7 *THE BATTLE BOX MUSEUM*

Saturday came quickly. It was the day when 3E3 and 3E4 would be going on an excursion to Fort Canning Park. Jing Yang and Angelina arrived in school at ten o'clock. They joined the other students in waiting for their transport in the open area next to the carpark. There were four teachers accompanying the classes for the trip. Mr Zee was the teacher-in-charge of the excursion. It was noisy as the students were chattering among themselves. They were excited, not just because they were going on a trip, but also because they were allowed to bring along their mobile phones and cameras. The teachers made little effort to keep down the noise. It was a Saturday after all and the students were not having any lessons. Soon two buses pulled into the carpark and the students boarded them. Jing Yang and Angelina were seated together on the first bus which held students from 3E3 as well as two teachers. On the second bus were students from 3E4 and two teachers.

The journey to Fort Canning Park took forty minutes. As the buses cruised along the roads and expressways, the students were busy doing their own things. Some passed the time engaged in casual conversation while others found time to read their favourite fiction. Some were occupied with snapping pictures of their classmates. Jing Yang and Angelina were among the few who were catching up on their sleep.

Soon the buses exited the expressway, entered Fort Canning Road, and turned left into Canning Walk. They were now going uphill. The buses made a right turn into Percival Road. The students had stopped what they were doing and were now peering out of the windows. Many, like Jing Yang and Angelina, had not been here before. Some had been here with their parents for leisurely walks while others who were members of uniformed groups had previously carried out field-study exercises in the area.

The buses pulled to a stop at a roundabout on top of the hill. In front of the roundabout was a small white building with glass doors in front. On top of the glass doors was a sign reading The Battle Box. This was the first stop for the students. On hand to greet the students were two guides, dressed in green T-shirts and trousers, from The Battle Box. The students disembarked from the two buses. Special arrangements had to be made to accommodate the group of eighty-two students and four teachers. One of the guides waved to students from 3E4 to follow him up a lane. The other guide showed students from 3E3 into the white building.

There were rows and rows of benches in the room. In front of the benches was a large television. On the walls were posters of World War Two stuff and pictures of tanks and ships. Hanging from the ceiling were mobiles with aircraft dangling from them. In a corner of the room sat a wooden counter. In another corner were coin-operated drink dispensers. Mr Zee and Miss Quek busied themselves ushering the students to their seats. Then they stood next to the door. Jing Yang and Angelina sat next to each other in the third row. Their backpacks were strapped to their backs. It was crammed in the room and some of the students were already fanning themselves with brochures as the air-conditioning was not very cold. The heat coming through the glass doors made things worse but conditions were bearable.

The guide who showed them into the room came up in front of the students. He was a tall man with strong arms along which were some tattoos. He kept stroking his thick moustache when he talked.

'Boys and girls, welcome to The Battle Box. I am Mr Craig Savage. I am your guide for today.'

'Class, please greet Mr Savage,' said Mr Zee.

'Good morning, Mr Savage,' the students chorused.

'Thank you. Your tour of The Battle Box consists of two parts. First, you will watch a ten-minute video on the fall of Singapore here. Then I will take you down into the underground bunker for a 45-minute guided tour. Please remember not to scream or shout when you are in the bunker; it's an enclosed space. Any questions?'

'Can we take pictures in the bunker?' asked a student, pointing at a sign on the wall disallowing the use of cameras.

'Yes, of course, you can. Please ignore the sign. But video-taping is not allowed,' Mr Savage replied.

'Is he an *Angmoh*?' Angelina whispered to Jing Yang.

'Nope! I don't think so. He looks Eurasian,' Jing Yang said.

'Class, stop talking and pay attention,' said Mr Zee.

Mr Savage turned on the video presentation and proceeded to close the glass doors. He then shut a pair of wooden doors parallel to the glass doors and switched off the lights in the room. It was dark in the room.

It was difficult for Jing Yang and Angelina to watch the video as the students in the front two rows were blocking their view. They contented themselves with listening to the commentary instead. Some of the students were not watching the video. They were fiddling with their bags. Some were looking around at one another. Others held their heads down.

After the video had ended, Mr Savage opened a side door and told the school group to follow him. He led the group up the lane next to the white building. The lane, which was paved with broad rectangular setts, was quite wide; it could allow a big truck to pass through. On both sides was greenery. On the left was a path leading to a carpark and on the right was a steep slope on top of which the students could see a low concrete wall. Also on the right, about a hundred feet away from the white building, was an entrance to a tunnel. There were some steps leading down to the open doorway which had a large metal door hinged to each side.

What attracted the students' attention was a life-sized mannequin in army uniform, complete with boots. It was standing at attention, guarding the entrance to the tunnel. On its right was a wooden rifle, painted black, which it was holding. The mannequin looked life-like. Its head, arms and legs appeared to be made of wax.

'Boys and girls, this is the entrance to The Battle Box. It was the underground command centre of the British forces in Singapore during World War Two. Please follow me down the stairs.'

The column of students entered the tunnel, walked up a short flight of steps and then down a long flight of stairs. Then everyone stopped moving. The front part of the column had reached the door downstairs and Jing Yang and Angelina, who were in the rear of the column, were standing near the top of the long flight of steps. From there, they had a good view of the tunnel. It had concrete walls on both sides and a screed floor. There was a long rectangular metal duct on the ceiling running all the way from the bottom of the tunnel to the top. On the left wall was a pre-1950 fuse box with big Bakelite fuses attached to it. The tunnel was lit by incandescent bulbs behind round domed glass with metal rims. These old wall lights were mounted on the right side of the tunnel.

The door to the bunker was locked. Mr Savage

punched some numbers on a pad installed on the left of the tunnel, next to the door. The door opened with a loud clicking sound. Suddenly the wailing of sirens permeated the tunnel. Some of the students covered their ears with their hands. The others were enjoying the experience, laughing or screaming in congruity with the wailing.

Mr Savage gesticulated to the students and teachers to follow him into the bunker. They found themselves at the beginning of a long wide brightly lit corridor. The bunker was air-conditioned. What a relief! It had been hot outside. Standing in front of them was another mannequin in army uniform. This one was armed with a wooden pistol holstered to its waist. The mannequin's left arm showed them the way into the first room on the right.

The group squeezed into the small room which Mr Savage introduced as the Orderlies Room. There they were told to sit on the tiled floor. Pushed against the walls of the room were some wooden benches on which their teachers and some classmates sat. There were some shelves on a wall on which an old black telephone sat at one end. There were basket trays next to it. Some helmets and messenger bags harking back to World War Two were hanging from a wooden rack on another wall.

'Boys and girls, this is the first of twenty-six rooms in the bunker that we will be visiting,' said Mr Savage. 'As I go through the main ones, I will explain the use of the rooms and their historical significance. Many of the things you see in the room have been recreated so that you can have a realistic experience.'

'You mean that the helmets are replicas?' asked Angelina.

'Young lady, the helmets are old stuff, but they are not originals in the sense that they were not originally in this bunker when it was built,' said Mr Savage. 'But there is one thing in this bunker that was originally here when the bunker was built.'

'Is it the door?' said Jing Yang, pointing at the metal

door.

'I said, in the room. The door is part of the structure,' said Mr Savage.

'The telephone?' said a girl seated in front.

'No, any more guesses?' Mr Savage said.

'Is it the wiring on the wall?' asked a boy.

'Is it the sink?' enquired another boy. He was pointing at a porcelain sink in a corner of the room.

'Yes, you are correct,' said Mr Savage.

'The sink has been here since the bunker was built,' said Mr Savage.

'When was this bunker built?' asked another student.

'This bunker was built in 1939, long before I was born, long before your teachers were born and perhaps, long before some of your parents were born,' Mr Savage retorted.

'*Wah*!' some students exclaimed.

Mr Savage handed some stacks of brochures on the bunker to the students in front of him and asked them to pass these around.

'We are now going to move through the rooms in the bunker. Please stand up,' he said.

The room erupted into activity as students of 3E3 stood up.

'Follow me into the next room,' Mr Savage commanded. He walked into the adjoining room.

This room was smaller than the first and it could not hold all the students, so some spilled into the corridor outside. It was also not as brightly lit as the first. There was a big old telephone switchboard occupying a quarter of the room on one side and some low bookcases on its side. An old fan and a hurricane lamp sat on top of the bookcase. Seated at the switchboard was a mannequin frozen in movement. It was apparently trying to connect a call, for in its hands were wired plugs which seemed about to be slotted into small holes on the switchboard. Messenger bags were hanging off some wall hooks. On the right wall was a big metal cabinet with centre-opening doors.

'This was the telephone exchange. This was where the operator would place calls using land lines laid across the island,' Mr Savage said. 'The telephone exchange was connected to all these places you see listed on the wall over there.'

'The telephone exchange equipment you see here is not the original one. The original one was pretty big. To get an idea of just how big it was, take a look at the floor,' Mr Savage continued, shining a torch at the floor around him. The cool light from the torch illuminated the floor in the dimly-lit room, spotlighting the ceramic floor tiles and some wooden planks on the floor as it panned the floor. The planks covered more than three-quarters of the room.

'The original telephone switchboard rested in gaps beneath these wooden planks,' Mr Savage explained.

Suddenly a loud boom rang in the room. The room seemed to reverberate. Another loud boom sounded. The girls in the crammed little room screamed. Some covered their ears. The boys shouted in joy. Mr Savage had not warned them about the simulated bombing.

Angelina held Jing Yang's hand tightly. Nobody noticed this as it was too crowded in the room. All that could be seen were students huddled together.

Mr Savage was clearly pleased. He seemed to enjoy surprising the students. Beaming, he led them out into the corridor and then into a series of three inter-connected rooms. Jing Yang, Angelina, and a few other stragglers remained in the telephone exchange to snap some photographs. Angelina asked a classmate to take a picture of her and Jing Yang standing in front of the mannequin.

The first of the three inter-connected rooms had desks arranged parallel to the walls of the room. There were old typewriters on these tables, with slips of paper around them, as if the room was still being used. The students filed into the middle room where Mr Savage told them to gather. On one side of the room was a wall-to-wall table-top, on which sat old army-style telephone sets. There were slips of paper on the table-top. Some wicker baskets sat on the floor which was of wooden planks evenly placed across the length of the room. The planks vibrated under the weight of the students as they stepped on them. This longish room was slightly bigger than the telephone exchange but still could not hold everyone in the group. Both ends of the room were bulging with students.

'The room on my left was for sending telegrams. On the other side was the Cipher Office, for decoding and encoding messages. This room that we are in was the Signals Room. This was where telephone messages were sent or received. Once they were received, decoded and scribbled onto these forms here, they were then inserted into tiny capsules, with a rubber base,' Mr Savage explained, raising the torch he was holding to demonstrate the insertion of messages.

'The messages were then shot into the rooms here using this pneumatic tube system,' he continued, shining the torch at a tube-like contraption running up the wall, and across the ceiling to one end of the room where it penetrated the wall.

Flashes were popping as Mr Savage talked.

'Wow! Thanks very much,' he said.

'I feel as if I am a movie star, and all of you are my fans, with all those flashes popping off on your cameras,' he quipped.

The girls giggled. He was funny now. Their impression of him had been that he was a no-nonsense type of person.

Mr Savage was smiling now. This was the first time the group saw him smiling. His discoloured teeth showed through the smile. They were stained dark brown, with sticky tar deposits on them, alluding to his heavy smoking habit. He was stroking his moustache again.

'Come follow me into the next room,' he said, waving a hand in the air.

The students and teachers crowded into the room

which also had a floor of wooden planks. On one long wall was a wall-to-wall table top. There were some old instruments amidst strewn slips of paper on the table top. Two rows of shelves lined the wall above these things. On these shelves lay some old helmets and wicker trays. A wooden cabinet stood in a corner of the room. On the other long wall were what appeared to be graffiti in pencil, protected behind Perspex sheets. These graffiti were regularly spaced along the wall. There were English translations on top of the writings.

'This was the Signals Control Room. This was where telegrams were sent or received using these morse code transmitters,' Mr Savage said. 'After the surrender of Singapore, Japanese soldiers were seen in this room using it as their communications centre for a short while, but they were here long enough to leave for posterity evidence of their being here,' he added, illuminating the graffiti on the wall with his torch.

'Why did they stay here only for a short while?' asked a student.

'Well, it was pretty hot and stuffy in it. There was no air-conditioning in those days,' he replied.

'How did the British manage to stay here for so long?' asked Jing Yang.

Mr Savage was stumped. He had no ready answer. For the first time since the group arrived in the bunker he was unable to deliver a reply immediately. He pondered for a while, searching his mind. There was chattering in the room as the students waited for his reply.

'Er...because they were used to the place,' he said lamely.

Then he changed the subject abruptly.

'This bunker was built in 1939. After the wall, it was left abandoned and forgotten for many, many years,' he said. 'Nobody stepped foot into this bunker for well over forty years. In 1988, this bunker was rediscovered.'

'*Wah*! So long,' a girl in the group remarked.

'When this place was rediscovered, it was also found that some of the rooms had their floors dug up,' he continued.

'Who dug up the floors? Why did they dig up the floors?' Jing Yang asked in succession.

'Well, well...' Mr Savage was trying to find the words. He was frowning. 'Perhaps, they were looking for treasure,' he said. Then he abruptly stopped talking.

'Who were looking for treasure? Was it the Yamashita treasure?' asked Jing Yang.

Mr Savage turned red in the face. Obviously, he thought he had talked too much. Jing Yang was sure that Mr Savage was not comfortable talking about the Yamashita treasure. But, he did not know why and he could not ask more about the treasure, for Mr Savage had moved on to other things in his commentary.

"When it was rediscovered, it was found that many rooms were flooded, with water this deep,' Mr Savage said, using both hands to measure roughly one feet of air between them.

'Even today, after we shut our doors every evening, we need to pump out the excess water,' he said, spotlighting a metal drain cover on the floor in the corridor outside the room. The students craned their necks to look at where the light from the torch fell.

"Beneath this drain cover is a network of drains covering the entire bunker. Every evening, we put in portable pumps to pump out the excess water. The danger is particularly great because behind this wall,' he said, pointing at the long wall adjacent to him, 'say about seventy feet away lies a big reservoir of water. Any over-flooding from that reservoir could adversely affect this bunker.'

'Most probably, the British, when they built this bunker, put in this underground drainage system to take care of that eventuality,' Mr Savage said.

Jing Yang was listening hard and scribbling notes as he

listened. He did not have a portable MP3 recorder as did some students who were pointing these things at Mr Savage as he spoke. He resolved to buy one of these electronic devices.

'Weren't the underground drains installed to take away groundwater too?' asked Jing Yang.

Mr Savage was clearly irritated this time. This boy was getting into his nerves, always asking questions for which he had no answers, he thought to himself. He did not know what groundwater was in the first place but tried hard to look as if he did. There was a long pause before he answered the question.

'In case the reservoir spills over, the water coming towards the bunker would be drained away,' he squeaked feebly. He was clearly uncomfortable.

'What if the reservoir doesn't spill over? What if it was just raining? What happens to the rainwater?' asked Jing Yang. Angelina nudged him. She had seen the displeased expression on Mr Savage's face.

'Stop the questioning,' Angelina whispered under her breath.

'Er…er,' muttered Mr Savage, 'we are falling behind on the tour schedule. Let's move on.' He exited the room in a huff, waving the students to follow him into the corridor. He then entered a room on the left.

This room was bigger than the rest of the rooms they had visited. Some of the students touched the thick metal door as they entered the room. In the far end two mannequins were seated at a large wooden desk. They were more life-like than the others the students had seen earlier. The one with a moustache sat in a wicker armchair behind the desk. The other sat in another wicker armchair at one side of the desk. They appeared to be in conversation as their mouths were open. The one on the side was wearing a peaked cap.

"This was the office of the fortress commander. That's the gentleman seated at the side of the table,' said Mr

Savage. He shone the torch at the figure wearing the peaked cap next to him.

'As the fortress commander, he was in charge of all the coastal and beach defences. The anti-aircraft defences, including the search lights, were also under his control,' he continued.

'Though he was the Fortress Commander, notice he is not seated behind the desk. That's because his superior, Lt General Arthur Percival, made this room his office in the last few days preceding the fall of Singapore. General Percival was the GOC Malaya. He was the General Officer Commanding Malaya and had about 88,600 soldiers under his command,' Mr Savage said.

Pointing to a sink in a corner of the room, just behind General Percival's look-alike, Mr Savage said, 'This sink has been here since 1939. There are six of these sinks which have survived to this day.'

'You mean all the other things in this room were not originally in this room?' asked Jing Yang.

'Next time, ask questions only when I have finished talking,' Mr Savage said in a loud voice. His eyebrows were now contracted. He was scowling at Jing Yang.

'Sorry,' uttered Jing Yang.

Mr Savage ignored Jing Yang and walked through a doorway behind him into the next room. He beckoned everyone to follow him.

This room was big enough to accommodate the students and teachers even though occupying its centre was a large rectangular table – its longer side was the length of five classroom desks placed side by side and its shorter side could fit four such desks – atop which was a large white map of Malaya and Singapore framed by a one-foot wide wooden surface. There were some wooden blocks and model aircraft scattered on the map. On the wooden sides of the table were more wooden blocks and thumb-length letterings in plastic. On the walls of the room were big maps of the Asia-Pacific region, Malaya and

Singapore. There was a metal door on each of the walls.

'This was the Gun Operations Room,' said Mr Savage. 'This was where information on enemy aircraft was received by these two soldiers – the ones wearing the headsets. The information came from secret stations located along the coast of Malaya and also along the coast of Singapore. Men at work in these secret stations would be on the lookout for enemy aircraft flying in from the sea, in this case, the South China Sea.'

'In those days, the equipment was not so advanced, so these men had to rely on their eyes to gauge the heights at which the aircraft were flying. For instance, on this block you see the reference number H10, H for hostile, enemy aircraft, 25 of them, flying at 22,000 feet. For their own aircraft, they used the letter F – denoting friendly aircraft,' Mr Savage went on.

'Once the information was plotted on this map here, it was the turn of these two tellers, the ones manning the telephones, to relay the information to anti-aircraft positions which would then bombard the enemy aircraft,' he concluded.

Mr Savage was happy that no one had interrupted him in this room. Even the mousy thin boy who kept peppering him with difficult questions had remained quiet, he thought. Actually, Jing Yang was busy writing down the things that Mr Savage was saying about the room. He had no time to think of questions. Jing Yang was still scribbling when the group left the room to go into the corridor. Angelina was on hand to help carry the notes he had scribbled earlier. They worked together as a pair.

The students straggled along the long corridor, past two locked metal doors, and entered a room on their left at the end of the corridor. In the room were two rows of wooden benches arranged parallel to one wall of the room, from one side of the room to the other – ending at another open doorway, beyond which was another room housing a big metal contraption.

Mr Savage commanded the students to sit on the benches. The room could barely fit all of them so they were huddled together. In front of the students was a very long wooden table around which sat several uniformed mannequins. At each end of the table stood two of these mannequins, one of which was holding some paper files. These mannequins were apparently attending a meeting. On the table were scattered pieces of paper, a clock and a telephone.

'This was the Surrender Conference Room,' said Mr Savage, his voice booming across the room. 'Earlier, in one of the rooms, we saw General Percival, that's this gentleman over here, calling for a conference of his commanders whom you can see seated around him. This wasn't a proper conference room. This was an office.'

Then Mr Savage, who was standing next to the doorway they had come in through, shone his torch at the top of the doorway.

'On top of this doorway, you will see the original letters CAAD. This was the office of the Commander, Anti-Aircraft Defences. That's this gentleman over here – Brigadier Wildey,' he said, pointing at the figure seated at the long table next to him.

'The reason they used his office as a conference room was that it was pretty noisy in here, what with the noise coming from the air filtration plant over there – there were three such plants in the bunker – and more noise coming from the oil tank up there.'

'Why was noise good?' he asked the visitors in the room. Mr Savage had summoned enough courage to ask questions of his young audience. He seemed quite sure that Jing Yang would not pester him with those silly questions of his again. This boy was busy writing down something. He had not held up his head even once in the room. Mr Savage looked pleased. He fiddled with his moustache.

'Because they could not be heard by other people?' said

a boy at the far end of the room.

'Yes, exactly,' Mr Savage said. 'Noise was good because it would drown out their voices. You never knew whether there were any spies among the men working in the bunker.'

'At first, General Percival was against surrendering. When I turn on the broadcast, you will hear over the speakers his commanders voicing their disagreement with him. So finally, General Percival made the decision to surrender. This room is historic in that the decision to surrender Singapore to the Japanese forces was made in this room, but the signing of the surrender took place many miles away in Bukit Timah in a building called the Ford Motor Factory,' he continued.

'If you have the time, please pay a visit to that place, but do not be confused with the two places. History was made in this room when General Percival made the decision to surrender Singapore to the Japanese forces. And history was also made in the Ford Motor Factory when the signing of the surrender took place there,' Mr Savage said.

There was so much to write down. It was information overload for Jing Yang who could barely keep up with what Mr Savage was saying. Jing Yang's handwriting was now barely legible, even to him. But he would not stop writing; he could not stop writing. It was information that was important for their project. Angelina could only look on helplessly. She could not write as fast as he could so she did not volunteer to help.

'After the surrender decision was made, they nominated a small group of officers to approach the Japanese forces to discuss surrender terms. The Japanese commander, Lt General Yamashita, who was the commander, 25th Japanese Imperial Army, was impatient. General Yamashita had set a target date for taking over Singapore. He had set 11th Feb 1942 as his target date for taking over Singapore. This meeting was held on 15th Feb

1942. General Yamashita was already four days late in meeting his own target, so he was impatient, tough and uncompromising and would accept nothing less than an unconditional surrender from the British forces,' said Mr Savage.

'Why did General Yamashita set 11 Feb 1942 as his target date? It was, and I believe it still is Japan's National Day, their National Foundation Day, commemorating their very first emperor many centuries earlier. General Yamashita wanted to bring good news to his emperor on that day, and he was already four days late,' he concluded.

Then Mr Savage pressed a button on a panel mounted on the wall next to the doorway. He stood outside the doorway, looking at the visitors in the room. A loud voice boomed from the speakers in the room. The commentary on the goings-on during this important conference had started. This was followed by a short video presentation on an LCD monitor mounted on the wall across the room.

'After this broadcast, we will go out from the other doorway,' Mr Savage told Mr Zee who was standing next to him. Mr Zee nodded.

In the room, most of the students were listening to the commentary. One or two were typing away on their netbooks. Some were nodding off, while others were taking pictures of the mannequins at the table. There was not a sound from Jing Yang. He was still scribbling on a notepad, taking down the conversation between the generals in the meeting. Angelina snapped some pictures of the students and the wax figures. She wanted a picture of Jing Yang and her, but dared not ask. Her partner was busy and should not be disturbed, she decided.

Mr Savage appeared at the doorway at the far end of the room. He beckoned the students to follow him into the room he was in. Taking centre-stage in this room was a big contraption which he introduced as an air filtration plant. He said that the plant was one of three in the bunker. It filtered the air of poisonous gas dumped in the air above the bunker by Japanese aircraft. The filtered air would then be circulated in the bunker. In those days, the British would burn charcoal in the big container into which were fitted metal ducts on both ends. The students touched the metal structure as they moved around the room.

Then Mr Savage led them into another corridor. On the left was a mini-museum and on the right, after a short passageway was an emergency escape route, which Mr Savage said only the commanders of the bunker knew about. As the students wanted to take a look at the escape route, he led the way through a passageway which then bent at right angles and straightened again. At the end of the passageway was a stairwell. There was a cat ladder on the wall. It led up to the ground level. From where the students were, they could see that the bunker was about three storeys deep underground. Three metal platform landings marked the different storey levels along the cat ladder. At the top landing was a metal door. There were railings on each of these platform landings. The students took turns to approach the end of the passageway as it was only wide to accommodate students standing four abreast. They looked up at the skylight on top. Sunlight was streaming in. They could hear some music echoing through. Evidently, there was a band playing up on top of the hill.

The students turned around and retraced their steps into the corridor. Mr Savage led them into an open area on the right of the corridor. There were display cases on both sides of the open area. These effectively created an enclosed space for viewing exhibits out of sight of traffic along the corridor. There were old uniforms, peaked caps, incomplete old rifles which had seen better days and bullets. Adorning the wall were photographs of generals with information on them directly below their photographs.

Mr Savage told the visitors that the mini-gallery was

originally a power house, where large generators were located. These generators supplied electricity to the bunker when the power supply from outside was cut off. There were tell-tale marks on the screed floor showing where the generators were placed.

Opposite the mini-gallery was an open doorway positioned midway along the corridor. It was dark inside. The room was cordoned off with a thick rope dangling between two metal queue posts.

Jing Yang and Angelina peeked inside. The room was an empty shell. The walls were plain. They were curious. Why was the room in darkness?

Jing Yang approached Mr Savage who was standing in the middle of the mini-gallery.

'Why is that room in darkness?' he asked the guide.

'Oh that one!' Mr Savage said. 'It's not being used, that's all.'

'Why is it not in use?' Jing Yang asked again.

'Er…because,' Mr Savage paused. He had no ready answer for the boy. This boy was persistent. He had to get away.

'Oh – look at the time,' he said, pretending to look at his watch. 'We should be moving along. Come along with me, everyone.' He walked off in a huff. He led the group along the corridor, past the lavatories and some of the rooms they had been to. But Mr Savage was having a hard time keeping the group together. There were too many stragglers. Some students were still in the mini-museum with their teachers. They were discussing events leading to World War Two. Some were posing with the mannequins standing at attention along the corridors. Jing Yang and Angelina had popped into the fortress commander's office to pose for photographs with the mannequins in the room. These two wax figures looked so real that they could not resist taking a second look. There was that sparkle in General Percival's eyes and the worried expression on General Simmons' face seemed too real. It was a surreal experience for the couple.

Meanwhile. Mr Savage had led the students following him through the officers' mess, back into the corridor and then into the last two rooms – the autograph room and the souvenir shop. He left them in the two rooms and went back into the corridor.

'Who says you can touch the mannequin?' Mr Savage shouted. His voice thundered down the corridor. Three boys were next to a mannequin stationed along the corridor. One was fiddling with a wooden pistol that he had lifted from its holster. They had not seen Mr Savage. The boy dropped the pistol which landed with a thud on the screed floor.

The boys stood still. By now Mr Savage was standing in front of them. He reprimanded them before letting them go off to join the others. Then he bent down, retrieved the pistol and replaced it in the holster. He buttoned the holster and continued on his way to the mini-museum to pick up the other stragglers. These kids were a pain in the neck, he thought to himself. He did not like children. To him, they were a load of trouble. But he had no choice. His job as a guide entailed interaction with young children, teenagers and young adults.

It was now quarter past eleven. By now, Mr Savage had rounded up all the stragglers and brought them into the souvenir shop. It was the students' last stop in the bunker. The longish room was brightly lit, unlike the other rooms. There was a massive L-shaped wooden counter occupying pride of place on one side of the room. On display in its glass cabinets were World War Two posters and stacks of playing cards. There were postcards slotted into a row of Perspex holders on top of the counter. A cash register sat at one end of the counter. On the wall behind the counter was a large notice board, on which were mounted several World War Two posters and pictures of aircraft. Flags of Singapore and the United Kingdom adorned both ends of the notice board.

The students and teachers browsed the books on display in the bookcases and on the shelves. Two boys were handling model aeroplanes on the shelves.

'Is this for sale?' asked one of the boys. He was holding up a model aeroplane in his hands.

'No, the aeroplanes and the tanks on display are not for sale,' said the cashier at the counter who was keeping an eye on the students and attending to a student who had purchased some postcards and a fridge magnet.

'Let's go, class,' said Mr Zee. He turned to Mr Savage and said, 'Thank you for the tour, Mr Savage.'

'My pleasure,' Mr Savage replied.

The students and teachers shuffled out of the shop into the corridor and made their way up the flight of steps on the left of the corridor. It was a different staircase from the one they had come in. This one led to the other side of the hill. The bunker sat beneath the top of the hill.

The students formed a column along the lane, just outside the exit to the bunker. Mr Zee did a head-count and, satisfied that everyone was accounted for, told them to wait there for 3E4 who had finished the tour of the bunker earlier and were now watching a video in the white building at the end of the lane.

It was a cloudy day and this side of the hill was in the shade. The students milled about, chattering and drinking from their water bottles. From the lane, they had a clear view of the surroundings. The YWCA building and Park Mall lay in the background on their right, behind rows of trees and some low buildings.

'What's this building?' asked Angelina, pointing at the massive white building looming in front of them.

Jing Yang opened a brochure he was holding. When fully unfolded, it was A2 size. On one side of it was a map of the area. He pored over the map.

'Let's see, we are here,' he said, pointing at a thick blue line on the map. 'That's the building, alright. It says Little Rocket Hotel.'

'What's that in brackets below the name?' asked Angelina.

The words were in fine print. Jing Yang focused on the words.

'It says, HQ Far East Command,' he said. 'Evidently, this must be the headquarters of the British command during World War Two. See this flight of steps in front of us? It leads to the big building and the exit to the bunker faces the steps directly.'

'What does that mean?' asked Angelina.

'Simply that the generals entered the bunker using this tunnel,' he said, pointing to the tunnel exit. 'So this was not the exit but an entrance as well as an exit for the generals. It was a convenient way for them to access the bunker.'

'The students from 3E4 are coming out now,' said Mr Zee.

A column of students had emerged in the distance. Mr Zee told 3E3 to line up in twos. When 3E4 was just behind them, he led the way up the lane which was also paved with broad rectangular setts. The long train of students shuffled along the wide lane, taking in the sights. Two teachers walked behind the students, chatting as they moved at a leisurely pace.

Mr Zee was obviously familiar with the place. He was not using a map. The group walked up a flight of steps along the left slope to the top of the hill. From there, they had a clear view of the surrounding low lying area. They walked past Fort Gate and the Old Married Soldiers' Quarters. Mr Zee explained the significance of the buildings around them as they moved along the footpath. On their right was a big reservoir – the one that Mr Savage was talking about in the Signals Control Room. It lay on top of a slope. The perimeter was fenced off and there was a sign reading 'Protected Area'. Mr Zee explained that the reservoir was a secure area, patrolled by Gurkha soldiers.

By now what had begun as an orderly column of

students and teachers moving along the footpaths in the park had become a straggling procession. Farther down along the winding footpath were some nine-pound cannons and a memorial to James Brooke Napier. The students and teachers turned into Cox Terrace and stopped in front of a long building. Mr Zee told them this was formerly a British army barracks. It was now Fort Canning Centre, a venue for the arts. The building housed theatre facilities and function rooms which were open for wedding and other bookings. Mr Zee explained the historical significance of the building. He told the group it was constructed in 1926.

'Let's take a break here,' said Mr Zee. 'The toilets are on both ends of the building if you need to use them.'

The weary students dispersed, some running and others walking towards the toilets. Several queued up to buy canned drinks from a coin-operated vending machine at one end of the corridor. Some students sat on the wooden benches placed along the corridor. Others sat on the floor, leaning against the wall; they were tired after a long morning on the hill. Jing Yang bought cold canned drinks for Angelina and himself. They sat leaning against a pillar in the corridor.

It was almost one o'clock. Everyone was hungry but there were no kiosks or eating places on the hill, not even snack vending machines.

'Don't worry about lunch,' Mr Zee said. 'Lunch is on the way. Correction! It's here!'

A van had pulled up in the open space in front of the building. A man got off and opened a side panel door. Mr Zee approached the man, smiling. Then he chatted with the man.

'3E3 and 3E4, queue up in two lines. 3E3 on my left and 3E4 on my right,' Mr Zee said.

The students formed two long lines, trailing from the van. Their lunch was here. They were famished!

'Remember to throw the Styrofoam containers into the

dustbins after you have eaten,' Mr Zee said as he spooned some rice into his mouth. 'And don't leave your empty drink cans lying around. This is a public place, not your house.'

As Jing Yang and Angelina ate, they reflected on the morning's happenings in the bunker.

'You were giving him a hard time in the bunker, you know?' said Angelina.

'Who?' Jing Yang asked.

'Mr Savage,' Angelina replied. 'You kept asking all sorts of questions.'

'But he didn't know the answers,' Jing Yang said.

'That's because you asked all the difficult questions,' quipped Angelina. 'You sure know how to torture people.'

'Ha! Ha! Ha! You call that torture?' Jing Yang exclaimed.

'I think this guide doesn't like you,' Angelina added. 'He kept glaring at you. Luckily you were too busy writing down all these notes, otherwise, if you had disturbed him some more, goodness knows what he would have done to you.'

'So what could he do to me?' Jing Yang asked.

'Eat you for lunch, like this and this,' said Angelina. She put down her packet of food and mimicked Jing Yang's scratching and pawing motions with her two hands.

'You sure know how to act,' guffawed Jing Yang. Then he coughed. He had almost choked on the food.

'You have five minutes left for lunch,' Mr Zee announced to the group. 'We set off in five minutes.'

Jing Yang looked at his watch. It was almost half past one. They had been on the hill for over three hours.

'Make sure you dispose of all the empty containers in the dustbins,' Mr Zee shouted. 'Line up in twos in front of me, 3E3 on my left and 3E4 on my right.'

The students gathered in front of the four teachers. When everyone was accounted for, they filed down the lane towards the roundabout. Their buses were waiting for them at the roundabout.

A guard was standing at the guard post situated next to the white building where they watched a video. He assumed an air of importance, scanning the students and teachers as they passed him. It was as if he was inspecting them. Jing Yang could not help looking at the guard. This middle-aged Chinese man had wavy hair which did not look real – it looked perfectly combed. There was hardly a strand of hair out of place. Was he wearing a toupee? He was rather short for a guard; he was a head shorter than Jing Yang. He was rotund too. Was it a beer belly that was above his waist? Could he run after a thief? Jing Yang was asking himself in his thoughts. Angelina noticed Jing Yang seemed to be pre-occupied. She elbowed him gently in his ribs. That got his attention. He was now looking at her.

'Just observing the guard. He seems strange; doesn't look like a guard at all.'

'Busybody!' said Angelina. 'Look ahead; we are supposed to board the bus now.'

Jing Yang took aim at the guard with his mobile phone and clicked the shutter.

'Why did you take a picture of the guard?' asked Angelina.

'For fun,' said Jing Yang gleefully.

With the students from 3E3 and 3E4 and the four teachers safely deposited on them, the two buses made their way down the winding road to the expressway, heading for Punggol housing estate. It had been a fruitful half-day for Jing Yang and Angelina. For the others, it was an enjoyable trip.

8 *RESEARCHING THE BUNKER*

Saturday afternoon was rest time for Jing Yang and Angelina. Both of them had trudged home, dumped their bags on the floor and thrown themselves into bed for a badly needed nap. They were too tired to do anything else. It was a long nap but what a difference in environment for both of them! Jing Yang had the air-conditioning on at full blast; he had come home feeling too hot. Angelina had the fan on at full blast too. By the time they woke up, it was getting dark outside. Jing Yang was up first. He had slept four hours. He slipped down the stairs for dinner. Angelina was up half-an-hour later. She spent another few minutes sitting on her bed. It was her habit – for some strange reason she liked to give her body some time to adjust itself to waking up. Angelina took her dinner seated on the floor in front of the television in the living room. Her mother was having hers at the table in the living room. Both were watching the seven o'clock Korean serial, 'Thank Heavens!'

'Beep! Beep!' went the mobile phone in Angelina's room. Angelina got up to go into the room to retrieve the phone. It was an SMS message from Jing Yang. He had texted that he wanted to make a trip to the National

Library in Victoria Street at ten o'clock the next morning. Tim would be going along. Angelina replied that she would like to go too. Then Jing Yang texted again, telling her he would be hard at work that evening putting his notes on the Battle Box in order. He also said goodnight to her. She texted the words 'sweet dreams' to him. This was the way the pair communicated with each other. It was not as good as calling each other and whispering sweet words into each other's ears but it was easy on Angelina's pockets. Besides, this method worked too.

It was a sunny Sunday morning when the trio met at the footpath near Jing Yang's house. Angelina looked fresh. She had recovered from the fatigue of the trip the day before. She was in a pink T-shirt and white shorts. Jing Yang was wearing his favourite red Nike T-shirt and brown Bermudas, and carrying a black neoprene case. Tim was in a loud T-shirt and checked Bermudas. They made their way to the bus-stop, chattering along the way. Today, they would take a bus to Kovan MRT station where they would switch to the MRT for the journey to Bugis MRT station which was a stone's throw away from the National Library.

'What are we researching on today?' asked Angelina.

'The bunker,' said Jing Yang. 'Remember the guide said the bunker was rediscovered in 1988?'

'Yes, but how are we going to find out more about the rediscovery of the bunker?'

'Through the newspaper! The local newspapers will likely have news stories on the bunker. We just need to go through the whole year for 1988.'

'*Wah*! That's a lot of paper to browse through.'

'No, silly. We are not going to browse through the actual newspapers. We are going to look through microfiche copies of the newspapers.'

'You mean I have to help out too?'

'Yes Tim. Otherwise why did I ask you to come along?'

'Alright. Okay.'

'Jing Yang, what's microfiche?'

'Microfiche is an archival format, like microfilm, but better. The National Library in Victoria Street has an archive of all newspapers ever printed in Singapore. There are special microfiche readers to help us browse through the microfiche copies of the newspapers.'

'I see. Can we make a photocopy of the newspaper if it is on microfiche?'

'Yes, of course. There is an attendant in a special room to help us make copies.'

The journey to Bugis MRT station took an hour. From Bugis MRT station, the three friends walked through Bugis Junction, a shopping centre above the station, and exited the building at the junction of North Bridge Road and Middle Road. The National Library building was just across the road. It was a spanking new white building towering above the pre-war shophouses along North Bridge Road. The microfiche archives were located in the reference section of the library on the eleventh storey. They took a lift up to the eleventh storey. When they came out of the lift, they found themselves in front of the entrance to a very large hall. It occupied an area of about 65,000 sq ft.

Above them was a large sign reading 'Lee Kong Chian Reference Library'. There was a guard seated next to the entrance. Jing Yang passed his case to Angelina and told them to follow him into the hall. Jing Yang seemed to know his way around the reference section. He led them past row upon row of bookshelves to a corner where some rows of metal cabinets were stacked against the wall. These stored card catalogues. He bent over the cabinets to browse the titles on them. Then he opened one and fingered the paper catalogues in the box. He jotted down some numbers and walked across to a long row of metal cabinets on the other side of the room. In these cabinets were stored microfiche. He seemed to know what he was doing. Angelina and Tim merely tagged along silently. Jing

Yang looked at the numbers at the top of each drawer and compared them with those he had scribbled down. Then he opened a drawer and fingered the plastic containers in it. He pulled out a few of these containers and handed them to Angelina.

'Come, let's go to the microfiche readers,' he told the two of them. He took back the containers from Angelina and walked towards a door-less room on the right. In this dimly lit longish room were several microfiche readers.

Jing Yang walked to one of the readers. He sat down in a chair and beckoned them to join him. They sat next to him.

'Watch carefully what I am going to do. Afterwards, you will need to do the same thing. We will split our work into three parts so that we can all do the searching for information on the bunker,' he told them.

Then he opened one of the containers and took out a reel of microfiche. He stood up, fitted the roll of microfiche onto a metal revolving structure on top of the reader and fastened the catch. He turned on a switch at the side of the revolving structure and sat down. He pressed a button on his right and, hey presto, an image of the The Straits Times newspaper appeared on the white board at the base of the reader. He adjusted a lever next to the button and the image appeared bigger so that the text was readable.

'See? This is how I do it. To scroll from page to page, simply move the lever up or down. To scroll quickly, depress the lever.'

It looked so easy when Jing Yang did it but when it came to their turn, Angelina and Tim were hopelessly lost. In the end, Jing Yang had to set up the readers for them. The three sat at their own microfiche readers, browsing through the pages of the newspaper. Each had different months of 1988 to go through. Jing Yang had to go through the months from January to April; Angelina had to do the months from May to August; and Tim, the rest of the year.

Jing Yang and Tim did not have any luck with their rolls of microfiche. They had spent an hour going through the newspaper archive and were a little groggy from the repetitive flipping of the images on the reader. Angelina was the first to discover news of the bunker. She had been flipping the images and had almost let the page with the news pass. It was the picture that accompanied the news story that caught her attention. She waved frantically to Jing Yang to come see the image on her reader. Both boys crossed over to her screen to take a look.

There in the image of the 26th July 1988 issue of the newspaper was a news story headlined Percival's Last Stand. It occupied almost half the page. On the left of the article was an illustration of the underground structure of the bunker. It was the story that they were searching for! Jing Yang lapped up the news story. Then he noted the edition date and the page number of the newspaper.

'Let's go!' he told the others. 'We have finished our work here.' He grabbed the container with the microfiche that had the newspaper edition that they wanted and asked Tim to help him carry the rest of the containers.

Tim returned the containers of microfiche to the cabinets. Then Jing Yang led the way to a room at the end of the hall. There was an elderly attendant in it. He was seated next to a large machine.

'Can I have a copy of this page, please?' Jing Yang said to the man, handing over the note that he had written, and the roll of microfiche.

The attendant inserted the microfiche into the machine and pressed some buttons. Then he flipped the images till he got to the date and page that Jing Yang had written down.

'Is this the page you want?' he asked Jing Yang.

"Yes, and that is the article I want copied,' Jing Yang replied, pointing at the article on the bunker in the image.

'That will be ninety cents, please,' the man said. He

zoomed in on the article so that the print was big enough to be read.

Jing Yang dug into a pocket for some coins and passed them to the attendant who then printed the article and handed it to Jing Yang.

'Thank you, Uncle,' said Jing Yang. He folded the paper into half and placed it into his neoprene case.

'I will study this piece of information tonight,' he told Angelina.

The three friends made their way down to the lobby and left the building.

'Let's get a bite,' said Jing Yang. It was now half past eleven.

Jing Yang suggested walking to Raffles City Shopping Centre, about a five-minute walk away. Everyone agreed so they did a brisk walk to the building. It was too hot for a leisurely walk that morning.

At Raffles City, they rode the escalator down to the basement where there were many eating places they could choose from. But there was no food court. Jing Yang suggested going into a fast-food outlet in front of them. Angelina was hesitant. Jing Yang knew at once the reason. He grabbed her hand and strode into the restaurant with Tim following.

'My treat,' Jing Yang said to the two. Then he placed his case on a vacant table and motioned them to sit.

'I am not eating,' said Angelina. 'I'll just get a drink.'

Angelina kept shaking her head but he did not bother to look at her. He knew what she liked – fish burger and a Coca-Cola – and after asking Tim what he wanted, left the table to go to the counter.

Jing Yang thought to himself that he was not being insensitive to her feelings. After all, he was not giving her treats because he wanted to get things out of her. He was doing it simply out of the goodness of his heart. But it was not compassion. It was simple sharing of resources between two bosom friends. He had to make her understand that, but it would not be easy, given Angelina's fierce independent streak.

As they ate, they talked about the events of the previous day. Tim sat listening.

'Looks like we have to pay another visit to the bunker,' said Jing Yang. He had not managed to take down all the information that was proffered that day. He also did not have time to look at the exhibits – he had been too busy writing notes.

'Can I come, too?' asked Tim. He had not been to the bunker before. Moreover, after the incident at school in which Jing Yang defended him against a bully, he was amenable to associating with this cousin of his.

'Sure,' said Jing Yang. He was glad Tim and he were no longer at loggerheads, at least not presently.

'So when are we going there?' asked Angelina.

'How about Wednesday after school?' suggested Jing Yang. 'We will go directly after school.'

'Okay by me. Remember to bring your camera,' said Angelina.

'That reminds me, I need to print some photographs that I took yesterday,' said Jing Yang. 'Can we hop by a digital imaging outlet afterwards?'

'Sure,' said Angelina.

'By the way, shall we ask Mabel and Fanny to come along?' asked Angelina.

'They were with us at the bunker yesterday but did not seem at all interested. I doubt they want to go again,' said Jing Yang.

'In fact, I'm not too happy about these two girls. They don't seem to be keen on doing the project,' he continued.

'Seems to be the case, I was talking with Mabel last week and yesterday too. She kept giving me a lot of excuses when I asked to meet her. One time, she said she had to attend piano lessons. Another time she told me she had to attend some function.'

'Might be, she wants us to do all the work and then she

would share all the credit. It's common practice you know,' said Jing Yang.

'Likely,' said Angelina. 'But it's not fair that we do all the hard work and they get the benefits. So how do we deal with this?'

'Remember – you were the one who recommended them to be in our group,' said Jing Yang.

'I know. But at the time they seemed interested,' Angelina said.

'Yes, interested in letting us do all the work and letting themselves get the credit too,' exclaimed Jing Yang.

'Sorry. So how now?' asked Angelina.

'I may ask Mr Chan if we can work alone – that is, just the two of us.'

'May?' Angelina said.

'Alright, I will ask him tomorrow,' Jing Yang replied.

'Let's walk around this place,' said Tim, tapping a finger on the table. They had finished having lunch ten minutes ago and he was bored sitting there while Jing Yang and Angelina chatted away.

'Okay, let's go,' said Jing Yang. They went out of the restaurant and browsed through the shops in the basement, talking as they moved along. They were not thinking of buying anything, just window-shopping to pass the time in air-conditioned comfort. They went into a digital imaging outlet and Jing Yang made some instant prints of the photographs he had taken during the excursion. Then they sat next to a fountain, looking through the photographs.

'Rrrring! Rrrring!' Tim's mobile phone was ringing. He took out his phone and pressed a button on it.

'Hi Mum,' he said.

'Dear, is Jing Yang with you?' asked his mother.

'Yes, Mum,' said Tim.

'Pass the phone to him. I want to talk to him,' said his mother.

'My mum wants to speak to you,' Tim told Jing Yang,

handing him his mobile phone.

'Hi Aunt Dorothy,' said Jing Yang.

'Jing Yang, Mr Wang just called me. He can't make the appointment next Thursday and wants to know whether he can come tomorrow afternoon at four o'clock instead,' his aunt said.

'Sure! Aunt Dorothy. Tomorrow's Monday. I will be back by two o'clock,' said Jing Yang.

'But I won't be around when Mr Wang comes. I'm going house-hunting with Tim. Is it alright with you?' his aunt said.

'No problem, Aunt Dorothy,' said Jing Yang.

'Thanks, Jing Yang. Let me speak with Tim,' said his aunt.

Jing Yang passed the phone to Tim.

'Yes, Mum,' said Tim.

'Remember to come home early tomorrow, dear. We are going house-hunting,' his mother said.

'Yes, Mum,' said Tim.

Tim ended the call and slipped his mobile phone into a pocket.

'I need to go to the restroom,' said Tim.

'We'll wait for you here,' said Jing Yang.

Jing Yang waited until Tim had moved out of sight before turning to Angelina.

'Open your right hand,' Jing Yang said.

'Why?' Angelina asked. 'Is it a trick?'

'Do as I say, please,' Jing Yang replied. Angelina opened her right hand.

'Here!' Jing Yang said, placing in Angelina's hand a top-up phone card.

'What's this for?' Angelina asked.

'For your mobile phone!' Jing Yang replied. 'We are always SMSing each other. With this, you can SMS me all you like.'

Angelina blushed. She did not know what to say. She wanted to return the card to him. It was in her character not to accept things from others, even good friends. But, at the same time, she felt that Jing Yang and she were more than just good friends. Jing Yang was trying to get closer to her and she was finding it difficult to reject his moves. She was in two minds. Should she return the card and risk losing this closeness between the two of them, or should she accept the card to send the message that they were in a relationship.

'Angelina,' said Jing Yang. 'What's on your mind?'

'I...I,' muttered Angelina. She was lost for words. She did not know why she did what she did next – she slipped the top-up phone card in a pocket.

Jing Yang was expecting her to put up some resistance; it was so like her to do so. So he was pleasantly surprised by her action. He smiled and clasped her hand in his.

'Shall we go out of this place or do you guys want to hang around here some more?' said Tim. He had just returned after using the restroom.

'Jing Yang, let's go somewhere else,' said Angelina.

They took the MRT to Hougang Mall and spent the rest of the afternoon loitering around the shopping centre.

Jing Yang was in his bedroom the whole evening going through the notes he had made when he was in the bunker. Then he wrote down the important points. By now, he had known about the significance of the bunker in Singapore's history. This was the place where British General Percival had made the decision to surrender Singapore to the Japanese invading forces. But he had doubts in his mind. The information they had collated showed that the British had some 88,600 soldiers and the Japanese had only about 30,000 soldiers. Why then did the British surrender to the Japanese? It just did not make sense to him. Did General Percival have the authority to surrender his forces?

Also, questions about the famed Yamashita treasure abounded in his mind. He had found that General Yamashita stayed in Singapore for only about six months and then left for Manchuria. He was in Manchuria till late 1944. How did he manage to amass so much treasure? It seemed impossible. Surely, he could not have trusted his men to take care of the treasure for him while he was assigned to a post so far away. As for the Philippines part of the treasure story, he had found out that General Yamashita went to the Philippines only in October 1944. In the same month, the United States Army entered the Philippines so General Yamashita was pre-occupied with fighting fierce battles with the United States Army. Certainly he could not have the time to hide the treasure there. It did not make sense to Jing Yang.

Perhaps, Mr Wang could help him with answers to his questions the next afternoon. Jing Yang listed in a piece of paper all the questions that he needed answers for.

Jing Yang had some photographs of the bunker but these were not enough. He needed more so that he could pick the best to be included in the project's report. He had to remember to take more pictures when he next visited the bunker.

Meanwhile, Angelina had texted him about the progress in the project, and he had shared with her his doubts. The couple sent quite a few SMS messages between them. Jing Yang was glad he had got Angelina the top-up phone card and Angelina was happy she could SMS Jing Yang more often, instead of rationing her SMS messages as before. The top-up phone card did help bring the two closer.

9 *MR WANG AND MR SAVAGE*

In school the next day, Jing Yang remembered to see Mr Chan about reducing the number of members in his group to two – he and Angelina. He could have approached the two girls instead, but he thought it would not work. Angelina had wanted to talk to the girls first, but Jing Yang did not let her. He did not want her to complicate matters. They might not agree to being taken out of his group. However, he was determined not to let the girls hitch a free ride.

Angelina wanted to come with him to see Mr Chan, but he thought it was not a good idea. Angelina was a little on the soft side, especially when it came to matters concerning her friends. She might just spoil his plans.

Jing Yang used the intercom on the wall outside the teachers' room to contact Mr Chan. Fortunately Mr Chan was in the room. He did not have a period in class. When Mr Chan came out, Jing Yang told him about his problems with Mabel and Fanny in the group. He pleaded with Mr Chan to take the two girls out of his group. Mr Chan appeared sympathetic. He knew that in some student groups there were some members who would rather depend on others to do the work for them.

When Mr Chan was doubtful that he and Angelina could handle the project alone, Jing Yang produced a stack of notes that he had compiled on the project to prove that both of them could handle the project equally well without additional support from other classmates. Mr Chan at last gave his consent. He said he would inform Mabel and Fanny himself.

When Jing Yang returned to class, he wrote a note and passed it to Angelina. In it he told her Mr Chan had agreed to take Mabel and Fanny out of the group. Angelina beamed when she read the note.

That afternoon, after school, Angelina went over to Jing Yang's house to keep him company. Tim and his mother had gone house-hunting and the two of them were alone in Jing Yang's room. They were going through the photographs taken in the bunker when Angelina held up one in a hand. It was a picture of her and Jing Yang standing in front of the mannequin in the telephone exchange.

'Isn't this photograph nice?'

'Yes, it is.'

'Can I have this one?'

'Sure you can.'

'Where's the scissors?'

Jing Yang took out a pair of scissors from a drawer and placed it on his desk. Angelina took the scissors and cropped some parts of the photograph. What she had left was a picture of her and Jing Yang. Even the mannequin had been cut out of the photograph. She showed the photograph to Jing Yang.

'Where's the mannequin?'

'There, on the table.' Angelina pointed to the cropped pieces on the table.

'*Alamak*! It was a nice photograph.'

'You mean, it's not nice now?'

Jing Yang sensed he had said the wrong words. He looked sheepishly at Angelina, hoping she would not flare up.

'Don't you think it looks nicer – now?'

'Yes, of course.'

'Really?'

'Really.'

'Good!' Then Angelina took out her wallet and inserted the cropped photograph in a clear plastic holder in the wallet. She held up the wallet, pleased with her work. Then she looked at Jing Yang who flashed a smile at her. He did not want to offend her. Sometimes, a smile worked wonders, he thought to himself.

Ten minutes before four o'clock, Jing Yang had tidied his desk and placed the notes and photographs for his history project neatly on his left.

'Wait for me in the living room afterwards. You can watch TV there.'

'Okay. Where shall I leave my bag?'

'Beside the bed, on the left.'

'We need to go down now. This guy is a stickler for punctuality.'

They went down to the living room and Jing Yang turned on the television. He walked into the kitchen to make a cup of tea using hot water from a flask. Then he took it up into his bedroom.

'Ding Dong. Ding Dong.' Mr Wang was at the door! Jing Yang clambered down the stairs. Standing at the doorway was Mr Wang. Angelina had opened the door for him.

'Hi Mr Wang.'

'Hello.'

'Mr Wang.'

'Hello, Jing Yang. Who's this young lady?'

'This is my classmate, Angelina.'

Mr Wang nodded at Angelina. Jing Yang led him up the stairs.

'Aunt Dorothy says she can't be home this afternoon. She has gone house-hunting.'

'Is that so? Is that so? Will she be moving to somewhere nearby?'

'I don't know.'

'Please go in.' Jing Yang stood at the doorway waiting for Mr Wang to enter his bedroom. Then he sat on the left of Mr Wang.

'Let's start, shall we?'

Once settled into the chair, Mr Wang placed his mobile phone and a thick plastic file he was carrying on his right and proceeded to talk at length on the history topics that Jing Yang's teacher had covered the last three months with his classmates. He took out some notes from the thick plastic folder on the desk. He handed a set to Jing Yang and referred to another set when talking to him. These were photocopies of PowerPoint presentations, with six slides printed per page, stapled together. The topic titles were positioned on top of each page.

When he had finished delivering his lesson, he summarised the points and then asked for questions from Jing Yang. But Jing Yang did not have any. Mr Wang's explanation was lucid and the notes he had prepared were detailed, yet not confusing to him. When Mr Wang asked him what he had understood of the lesson, Jing Yang regurgitated what Mr Wang had told him. Mr Wang was clearly pleased. This student had been paying attention. He was different from many others he had tutored at university.

'Mr Wang, can we discuss my history project, please?'

'Of course, Jing Yang. In fact, I have set aside fifteen minutes for this.' Mr Wang was looking at the mobile phone on his right. He did not wear a watch and would occasionally pick up the phone as the lesson progressed.

'And, don't call me Mr Wang – remember?'

'Yes.'

'Good! Now, show me what you have got so far on the project.'

Jing Yang picked up the stack of notes and

photographs on his left and placed it neatly between them. On top was a summary of the salient points he had gleaned from the notes. There were some questions listed below the summary. Mr Wang glanced at the front sheet and flipped through the notes. Then he took the photographs and went through them one by one.

Suddenly, he stopped at one of the photographs. He held the photograph in his hands. He had recognised something in the photograph. He gazed at it.

'Where did you take this photograph?'

'This one? In the bunker at Fort Canning Park.'

'I see. I see.'

Mr Wang was deep in thought. Jing Yang glanced at the photograph. It was one showing the Orderlies Room. The guide and some students and teachers were in the photograph.

'This chap,' Mr Wang said, pointing an index finger at the guide. 'This chap was a classmate of mine – long, long ago.'

'You mean, Mr Savage?'

'Yes, that's his name alright, Savage.' He paused. 'Craig Savage. Bright chap, but dropped out of school. So he's working in the bunker now.'

'Were you together in secondary school?'

'No – university. He was in the same class. A brilliant chap he was.'

'Was he studying history too?'

'Yes.' But he left abruptly in the second year. Let me think. Yes, I believe he said he was on a quest for something.'

'Our class had been doing a project for a history module. Let me see. It had something to do with World War Two, I believe. It was so long ago; I can barely recollect.'

'Was it about the Yamashita treasure?'

'Yamashita treasure? Mmm…'

Mr Wang fisted his hands against his chin. He was deep

in thought now.

'Yes, I think he was doing research on the Yamashita treasure. I was not on his team. He was a loner and did not get along well with others. He didn't like to share his research with the other members of his group.'

Old memories were flooding into his mind as he spoke of Mr Savage. He looked slightly disturbed.

'Called me a busybody. Always poking into his affairs – he was complaining to everyone.'

'I had said he was wrong – there was no Yamashita treasure to be found. But he was adamant that there was.'

'What happened then? Why did he drop out of university?'

'Let me see, now. One day he simply disappeared without a word. His group members said something about him discovering a lead to some treasure. They said that he was crazy.'

'I guess they were right.' Looking at the photograph in front of him, he continued talking.

'He's still working on the treasure leads. That means he has not found any treasure yet. Otherwise, he will be living a life of luxury now.'

'Beep! Beep!' The alarm on Mr Wang's mobile phone had been activated.

'Gosh! How time flies!'

Mr Wang got up, pocketed his phone, and picked up the file from the table.

'That's it for today, Jing Yang.'

He moved towards the open doorway. Jing Yang followed him.

'If you want to know more about this chap, come over to my place this evening, after dinner.'

'Thank you, Mr Wang.'

'There you go again, Mr Wang indeed. Just make sure you let your aunt know that you are coming over. Manners, you know.'

'Yes.' Jing Yang followed Mr Wang down to the living

room and saw him to the door.

'Did you get the answers to your questions?'

'Didn't get a chance. He was talking about Mr Savage.'

'Mr Savage? Has Mr Wang been to the bunker before?'

'No. He saw Mr Savage's picture. He said that he was Mr Savage's classmate.'

'What? Are you kidding?'

'No! It's true. He and Mr Savage were classmates at university.'

'What a small world!'

'Yes, indeed. It seems they were both history students.'

'But, why then is Mr Savage working as a guide?'

'Because he dropped out of university.'

'Really? Why?'

'I'm not sure. Mr Wang said something about Mr Savage looking for treasure.'

'What? You mean there is treasure?'

'I think so.'

'Tell me more. Tell me more.'

'I can't. Mr Wang only told me so much. Then the alarm on his phone went off and the lesson ended.'

'Gosh! We have to wait another week to find out more.'

'No need. Mr Wang said I could visit him this evening for a chat.'

'He did? Good! Can I come along?'

'Sure. We'll go together after dinner.'

Angelina looked at her watch. It was showing half past six.

'It's late. I had better get going. So what time are we going there?'

'Meet me outside my house at eight o'clock, okay?'

Angelina strapped her bag behind her and, waving at Jing Yang, walked out of the house.

It was eight o'clock when Angelina arrived at the gate outside Jing Yang's place. She was dressed in a white tank top and dark blue shorts. Jing Yang and Tim were already there waiting for her. They were in T-shirts and Bermudas.

'Tim, you are coming along too?'

'Yes. Jing Yang asked me to follow along. He says since I'm helping out with the project, I should tag along.'

They walked to Mr Wang's house which was two doors away from Jing Yang's. From the outside, the house looked the same as theirs. It was the same size. The gate was of the same design, only painted in a different colour. The house also had balconies in front and behind. And there were bay windows in front of the house. But the house was not as brightly lit as Jing Yang's. There was an old white Volkswagen Beetle in the porch.

Jing Yang pressed the doorbell on a pillar next to the gate. There was no answer. He pressed the doorbell again. Mr Wang came ambling to the gate. He greeted the teenagers with a smile.

'Nice of you young chaps to visit me. Come in, please.' Mr Wang opened one side of the gate to let them in.

'This way please.' He led them into the living room and showed them to a large black leather sofa on the right of the room. The room was lit by wall lights and a large table-lamp which sat on a side table nested between a large sofa and an equally large black leather armchair.

'*Wah*! This house looks the same as yours, Jing Yang.'

'No. It's not the same – the decoration is totally different.'

'Sit down, please.'

The three friends sat together in the large sofa with Angelina in the middle. Mr Wang made himself comfortable in the armchair. There were packets of drinks on the coffee-table in front of them.

'Help yourselves to the drinks.' He bent forward to move the drinks nearer to them and rested his back in the armchair again.

'Who's this?' Mr Wang was pointing at Tim. 'He looks familiar.'

'This is my cousin, Tim. He is Aunt Dorothy's son.'

'Oh, I see. I have seen you around.'

'So how's the house-hunting progressing?'

'Mr Wang, my mum and I have found a suitable house near here.'

'Is that so? Very near here?'

'It's across the main road, in Jalan Nuang.'

'That certainly is near. Good for you cousins. You can visit each other every day then.'

'Yes. Mr Wang.'

'I have already told Jing Yang not to call me Mr Wang. You should do the same too. Just talk to me without mentioning my name all the time. I like it better this way.'

'Yes.'

'Mr Wang, are you living alone?'

'Angelina, Mr Wang told us not to call him Mr Wang.'

'Jing Yang, you are also calling him Mr Wang.'

'Are you living alone?'

'Yes, of course. Been living here since the 1990s. It's quiet and the neighbours are friendly. I like it here very much.'

'Are you married?'

'Angelina!'

'Jing Yang, I just wanted to know whether he is married – whether he has children.'

'Sorry, Angelina can sometimes be blunt.'

'It's alright, Jing Yang. Angelina, I am a bachelor so I have no children.'

'Don't you wish you have children? I mean, they can keep you company.'

'Ha! Ha! Ha! Angelina. Thanks very much for your suggestion. I'm contented with what I have now. Perhaps, it is fated that I remain unmarried. I have had no time for things other than my history books and research projects for ages. But, I don't regret it one bit.'

'Don't you think it's a…' Before Angelina could complete her sentence, Jing Yang had cut in.

'We actually came here to find out more about Mr

Savage.'

'Yes. I am sure you are anxious to ask me some questions about my classmate Craig Savage. Go ahead. Fire away.'

'Are you sure the person in this photograph is your classmate?' Jing Yang showed the photograph to Mr Wang again.

'It's him alright. Didn't you say that he called himself Craig Savage? Then I can't be wrong.'

'If like you said, he dropped out of university to look for treasure, then why is he at Fort Canning working as a guide?'

'You got me there, Jing Yang. I have been thinking about it since I returned home this afternoon. I thought perhaps that he had to be working because he did not strike it rich. And because you had said he was a museum guide, I thought he had become a museum guide because of his background in history. He was knowledgeable in history so it was easy getting the job, and even easier doing the job.'

The three visitors were all ears, taking in every word that Mr Wang was saying. Jing Yang kept looking at the list of questions in a piece of paper he was holding on his lap. It was getting late, and there were many more questions he wanted Mr Wang to answer.

'But, when I heard that he was a guide at the bunker, which is connected to World War Two, something in me told me things were not that simple. You see, Craig Savage had been doing research on the Yamashita treasure when he disappeared without a trace. And this bunker was where the British general surrendered to General Yamashita. General Yamashita must have had access to the bunker after the fall of Singapore.'

Mr Wang paused for a long while. Then he continued talking.

'Just too much of a coincidence. Too much of a coincidence.'

'Could it be that there's treasure in the bunker?'

'Yes, Jing Yang, it could possibly be the case. Otherwise Craig Savage would not be working there. He is not the kind of person who would give up easily. He could be there looking for the Yamashita treasure. Likely so, I think.'

Mr Wang paused again.

'Jing Yang, do you know how long he has been there?'

'No, but I can try to find out. We guys are going to visit the bunker again soon – like on Wednesday.'

'Yes, please. Come to think of it, as a museum guide at the bunker, he's got access to all parts of the bunker and if he wants to search the bunker, no one will be suspicious of him.'

'Where do you think the treasure is buried?'

'Buried? Oh yes, buried. It's just possible that it is buried somewhere under the bunker.'

'Is that why Mr Savage was uttering something about some of the rooms in the bunker being dug up, Jing Yang?'

'Yes, I remember now. Angelina has triggered my memory of that day's happenings. Mr Savage was telling us students that after the bunker was rediscovered in 1988, they found that some of the rooms had been dug up. Then he stopped abruptly, and tried to change the subject when we pestered him to tell us more.'

'Is that so? Is that so?' Mr Wang had rested his elbows on both sides of the armchair and was now clenching his fists against his chin.

'Yes.'

'Did you guys see anything suspicious about the bunker when you were there?'

'Mr Savage was stamping his foot on the wooden floorboards in one of the rooms.'

'Yes, Angelina is right. Most of the rooms had screed flooring, but there were three rooms in the bunker that had wooden floorboards. Also, I noticed that one of the rooms was locked. And the guide did not take us into the room.'

'Which room was it, Jing Yang? Why didn't I notice it?'

'Angelina, you were busy taking photographs of the mannequin in the corridor outside the Gun Operations Room, remember?'

'Oh yes, I remember now. You are talking about the room between the Gun Operations Room and the Surrender Conference Room.'

'Right, Angelina.'

Mr Wang had been listening intently to the verbal exchange between Angelina and Jing Yang.

'Was there any light in the room, Jing Yang?'

'The metal door had a small window but it was boarded up. There was no way to see inside.'

'I see. I see. Looks like there may be something in that room after all. Try to get inside, if you can.'

'I will. I will.' Jing Yang noted this in the piece of paper he was holding. Angelina was now nudging him.

'Why are you mimicking him?' Angelina had covered her mouth. She was muttering under her breath.

'There is something that just doesn't make sense to me about the Yamashita treasure.'

'What is it, Jing Yang?'

'General Yamashita was in Singapore for only about six months, and after that he was in Manchuria until late 1944. Just how did he manage to amass so much treasure?'

'Good question, Jing Yang. Good Question.'

'Come – follow me.' Mr Wang got up and led them into his study. It was a dimly lit room. A table lamp atop a big wooden desk in front of the window was the only illumination in the room. Behind the desk was a leather armchair. There was a wall-to-wall wooden cabinet behind the armchair. In front of the desk was a chaise lounge in black leather. It had wooden legs. There were floor to ceiling bookcases on both sides of the room. On their shelves were row upon row of books – thick books, thin books, hard-cover books, paper-backs, and casebound books.

Mr Wang walked up to his desk and opened a cabinet behind it. He pulled out a thick brown paper folder and set it on his desk. The three visitors stood beside him at the desk. Mr Wang opened the folder and flipped through the papers in it.

'Here it is.' He was looking at a handwritten note. It had yellowed with age and the ink was fading but the handwriting was still legible. He switched on another table lamp and adjusted its arm so that the piece of paper was illuminated. Then he fingered the text in it.

'This is a page from research that Craig Savage had been doing at university.'

'How did you get hold of it?'

'It was found among the stuff he had left behind. I have been keeping it for many years. It is the only clue to why he had left so suddenly.'

Mr Wang took off his spectacles. He was short-sighted but he could see small text clearly without the need for reading glasses.

'Here it is. There is mention about a map showing the location of the treasure. From this note, it seems Yamashita might not have known about the treasure after all. A secret group working in the military was in charge of loot collected from the conquered countries. This group had secret operatives in the Kempeitai – the Japanese secret police.'

'Kempeitai? The name sounds familiar. I have heard it somewhere.'

'Of course, you have, Jing Yang. Remember the Signals Control Room? Remember Mr Savage was showing us the graffiti on the wall before he started stomping on the floorboards?'

'Yes, I remember now. There were some Japanese words scrawled on the wall in that room.'

'Can you take pictures of them when you are there, Jing

Yang?'

'Sure.' Jing Yang wrote this down in his to-do list.

Just then, Tim's mobile phone rang. It was his mother calling to ask them to return home. It was already half past nine.

'Gosh! I didn't realise it is so late. Get going now, young lads. Get going now.'

'Thank you,' they chorused.

Mr Wang walked with them to the gate and said a goodnight to them. Then he returned to his house. Tim went home while Jing Yang accompanied Angelina to her flat. They lingered in the void deck for a while. Then after seeing Angelina up to her flat, Jing Yang returned home. That night, he texted her on his mobile phone. He told her that he would be paying for the admission tickets to the bunker. She needed not worry about it. Angelina did not reply. She did not know what to say. She felt it best to remain silent as silence also denoted consent. She did not want to reject his offer. They had become too close for her to say no to many things.

10 *A SECOND LOOK IN THE BUNKER*

It was Wednesday in week two of the third school term. After school, Jing Yang, Angelina and Tim met at their regular meeting place outside the art room. It was half past one. The museum closed at six o'clock so there was still time for them to go home first to change out of their uniforms before making the trip to The Battle Box. Jing Yang thought it better not to be in school uniform as he did not want the museum guide to recognise him or Angelina. The guide did not have a good impression of him the other day, as he had asked too many questions of the guide.

When they had changed into their casual outing attire, Jing Yang and Tim walked out of the house. As usual, Angelina was waiting at the gate. Jing Yang was the only one carrying a bag. He had his backpack strapped to his back. In it were a netbook, a water bottle, his notes and a notepad.

'Don't forget the camera,' Angelina reminded Jing Yang.

'It's in my bag,' Jing Yang answered.

To get to Fort Canning Park, where The Battle Box was located, they had to take the MRT to Dhoby Ghaut MRT Station. They took a bus at Upper Serangoon Road and alighted at the bus-stop outside Kovan Heartland Mall. Then they rode an escalator down to Kovan MRT Station and boarded the train to Dhoby Ghaut MRT Station.

It was half past two when they emerged from Dhoby Ghaut MRT Station. Though it was their first trip to the bunker by themselves, Jing Yang could find the place because he had gone on the Internet to find out the way there. He was lucky. There was help at local search engine and directory getforme.com. It had a detailed description, complete with pictures, of how to get to the bunker on its local attractions Web page.

The trio walked to the junction opposite Park Mall, a shopping centre in Penang Road. They crossed the junction and entered the shopping centre. In the lobby, they took a lift to the fourth level and walked into the carpark. They made their way to the entrance of the carpark and crossed the road outside it. They were now at the foot of Fort Canning Park. There was an open carpark on the right. Jing Yang pointed to the left and they moved along the side of the road. About one hundred steps ahead, on their right, was a flight of steps. Jing Yang led the way up the steps. They were now at a zebra crossing. There was little traffic here so they crossed the road quickly. They were now at the beginning of another two flights of steps. The steps looked rather steep. It was going to be a long tiring climb up the steps. They clambered up the first flight of steps and paused. Angelina was getting tired. Then they continued up the second flight of steps. By the time they were almost at the top of the slope, they were panting. It was not an easy climb though they were young. At the top of the steps, they stopped to look back. There below them were the three long flights of steps they had conquered. They would have to go down these steps later, on the way back.

'*Wah*! That is tiring. I don't think I can do this climbing every day,' said Angelina. She sat on a wooden bench next to the steps to rest her legs.

'Exactly ninety-three steps in all,' cried Tim, bending down.

'Really? That many steps?' exclaimed Jing Yang. He too was exhausted.

Ahead of them, they could see a roundabout. The white building that Jing Yang and Angelina had been in sat behind the roundabout.

'Let's rest here for five minutes,' suggested Angelina. She was wiping her forehead.

'It certainly is hot up on the hill,' said Tim. He was still not accustomed to the hot weather in Singapore. It was only the first time he had climbed a hill here. It seemed to be hotter up the hill than elsewhere in Singapore.

'Are we going to be seeing the guide again?' asked Angelina. She did not relish the idea of meeting the guide.

'Hope not,' Jing Yang replied.

'Why are you so afraid of him?' asked Tim.

'We are not! We just don't like him,' said Angelina.

'Yeah! He's so unfriendly. He also looks fierce, especially when he contracts his eyebrows – like this,' said Jing Yang. He pulled a funny face for the other two to see. They roared with laughter when they saw his contorted face.

'How many guides do they have there?' asked Angelina.

'I have no idea,' Jing Yang replied. 'I suggest we do not take the guided tour. This way, even if Mr Savage is there today, we do not have to face him constantly. Besides, it's cheaper this way, only five dollars per head, instead of eight dollars.'

'Yes! I agree,' said Angelina. 'We can just walk around the bunker on our own.'

'That would be great,' said Tim. He did not want any stranger by his side in the bunker.

'Shall we make a move?' asked Jing Yang. He was eager to get into the bunker.

They sauntered to the white building and stood outside taking some pictures of themselves in front of the building.

Suddenly, Tim was scratching his legs.

'Bloody mosquitoes!' Tim exclaimed. 'Why are there so many mosquitoes here?'

'Yeah!' cried Angelina in agreement. Her arms were getting itchy too.

'Here! Use this,' said Jing Yang. He handed a small bottle of medicated oil to Angelina who applied some on her arms. She passed the bottle to Tim. By now he had had five bites – three on his legs and two on his arms. Angelina was luckier – she only had two bites. But, the mosquitoes had left Jing Yang alone.

'Isn't this a public park?' asked Tim, scratching his legs again. 'There shouldn't be so many mosquitoes around.'

'Why aren't they biting you too?' Angelina asked Jing Yang. She was stamping her feet on the ground.

'Let's go into the building,' said Jing Yang, smiling. He did not answer her.

They opened the glass doors and entered the building.

They looked at the cardboard clock showing the time for the next guided tour. The hands on the clock told them the next guided tour would be in an hour. That would mean they would not be seeing a guide here for some time. Jing Yang went up to the cashier behind the counter in the corner of the room. Tim and Angelina looked around the room.

'Look! Angelina. These pesky mosquitoes are trying to come in through the glass doors,' Tim exclaimed. He was gazing at some mosquitoes on the other side of the glass doors. 'Don't they know it's glass? That they can't go through glass? They are trying like mad.'

'*Wah*! I can count six, no, eight of them,' said Angelina. She opened a glass door slightly and used a piece of tissue paper to press against the mosquitoes, killing them. Then she closed the door again. She had given up. There were more coming. Fortunately they were in the room and out of reach of these pesky mosquitoes, she thought to herself.

'I have got the tickets. Do we wait for the next video presentation or go in now?' Jing Yang asked.

'Tim has not watched the video yet,' said Angelina.

'I'm not watching,' said Tim. 'Let's go in now.'

'Alright. Let's go. I'll inform the cashier.'

The cashier came out of the counter and led them up the lane outside. She stopped at the entrance to the bunker and told them that video cameras were not allowed in the bunker.

'How long can we remain in the bunker?' asked Jing Yang.

'As long as you like, but we close at six o'clock. You will have to be out by then,' the cashier replied.

They descended into the tunnel. After punching some numbers on a pad on the wall next to the door, she opened the door to let them in.

Sirens wailed through the corridor. Men were shouting commands overhead through the speakers mounted on the wall. Jing Yang and Angelina had heard these sounds before so they were not alarmed. Tim was surprised initially, but he was not alarmed.

'Follow the arrows on the wall so you will not be lost,' she said nonchalantly, oblivious to the din reverberating in the corridor. 'Here's a plan of the bunker for your reference.' The cashier handed to Jing Yang an information sheet and then left the bunker.

'Whoopee! We are alone now!' exclaimed Angelina.

'Shh. Not so loud. It's an enclosed space; there will be echoes,' warned Jing Yang.

'What's that on your arms, Tim?' said Angelina. She had noticed a red swelling extending from the wrist of Tim's left arm to the elbow. The swelling seemed to follow the direction of the veins beneath the skin.

"Oh! It's those pesky mosquitoes. They have got into my blood system,' said Tim. He applied more medicated oil to the affected area.

'They will go off in a while,' said Jing Yang. 'Shall we move along now?'

'Come, let's move around,' said Angelina.

As far as they could see, there were no other people around. They appeared to be the only ones around.

They were now in the first room, next to the entrance. On their left was an open doorway to the next room – the Telephone Exchange. There was a door at the end of the room directly opposite them. A cupboard sat on its right. Jing Yang turned the knob on the door. It opened. Suddenly a strong breeze gushed past him into the room. There was a howling sound.

'Must be the return air for the air-conditioning,' Jing Yang said.

He peeked inside the room. It was a large room, almost three-quarters the size of their classroom. There were row upon row of shelves and a myriad of things on them – paper, forms, baskets and more. Angelina and Tim popped their heads into the room.

'Boy! Sure is windy in here,' said Tim.

'Yeah!' agreed Angelina, fingering her hair. It was getting into her face.

'Nothing much to see,' said Tim.

'Look down!' said Jing Yang. 'Screed flooring.'

Jing Yang closed the door. There was nothing of interest to them in there.

They looked around the room. There were some benches and a wooden rack on one side. A porcelain sink sat in a corner.

Angelina tried the doors on the cupboard. They were locked.

Then they walked through the open doorway into the Telephone Exchange Room.

Tim stretched his hands to touch the mannequin sitting

behind the old telephone exchange equipment. It looked real, more real than the one in the corridor outside.

Jing Yang examined the planks lying on part of the floor. He took a torch from one of his pockets and shone it at a gap between the planks. It was cement screed beneath. He shone it through some other gaps. He checked the cement grouting between the ceramic tiles. It was sealed tight. There were no gaps in the joints so there could not be a secret door below.

Then he touched the walls in the room. There did not seem to be any hidden doors in them.

'*Wah*! Are you really going to inspect all the rooms like that?' Angelina asked. 'It would take forever, you know.'

'Not all the rooms – only the ones that look suspicious to me.'

'What if the guide sees us doing it?' asked Tim.

'Just pretend to look for something we had dropped.'

'Your mind works pretty fast,' said Angelina.

Jing Yang flashed his trademark smile at her.

They were now in the corridor, heading towards the other rooms.

'If you see anything suspicious looking, tell me,' Jing Yang told the other two. 'Anything at all.'

They nodded to signal they had heard him.

The three of them entered the Cipher Office. This room had wooden planks laid on top of a screed floor. Jing Yang squatted down and peered into the gaps. There was nothing suspicious.

The next room they went into was the Signals Room. It also had a raised wooden floor. Jing Yang checked the gaps here too. Angelina pushed aside a framed poster hanging on the wall to see behind.

The Signals Control Room was the last of the interconnected rooms that they entered. This was the room which had graffiti in Japanese scribbled on the wall. Jing Yang remembered that Mr Wang wanted him to take pictures of the graffiti. There were eight sets of graffiti on the wall in this room. Jing Yang took pictures of all eight sets. He also checked the gaps between the wooden planks on the floor. There were no trap doors beneath. The three notice boards on the wall were nailed to the wall. Jing Yang ran his finders around the lower edges of the notice boards.

They went out into the corridor. The toilets were on their left. Right under their feet was a metal drain cover about two feet long and one-and-a-half-feet wide. There was a fork in the corridor here. Straight ahead was another corridor leading to two places: the mini-museum on the left and farther up at the end of the corridor, the secret escape route. Turning right from where they were standing would take them to the Fortress Commander's room and other parts of the bunker.

'It's possible for a tunnel to be under this drain cover,' said Jing Yang. He noted this down.

'Keep a lookout for me,' he told Angelina and Tim.

Then he squatted down next to the drain cover and lifted it up to his shoulder.

'Yes, there is a low tunnel underneath,' he said. 'Come look!'

They looked inside. There was a tunnel beneath. It was about three feet wide and two feet deep. In the middle, there was a small culvert about eight inches wide and four inches deep, running along the length of the tunnel. The water in the tunnel was about ten inches deep. A person could move through the tunnel, but had to crawl through it. He took a picture of the tunnel and placed the cover back into position. Then he got up and flicked the dirt off his knees.

'Where do you think the tunnel leads to?' asked Angelina.

'From the direction of the tunnel, I would say all the way to the end of that corridor,' Jing Yang said, pointing to the bend in the corridor leading to the escape route. He scribbled something on the plan of the bunker. He would need to study this bit of information when he got home.

'Let's go into the Fortress Commander's Office,' said Jing Yang.

They turned into the room on their left. It was a big room, almost half the size of a classroom. A large desk sat about four feet away from the end wall which was facing them. Behind this desk was a mannequin who was seated in a large wicker cane armchair. On the right, at the side of the desk, sat another mannequin, also in a large wicker cane armchair. Behind the second mannequin was a wooden open cabinet, placed against the wall. There was a hurricane lamp and a gas mask on top of the cabinet. Resting in that corner of the room was a wooden cabinet. On the walls of the room were three large notice boards – two on the left wall and one on the wall directly opposite the teenagers.

As Jing Yang ran a hand over the surface of the walls, he shone his torch over it to illuminate the area he was examining. The room was dimly lit and the torch was a great help. He was about to move to the wall behind the desk when a loud voice startled him.

'Boy there! What the dickens are you doing?' said a booming voice behind him. Jing Yang turned around. He had been discovered, he thought. But the man was not looking at him. He had his eyes fixed on Tim. Tim had been adjusting the peaked cap on the second mannequin's head when the voice from behind startled him. He dropped the cap he had been holding. Jing Yang looked at the man at the doorway. It was Mr Savage.

'Who says you can touch the mannequin?' Mr Savage bellowed.

'I…I was just adjusting the cap. It was tilting over,' said Tim.

'Don't lie, boy,' Mr Savage boomed. 'I saw you playing with the cap.'

'No! I was not!' cried Tim. 'Someone else must have played with it. I was merely putting it back nicely when you surprised me.'

'Yes! Someone had played with the cap before we came into the room. He was just helping to adjust it. It's not his fault,' said Jing Yang.

Mr Savage walked up to Tim, picked up the cap and placed it on the mannequin's head. Then, one by one, he looked over Jing Yang, Angelina and Tim. Then his eyes turned to Jing Yang. There was recognition in his eyes.

'I remember you now. You are that boy!' exclaimed Mr Savage. 'The smart aleck who asked me so many questions the other day. Don't think I can't recognise you just because you are not in school uniform.'

Mr Savage cursed Jing Yang under his breath. That wretched boy had come again to irritate him. He would put him in his place.

'Why are you here again?' he asked Jing Yang.

'Why can't I be here again?' Jing Yang asked Mr Savage. He was determined to argue it out with the guide. After all, he was in the right. He had paid for admission to the museum and he was not going to let the guide question his right to be in the bunker.

'Don't tell me you own the bunker,' Jing Yang continued.

Mr Savage was furious this time. This boy had the gall to talk back to him.

'You have that right but you have abused it,' said Mr Savage. 'You guys fooled around with the mannequin's cap. For that reason alone, I can throw you all out.'

'No, you can't,' said Jing Yang. 'We were doing a good deed helping to place the cap properly on the mannequin's head. You just can't blame us like this.'

'I can and I will,' said Mr Savage. He caught hold of Jing Yang's arm and pulled it along as he walked out of the room. 'All of you – get out of this bunker.'

'Says who?' cried Tim.

'Says this fist of mine,' said Mr Savage and he raised a fisted hand to Tim's face. Tim fell into silence. He had been intimidated by the heavily built man in front of him.

Mr Savage dragged Jing Yang along as he marched towards the main door. Angelina and Tim had no choice but to follow them; they were afraid Jing Yang would be harmed. Mr Savage opened the door and pushed Jing Yang out. He waited until Angelina and Tim had passed him before slamming the door shut.

Jing Yang nursed his bruised arm. It was hurting him. Angelina pulled back the sleeve on his T-shirt to look at the arm. The skin around the area was red and swollen. That man had brute strength and he was not afraid to use it. Angelina touched the skin.

'Ouch!' cried Jing Yang. 'Don't do it. It's painful, you know.'

'Sorry! That man really showed no mercy,' Angelina said.

'Yeah! He's not one to mess around with,' agreed Tim. 'Savage! What a fitting name! He sure is savage, alright.'

'Shall we lodge a complaint against him?' asked Angelina.

'No! I'm alright,' said Jing Yang. 'Really!' He was afraid that if they went ahead to complain about the guide, his parents would come to know about it and he might be grounded though it was not his fault. He just did not want to take the chance of the matter blowing up.

'Why not?' asked Tim.

'Because... because we will get an earful from your mother and my mother when they find out about it,' said Jing Yang. 'Come, let's go back. We have done enough work today.'

'But, we haven't finished with all the rooms yet,' said Angelina.

'Never mind, we can always come back another day, when this guy is not around,' said Jing Yang.

'Let me carry your bag,' said Tim. He reached for Jing Yang's backpack and helped him to take it off him. Then he strapped the bag behind him.

'Come, let's go home,' said Jing Yang.

It was a quiet journey back to Hougang for the three teenagers. All three had been unsettled by the way the guide had man-handled Jing Yang and then thrown them out of the bunker.

'Tim, don't say a word to your mother, okay?' said Jing Yang. 'I don't want her to worry.'

'Sure thing,' said Tim. He felt sorry for Jing Yang. This was the second time that his cousin had helped him out. He was the one who had got his cousin into trouble and he did not feel good about it. His cousin, however, had not blamed him for what had happened. When confronted by the guide, his cousin also did not pass the blame to him. For this, Tim was grateful.

'Jing Yang, can I come to your house?' asked Angelina.

'Sure,' Jing Yang replied. He knew he could not refuse her request. She had been looking worried since she saw the bruise on his arm. He did not want her to go home in that state. Somehow, that evening, he had to get her smiling again. Subconsciously, he had begun to be intimately concerned with giving this girl happiness.

Back in the boys' home in Hai Sing Close, the three schoolmates gathered in Jing Yang's bedroom for a discussion on the bunker visit. Jing Yang and Angelina sat on the bed, while Tim made himself comfortable in a chair in front of the computer. Angelina kept looking at the bruise on Jing Yang's arm. It had become more prominent; it was now black and blue.

'That man was very rough towards you,' she said.

'Yeah!' Tim agreed. 'Sorry about it, Jing Yang. Wish I was bigger than him. I could have punched out his lights.'

'You did no wrong, Tim,' said Jing Yang. 'He was the one at fault, hitting out at us for no rhyme or reason. Didn't even bother to hear us out.'

'An unreasonable man, that's what he is,' said Angelina.

'This discoloration on my arm will take a few days to go away,' said Jing Yang. 'I am worried Aunt Dorothy will see it. It's so conspicuous.'

'Yeah!' Tim agreed. 'Mum's very sharp, you know. Nothing escapes her eyes. You were lucky just now; she was busy in the kitchen.'

'You have got to think of an excuse for the bruise,' said Angelina.

'Yes, of course,' said Jing Yang, thinking hard. 'It's difficult to hide it. It's midway between the shoulder and the elbow; there's no T-shirt that can fully cover the bruise.'

'Why don't you tell my mum that you knocked against something? It causes this type of discoloration, you know,' said Tim.

'I'll just tell Aunt Dorothy that I lost my balance and fell while climbing the steps out of the bunker. I'm sure she will believe me,' said Jing Yang.

'That's a good one,' said Angelina. 'Aunt Dorothy won't question that excuse.'

'By golly, Jing Yang, you sure know how to cook up an excuse,' said Tim.

'Yes, sometimes, I do surprise myself,' said Jing Yang.

'Self praise is international disgrace!' cried Angelina. She had lightened up enough now to be poking fun at Jing Yang.

'Ha! Ha! Ha! I was just joking, just joking,' laughed Jing Yang. He was pretending to be in good spirits; he wanted Angelina to smile. It was working. Angelina was smiling. Jing Yang had to change the subject now, to get Angelina's mind off his bruise.

'Remember the drain cover in the corridor outside the toilets?' said Jing Yang. 'It looked suspicious.'

'Yeah!' said Tim. 'It looked suspicious to me too.'

'The tunnel in it is big enough for a man to crawl through. And it looks like it runs all over the bunker. It must lead to some secret place also.'

'But, there's water in the tunnel. How on earth can anyone move through?' said Angelina.

'By swimming through,' joked Jing Yang, 'wearing snorkels.' Then he began gesticulating in the air with his hands, making as if he was executing a freestyle swimming technique.

Everyone broke into laughter. Jing Yang was simply hilarious. Jing Yang was glad Angelina was enjoying herself now. His antics with his hands were effective after all.

'By George, you certainly are crazy. Fancy coming up with that idea. Why, there isn't even enough water to wade through,' said Tim.

'That reminds me,' Jing Yang said. 'The bunker is on a hill. There could be groundwater moving into the underground drains so sometimes the tunnel may be filled to the brim with water.'

'So?' said Tim.

'So, it may be impossible to move through the tunnel when it's full of water. We may have to wait for a suitable time to explore the tunnel,' said Jing Yang.

'We?' asked Tim.

'I mean – I,' replied Jing Yang. 'I have got to see where the tunnel leads to. Perhaps, there's some secret opening or door somewhere that leads to hidden treasure under the tunnel.'

'You mean, you believe in that treasure story?' said Angelina disbelievingly.

'Yes! I do. Otherwise why is that man working there as a museum guide? There's too much coincidence.'

'Too much coincidence?' asked Tim. 'I don't get you.'

'Here are the suspicious points about him: Number one, this Mr Savage is a history academic who specialised in World War Two history. Number two, he has been looking for treasure since his university days. Number three, this bunker happens to be a World War Two structure. And number four, a guy like Mr Savage just simply couldn't be happy working in such a low-income job; he is too ambitious and greedy as well,' said Jing Yang. He was intellectually curious about things. His mind was not closed. He was good at unravelling mysteries and he persevered in his investigative work. These were, perhaps, qualities that he had inherited from his parents' genes.

'It's too dangerous for you to crawl around in that tunnel,' said Angelina. 'I don't like the idea.'

'But, it's the only way to find out whether the bunker holds any secrets to its past,' said Jing Yang. 'Notice anything else suspicious about the things in the bunker?'

They had stopped at Fortress Commander's Office. They had yet to go to the other rooms.

Tim did not like the idea of poking around in the bunker. He did not have that spirit of adventure in him. But he did not let it show. He had to go along with whatever his cousin wanted him to do. It was the least he could do, after all, his cousin had stood by him a few times when he was in trouble. The two boys' family ties were finally beginning to work its magic now.

'Are you going to tell Mr Wang about your discovery later today?' asked Angelina.

'Perhaps tomorrow,' Jing Yang replied. 'Let me study this information first.'

'Did you guys see anything else suspicious when we were in the bunker?' Jing Yang asked them.

'Angelina?' he continued.

'Still thinking,' she replied.

'How about you?' he asked Tim.

There was silence in the room for the next few minutes. Angelina broke the silence.

'Do the graffiti on the wall in the Signals Control Room hide any secrets?' she asked.

'I don't know. I have got pictures of them here,' Jing Yang said. Then he picked up his camera, removed a portable memory card from it and inserted the card into a slot in his computer. He fired up the image browser program on his computer and scrolled through the images he had taken.

'Here they are,' he said. The pictures of the graffiti

appeared on the screen, one by one, as he clicked on the mouse.

He stopped at one of them, zoomed into the image and looked at it carefully. Angelina and Tim stood next to him at the computer.

'Looks like nothing out of the ordinary,' Jing Yang said.

'Yeah!' Tim agreed. He was gazing at the English translation on a card on top of the graffiti.

'Are you going to show these to Mr Wang?' asked Angelina.

'Yes. Remember he was the one who asked me to take these pictures?' said Jing Yang.

'Sorry!' said Angelina.

'I've yet to take a look in the locked room – the one next to the Gun Operations Room,' said Jing Yang. 'Looks like I have to make another trip there.'

'You?' repeated Angelina.

'Yes, me. It would be better if I went alone. Too many people would attract the guide's attention. Besides, I plan to go in secretly,' Jing Yang said.

'Secretly?' repeated Angelina.

'Right, secretly. I will make sure Mr Savage is not around when I go in so there will be no unpleasant surprises for me,' Jing Yang said.

'Can I tag along?' asked Angelina.

'It's too dangerous if we go in together. We won't be able to react fast enough if something happens inside,' Jing Yang said. What he actually meant was that if he was alone he could bolt out of the place immediately, but if Angelina went along, she would be in danger's way.

'Please, can I?' pleaded Angelina.

'Oh, alright. You can come along but stay outside. Keep a safe distance and help me observe the bunker from the outside,' said Jing Yang. He had relented. Besides, it would be a good idea to have someone keep an eye outside, just in case something happened to him, he thought. But he had better not talk to her about this. He did not want to frighten her.

'I also want to come along,' Tim said.

'Good! You can keep her company outside,' Jing Yang said.

'Sure,' Tim replied. He turned to Angelina. 'Don't worry, I will watch over you.'

'When are we going there again?' asked Angelina.

'Tomorrow, perhaps,' said Jing Yang.

'But, tomorrow's Thursday. Don't you have a tuition lesson tomorrow?' Angelina asked.

'Tsk! Tsk! Aren't you forgetful,' Jing Yang replied. 'I just had a lesson two days ago, remember?'

'Oh yeah! I forgot,' she exclaimed. 'So we go straight after school?'

'Of course not. I don't want to be caught sneaking around in school uniform,' said Jing Yang.

'Oh!' said Angelina. Then she looked at the clock on the bedside table. Suddenly, she jumped up. 'Sorry, guys. I've got to go home or my mother will worry.'

The three of them went downstairs. Hearing their footsteps, Dorothy came out of the kitchen. She saw Jing Yang and Angelina heading for the main door.

'Where are you going?' Dorothy asked Jing Yang. 'Dinner's ready.'

'I'm seeing Angelina home, Aunt Dorothy,' Jing Yang said.

'Alright. See you, Angelina,' said Dorothy.

'See you, aunty,' said Angelina. The couple went out of the house.

When Jing Yang returned home, dinner was on the table. Dorothy and her son Tim were waiting for him in the living room. Mother, son and nephew sat down to a traditional Chinese meal of three dishes and a soup. There were stir-fried Kangkong, fried grey pomfret, fried chicken wings and watercress soup. It was a change from the typical British fare that Dorothy usually prepared for them. It was her plan that she would slowly wean Tim off the

British food that he had been accustomed to. As the weeks progressed, Tim would find more and more Chinese food on the table. Eventually, there would only be a British meal every week. She did not need to worry about Jing Yang as he had grown up eating the Chinese food that his grandmother cooked.

'How's the food?' Dorothy asked the two boys.

'Very nice, Aunt Dorothy. I especially like the chicken wings.'

'Okay,' said her son. He was still trying to get used to the stir-fried stuff that she cooked.

'I had thought of frying some sausages but changed my mind. Jing Yang likes chicken wings and the ones at the market looked big and juicy so I bought them instead.'

Jing Yang reached across the table to fork a chicken wing.

'Jing Yang,' said Dorothy. 'What's that on your arm? Have you been fighting?'

'No, Aunt,' Jing Yang replied. 'I fell down.'

'Did you apply any ointment?' she asked.

'Yes, Aunt,' Jing Yang said.

'Let me have a closer look after dinner, will you?' said Dorothy.

'Yes, Aunt.'

'Your grandma called earlier. She said she would be back on Monday,' Dorothy said.

Jing Yang nodded.

'Mum, does Grandma know how to cook English food?' Tim asked.

'I doubt so, dear. But, she can fry French fries and pork chops quite well,' said his mother.

'Pork chops with apple sauce?' Tim asked.

'No, dear. Just plain pork chops,' his mother replied.

'Will you be doing the cooking or will Grandma?' asked Jing Yang.

'Both of us will,' said Dorothy. 'Now, finish your food quietly, we shouldn't be talking so much when eating.'

After Jing Yang had had his bath, he plunked onto his bed and got down to looking through the notes that he had prepared on the bunker. He did not notice his aunt standing at the doorway.

'May I come in?' she said. She was holding a bottle of medicated rub in her hands.

'Sure! Sorry, I did not notice you earlier,' said Jing Yang.

Dorothy sat next to him on the bed and placed the bottle on the bedside table.

'Let me see your arm,' said his aunt.

Jing Yang stretched out his bruised arm. Dorothy rubbed some ointment between her palms and massaged it over the discoloured skin. He felt pain first, then some warmth radiating through his arm.

'Don't wait till you land in big trouble before you come clean with me, okay?' Dorothy said. Somehow, she had seen through his lie. Jing Yang wondered whether Tim had leaked out the incident, but thought it not likely, after all he got this bruise all because of him. Moreover, Tim was not one to squeal on his friends, Jing Yang had learnt.

'Your mother and I were pretty naughty when we were young. We gave your grandma lots of trouble with our fooling around,' Dorothy said.

'But, we never got over our heads,' she continued. 'We knew when to stop giving your grandma worries.'

'So if you have anything that you need help in, just open your mouth and ask,' she said.

'Yes, Aunt,' said Jing Yang.

Dorothy took two bracelets out from a side pocket and handed one to Jing Yang. It was a string of crystal beads with golden needles in them.

'This is for you to wear on your left wrist,' she told him.

'Thanks, Aunt Dorothy,' said Jing Yang. 'What are these crystals?'

'These are rutilated quartz crystals. They give the

wearer luck and protection,' said Dorothy.

'Protection?' asked Jing Yang.

'Yes, protection against psychic attacks, that is protection from dark and negative energetic vibrations, such as spells and spirits,' added Dorothy.

'Are there such things as spells and spirits, Aunt Dorothy?' asked Jing Yang.

'We are surrounded by all sorts of energies: good, dark, negative, supernatural and mysterious ones. These can be transferred from one person to another. Spells and spirits belong to the group of dark, negative energies. They are real. These crystals neutralise these dark energies,' Dorothy said.

Jing Yang looped the bracelet around his left wrist.

'Good,' said Dorothy. 'Give this bracelet to Angelina for me.' Dorothy handed the other bracelet to Jing Yang.

'Thank you,' said Jing Yang.

'Sleep early. You have got school tomorrow.'

Then she crossed over to her son's room to have a chat with him.

'Dear, are you awake?' said Dorothy, knocking on Tim's door. Tim yelled something from inside the room, and she opened the door.

'Not going to bed yet, dear?' Dorothy asked her son.

'No, not yet, Mum. I am surfing the Internet,' said Tim. He had craned his neck to talk to her as he was at his computer. Dorothy sat on the bed which was adjacent to the desk where the computer was.

'Dear, can I talk to you about your cousin?' she asked Tim.

'Sure, Mum,' Tim said and swung around in the swivel chair to face his mother.

'Dear, both you and Jing Yang are related by blood. Remember the saying, blood is thicker than water?' said Dorothy.

'Yes, Mum. I know that,' said Tim.

'So you should look after each other like brothers,' said

Dorothy.

'Yes, Mum,' said Tim.

'You keep saying that you know,' Dorothy said. 'Then how in heaven did your cousin end up bruised?'

'I...I,' said Tim.

'I know you young people like to keep secrets, but can you promise me something?' said Dorothy.

'What Mum?' Tim asked.

'Promise me if something really bad happens to either of you, you will come running to tell me. Can you do that, dear?' said Dorothy.

'Yes, Mum,' Tim promised.

'Do you mean it, dear?' asked Dorothy.

'Yes, Mum. I really mean it,' said Tim.

'That's great. Here, wear this bracelet on your left wrist,' said Dorothy. She took a bracelet out of a pocket.

'Now?' asked Tim.

'Yes, dear,' said Dorothy.

Tim placed the bracelet of rutilated quartz crystal beads on his left wrist.

'Thanks, Mum,' said Tim.

'Goodnight dear,' Dorothy said, closing the door behind her.

11 *ESCAPE FROM THE LOCKED ROOM*

It was a wet Thursday morning. The thundery weather worried Jing Yang. If the bad weather persisted into the afternoon, he would have to cancel his plan to visit the bunker. He prayed hard that the wind would blow the rain clouds away. Indeed, the rain clouds fleeted away by late morning and sunshine broke through the clouds at noon. It was a hot afternoon that day.

When the bell rang for dismissal, the three friends met in the school canteen for lunch. Then they went home as soon as they could and changed out of their uniforms. They met as usual outside Jing Yang's house and headed off to Fort Canning Park, where the bunker was located. Angelina was wearing the bracelet that Jing Yang had taken from his aunt. Jing Yang and Tim were wearing their bracelets too. Jing Yang had tried to explain to the other two the significance of the bracelets on their wrists, but though they nodded, he was quite sure they did not understand what he was telling them. However, all could agree on one thing – if these could help ward off evil, especially the evil Mr Savage, they were all for wearing the bracelets.

It was three o'clock when they reached the top of the three flights of steps on Fort Canning. They were tired after the climb and sat on a bench next to the road. Ahead of them was the roundabout.

They ran through their plan as they drank from their water bottles. Jing Yang was to sneak into the bunker from the exit door on the right side of the hill. This exit door was not locked as visitors would use this door to leave the museum. All three would perch themselves on the top of the hill. Angelina and Jing Yang would station themselves on top of the slope above the exit door. Tim would stand guard on top of the slope above the entrance door. If Tim saw Mr Savage leaving for a break, he would text an SMS message to Jing Yang. Angelina and Jing Yang were together so if they saw Mr Savage coming out of the tunnel for his break, Jing Yang would sneak into the bunker using the exit door. Once Jing Yang was in the bunker, the other two would keep watch for Mr Savage and SMS Jing Yang if they saw Mr Savage returning to the bunker. The plan looked foolproof, except for one important point. Alas, all three did not realise that signals from the mobile phone network could not penetrate the bunker – it was twenty-seven feet underground. Their plan was doomed to failure from the start.

It was Tim who saw Mr Savage emerging from the entrance door some fifteen minutes after they had stood watch on top of the hill. The guide turned left and headed down the lane, walking towards the roundabout. Tim SMSed Jing Yang immediately, telling him the good news. Jing Yang wanted to be sure that Mr Savage was indeed gone so Tim waited till Mr Savage had walked past the roundabout, and disappeared down the flight of steps beyond the roundabout. Tim SMSed Jing Yang again.

Jing Yang looked at his watch. He reckoned that Mr Savage would be away for about half-an-hour. It was now quarter past three. He had to be out of the bunker at quarter to four. Jing Yang walked down the flight of steps next to him. Then he dashed to the exit door, turned the knob and opened the metal door slowly. He was careful not to let the door squeak. He stole a look at Angelina above him, gave the thumbs up and went down into the bunker.

The souvenir shop was the first room on his right. He stopped next to the doorway to listen for sounds from the room. There was music being played in the room. He tip-toed across the doorway and moved towards the end of the corridor. Here it branched into the left and the right corridors. He took out a plan of the bunker. He glanced at a marking on the plan he had made the other day. He had to make a left turn, followed by a right turn. The drain cover should be somewhere in the corridor after the right turn, he thought. He folded the plan in one hand and walked along the left corridor. Then he made a right turn at another turning in the corridor. This bunker was like a maze, he thought to himself. He had moved only about ten steps when he saw the drain cover on the floor.

Business was slow today at the bunker. There was no one in sight. This was good news for Jing Yang. He bent down beside the floor trap and lifted it. Then he pushed it aside onto the floor. He took out his torch and shone it into the drain tunnel. Alas, there was water in the drain tunnel. It was about a foot deep. There was no point going down. It was too dangerous to crawl through the drain tunnel. Disappointed, he put back the drain cover.

Jing Yang looked at the plan again. His next target was the locked room. He had to turn back into the earlier corridor. It was the second door on the left of that corridor. He looked at his watch. It was almost half past three. He had another fifteen minutes left in the bunker. He retraced his steps to the break in the corridor and turned left. He had just passed the first doorway – leading to the Gun Operations Room – and now he was outside the second door. It was the locked door alright. He tried the doorknob. It turned but the door would not open.

'Why is it locked all the time?' Jing Yang wondered. All the other rooms were open. There had to be some secret in this room, he thought to himself.

Then he remembered that the third door also opened into the locked room. He walked to the third door. He looked up. There was a label on top of the doorway. It said Gun Operations Room. So this was indeed the real McCoy, he thought to himself. The present Gun Operations Room was not the real one after all. He twisted the doorknob. The door would not open. He looked in the keyhole but it was dark through it and he could not see a thing. Frustrated, he turned around to try the second door and, and lo and behold, who should he see but Mr Savage standing in front of him.

'Ticket? Ticket? Where's your ticket?' the guide demanded.

'You have no ticket and you dare to barge in here?' he bellowed.

'Since you like this room so much, I shall let you spend some time in it,' Mr Savage roared.

Grabbing Jing Yang's collar, he unhooked a bunch of keys from the belt on his waist, picked one and opened the door with it. He pulled Jing Yang into the room and kicked the door shut behind him. This boy was getting too nosey for his own good, he declared. He might discover his secret.

'You can't do this to me,' shouted Jing Yang. 'You are abusing your power.'

'I'll teach you to be rude,' said the guide. Then he raised a hand and slapped Jing Yang across the face. It landed heavily on his cheek. The boy screamed in pain. He almost cried. Poor Jing Yang, first he had suffered a bruised arm from Mr Savage; now it was a bruised cheek.

Mr Savage took a ball of string from a box on the floor. Then he tied Jing Yang's hands behind him and pushed him onto the floor. Next, he tied Jing Yang's legs. When

Jing Yang screamed in protest, he gagged Jing Yang's mouth. Satisfied with what he had done, the man walked out of the room and locked it.

Jing Yang was now lying on the floor, all tied up. He bent his knees towards his stomach and tried to sit up. He failed the first time. Then he tried again and succeeded. He leaned against the wall next to him. It was dark inside the room. It was also cold, much colder than the corridor. It was because the room was shut all the time, he told himself. He could make out the outlines of the walls of the room. There was no interruption in these outlines. He figured that there was no furniture in the room. It was stark empty. No wonder there were echoes when he and the guide spoke earlier. This room certainly was bigger than the others he had been to in the bunker. It was about double the size of the room next door.

Jing Yang's thoughts wandered to his cousin and Angelina who were outside the bunker. Why had they not warned him about Mr Savage's return to the bunker? Horror of horrors, had something happened to them? His mind was in a muddle. He had to clear his thoughts to find a way out of the situation he was in. First things first – he had to figure out how to untie himself. He wriggled his hands. Then he struggled. It was of no use; this man had experience in this area – the knots were tight.

Then he tried the same thing with his legs, but the knots on the string would not bulge too. What was he to do now? Yes, he had to look for something sharp with which to cut the strings. But, it was an empty room. He looked around in the darkness. Except for the box next to him, there did not seem to be anything else in the room. Was there anything of use in the box? He shifted towards the box and tilted his head to look inside it. There were hazy outlines of a ball of string, and something which looked like a tape measure. Just what did Mr Savage use to cut the string? He did not tear the string apart with his bare hands; it was just too thick. Jing Yang thought hard for some minutes. He tried to recall the previous few minutes in the room. Oh, yes, Mr Savage had taken a pen knife out of a back pocket and used it to cut the string. Where was the pen knife now? He squinted his eyes and looked around the screed floor. Other than the box, there was no silhouette of anything solid on the floor. But there was the glitter of glass on the screed floor. There were glass shards embedded in the floor and these were reflecting light. Yes, he told himself, there was some light peeking through the gap between the floor and the metal doors. It was the light from the corridor.

Just then, he heard the shuffle of feet out in the corridor. There was chattering too. He struggled to loosen the gag around his mouth. It was too tight and would not bulge too. Ouch! He felt pain in his right cheek. He had forgotten about the slap he had received earlier and his attempt to unravel the gag now had caused the pain to intensify. The footsteps soon faded away. It was quiet again out in the corridor. This museum did not have many visitors; it would be ages before anyone discovered him. Jing Yang sighed heavily.

Outside on top of the hill, Angelina and Tim had been keeping vigil over the space outside the bunker. Fifteen minutes after Jing Yang had entered the bunker, Tim had seen Mr Savage returning to the bunker. he had SMSed Jing Yang immediately with the news. Then he had run over to where Angelina was to tell her the news. Both of them had stood on top of the slope above the exit door waiting for Jing Yang to appear. When he failed to appear, Angelina in desperation had called him on his mobile phone. It was then that she realised there was no network in the bunker. It was also then that she recalled Mr Savage had told her class the bunker was sited twenty-seven feet underground. There was no way any mobile network signals could penetrate that deep into the ground. They were helpless! They could not contact Jing Yang. He was in imminent danger.

Tim had thought of dashing into the bunker in that instant but Angelina held him back. She figured that Jing Yang might have seen Mr Savage coming into the bunker and could be hiding somewhere. It would not help matters if Tim had charged into the place. Besides, Tim was no match for the burly man. Angelina was now worried that something serious had happened to Jing Yang for it was now past four. Jing Yang had been in the bunker for an hour!

They deliberated on what to do next. Should they barge into the bunker? Should they go for help? Or should they wait a little longer? Jing Yang could have hidden himself and was perhaps waiting for an opportunity to escape. They decided to wait another fifteen minutes.

It was now half past four. There was still no sign of Jing Yang. It was highly possible that Jing Yang had been caught sneaking around in the bunker. As the older of the two friends, Angelina took the lead in making decisions. She decided to go into the bunker with Tim to look for Jing Yang. If they could not find him, they would leave the place and ask Aunt Dorothy for help. It was the best plan she could come out with.

'Are we going to buy tickets to enter the bunker?' asked Tim.

'Better not take the risk,' said Angelina. 'The cashier might be in cahoots with Mr Savage. We might end up getting caught.'

'So, do we go in now?' asked Tim. Angelina nodded.

'Come, let's go down,' said Angelina.

They moved down towards the exit door. Tim swung open the door carefully so as not to make a sound. Then they tip-toed down the steps to the corridor. There did not seem to be anyone around.

'Can you remember which rooms Jing Yang said he would check out?' Tim said.

'The locked room,' said Angelina. She tried recalling the location of the room in her mind. 'Should be the room next to Gun Operations Room.'

'Which room is the Gun Operations Room?' Tim asked. He simply could not remember.

'It's the one with the big map on the table,' said Angelina. 'There, that room on the left.' She pointed at the open doorway in the corridor. Then she pointed at the room next to it.

'The door next to the open doorway is the room we are looking for,' said Angelina. 'Come with me.'

They sidled to the locked door and Angelina tried turning the knob. The door did not open.

'It's locked,' said Angelina.

Jing Yang was on the other side of the door but he did not know it was Angelina making the noise at the doorway. He thought it was the guide opening the door to come in so he kept quiet. He did not want to be hit again. The sound stopped. Perhaps, it was not Mr Savage after all. Perhaps, it was someone else. It might have been Angelina and Tim looking for him! He chided himself for not having thought of that. Alas, it was too late. The corridor outside was quiet again.

The room seemed to be getting colder by the minute. Jing Yang wondered whether it could be because he was sitting on the floor. He touched the floor with his bound hands. It was cold. The air-conditioning had cooled the floor, he told himself. But, it was a strange coldness. Unlike the cold air he was accustomed to in his air-conditioned bedroom, this cold air kept giving him goose pimples.

Jing Yang felt jittery all of a sudden. Something in him told him things were not right in this strange room. He felt scared. He seldom got goose pimples. He closed his eyes. But it was no use. There seemed to be a light breeze blowing past him in the room. It could not have come from the air-conditioning vent on the ceiling, for the vent was many feet away.

'Is it what Aunt Dorothy calls dark negative energies?'

Jing Yang asked himself. '*Alamak*! That would mean spirits!'

Jing Yang was frightened all of a sudden. He was trapped. First he had no way of escaping from the room. Now, he had no way of escaping from these spirits. He trembled.

Out in the corridor, Angelina and Tim had just entered the next room.

There was nothing suspicious looking in it. The table on which the map lay was so big that it could possibly hide things underneath. They bent down and crawled under the table. It was dark in there but groping around in there did not yield any results. Mr Savage could not have hidden Jing Yang there. There were also no trapdoors. Suddenly, they heard footsteps. They kept still. There were people in the room now.

'I want you to explain the strategy used by the Japanese invading forces in Malaya and Singapore to the two school groups coming tomorrow,' said the first man.

'Yes,' said the second man.

'And be sure to tell them about the Japanese tricking the British forces into thinking that they would be attacking Singapore from the east,' said the first man.

'I will,' said the second man.

'Have you shut the main doors? It's five o'clock already,' said the first man.

'Sorry, I forgot. I will do it now,' said the second man.

They heard the man shuffling out of the room. The other man lingered in the room. They heard some sounds coming from the table top. He seemed to be moving things on the table. Then there was a loud thud sound. Something had fallen off the table onto the floor. It was a wooden block. Angelina and Tim shrank. The man was now bending down to retrieve the block. Would he see them under the table? They kept perfectly still. The man resumed what he was doing. Soon he also left the room. They sighed loudly. It was a close call. They waited for a few minutes before crawling out.

Both of them were perspiring. It was too hot underneath the big table. They wiped off the sweat with the sleeves of their T-shirts as they walked into the next room, Fortress Commander's Office. The other door facing the corridor was shut. They peered through the grille window on the door. There was no one out in the corridor. Tim and Angelina looked around the room. It did not seem to hold any secrets. There were no other doors in the room so Jing Yang could not be hidden here.

Tim went behind the desk where the wax model of General Percival was. First he felt the edges of the large notice board. They appeared to be nailed tightly to the wall. Next, he squatted down behind the wax model and duckwalked around, examining the tiled floor carefully.

'Ouch!' said General Percival's look-alike.

Tim was startled. He fell onto his knees. He gazed disbelievingly at the mannequin. So did Angelina, who had been looking through the wooden cabinet next to General Simmons' look-alike.

'What's that sound I heard?' Tim said to Angelina.

'It came from him,' said Angelina, pointing at the mannequin.

Tim stood up at once.

'You just stepped on my foot; that's what you did,' said General Percival's look-alike.

Tim froze in his tracks.

'Young lad, I say, look sharp. Don't just stand there staring at me,' said General Percival's look-alike. 'Say sorry, that's what I want. An apology, that's all.'

Tim's jaws opened wide. The mannequin was not moving. But the voice did come from it.

'Tim, come over,' Angelina stammered. 'I'm scared.'

Tim wobbled over to Angelina's side. They stood almost touching each other. Angelina was dumbfounded.

'I say, why are you turning away from me?' said General Percival's look-alike. 'For goodness' sake, look at me when I am talking to you.'

'Ar...Are you talking to us, sir?' asked Tim.

'Of course, I am. There's nobody else here, is there?' said General Percival's look-alike.

'Ar...Are you for real, sir?' asked Angelina.

'Don't patronise me, young lass,' said General Percival's look-alike. 'I'm not a dummy.'

'Sorry, sir,' said Angelina. 'What I mean is, who are you, sir?'

'Oh me? I say, it's been a long time since someone asked me that question – an awfully long time, if I may say so,' said General Percival's look-alike.

'You still haven't told us who you are, sir,' said Tim. He had more or less recovered from shock.

'Oh, sorry, old chap. I am Colonel Walter Henry Cooper of His Majesty's Royal Engineers. I was stationed here in 1939,' said General Percival's look-alike.

'That's a mighty long time ago, if I may say so, sir,' said Tim.

'Is it now?' said General Percival's look-alike. 'What year is it now, young lad?'

'It's 2009, sir,' said Tim.

'I say, did you say 2009?' said General Percival's look-alike.

'Yes, sir,' said Tim.

'That makes me,' said General Percival's look-alike, 'ninety-one years old. But, I don't feel that old. I'm so energetic.'

'Sir, you are not real,' said Tim bluntly.

'What do you mean,' said General Percival's look-alike, 'I am not real?'

'Well, sir, I think, I think you are..,' said Tim. He stopped talking as Angelina was elbowing him.

'Sir, what he means to say is,' said Angelina, 'you do not look ninety-one years old. You look much younger.'

'Do I now?' said General Percival's look-alike. 'Where's the mirror? Why can't I move my arms?'

'Sir, I think you are too tired,' said Angelina. 'You have been sitting in that armchair for too long.' Angelina was right after all. The wax model had been in the armchair since 1997. Tim tried hard not to laugh. He was tickled by that last remark.

The funny look on Tim's face attracted the mannequin's attention. He looked at Tim in the eyes. There was something different in those eyes.

'Oh I say, you speak with a British accent, but you look –different,' said General Percival's look-alike.

Tim was peeved. He did not like being called different. Some of his schoolmates in England had teased him about being different from the other British kids and he did not like it one bit.

'His mother is Chinese, sir,' said Angelina, 'and his father British.'

'Oh I see, you are of mixed parentage,' said General Percival's look-alike. 'And young lass, you must be Chinese.'

'Yes, sir,' said Angelina.

'What are you two doing in the command centre? Children are not allowed in this bunker,' said General Percival's look-alike.

'We are looking for our friend. He's in here somewhere,' said Angelina.

Just then, the wax model of Major-General Keith Simmons suddenly spoke.

'You mean the tall lad in a white oversized shirt and khaki shorts?' said General Simmons' look-alike.

The two teenagers who had been standing next to the wax model of General Simmons were startled by the new voice in the room. Now there were two spirits in the room, they thought. This one was just next to them. Angelina and Tim edged closer to the side doorway, away from the wax models.

'I say, don't stand there looking dumb,' said General Simmons' look-alike, 'I'm talking to you.'

'Sir, what did you say?' asked Angelina. They had not heard him.

'I asked whether you were talking about the lad in a white oversized shirt and khaki shorts,' said General Simmons' look-alike.

'Yes, sir. That's the one,' said Angelina excitedly, 'Have you seen him, sir?'

'Of course, I have,' said General Simmons' look-alike, 'otherwise, I would not know what he looks like, would I?'

'Sorry, sir,' said Angelina. 'Can you tell us where he is? We are worried sick about him, sir.'

'I see. He's in the Gun Operations Room now,' said General Simmons' look-alike.

Angelina and Tim turned their heads to look at the room on their right. There was nobody in there.

'Sir,' said Tim. 'There's nobody in the room. We searched it just now.'

'Yes, sir,' said Angelina. 'Is there a secret passage in that room?'

'Secret passage?' uttered General Percival's look-alike. 'How do you know about the secret passage?'

'I...I didn't, sir,' said Angelina. 'I merely thought that there would be one since there's nobody in there right now. See?' Angelina pointed at the empty room on her right.

'Oh my, you are confusing me, young lass,' said General Simmons' look-alike. 'That's not the Gun Operations Room. That's the Fortress Plotting Room.'

'But...but, we were told it was the Gun Operations Room,' said Tim.

'Who told you so?' asked General Simmons' look-alike. 'The soldier who told you ought to be shot. Fancy getting the rooms mixed up like that. How are we going to fight a war with such imbeciles?'

'I agree with you, Todds,' said General Percival's look-alike.

'Sir, then where is the Gun Operations Room?' asked

Angelina.

"Don't you know? It's the room next to Fortress Plotting Room, said General Simmons' look-alike. 'I don't blame you for getting confused. There are twenty-six rooms in the command centre.'

'The room next to Fortress Plotting Room? Is that the one that is locked?' asked Angelina.

'Is it locked? Must be, I guess,' said General Simmons' look-alike. 'Sir, do you know how these kids came into the command centre?'

'Search me, Todds,' said General Percival's look-alike.

'Yikes!' said General Simmons' look-alike.

'What's that all about?' said General Percival's look-alike.

'Sir, you haven't shaven today,' said General Simmons' look-alike.

'Oh lord, I haven't?' said General Percival's look-alike. He was trying to move his left hand but it would not bulge. He wanted to retrieve the mirror in the drawer next to him. 'Why, I can't seem to move, Todds.'

'Sir, me too. I also cannot move. My body seems to be stuck in this armchair,' said General Simmons' look-alike.

'Sirs, perhaps, both of you have been in the armchairs for too long,' said Tim. He was trying to hide a smile. Tim had forgotten about the remark on him being different.

'Mr Todd, sir,' said Angelina. She had heard General Percival's look-alike addressing General Simmons' look-alike by this name. 'Is our friend in the locked room?'

'Why, yes, of course. He's still there – all tied up,' said General Simmons' look-alike.

'All tied up?' asked Angelina. She was looking worried now.

'Yes, bound and gagged,' said General Simmons' look-alike.

'Bound and gagged?' repeated Angelina.

'I say, young lass, don't go repeating every word I say,' said General Simmons' look-alike. He sounded annoyed.

'Sorry, sir. I didn't mean to, sir,' said Angelina. 'It's just that I am worried sick about Jing Yang.'

'Jing Yang? Is that the name of the lad you are looking for?' asked General Percival's look-alike.

'Yes, sir,' said Angelina.

'Don't worry your heads off,' said General Percival's look-alike. 'He's fine. Just minor injuries, that's all.'

'Minor injuries?' said Angelina in a shaky voice.

'Yes, he's been slapped you know,' said General Percival's look-alike. 'The bloke who slapped him ought to be punished. Fancy bullying a young lad like that. We do not condone such despicable acts in the command centre.'

'How do we get inside?' asked Angelina. 'The room is locked.'

'Mmm. Now that's a problem. The bloke's always carrying the keys to the place with him. You just can't flit in and out like us,' said General Percival's look-alike.

At times, it appeared that these two spirits knew they were not human, and yet at other times, they seemed to think they were still young, alive and fighting the war in the 1940s. They had not quite come to terms with knowing that they were dead.

'That bloke is taking a nap now,' said General Simmons' look-alike. 'It's that time of the day now. That's the best time to get the keys from him – when he's asleep.'

'Thank you, sirs,' said Angelina. 'We'll go find him right now. Thank you for your help, sirs.'

'Now, isn't she such a polite lass?' said General Simmons' look-alike.

'Go on, now, before the bloke wakes up,' said General Percival's look-alike.

Angelina and Tim turned into the next room.

'That's the wrong way,' said General Simmons' look-alike. Use the other door. Go into the corridor. He's in the second room on the left.'

'Thanks, sir,' said Angelina.

'Thank you, sir,' said Tim.

They opened the metal door, checked that the coast was clear before walking up the corridor. They passed the first room, peeped inside and then proceeded towards the second room. They stopped just before the door opening. Tim was in front, followed by Angelina. Tim poked his head into the room. It was dark but the corridor light was enough to illuminate the area around the doorway. He could hear snoring. He saw an empty bench on the left end of the room. The open door was blocking his view of the rest of the room. Tim crouched down on the floor; Angelina followed suit. They duckwalked across the doorway and leaned against the open door. Tim poked his head out. He could see the outlines of a wooden bench below the white wall in the far end of the room. There was a silhouette of a figure on top of the bench. The snoring came from the figure. Tim signalled to Angelina to keep still. He prostrated himself on the floor and crawled towards the figure. Tim was breathing heavily; he was nervous. He was also afraid his breathing could be heard so he paused for a moment. Then he crept up close to the figure. Now he could hear the figure's breathing. He was near enough to see it was Mr Savage. Mr Savage was sleeping on his back. Alas, there were no keys hooked to his belt.

'Where could they be?' Tim wondered. 'Could they be in his side pocket?'

Tim dragged himself along the floor till his eyes were just above the man's side pocket. The pocket was not bulging. The keys were not in it. Tim wondered what to do next. He did not have any idea how to proceed next. It was while he was deliberating his next course of action that Mr Savage suddenly turned towards him. Tim was startled. He thought Mr Savage had seen him. Tim blinked. It was a moment before he realised that Mr Savage was not awake; he was in dreamland. Mr Savage was not looking at him, for his eyes were shut.

'Lucky me,' Tim told himself, 'That certainly was close!'

Then Tim smiled. It was not that he was priding himself on that close shave. He had struck pay dirt! The other side pocket was now facing him. And it was bulging alright. Tim could see the outlines of some keys on the fabric of the side pocket. Now he had to be very careful. He did not know when Mr Savage would decide to turn to the other side so he had to work fast.

Without a moment's hesitation, he raised his left hand, and using the palm of his right hand to support his left elbow, gently lowered his left hand into the side pocket, careful not to lean it onto the body. His fingers felt something cold. He inserted a finger into what felt like a key ring and using his thumb and finger, gripped the object and withdrew it from the side pocket. He had no time to lose, for any moment Mr Savage might turn to the other side.

Then he allowed his head to fall back onto the floor again. The job had been done. The keys were in his left hand now. Mr Savage was still asleep. Tim turned onto all fours and crept along the floor to the open door where Angelina was. He motioned her to move off first. Then he followed her into the corridor. There, he placed a finger to his lips; they were not to say a word. He led her down the corridor to the next turning, and seeing the path was clear, waved her to follow him into the right corridor. Then they made a left turn to the locked door. Tim whispered to Angelina to keep a look out while he tried opening the door. There were four keys and he had to try them one by one. Finally, one worked; Tim twisted the doorknob and pushed open the door.

It was dark inside; but the corridor light provided enough illumination for them to see that it was empty, except for a dark outline below the white walls in the far end of the room. It was wriggling! It could be Jing Yang! They approached it with haste. It was Jing Yang. Angelina grabbed hold of him and cried uncontrollably. Tim placed a palm over her mouth to shut her up.

'For goodness' sake, we have no time to spare,' he whispered to Angelina. 'Quick, remove the gag.'

There was no time to waste. Tim untied Jing Yang's hands and legs while Angelina removed the gag around his mouth.

'Glad to see you guys,' said Jing Yang.

'Your face, Jing Yang,' said Angelina. She had noticed a black patch on his face. 'Does it hurt?'

"No, not so much now,' said Jing Yang. Suddenly he remembered the bruise on his cheek. He nursed his cheek. It was still tender.

'Let's go,' said Tim. 'We have no time to lose.'

They rushed out of the room. Tim was in front. Angelina was behind him and Jing Yang behind her. As Mr Savage was in the room next to the entrance door, Tim did not want to use that way to escape so he led the others up the steps to the exit door. It was padlocked. He tried the keys one by one. One of them opened the lock on the door. He unravelled the chain around the door handles and opened the door. All three dashed out of the bunker. They ran as fast as their legs could carry them. They ran to the roundabout, and down all ninety-three steps. Only when they had reached the bottom of these steps did they stop. All three were panting heavily. Angelina threw herself into Jing Yang's arms and cried again. Jing Yang himself was also tearing in his eyes. It had been a nightmare turned real for him. He thanked Tim and Angelina. They were all thankful that evening, for they were safe now.

The boys' mobile phones were now beeping madly. There was no network in the bunker so the SMS messages could not be received earlier. Now that the boys were out in the open, the messages were flooding in. Some of the messages in Jing Yang's mobile phone were from Angelina, some from Tim, and the rest from Aunt Dorothy. The messages in Tim's mobile phone were all from his mother. His mother had also called a few times for there were some missed call notification messages. She was furious that the boys had not come home for dinner. She thought that they were having fun and had forgotten to call home to tell her they would be back late. They had kept her waiting.

'I had better call Mum now,' said Tim. 'She will be worried sick if I do not call her.'

'Let's get out of this place first,' said Jing Yang. 'That monster might be looking for us any minute now.'

'Yes, let's,' said Angelina.

They ran to the road where they hailed a taxi. In the taxi, Angelina called her mother to tell her she would not be coming back for dinner. Then she ended the call.

'Did your mother scold you?' asked Jing Yang. He was seated next to her in the back seat. Tim was in the front seat, next to the driver.

'No,' said Angelina. 'My mother knows I can take care of myself. She also knows that I won't fool around.'

'Lucky you,' said Tim. He had turned his head to look at them. 'We are bound to get hammered left, right and centre when we get back.'

'Aren't you calling Aunt Dorothy now?' asked Angelina.

'Er...yes. I am wondering what to tell her,' said Jing Yang. 'I think I have to be honest with her. This thing's gone too high above our heads. It is better if an adult knows about it. Besides, I promised her I would ask for help when I need it and we really need help.'

Jing Yang called Aunt Dorothy to tell her they were on the way back in a taxi. He said that he would explain things when they got home. Then he ended the call.

'Was my mum very angry?' asked Tim.

'She sounded angry,' said Jing Yang. 'I think that we will both get an earful when we get home.'

'Can I come with you, Jing Yang?' asked Angelina.

'No, better not,' said Jing Yang. He did not want her to see him being scolded. 'I will call you when everything is over.'

'I want to, Jing Yang,' said Angelina. 'I don't want you to suffer a scolding alone.'

'I won't be alone,' said Jing Yang. 'Tim will be with me.'

'Please let me come along,' Angelina pleaded. 'I won't be in the way.'

'Aw! Let her come along, Jing Yang,' said Tim. 'Besides, with her around, Mum won't be so harsh with us.'

'Oh, alright,' said Jing Yang.

In the taxi, Angelina could see the bruise on Jing Yang's cheek more clearly now. It was one big red patch stretching from behind the eye to the jaw. The shape of the discolouration resembled the palm of a hand.

'It must be very painful,' said Angelina. She raised a hand to touch the bruise on his cheek.

'Ouch!' Jing Yang exclaimed. The bruise was still tender.

'Sorry,' said Angelina. 'Does it hurt very much?'

'Of course, it does,' said Tim from in front of the taxi. 'That guy had brute strength, you know.'

'Aunt Dorothy is going to be very mad at you. First, there was the bruise on your arm, and now this one on your cheek,' said Angelina.

'Don't worry. I can handle it,' said Jing Yang.

'It's not your fault, anyway. This guy was rough,' said Tim. 'I will tell Mum all about him. She will side us for sure.'

'Why didn't you guys SMS me when the guy came back?' asked Jing Yang. He had remembered to ask them now.

'We did. We did,' said Angelina. 'We sent several SMS messages but you did not come out of the bunker.'

'I did not receive any SMS messages,' said Jing Yang. 'My phone was on silent alert, but I kept an eye on it and it didn't beep at all. No messages were coming in at all.'

'That's because you were in the bunker,' Tim explained.

'There's no way any SMS messages will get into the bunker.'

'Yes, Jing Yang. The bunker is very deep underground,' said Angelina.

Jing Yang remembered now. As he was running out of the bunker with Tim, his mobile phone was beeping furiously. He ran through the SMS messages in the inbox of the phone. He scrolled through the messages from Angelina, Tim and Aunt Dorothy.

'Sorry, guys,' said Jing Yang. 'I forgot the phone network could not penetrate the tunnel.'

'Your plan was good. Only you forgot that mobile phones could not be used in the bunker,' said Tim.

'Yes, yes,' said Jing Yang, nodding in agreement.

'So how did you get caught?' Angelina asked.

'Mr Savage came up from behind me and grabbed hold of me,' said Jing Yang. 'I tried to escape, but he was too strong.'

'How did you know I was in the room?' asked Jing Yang. 'Were you outside the room earlier? Was it you I heard outside the room?'

'Yes,' said Angelina. 'At first, we went to the locked room, but could not open the door. We didn't know you were in the room.'

'Then how did you find out?' asked Jing Yang.

'A…a spirit told us,' said Tim.

'A spirit?' said Jing Yang in disbelief. 'What are you talking about? There are no spirits in this world.'

'Yes, there are,' exclaimed Angelina. 'Believe me, we saw two spirits. It was they who told us you were in that room.'

'Yeah! We were shocked when they spoke. I froze for a minute, you know,' said Tim. 'The first one gave me the shock of my life.'

Jing Yang remembered it was chilly in the room he was tied up in. He remembered the light breeze. Was it the spirits flitting around him?

'I was shocked too,' said Angelina. 'But they were so friendly, I forgot they were spirits.'

'Did you see them?' asked Jing Yang. He was in the room with them but he did not see anything. It could be it was too dark in the room, he told himself.

'Yes. Well, how should I put it? The spirits entered the wax models, I think. We did not see the spirits. We only heard voices. They came from the wax models,' said Angelina.

'The wax models talked?' asked Jing Yang.

'They did not open their mouths but I know the spirits were in them,' explained Angelina.

'And they were British,' Tim added. 'They spoke with a British accent.'

'Really?' said Jing Yang. 'Did they say anything else?'

'Let me think. We were so afraid then, so I can't remember what they said at first. They were soldiers I think. One of them was a Colonel something,' said Angelina.

'Colonel Walter Henry Cooper,' Tim chipped in.

'He said he was from His Majesty's Royal Engineers,' he continued.

'We are home already,' said Jing Yang. The taxi had turned into Lorong Low Koon. Jing Yang told the driver to stop in front of his house. He paid the driver and they got off.

Dorothy was waiting in the porch. Mr Wang was with her. She was frowning.

'Hi Aunty,' said Angelina.

'Hi Angelina,' said Dorothy.

'Hi Mr Wang,' the teenagers chorused.

Mr Wang nodded.

'Boys, what happened to you? Why didn't you answer my calls?' asked Dorothy. 'Jing Yang, why is your face bruised like that? Let me look at you.'

Dorothy was talking in succession. There were so many things she wanted to know. She did not give them a chance to answer. She placed her hands on Jing Yang's jaws and tilted them.

'How did you get this?' Dorothy asked Jing Yang. 'This looks like a palm print. Did someone slap you?'

Then she realised they were all still in the porch. She released her grip on Jing Yang's face.

'Come in quickly, all of you. Mr Wang, this way please,' said Dorothy. 'Take a seat, please.'

Dorothy herded the teenagers into the large sofa. Mr Wang and she sat in the two armchairs in the living room.

'Dear, let me take a look at you,' Dorothy said to her son. She leaned towards him. Satisfied, she turned to the others. They were ready for a long lecture.

'I was so worried about all of you,' Dorothy said. 'So worried that I went over to ask Mr Wang for help. I didn't know what to do.'

Mr Wang and the three friends sat listening. None interrupted her.

'You, Jing Yang – I told you repeatedly that you should always call home if you are going to be late for dinner. Fancy you not answering my calls,' said Dorothy. 'You are the older of the two. Surely you should have some sense of responsibility.'

'Mum, it's not his fault. He was locked up so we couldn't come back,' said Tim.

'Locked up?' said Dorothy in surprise. 'What do you mean – locked up? Jing Yang, tell me everything. Don't leave out anything.'

'Aunt Dorothy, I was caught by the museum guide. He locked me up in a room. Tim and Angelina rescued me.'

'You went to the museum again?' Dorothy asked.

'Yes,' Jing Yang replied.

'Mr Wang was talking about the museum with me just now. He said you wanted to get some information. How did you get into trouble with the guide? Did you go into the place illegally?' asked Dorothy.

'Yes, Aunt,' replied Jing Yang.

'How could you sneak into the place? Don't you know it's wrong to do that?'

'We had no choice, Mum, the monster threw us out the first time,' said Tim.

'Monster?' said Dorothy in surprise. 'What monster are you talking about?'

'Aunty, Tim means the museum guide,' said Angelina. That man was very rough towards us. We paid for the tickets into the bunker and he threw us out. We had no choice but to go in quietly.'

'He was the one who grabbed Jing Yang's arm the other day,' said Tim.

'He did that too?' said Dorothy. How could he do that to a boy?'

'Are you talking about Mr Savage,' asked Mr Wang. He had been listening intently to the conversation and thought it was time to join it.

'Yes,' said Tim.

'Mr Savage had a hot temper when he was young. I am surprised he has not changed. He used to bash up people for no rhyme or reason but he shouldn't go around hitting children,' said Mr Wang.

'Do you know him, Mr Wang?' asked Dorothy.

'Yes, indeed I do. He was my classmate at university,' replied Mr Wang.

'How can he be so violent – going around hitting children?' said Dorothy. Turning to the youngsters, she said, 'I don't want you people to go near that man again, is that clear?'

Jing Yang, Tim and Angelina looked at one another in silence. It was a difficult order for them to follow.

'Boys, is that clear?' Dorothy repeated. 'I can't have you boys coming home with bruises all over every time, can I?'

Turning to Jing Yang, she said, 'This time you were locked up; what about the next time? By the way, Jing Yang, you haven't told me how you managed to get free.'

'The spirits helped us,' said Tim. He was beaming.

'They told us where Jing Yang was being kept and we went to rescue him.'

'Spirits?' asked his mother.

'Yes, there were two of them – both British. I think they must be over ninety-years old,' said Tim.

'Dear, you saw spirits?' Dorothy. She looked doubtful. She turned to Jing Yang. 'What did they look like?'

'Aunt Dorothy, I did not see them. Tim and Angelina saw them,' said Jing Yang.

'Dear, describe them to me,' said Dorothy to her son.

'Mum, they were wax models,' said Tim.

'Aunty, actually, they were voices coming from the wax models,' Angelina corrected him.

'I see. So you did not see the spirits, right?' said Dorothy.

'How did you know, Mum?' asked Tim.

'Because spirits are manifestations of dark negative energies,' said Dorothy. Seeing they did not understand, she continued, 'Think of spirits as moving air. You know – a light breeze.'

'Does that mean I encountered spirits in the locked room too?' asked Jing Yang.

'Did you feel something in the room?' asked Dorothy.

'Yes, Aunt. Just like you described it – a light breeze. It was a cold breeze.'

'That's it. But, they would not harm you, for you are wearing the bracelet I gave you.'

'Why did they not talk to me?' asked Jing Yang. 'Why did they talk to Tim and Angelina?'

'That's because they need to enter something and use it to talk to people. They entered the wax models to talk to Tim and Angelina,' said Dorothy. 'Perhaps, in the room you were in, there was nothing suitable for them to enter.'

'Do they talk to just anybody?' asked Angelina.

'No. It is the bracelet, Angelina,' said Dorothy. 'The bracelet has powers. It lets you access the spirits' world so you can hear them. Gosh! I have forgotten about dinner. It's getting cold.'

Dorothy got up and ushered all of them to the dining area next to the living room.

'Mr Wang, I am sorry I forgot about dinner,' said Dorothy.

'No worries,' said Mr Wang. 'Here, let me help you.'

Mr Wang helped Dorothy to lay the plates and cutlery on the table. Jing Yang and Tim got the dishes of food from the kitchen.

'You must be famished, all of you,' said Dorothy. 'Please help yourselves to the food.'

There was hardly any conversation as they sat down to dinner, tucking into the food. They were all too hungry. After dinner, Mr Wang suggested that the three of them hop by his place after school the next day so that he could hear more about their little adventure. They were too glad to visit him. Then he returned to his house. By the time Jing Yang took Angelina home, it was already ten o'clock.

12 *A STRANGE TALE*

Friday at school was a bad day for Jing Yang. His classmates teased him about the palm-sized blue-black mark on his cheek. One remarked that he had been smacked by some girl who had spurned his advances. Word spread so fast that there was a continual flow of curious traffic outside his classroom; his schoolmates wanted to take a look at what they called a love-smack. They were accustomed to seeing love-bites so this love-smack was a novelty.

Jing Yang was glad it was a Friday that day. He only had to endure a morning of ridicule, for there would not be school till Monday which was two days away. He could have some respite from the teasing. He heaved a sigh of relief when it was dismissal time. The three friends met at their regular meeting point to discuss where to go next. They had been too tired that morning so they barely talked on the way to school; they were trying to conserve energy. They sat at a wooden table outside the art room.

Tim was first to bring up the topic of the bunker. He had some news for them.

'I wanted to tell you guys last night but didn't have the chance; Mum was around all the time,' Tim said.

'What is it?' asked Jing Yang.

'Remember the keys I took from the monster?' said Tim.

'The ones for the locked room and the exit door?' said Angelina.

'That's correct,' said Tim. He fished out a bunch of keys from a pocket and placed it on the table. Jing Yang and Angelina stared at the keys.

'You didn't return the keys to Mr Savage?' said Jing Yang.

'I didn't get a chance,' said Tim. 'We were too busy rescuing you and then making a getaway that I plain forgot about it.'

'Boy! Mr Savage is going to be very mad at us,' said Angelina.

'So what? Serves him right for doing what he did to us,' said Tim.

'What are we going to do with the keys? Return them to Mr Savage?' asked Angelina.

Jing Yang had other ideas. He was busy thinking.

'Jing Yang, are you listening?' asked Angelina.

'Why, yes, of course,' said Jing Yang. 'I was just thinking that it would be a good opportunity for us to go into the bunker to find the secret passage.'

'What? Go in again?' Angelina stammered. 'No way! It's too dangerous!'

'It won't be dangerous. We have the keys to the bunker. We can always wait till the guide has gone off before going in,' said Jing Yang. 'That way, it will be perfectly safe.'

'But, your aunt has told us not to go in there anymore,' added Angelina.

'What about you, Tim?' asked Jing Yang. 'Do you think we should go into the bunker one more time?'

'Anything,' said Tim. 'I don't mind. Besides, Mum won't know if we don't tell her.'

'What if we are caught again?' asked Angelina. 'Mr

Savage will skin us alive.'

'Don't be so negative,' said Jing Yang. 'We'll wait till there's nobody around.'

'But, it's illegal, going in like that,' said Angelina.

'Angelina, you can stay at home while we go there,' said Jing Yang.

'I don't want to be left behind. I want to go where you go,' said Angelina.

'It won't be convenient with you around. It won't be safe for a girl to come along. We are going in at night,' said Jing Yang.

'But will Aunty let you guys go out at night?' asked Angelina.

'We won't tell her. We'll just sneak out of the house when she's in the bedroom,' said Tim. 'We'll take dinner with her and then go to our rooms to do our homework. This way, Mum won't suspect a thing.'

'What if something goes wrong?' asked Angelina. 'What if?'

'Angelina's right, Tim. We have got to have contingency plans,' said Jing Yang.

'Con-what?' asked Angelina.

'Contingency plans – backup plans so that in case anything goes wrong, we have a way out already prepared,' said Jing Yang.

'When do you plan to go to the bunker?' asked Tim.

'Monday,' said Jing Yang.

'That's three days away,' said Tim. 'Why wait so long?'

'We can't go now. That Mr Savage will be on the watch for us. He will be waiting for us so if we go now, we will definitely fall into his trap,' explained Jing Yang.

'So we should wait till he has relaxed his guard before making our move?' asked Angelina.

'That's right,' said Jing Yang. 'It will also give us enough time to recce the surroundings so that we are fully prepared for all situations when we make our move.'

'So we are going to Fort Canning Park these few days?'

asked Angelina.

'Correct!' said Jing Yang. 'We need to study the place. We need to find out the best time to enter the bunker. We also need to find out which door into the bunker to use for getting in and which one for our escape,' said Jing Yang. 'So we cannot hurry along. We must plan carefully so there will not be any mistakes.'

'Are you going to tell Mr Wang about this?' asked Angelina.

'I do not know yet,' said Jing Yang. 'What I am afraid is that he will tell Aunt Dorothy and that would spoil our plans. For certain, Aunt Dorothy will not allow us to go there.'

'When are we going to Fort Canning Park?' asked Tim.

'Let me plan first,' said Jing Yang. 'By tomorrow, I should be able to tell you everything,'

'So what do we do now?' asked Angelina.

'Enjoy ourselves,' said Jing Yang. 'We need to relax ourselves. We deserve a nice rest after what happened yesterday.'

'Don't forget we have to go visit Mr Wang today,' said Tim.

'Oh! I forgot!' said Jing Yang. 'I knew there was something we had to do today.'

'Let's go for lunch. I am hungry,' said Tim.

The three friends headed for lunch at the nearby Punggol Plaza. Then they browsed through the shops in the shopping centre till three o'clock before going to Jing Yang's place. They put their bags down in the living room and crossed over to Mr Wang's house two doors away. Mr Wang was waiting for them at home. He was eager to learn what they had found out. He also wanted to know the previous day's happenings in detail. He did not have a chance to ask many questions that were in his mind as Tim's mother had dominated the discussion the night before. By the time they had had dinner that night, the teenagers were tired and he did not want to wear them out further.

Mr Wang kept pacing the study. He was curious about the spirits that the children had been talking about the whole night. He was so excited he hardly slept a wink the night before. Did such things really exist? Also these were World War Two spirits so if they did exist there was plenty that they could tell him about the war past. As a historian, he had been researching past events, looking for facts or purported facts to back up his analysis of historical happenings. So far he had had to rely on sources such as diaries, libraries and government archives for these facts.

Now, he had a chance to learn first-hand what happened in the past – from the mouths of persons connected with the past. He could interview these spirits to get their oral recollection of important points in history. And if there were such things as spirits in this world, he could find a way to contact other spirits who had intimate knowledge of important historical events. The benefits of learning history from them would be immeasurable. Right now, he wanted to find out more from the children to satisfy his curiosity. Mr Wang looked at the clock on the wall. It was almost half past three and the children were not here yet. Most probably, they were on their way, he thought to himself. He picked up the piece of paper on which he had scribbled some notes and glanced through a list of points he had penned. He wondered what else he had forgotten to write down.

Just then, the doorbell rang. It was the children arriving, he thought. He walked towards the main door of the house. Standing at the doorway were Jing Yang, Tim and Angelina. They greeted Mr Wang and followed him to his study. There they seated themselves in some chairs that were not in the study the last time they visited him. He had carried these chairs in specially for them. He was more comfortable talking in the study than in the living room. Mr Wang pushed a plush swivel chair out from behind his desk and placed it next to the children. Then he passed to each of them a packet of drink before seating himself. They were all comfortable now, he thought. He could start getting them to fill in the gaps in his knowledge of the previous day's events, he decided.

'You have all had an exciting time yesterday afternoon,' said Mr Wang. 'I am sure you have lots to tell me about your little adventure in the bunker. Who wants to start first?'

'Jing Yang, you start first,' said Angelina. 'Tell Mr Wang what happened to you in the bunker.'

'Yes, and then I will talk about the rescue,' said Tim.

'That would be fine,' said Mr Wang. 'Go ahead, Jing Yang, tell me what you know.'

'Well, I went into the bunker to take a look at the locked door,' said Jing Yang. 'I was curious about what lay hidden behind the locked door.'

'So what did you find out?' asked Mr Wang.

'I couldn't get the door to open and suddenly Mr Savage was behind me. He grabbed hold of me and pushed me into the locked room,' said Jing Yang.

'He had the keys to the room?' asked Mr Wang.

'Yes,' said Jing Yang.

'What was in the room?' asked Mr Wang.

'It was dark inside. I could not see clearly, but from the little light that came in through the openings between the doors on each side of the wall and the floor, I could make out the room was empty – devoid of furniture,' said Jing Yang.

'There was nothing in there?' said Mr Wang.

'There was a small cardboard box on the floor. It contained a ball of string and a tape measure,' said Jing Yang.

'Did you notice anything else about the room?' asked Mr Wang.

'It was big – more than half the size of a classroom. But, it was too dark for me to see whether there were any hidden doors,' said Jing Yang. 'On the four sides of the room were metal doors. I think these led to the other rooms. It was cold in the room. It was chilly. I had goose pimples running through my arms but I did not know why. I felt a little breeze going past me time and again, but the air-conditioning vents were so far away – in the centre of the room. Now, I know it was these spirits that Tim and Angelina had talked about.'

'Mmm. Now tell me why Mr Savage hit you,' said Mr Wang.

'I don't know. I really don't know,' said Jing Yang. 'I think I said something about him abusing his power and this got him angry.'

'Did you see anyone with Mr Savage?' asked Mr Wang.

'No! I think he was all alone,' said Jing Yang.

'What about the drain cover? Did you find out anything about the drain cover?' asked Mr Wang.

'I wanted to crawl through the tunnel to see where it led,' said Jing Yang. 'But it was flooded with water up to about one foot deep. It was too dangerous to go inside.'

Mr Wang was now leaning back in the swivel chair. He was thinking hard.

'There may not be anything interesting down there,' said Mr Wang. 'If there is water in the tunnel, it is likely that the tunnel is a bona fide drain tunnel functioning as a means of transporting ground water out of the tunnel, to prevent flooding in the tunnel, you know.'

'Why should there be water in the drain tunnel?' asked Angelina. 'Why should they let water go into the bunker? It is dangerous!'

'Most likely, when the British designed the bunker, they put in the drainage tunnel to take care of the possibility of a flood hitting the bunker. They had to find a way to channel the water out of the tunnel. It may be bomb-proof but I don't think it is flood-proof,' said Mr Wang.

'Yes, Mr Savage had said there was a big reservoir of water about seventy feet away from the bunker,' said Angelina.

'Nevertheless, I still want to go into the drain tunnel when there is a chance,' said Jing Yang.

'You certainly are persistent in your goals,' said Mr Wang. Turning to the other two children, he asked, 'So what have you got to tell me about your adventure?'

'We were waiting for Jing Yang to come out of the bunker. We waited and waited. In the end, we decided to go in ourselves,' said Tim. He was eager to tell his story. Life for him in Singapore these few months had been too monotonous – till the previous day.

'We were poking around in one of the rooms, Fortress Commander's Office, I believe, when a voice spoke to us,' Tim continued. 'It was eerie. It startled me.'

'Yes, it was frightening,' Angelina interjected.

'What did the voice say?' asked Jing Yang. He too was eager to learn about the spirits. They had not told him everything when they were in the taxi with him after their escape the previous day.

'Remember, I told you he introduced himself as a colonel something,' said Angelina.

'It was Colonel Walter Henry Cooper of His Majesty's Royal Engineers,' said Tim. 'He said he was stationed here in 1939.'

'Yes, that was what he said,' said Angelina.

'Then another voice spoke,' said Tim. 'This voice belonged to a chap called Todds. He was the one in the wax model of General Simmons. The first voice came from the wax model of General Percival.'

'I see. I see,' said Mr Wang. 'Royal Engineers. He must somehow be connected to the building of the bunker. He's a colonel so he must have intimate knowledge of the bunker. What else did they say?'

'The second spirit, the one in General Simmons, said that the Gun Operations Room – the present one – was not the real one. The real Gun Operations Room, was the next room, I mean the locked room,' said Angelina. 'The present Gun Operations Room was actually the Fortress

Plotting Room.'

'Why was the original Gun Operations Room locked and unused? Why did they use the Fortress Plotting Room as the Gun Operations Room instead?' asked Mr Wang. He was deep in thought now searching his mind for some answers to his questions. There had to be some important reason for the designers of the museum not to use the real Gun Operations Room as an exhibit room. It had to have some hidden secrets, he thought.

'Could it be, could it be?' Mr Wang thought aloud, 'that they realised that the room was haunted?'

'Haunted?' the three teenagers chorused in unison.

'Oh, I did say that, didn't I?' said Mr Wang. He suddenly realised that the children had heard him. 'It is likely that they locked up the room and did not use the room because it was haunted.'

'They saw the spirits too?' asked Jing Yang.

'I am not sure, not really sure,' said Mr Wang. 'Someone or some people might have seen something, or they would not have done something as drastic as changing the original functions of the rooms. This is after all a historical site. They can't just change history.'

'The spirits have been haunting the room for a very long time, then?' asked Angelina.

'Yes, perhaps since after World War Two,' said Mr Wang.

'Don't they know they are dead?' asked Tim.

'Now, that's a question I as a historian cannot answer,' said Mr Wang. 'Your mother should know the answer; she's a paranormal specialist.'

'A para-what?' asked Angelina.

'Paranormal simply means experiences or happenings that cannot be explained by scientific means, like spirits and magic,' interjected Jing Yang. He was always eager to boast his wide vocabulary.

'Yes, Jing Yang is right,' said Mr Wang.

'Ah! I remember something strange now,' exclaimed

Angelina.

'What?' Jing Yang asked. He was seated next to her and her sudden excitement had surprised him.

'We were talking to the spirits about where Jing Yang was. Then there was confusion about the Gun Operations Room. One of the spirits told us Jing Yang was in the Gun Operations Room, so we looked in there – it was next to where we were standing,' said Angelina.

'And?' said Jing Yang.

'Let me think,' said Angelina. 'The spirit mentioned something about a secret passage.'

'He did? Did he say where it was?' asked Jing Yang.

'Why did he suddenly talk about a secret passage?' asked Mr Wang.

'I asked him where Jing Yang was,' said Angelina. 'He said Jing Yang was in the Gun Operations Room but we saw nothing in the next room. So that was when I asked whether there was a secret passage in the room.

'You asked him whether there was a secret passage in the Gun Operations Room?' asked Jing Yang.

'I think when the spirit talked about a secret passage in the Gun Operations Room, he was referring to the locked room – the real Gun Operations Room,' Mr Wang interjected.

'Yes, that's what I think too,' said Angelina.

'Why didn't you tell us earlier?' asked Jing Yang.

'So which spirit told you about the secret passage?' asked Mr Wang.

'Let me see. It was General Percival,' said Angelina.

'You mean the spirit in the wax model of General Percival,' said Mr Wang. 'Colonel Walter Henry Cooper. That makes sense. Colonel Cooper was a senior engineer. He had to have intimate knowledge of the bunker's secrets.'

'Should we go see him?' asked Jing Yang. 'Perhaps, he could tell us where the secret passage is.'

'That is a good idea,' said Mr Wang. 'But these are

spirits; it will do us no good to get near them.'

'But, it's the only way to find out about the secret passage,' said Jing Yang.

'Yes, it is. Yes, it is,' said Mr Wang.

'Now, the problem at hand is how to get them to talk to us,' said Mr Wang. 'We can't just barge in and say hello to them. We don't even know where they are.'

'We can start with the Fortress Commander's Office. That's where Angelina and Tim met them.'

'We could use my mum's Godell prism to talk with them,' suggested Tim.

'Godell prism?' asked Mr Wang.

'Yes, Godell prism,' said Tim. 'My mum uses it often to communicate with what she says are dark and negative energies.'

'Dark and negative energies?' said Mr Wang.

'I mean spirits,' said Tim.

'I see. I see,' said Mr Wang.

'I don't think your mum will lend it to us,' said Mr Wang. 'Remember she told you guys not to go near the bunker anymore?'

'We could use it without her knowledge,' said Tim.

'That would not be good. That would not be good,' said Mr Wang.

'That would be stealing,' said Angelina. 'You would be stealing from your mother.'

'Yes, Angelina is right,' said Mr Wang. 'We need to find another way.'

'We are thinking of going into the bunker again soon,' said Jing Yang.

'When is that?' asked Mr Wang.

'Say Monday,' said Jing Yang. 'But first we are going to recce the area around the bunker. We need to find out how best to enter the bunker.'

'That's a good idea. You certainly wouldn't want to get caught again,' said Mr Wang.

So when do you plan to recce the hill?' asked Mr Wang.

'Tomorrow would be a good day,' said Jing Yang.

'Yes, it's a Saturday. It would be crowded. With so many people around, I'm sure we won't be noticed,' said Angelina.

'One more thing,' said Mr Wang. 'How are you going to get in this time?' asked Mr Wang. 'Sneak in by the exit door again?'

'We are thinking of a way,' said Jing Yang. Actually, they had found a way, for they had the keys to the bunker but they were not going to tell Mr Wang, just in case he told Tim's mother.

The three friends bade goodbye to Mr Wang and left the house. They walked to the bollards at the corner of the street and sat on them, talking about their meeting with Mr Wang.

'Luckily, you didn't tell Mr Wang about the keys,' said Tim.

'Yes, I purposely held back that bit of information,' said Jing Yang.

'What if Mr Savage has replaced the locks?' asked Angelina. 'We won't be able to get into the bunker then.'

'I am hoping he will not replace the locks. I am sure he hasn't told the other people in the bunker he held me prisoner in the locked room,' said Jing Yang.

I mean, it's a respectable place. Surely they can't be colluding with him,' he continued.

'Yeah,' said Tim. 'It's likely he works alone.'

'Maybe, he has reported that he lost the keys so they would change the locks without suspecting anything is amiss,' said Angelina.

'There is a suspicion in my mind that he won't do anything about the locks, not just yet,' said Jing Yang.

'Why?' asked Angelina. She was curious now.

'Because,' Jing Yang explained, pausing to find the words. 'Because he wants us to go into the bunker again.'

'He wants to catch us?' said Tim.

'Yes, I got away the last time,' said Jing Yang. 'He must

be fuming mad. He hopes to catch me again. He must think I know too much about his secrets.'

'He has secrets?' asked Angelina.

'He must still be looking for the Yamashita treasure,' said Jing Yang. 'I can feel it in my bones. I am certain I am right.'

'So he thinks you know he's looking for treasure?' asked Angelina.

'Of course, otherwise there is no reason for locking me up like that,' said Jing Yang. 'It just doesn't make sense.'

'I think you are right,' said Tim.

'I have been meaning to ask,' said Angelina. 'Why doesn't Mr Wang want to come along with us when we visit the bunker? I mean, he's so interested in what we are doing.'

'Mr Wang's interest in the bunker is only as a historian. He's not interested in the treasure stuff, silly,' said Jing Yang. 'Besides, he's old. What if he falls down the steps?'

All three friends broke into laughter. They just could picture Mr Wang rolling down the long stairs. They were not being mean. It was just like them, teenagers, to think of such funny situations. It was, perhaps, that spurt of youthful exuberance that propelled such imaginations in them.

'Tim, has your mother taught you how to use the Godell prism?' asked Jing Yang. He needed to find out whether Tim knew how to harness the power in the Godell prism. It was just in case they needed to borrow the crystal from Tim's mother.

'I could ask Mum to teach me,' said Tim. 'She would, you know. After all I am her son.'

'Then she would be suspicious of us immediately,' said Jing Yang. 'Your mother has got extraordinary powers of observation.'

'Yeah! You are right,' said Tim. 'I always cannot get away with my lies.'

'Does your mother keep notes on the Godell prism?'

asked Jing Yang.

'No idea, but I can find out,' said Tim. 'I will just look through her stuff when she's preparing dinner.'

'Isn't that sneaky of you?' said Angelina.

'For the sake of our little adventure, and for the sake of finding long-lost treasure, it's worth doing it,' said Tim. He extended his right hand to them. 'Let's shake on it.'

Jing Yang and Angelina also extended their right hands and all three grabbed one another's hands and formed a tight grip with them.

'All for one and one for all!' said Tim.

'What's that all about?' asked Angelina.

'Tim means we remain loyal to one another no matter what happens,' said Jing Yang.

'All for one and one for all,' yelled Angelina.

'Yes, all for one and one for all,' exclaimed Jing Yang. He was glad his cousin Tim was beginning to accept him as a bosom friend.

13 *ON A RECCE MISSION*

Saturday was the day that the three friends were going to Fort Canning Park on a recce mission. They resolved to wake up early in the morning, though it was not a school day and they usually slept till noon on this day. All three met outside Jing Yang's place at half past eight. They were in T-shirts and shorts. Angelina had suggested that they wear caps to help shield their faces. She had said that Mr Savage would not be able to recognise them so easily if they were dressed this way. So today they also donned caps.

It was lucky that they picked this day, for a company was having its family day in the park. There were many, many people – singles, couples, and families – in the park that morning when the three friends arrived on top of the three flights of steps near the roundabout.

'Remember guys, we have to keep out of sight of Mr Savage,' said Jing Yang. 'Our purpose today is to find the best way into the bunker. We need to stake out the two doorways into the bunker: the entrance door and the exit door. We also must take a look at the escape route door on top of the hill. Our goal is to decide which of the three ways is the safest for us to use to enter the bunker and which one to use for our escape.'

'Do we break into groups?' asked Angelina.

'No need. We are here to gather data only, not monitor the movements of the guides. Anyway, we will be going into the bunker at night when it is closed, so for today there is no need to know when the guides are on duty or taking their breaks. But, of course, we can take note of such things. Everyone clear on what to do?'

'Yes, sir!' said Angelina and Tim simultaneously.

'We'll just take a casual walk to the roundabout, up the lane on the left, and then up again to the top of the hill where we will have a good view of the surroundings,' said Jing Yang. 'Remember to blend with the crowd.'

They sauntered to the roundabout, careful to keep the brim of their caps turned down to hide part of their faces. As they moved, they mingled with the families straggling up the lane. They passed the guard post where the same guard was stationed and pretended to be busy taking pictures of the surroundings. Soon, they found themselves in front of the Fort Canning Centre. There were many make-shift games stalls along the long corridor, from one end to the other end. Manning these stalls were volunteers in dark blue T-shirts and jeans. They were busy putting the final touches to the stalls. There were round inflatable rubber dinghies in which could be seen rubber ducks floating on water. There was even a clown dispensing balloons at a stall smack next to the flight of steps leading up to the top of the slope. Already, families were milling around the area in front of the building but nothing was happening yet. There were children running around and maids minding their charges.

It was ten o'clock when the three friends climbed the steps to the top of the slope and sat on the low concrete wall encircling the top of the slope. From there, they could see all the way past the guard post to the roundabout on their left, and on their right, at the far end, they could see the high walls of the reservoir. Nobody coming up the lane could escape their notice. Satisfied with the location of their observation point, they settled down to observe the surroundings.

'Look! Over there!' Angelina was pointing to the lane next to the guard post. A figure in green was ushering a motley group of tourists onto the lane. They then headed up the lane towards the bunker entrance.

'Is it the monster?' asked Tim.

'No, this guy's Chinese,' said Jing Yang.

Soon the group arrived at the entrance to the bunker. The Chinese guide stopped in front of the entrance. He was now giving them some instructions.

'After the tour, if you need to use the ladies or the gents, the restrooms are over there, behind the window,' said the guide. Pointing up the slope on top of the entrance, he continued, 'The exit to the bunker is on the other side of the hill. Just make a big U-turn to get to the restrooms.' Then he led the tourists into the tunnel. Jing Yang noted the time on his watch. It was quarter past ten. The tours did not take place on the hour.

Soon they turned their backs to the building below and looked around the top of the slope. It was nothing but open space. There was a large tent pitched on one side. There were many chairs arranged in rows on both sides of an aisle in the tent. A platform sat in front of these chairs. Some people were moving around on the platform, putting up a banner and doing other stuff. Jing Yang unfolded the brochure he was holding. On one side was a map of Fort Canning Park. They pored over the map. On the far left, just in front of the reservoir, was a building which was labelled Old Married Soldiers' Quarters. The Fort Gate sat on its right. They matched the structures shown on the map with those they saw around them. No other buildings were shown on the map. However, about one hundred feet in front of the teenagers, was a tapering concrete structure about ten feet high and twelve feet wide. It sat under a large tree.

'Look! That concrete thing is not on the map. Let's take a look,' said Jing Yang.

They walked up to the concrete structure. On one side of the structure was an old metal door with rivets running alongside the edges of the door. The door's rivet design was similar to the doors in the bunker. It just was possible this was the exit from the escape route downstairs in the bunker. Jing Yang and Angelina recalled there was a cat ladder in the stairwell at the end of the escape route passage in the bunker. The cat ladder was served by three landings placed at equal intervals. One of the landings had a door next to it. It was probably this door that they were looking at now. They were elated!

'Now that we know this door leads into the bunker, we have to try the keys one by one to see whether one of them opens this door,' said Jing Yang. 'But, we can't do it now. There are too many people around.'

'Look! The doorstep is raised about one feet from the ground. Let's pretend to rest here first and decide what to do next,' said Tim.

'Good idea!' said Angelina.

The width of the doorstep could only take two persons so Jing Yang volunteered to stand. Then he found that he could conceal the key hole area just by leaning on the side wall next to the door.

'Tim, quick, hand me the keys,' said Jing Yang. 'I can put my hand behind me and try to turn the key in the keyhole. This way, nobody can notice what I am doing.'

Tim dug into his pocket for the bunch of keys and passed them to Jing Yang behind his back. All eyes were in front, for they were making as if they were admiring the scenery. Though others could not hear the sound of the keys rattling as Jing Yang inserted them into the keyhole one by one, it was quite loud to the teenagers. Finally, Jing Yang's face lit up. One of the keys had made a complete turn in the keyhole. It was possible the door had been unlocked. Now, they had to make sure it had been unlocked, without attracting undue attention from the passers-by and the occasional jogger going past them.

'I think the door is now unlocked,' said Jing Yang. 'But, I'm not sure.'

'What do we do now?' asked Angelina.

'I am afraid that this door may not have been opened in ages, so if we open it now, there's going to be a very loud creaking sound,' said Jing Yang.

'Why not wait awhile? Wait till the organisers of the family day event start using the public address system. The noise would definitely drown out the creaking sound,' said Tim.

'Thanks, Tim. Fancy me not thinking of that,' said Jing Yang.

'*Wah*! Tim, you sure are quick-thinking,' said Angelina.

'Not at all, just helping out, doing my share, that's all,' said Tim.

They did not need to wait long, for the festivities began barely five minutes later. The music blaring through the speakers not only drowned out the creaking of the metal door, it also made it difficult for them to hear each other. They had to resort to hand gestures to communicate with each other. Jing Yang gave the thumbs up to tell Tim and Angelina that he was ready to try opening the door behind him. He pulled the door knob slowly but it would not budge. He tried again, this time expending more strength. It yielded behind him. There was the familiar creaking sound which all three could hear. Satisfied with himself, Jing Yang pushed the door shut and turned the key to lock the door. Then he passed the keys to Tim, making sure Tim knew which key was used to open the lock.

With their mission accomplished, they moved away from the concrete structure towards the other end of the slope, just above the bunker's exit door. There, they sat on the low concrete wall, looking over the slope down to the area in front of the exit door and beyond, where the big building, the former HQ Far East Command, lay. From where they were, they could see the entire length of this building. It blocked their view of the other buildings surrounding the area. But, on their far right, they could see the nearby YWCA and Park Mall buildings, as well as the roundabout. The exit door could be their means of escape as, unlike the entrance door, this one did not have an access device installed. They had by now given up thinking of going into the bunker through the entrance door, for even if they could unlock the door, they could not go past the inner door which had a door access system installed on it.

Straggling visitors could be seen emerging from the exit door every half-an-hour or so. Apparently, this door was not locked; the visitors simply pushed a bar handle across the door to open it. The entire morning, they did not see Mr Savage on the hill.

'I think today's the monster's off-day,' said Tim.

'Likely so,' said Jing Yang. 'Only the Chinese guide is doing the tours today.'

'The guide seems to make a round every hour and there are only a handful of visitors each time, so the bunker is deserted much of the time,' said Angelina.

'It seems when there is only one guide, the guided tours are carried out at hourly intervals,' said Jing Yang. 'So, when two guides are around, we can expect the guided tours to take place every half-an-hour.'

'The Chinese guide doesn't know us so we can always wait for him to be on duty before going into the bunker,' said Angelina. 'At least, he won't chase us out even if he sees us.'

'But we'll still run into Mr Savage because there are two guided tours every hour – one done by the Chinese guide and the other by Mr Savage,' said Jing Yang. 'Unless, of course, we go into the bunker when it's Mr Savage's off-day.'

'There's no way to find out when Mr Savage will be off,' said Angelina.

'That's why, in spite of our findings today, I think it is still a good idea to go into the bunker at night, when nobody is around,' said Jing Yang.

'So you mean the night visit to the bunker is confirmed,' said Tim.

'What do you think, Angelina?' asked Jing Yang.

'You are the boss; you decide,' said Angelina.

'Tim?' asked Jing Yang.

'I'm with you,' said Tim.

'Good! Now, we need to decide which of the three ways into the bunker we are going to use on Monday night,' said Jing Yang.

'I suggest we use the escape route door,' said Tim. 'It's not so noticeable, especially at night when it's dark up here.'

'Angelina, what about you?' asked Jing Yang.

'We can't use the entrance door for sure. We don't have the access code to get past the inner door,' said Angelina. 'And the exit door is too open – it's opposite the Little Rocket Hotel. Anyone looking out of the window in the building can see us clearly. Also, there is a lamp post about ten feet away from the exit door, so we are bound to be seen at night. But, the escape route door is partly hidden under a big tree. That area is dimly lit. It is bound to be darker than the surroundings so we won't be found out easily.'

'So it appears we are all for using the escape route door to go into the bunker,' said Jing Yang. 'I also think we should use the same door to get out of the bunker.'

'Agreed,' said Angelina.

'Seconded,' said Tim.

'Right, we are finished with this place today. Shall we go back?' asked Jing Yang.

'Let's,' said Angelina.

It was noon when the three friends clambered down the steps on their left and made their way back to the MRT station. They were hot and tired after a morning's work.

They were also hungry. Instead of going back to Hougang, they decided to hop over to nearby Plaza Singapura for lunch. The shopping centre was connected to the MRT station. They only needed to walk through the underground station and enter the shopping centre using a basement entry point. There were some fast-food restaurants in the basement levels of Plaza Singapura. They chose McDonald's as it was their favourite restaurant. Also, there was an on-going promotion offering easy-on-the-pocket meals for less than five dollars. Angelina no longer had second thoughts about entering a fast-food restaurant. In fact, things had progressed such that Jing Yang would order food for her and she would eat whatever he ordered – no questions asked. Of course, he knew what she liked to eat – fish burger and Coca-Cola – and made sure he got them every time. As they sat at a table enjoying the food, Jing Yang wondered whether Angelina should participate in the night visit; it was a dangerous mission and he worried for her safety. She was rather headstrong so it would be difficult broaching the topic. Nevertheless, he had to talk about it.

'Angelina,' Jing Yang said to her, 'will your mother let you come out of the house at night?'

'You mean, Monday night?' asked Angelina.

'Yes,' said Jing Yang.

'I'll just tell her I am going to a friend's house for a project,' replied Angelina.

'She will let you?' asked Jing Yang.

'Of course, I have done it before, in secondary two,' said Angelina.

'But, we will be back quite late, maybe after eleven o'clock,' said Jing Yang.

'Are we going to be that late?' asked Angelina.

'Maybe,' said Jing Yang. 'I can't be sure.'

'It's not every time that I come home late; I am sure my mother won't mind,' said Angelina.

'But,' said Jing Yang.

'Jing Yang, I know what's on your mind,' said Angelina. 'Just don't think of going there without me. I won't let you.' Angelina certainly was blunt this time. She knew what she wanted. She also knew how to handle this boy. Jing Yang was lost for words. He did not know what to do next without greatly upsetting her. She was impossible to handle when she was upset.

'Remember our motto?' said Angelina. 'All for one and one for all. You had said yesterday that we should remain loyal to one another no matter what happened so you can't leave me out of this night visit.'

'Let her come, Jing Yang,' said Tim.

'Alright! You win,' said Jing Yang.

Angelina extended her hand to Jing Yang and he reluctantly shook it.

14 *CHATTING WITH THE TWO SPIRITS*

Monday evening came quickly. The teenagers had rested the whole afternoon knowing full well that that evening was going to be long and tiring. They were ready with their excuses. Jing Yang and Tim had their dinner and excused themselves to go into their bedrooms for schoolwork revision. When his mother was in the kitchen washing the dishes, Tim slipped into her room to borrow the Godell prism. Then he returned to his bedroom. He had already packed his bag; it contained a torch and a bottle of water.

He placed the Godell prism into a pouch and put it into the bag. Now the two cousins had to wait for Tim's mother to retire into the bedroom before going out of the house. She would usually pop into Tim's room to check on him before returning to her room. Tim had to wait for that to happen first. When his mother knocked on his door, he was ready for her. He appeared engrossed in some homework when she said goodnight to him. The moment she closed the door, Tim sidled up to the door to hear her footsteps going downstairs to her room.

Then he strapped his bag behind him and walked

across the corridor to Jing Yang's room. Jing Yang had also stood behind his bedroom door listening for Aunt Dorothy. He opened the door for Tim to go in. Then they went out into the balcony of the bedroom and climbed down a pipe. Tim's mother was watching television in her room behind the house so she would not be able to see them go out by the front of the house. They moved furtively to the gate and then climbed over it; they could not open the gate as the loud clicking sound would certainly alert Tim's mother.

Meanwhile, at dinner, Angelina had told her mother she would be going to a friend's house to do some urgent project. Her mother rarely questioned her so it was a simple process of telling her mother and then walking out of the house at the appointed time. She strapped her backpack behind her and dashed down the stairs to the carpark behind the block. She could see the two boys waiting for her at the bollards. She waved to them and strode towards them.

It was showing eight o'clock on Jing Yang's watch. Their plan was to take the MRT to Fort Canning Park and return by taxi. This way, Angelina would be home by eleven o'clock; she could only stay out that late without getting into trouble with her mother. They made a check of the things they needed for the trip.

'Have you got the Godell prism with you?' Jing Yang asked Tim.

'It's in my bag,' said Tim.

'Everyone has a torch?' asked Jing Yang.

Tim and Angelina nodded.

'The keys to the bunker?' asked Jing Yang.

'In my pocket,' said Tim, feeling the bulge in his right pocket.

'Let's go,' said Jing Yang.

The journey to Fort Canning Park felt longer than it was, mainly because the three of them were nervous. They were rather uneasy because they feared meeting with danger that evening. Soon, they were on top of the steps on the road leading to the roundabout. It was rather dark on the hill. The light from the lamp posts dotting the sides of the road was not bright but they did not complain. They would not be so noticeable wandering in the grounds of the park.

Ahead of them, they could see the guard post as it was the brightest place for as far as they could see. They could make out someone sitting behind the counter. They thought it was best to avoid contact with anyone connected with the park so they turned left into a carpark just before the roundabout. There were only a few cars in the carpark. From there, they walked up the kerb onto a dimly lit walkway which wound up to the lane midway between the guard post and Fort Canning Centre beyond them. Seeing no one in the lane, they crossed it to a Sally Port and clambered up the steps leading to the top of the slope.

When they were on the top few steps, they peeped at the open space in front of them. It was dark on top of the slope. Only a few lamp posts dotted the landscape and these were barely enough to illuminate the open space. This spelled good news to the teenagers. It was the perfect cover for them. There did not seem to be anyone around. They filed across the open space towards the escape route door of the bunker. Now, they could see some couples on the benches in the far right of the open space, hidden behind some trees. They leaned on the wall next to the door of the concrete structure. Luckily, the position of the door was out of view of the couples on the benches.

Tim took out a tube of lubricating oil from his bag and squeezed some on each of the two hinges along one side of the door. Then he fished a bunch of keys from his pocket and used one of them to open the door in front of him. The other two stood next to him. Then he turned the knob and pulled it. There was a slight creaking sound as the door opened.

'Trust you to bring along lubricating oil,' said Jing Yang. 'Who would have thought of that?'

'You sure are smart, Tim,' said Angelina.

'Quick,' said Jing Yang. He motioned them to enter the stairwell and closed the door behind him. They found themselves on top of a landing three storeys above the bunker. There was a cat ladder on their left. It led to two more landings and below the last landing was another cat ladder going down to the floor level. Though it was dark, they could see the outlines of the ladders and the walls around them, for above them was a skylight.

'Shh!' whispered Jing Yang. He gestured for them to follow him down the cat ladder. Tim was next, with Angelina behind him. When they reached the bottom of the stairwell, they paused. Jing Yang looked at the time on his watch. It was now quarter past nine. They had a little over an hour to spend in the bunker.

'Out with the torches,' said Jing Yang in a low voice. 'It's going to be dark from here on. We will move in single file, with Angelina between Tim and me. Stay close to each other.'

'Mmm,' mumbled Angelina. Tim gave the thumbs up sign.

They walked up the passageway, made a left turn and then a right turn. They found themselves at the beginning of a corridor. There was a doorway on their left. Jing Yang shone his torch into the room. It was where the air filtration unit was housed. The surrender conference room was in the next room beyond the unit. They were not going in there tonight. Jing Yang led the way up the corridor to the next opening on their right. It was the mini-gallery – an open space where display cabinets and standing partitions were placed. They were not going there either. On their left, directly opposite the mini-gallery was an open doorway into an empty room. There was a door at the opposite end. That door led to the locked room where Jing Yang was imprisoned the other day. The Fortress

Commander's Office would be farther up, after the bent in the corridor.

They had now reached the bent in the corridor. Jing Yang shone his torch onto the floor. The drain cover was right in front of them. Tim helped him lift the drain cover. They shone their torches into the drain tunnel. There was glitter in the tunnel. It was water! There was about half-a-foot of water in the drain tunnel – not enough to drown them. They could try crawling through it that night. But important things had to be done first. They had to try to make contact with the spirits in the wax models of Generals Percival and Simmons. It was their priority that night. They placed the drain cover back into position and continued on their way past the bent in the corridor.

They were now at a right-angle fork in the corridor. It was bright here with light coming from the corridor on their right in the far end. The light came from a spotlight located above a wax model standing some six feet from the inner door of the front entrance. They had no need for their torches here. But, they were not turning right this time. They looked into the grill window on the metal door on their left, which directly faced the right corridor. Inside was their destination for that night. It was the Fortress Commander's Office. It was dark inside. They were going to have a problem doing their work in the dark room as their torches were not bright enough to illuminate the entire room.

But, luck was on their side. When Jing Yang pushed open the metal door, it creaked loudly and the light from the corridor flooded the room, lighting it up. There was no need for torches after all. It was a godsend for the three teenagers. They piled into the room. The wax models of Generals Percival and Simmons were sitting at the desk in front of them. From where the wax model of General Percival sat, it had a full view of the corridor outside, all the way to the inner door at the front entrance. Apparently, the office was strategically located so that from where he sat, the fortress commander could see whoever was entering the bunker using that entrance.

The air-conditioning had been switched off for more than three hours, but the three teenagers could feel the lingering cold air in the room. It was not stuffy after all. But, the chilly coldness that Jing Yang had felt in the locked room was absent in this room. It was now half past nine on Jing Yang's watch.

'So these are the wax models which talked to the two of you,' said Jing Yang to Tim and Angelina. He was no longer whispering. They were now standing across the desk from where the wax models were seated.

'Tim, use the Godell prism now,' said Jing Yang.

Tim unstrapped his bag and retrieved a pouch from it.

'Where should I place it?' Tim asked.

'How about on the desk?' suggested Jing Yang.

Tim removed the crystal from the pouch and set it on the desk in front of the wax models. Then he stepped back to stand with his friends. A minute's silence prevailed in the room.

'They are not talking,' said Jing Yang.

'Let me try concentrating on the Godell prism,' said Tim. He stared hard at the crystal on the desk for the next few minutes, but nothing happened.

'They still won't talk,' said Jing Yang dejectedly. 'Is this the correct way to use the Godell prism?'

'Did you read the notes on the Godell prism?' asked Angelina.

'Yes, I did,' said Tim.

'This won't work. We are running out of time,' Jing Yang said. 'How did you get them to talk to you that day?'

'I...I think I stepped on General Percival's foot by accident,' said Tim.

'I see. Well, try stepping on his foot again,' Jing Yang said.

'Me? Again?' uttered Tim.

'Yes, you again. We have no time to lose. We have to

try this approach,' said Jing Yang. He was looking at his watch again. It was now quarter to ten. They had about three-quarters of an hour left in the bunker. Tim got behind the desk and looked for General Percival's feet. The other day he had accidentally stepped on General Percival's right foot. Tim thought that, perhaps, he should try stepping on the right foot first, and if it did not work, he could step on the other foot afterwards. He looked under the desk. General Percival was sitting cross-legged, with his left foot over his right. It was easier to step on his right foot as it was on the floor. The other foot was in midair. He could only kick it.

'Here goes,' said Tim and he stepped onto General Percival's right foot. There was no reaction from the wax model. He tried stepping again but to no avail.

'Step harder this time,' said Jing Yang. Tim stomped onto General Percival's foot.

'Hey! Why did you do that for?' asked General Simmons' look-alike. The three of them were startled by the voice. It appeared to be coming from General Simmons. But the wax model did not move.

'I say, are you deaf? Why did you step on his foot?' said the voice again.

'General Simmons, is that you?' asked Tim. He had regained his composure. He was no longer afraid as it was the second time he was meeting the spirit.

'Good lord! It's you kids again,' said General Simmons' look-alike.

'Yes, General Simmons,' said Angelina. She flashed a shy smile at him. She too was not afraid anymore.

'Look here! I'm not General Simmons. I am Major Norman Todds of the Second Australian Imperial Force,' said General Simmons' look-alike.

'Sorry, sir,' said Angelina.

'You haven't answered my question. Why did you step on his foot?' said General Simmons' look-alike.

'We…we just wanted to know whether General

Percival was here,' Jing Yang stammered. Jing Yang was a little apprehensive. He had never met a spirit in person before, let alone chat with one.

'Well, he's not General Percival. He's Colonel Walter Henry Cooper,' said General Simmons' look-alike. 'Why are you looking for him?'

'Sir, we...we wish to find out something from General – I mean Colonel Cooper, sir,' said Jing Yang.

'Hey! Now I remember! You were the chap in the locked room the other day,' said General Simmons' look-alike.

'Yes, sir,' said Jing Yang. Then after a pause, he said, 'Thank you for telling my friends here that I was in that room.'

'My pleasure,' said General Simmons' look-alike. 'Why the heck did that man lock you up?'

'I think he found me a nuisance, sir,' said Jing Yang. He was getting used to the voice now. 'I was poking around the bunker a lot,' he added.

'Why were you doing that?' asked General Simmons' look-alike.

'We are looking for treasure, sir,' said Tim.

'Treasure?' said General Simmons' look-alike. 'Is there really treasure in this bunker?'

'You mean there's no treasure in the bunker, sir?' said Jing Yang.

'Not that I know of,' said General Simmons' look-alike.

The three teenagers' hearts sank on hearing that bit of news. They were ill-prepared for such bad news. They had done all that work for nothing!

'Sir, are you sure there's no treasure in the bunker?' asked Tim. 'I heard that they buried gold bars beneath this bunker.'

'What gold bars?' asked General Simmons' look-alike.

'You know, gold bars from the Yamashita treasure,' said Tim.

'You have been too long out in the sun, dear boy,' said

General Simmons' look-alike. 'I have been here for an eternity and I have not heard of any such thing.'

'Perhaps, he doesn't know,' Jing Yang whispered to the other two. 'It could be that he doesn't know about the treasure.'

'Shall we try asking General Percival?' asked Angelina.

'You mean Colonel Cooper?' said Tim.

'Yes, after all, Colonel Cooper was the one who mentioned something about a secret passage when we were here with them,' said Angelina.

'Yes, Angelina. You are right. There is hope after all,' said Jing Yang. 'If there's a secret passage, there is bound to be some treasure somewhere. Besides, Mr Craig Savage is here so I smell treasure somewhere.'

'What are you children mumbling about?' said General Simmons' look-alike.

'Nothing, sir,' said Jing Yang. 'Is Colonel Cooper here? He isn't speaking to us.'

'Oh! The colonel!' said General Simmons' look-alike. 'He should be back soon. He's having his supper.'

'You take supper, sir?' asked Tim disbelievingly.

'Young chap, we have got to eat you know,' said General Simmons' look-alike. 'Can't be running around on an empty stomach, you know.' But the teenagers really did not know that spirits could eat or drink or even have a life.

'What can I do for you this evening,' said a familiar voice. Tim and Angelina recognised the voice. It was that of Colonel Cooper. It came from the wax model of General Percival.

'Colonel Cooper, sir,' Tim and Angelina chorused.

Looking at the watch on his hand, General Percival's look-alike said, 'It's so late already. Why are you kids still up? Don't you have school to go to tomorrow?' But the watch was not in working condition. It had stopped working even before it was strapped onto the wax model years ago when the wax model was brought into the bunker as a display unit.

'Sir, we came to talk to you,' said Angelina. 'My friend Jing Yang wants to thank you for helping him escape the other day.'

'Yes, sir. Thank you very much, sir,' said Jing Yang.

'Not at all! It was my pleasure, young lad,' said General Percival's look-alike. 'My pleasure.'

'Sir, the other day you talked to my friends about a secret passage,' said Jing Yang. 'Is there a secret passage in the bunker?'

'Secret passage?' said General Percival's look-alike. 'I did say that, didn't I?'

'Yes, you did, sir,' said Angelina.

'It's been a long time since anyone asked me about the secret passage,' said General Percival's look-alike. 'I almost forgot about it.'

'Where is it, sir?' asked Tim.

'The secret passage?' said General Percival's look-alike. 'It's just behind me.'

'Behind you?' repeated Tim. The teenagers were now looking at the wall behind the wax model.

'Yes,' said General Percival's look-alike. 'There's a secret door on the wall behind me. I designed it myself.'

'You did, sir?' asked Jing Yang. Now they could learn about the secret passage straight from the horse's mouth.

'Yes, of course,' said General Percival's look-alike. 'The entire bunker with its double walls, drainage system and secret passage were all my work. I'm pretty proud of it myself.'

'But, there's no secret door on the wall now, sir,' said Jing Yang.

'There isn't?' said General Percival's look-alike. He looked at the wall behind him. 'No wonder! The cabinet in the corner is blocking the secret door.' General Percival's look-alike was talking about a five-foot-tall-by-three-foot-wide wooden filing cabinet that stood in the corner on the left of the wax model. The other day, the teenagers had overlooked checking the rear of the cabinet. There was a big box next to it, blocking it. Tim pushed the box aside and stood by the side of the cabinet. He tried to move it but it would not budge. It was too heavy.

'Come help me,' said Tim. Jing Yang grabbed the other end of the cabinet and both tried to pull it out from the corner. They managed to move it out by a foot. Jing Yang shone his torch between the cabinet and the wall.

'There seems to be an outline on the wall,' said Jing Yang. 'A rectangular outline.' He fingered the outline on the wall and then directed the light from the torch onto the outline.

'Looks like a gap between both sides of the outline. This could be a secret door,' said Jing Yang.

'Of course, it is, dear lad,' said General Percival's look-alike. 'Surely, I can't be wrong about it. I may be very old, but that doesn't mean I have gone gaga.'

'There's no handle or lock on this part of the wall,' said Tim who had squatted next to the cabinet and was now peering into the gap between the wall and the cabinet.

'Can I have a look too?' asked Angelina. Jing Yang moved back from the cabinet so that Angelina could look into the gap.

'Sir, if there is no lock or knob, how can we open the door?' asked Jing Yang.

'Glad you ask,' said General Percival's look-alike. 'It is part of my proudest work. Am I not a genius? The secret door opens from a wheel somewhere else.'

'A wheel?' asked Jing Yang.

'Yes, a wheel mechanism,' said General Percival's look-alike. 'You turn a wheel and it turns another wheel which activates a pulley which in turn releases a locking mechanism.'

'I hate physics,' said Angelina. She could not understand a single word that General Percival's look-alike was saying.

'Search me too,' said Tim.

'He is talking about a door elevating wheel mechanism,'

said Jing Yang. Abstract matters posed no challenge to him.

'Glad to find someone who understands my work,' said General Percival's look-alike.

'Sir, where is the wheel located?' asked Jing Yang excitedly.

'It's in the drainage tunnel under the bunker,' said General Percival's look-alike.

'Is it the one outside this room, sir?' asked Jing Yang.

'Yes, that is the one all right,' said General Percival's look-alike.

'By golly! I never knew there's a wheel under the bunker,' said General Simmons' look-alike.

'There's so much that you do not know, Todds,' said General Percival's look-alike. 'I never tried telling you because you don't seem to understand engineering at all.'

'I do. I do,' said General Simmons' look-alike. 'It's just that you say things in a profound manner.'

'Sirs, may I interrupt, please?' asked Jing Yang. It was getting late. The time on his watch was showing half past ten now. If they did not leave the bunker now, Angelina would be very late getting home and she could get into hot soup when she reached home.

'Of course you may, dear lad,' said General Percival's look-alike.

'Just how far under the drainage tunnel do I have to crawl to get to the wheel?' asked Jing Yang.

'It's all in the map,' said General Percival's look-alike.

'Map?' asked Jing Yang. 'Is there a map on the location of the wheel?'

'Yes, the map shows the location of the wheel and the secret passage under the bunker,' said General Percival's look-alike.

Now that spelled good news to the three teenagers. They were getting somewhere at last.

'Sir, may I ask where the map is?' asked Jing Yang.

'Let's see now. Where did I leave it?' said General

Percival's look-alike.

'It's been so long ago. Can you really remember where you kept the map?' said General Simmons' look-alike.

'Of course, I can,' said General Percival's look-alike. 'I may be forgetful, but I am not gaga, you know. I just cannot remember right now.'

'Sir, is the map in this room?' asked Jing Yang.

'No, it isn't,' said General Percival's look-alike. 'I hid it behind a sink like this one here – next to me. I just cannot remember which one.' There was a porcelain sink in the corner behind General Percival. The teenagers remembered seeing a couple of these sinks in the bunker. There were altogether six sinks in the bunker. They had to look behind every one of these sinks and they were short of time.

'Pardon us, sirs,' said Jing Yang. 'We need to get home soon or we'll be in trouble. We need to look for all the sinks in the bunker now. Can we get your kind sirs' permission to leave you now?'

'Permission granted, young lad,' said General Percival's look-alike. He was pleased with the young man's manners.

'Be off now,' said General Simmons' look-alike. 'Don't forget to put back the cabinet before you leave. We can't have this room looking like a mess. It's our office, you know.' Jing Yang apologised and with Tim's help, pushed the wooden cabinet back against the wall. Luckily, General Simmons' look-alike had reminded him to do it. Otherwise, Mr Savage would discover this secret door when he came into the bunker the next day, Jing Yang thought.

'Don't forget to take your mother's crystal,' said Angelina, pointing to the Godell prism on the desk. Tim bowed to the two generals and grabbed the crystal from the desk. He inserted the crystal into a pocket and nodded to the other two.

The teenagers took leave of the two wax models and dashed off to the rooms around the bunker to look for the sinks. There was nobody else in the bunker. Noise was not a problem. Angelina and Tim were afraid to go off on their own so the teenagers decided to look for the sinks together. They checked for sinks in the rooms of the bunker. They found a sink in each of the places they checked out – the Orderlies Room, just outside the MOT Room, Fortress Commander's Office, Fortress Operations Room and the Fixed Defences HQ. There was nothing behind the sinks in these rooms. There was just one more sink that they found in the last room next to the corridor – the Surrender Conference Room. The sink was in the far right corner of the room, behind the wax models of the generals. Jing Yang climbed over some benches and squeezed between the wax models to get to the sink behind them. He shone his torch into the gap between the sink and the wall. He could see nothing. Was it a false alarm? There were no more sinks to search for; this was the last one, and their last chance to find the map.

'Do you have a ruler with you?' Jing Yang asked the other two. Angelina dug into her backpack and took out a plastic ruler. She handed it to Jing Yang. He inserted the ruler into the gap and pushed down gently. Suddenly, he stopped. The ruler had struck something; there was some resistance now. He dragged the ruler along the length of the gap, pushing it downwards as he dragged it.

'There's something coming out from underneath the sink,' said Tim. He was shining his torch at the area below the sink. It was something yellowish white. It was a parchment. Slowly, more of the parchment appeared. Jing Yang removed the ruler and used both hands to pull the parchment downwards. Finally, the parchment came out from the gap. The teenagers were overjoyed. Jing Yang crossed to where Angelina and Tim were and showed them the parchment. He shone his torch on it. It was no longer white; age and humidity in the bunker had taken its toll on it. Jing Yang unfolded the parchment. There was a large drawing on it; the ink had faded slightly but the outlines were still clear. There were no smudges. Occupying centre spot in the parchment was a plan of an underground passage, starting from a room in the bunker. The passage ran towards the reservoir and then appeared to go into it; there were dotted lines here. The teenagers did not understand the significance of the dotted lines. On the left of the map was a plan of a drainage tunnel. A wheel had been drawn in one of its bends.

Jing Yang looked at his watch. It was now eleven o'clock. They were already very late.

'No time to pore over the map now,' said Jing Yang. 'Got to get home now or Angelina will be in trouble.'

'What's the time now, Jing Yang?' asked Angelina.

'Eleven o'clock,' said Jing Yang.

'*Alamak*! I will be fried alive if I don't go back now,' exclaimed Angelina.

Satisfied with their find, the teenagers dashed out into the corridor and made their way to the escape route passage. The pattering of their feet echoed through the corridor. At the stairwell, Jing Yang lifted Angelina onto the cat ladder. He stood aside to let Tim climb up the ladder and went up last. Soon, they were out of the door on top of the slope. Tim slammed the door shut and locked it. They had no time to check the surroundings; they bolted towards the steps near the bunker's exit door, clambered down the slope and ran along the lane heading towards the roundabout. They did not bother to look out for the guard. When they were safely down the three flights of steps and on the roadside, Jing Yang hailed a taxi and they got into it.

They were exhausted by their little adventure and sat in the taxi with their eyes shut. By the time the taxi turned into Hougang Avenue 5, where Angelina's block of flats was, it was already half past eleven. Angelina looked up at her flat. Her mother was standing outside the flat, in the corridor. She was now looking down at the taxi. They got off the taxi, and the boys accompanied Angelina up to the fourth storey, where her mother was waiting. She was now glaring at the three teenagers.

'Don't you know it's past eleven o'clock?' Angelina's mother asked her.

'Aunty,' chorused the two boys. 'Sorry, aunty, we are late.'

Angelina waved them off. She was telling them she would handle her mother; she did not need their help.

'Bye, Angelina,' said Jing Yang. As Angelina walked into the flat with her mother, she waved her mobile phone at Jing Yang. He understood it to mean that he should SMS her that night.

The boys crossed the carpark behind Angelina's block and walked up to their house. The spotlights in the porch had been turned off. It meant that Tim's mother had gone to bed. She would always turn off the spotlights before she got into bed. It was safe for them to go into the house. They climbed up the gate and jumped into the garden. Then they scaled the pipe on one side of the façade. Tim was first to reach the balcony of Jing Yang's room. He was careful not to make any sound. It would be dreadful if his mother woke up and caught them red-handed. Jing Yang was the next to push himself into the balcony.

'Let's get into bed before your mother wakes up and spots us. We'll talk tomorrow,' whispered Jing Yang.

Tim nodded as he opened the door and peeked into the hallway. He tip-toed across the hall to his bedroom and entered it. Seeing Tim safely in his own bedroom, Jing Yang closed the door behind him and sat down at his desk. He pulled out the parchment from his bag and unfolded it. He looked at the map for a long while. Should he show the map to Mr Wang? There was no indication of any treasure on the map. It was just a plan of a secret tunnel with graphic instructions on how to enter it. The tunnel seemed to end under the reservoir. Obviously, the location of any treasure would be not on the map, Jing Yang told himself. After all, this was a plan of the secret tunnel made when

241

the tunnel was built. If the Japanese had put treasure in the tunnel, it would not show on the map. It would show on a map that the Japanese had drawn up. Where was this other map? For the moment, it was important to find out what lay in the secret tunnel. There just might be some clue in the secret tunnel. He had to go into it soon, perhaps, the next night. But, it would be too dangerous for Angelina. He had to leave her out of his plan to explore the secret tunnel.

Just then, Angelina texted him on his mobile phone. He had forgotten to text her. She was saying a goodnight and sweet dreams to him. He wanted to text her to find out whether she had got a scolding from her mother, but decided against it. He would talk to her the next morning on their way to school, he told himself. He also texted a goodnight and sweet dreams to her. Though he was good at English and therefore good at using words, when it came to things such as romance, he was a nerd. He put away the map and went to bed. It had been a tiring night for him. Everything else had to wait till tomorrow; he had to get his forty winks first, he said to himself. Soon he was in dreamland.

15 *THE TREASURE MAP?*

The next morning, when the three friends met outside Jing Yang's house, Jing Yang fired some questions at Angelina as soon as he saw her.

'Did your mother give you a big scolding?' Jing Yang asked Angelina. 'She looked so angry last night.'

Angelina shook her head. 'Actually, she wanted to, but when she saw us together, she changed her mind. She was not worried anymore,' said Angelina. 'She trusts you. She thinks you will take good care of me.'

'Are we going into the secret passage tonight?' asked Tim.

'Not just yet,' said Jing Yang. 'First we need to visit Mr Wang to get his advice.'

'Oh! That's right. I plain forgot about him,' said Tim.

'Are we seeing Mr Wang this evening?' asked Angelina.

'Nope. Sooner – after school today,' said Jing Yang. He was very anxious about the secret passage. If he could, he wanted to go into the secret passage straightaway. But, there were more important things to do first. He had to seek Mr Wang's advice first, after all the secret passage could be fraught with danger – booby traps and all that. Mr Wang, with his history background, could have some knowledge of such things and could tell them if it was safe in the secret passage. Now, he had to get Tim into his little plan for the night, but without attracting Angelina's attention. Jing Yang thought it best to leave that task till the afternoon was over, when they were home, just in case Tim should leak out his plan inadvertently. For Angelina's safety, he could not afford to let that happen.

In the school corridors, students were gathering in big and small groups, exchanging bits of gossip. It was noisy now in school as the three friends walked into the quadrangle from the corridor, heading towards their classes seated in columns on the tarmac.

'My last period ends at half past one. See you at the meeting point,' said Tim. Then he mingled with the secondary one students on the left of the quadrangle.

'See you,' said Jing Yang and Angelina as they headed for their class at the rear of the quadrangle.

Jing Yang was too excited that whole morning. He could not pay attention in class. Angelina noticed that Jing Yang could not keep still during their lessons. But, it was not that he was being playful. His mind was far away – beyond the topics for physical science, mathematics and the other subjects that were being discussed in their classroom. He was also oblivious to the din in the classroom when it was a free period as the subject teacher was absent from school.

Nobody, except Angelina, noticed his strange behaviour. To his classmates and teachers, he was his normal self.

After school, the three friends met at the table outside the art room. Jing Yang called Mr Wang to check whether he was free that afternoon. Mr Wang told them to come anytime after three o'clock. As they had some time on their hands, they decided to have their lunch at Compasspoint. The shopping centre was big so they could browse through the shops after their meal.

Going for lunch with the two boys was not simply

visiting the neighbourhood coffeeshop. It was invariably eating at fast-food restaurants. These boys had no qualms about spending six dollars on a meal. It was a different case for Angelina who had to scrimp and save on her lunches so that she could buy things she needed, things such as hair clips and stationery. Now that she was with Jing Yang every day and they would dine together in the afternoons, she no longer needed to buy her own lunches. There had been savings for her since she and Jing Yang got close to each other. The three friends went into the McDonald's outlet in the basement for a hamburger and Coca-Cola.

It was quarter to three when the three friends reached Hai Sing Close. Mr Wang expected his guests to be punctual as he himself was always punctual. But being too early for an appointment with him was another matter. Just in case Mr Wang might not like early birds, they stood outside his house waiting for three o'clock to arrive.

At three o'clock sharp, Jing Yang rang the doorbell. Mr Wang came to the gate. He was in a plain white singlet and brown shorts. Apparently, he did not like to dress up for visitors. He ushered them into his study and waved them to their seats. Then he sat back in his plush swivel chair and turned to Jing Yang.

'What have you got for me to look at this time?' Mr Wang asked Jing Yang.

Jing Yang reached into a pocket, produced the parchment, unfolded it and handed it to Mr Wang with both hands.

'Let's see now,' said Mr Wang as he removed his glasses and pored over the map in his hands. 'Mmm. This seems to be drawn many, many years ago. It looks like a plan of an underground tunnel originating from an underground bunker and terminating right under the big oblong thing here.'

'That must be the reservoir on top of Fort Canning Park,' said Jing Yang. 'Why are there dotted lines in the reservoir? Surely the tunnel cannot be underwater.'

'That's not underwater, Jing Yang. The dotted lines simply denote the tunnel burrowing in the ground under the reservoir,' said Mr Wang. 'Quite ingenious really,' he continued. 'The British had that type of technology as early as the 1940s.'

'Won't the tunnel collapse?' asked Tim. 'There's so much water above it.'

'Good question, Tim,' said Mr Wang. He paused for a long while. He was deep in thought. 'Ordinary soil will not take the weight of the water pressing down on the tunnel. It has to be limestone beneath the reservoir.'

'Limestone?' said Jing Yang.

'Yes, Limestone is stronger than concrete,' said Mr Wang. 'Most likely, the entire hill sits on a deposit of limestone. That's why the British picked this hill to build the bunker.'

'Is there treasure in the secret tunnel?' asked Tim.

'There's no indication of any treasure on this map,' said Mr Wang. 'But why would the British build a secret passage in a bunker that was already secret in the first place?'

'I don't understand what you are saying, sir,' said Tim.

'Tim, what Mr Wang means is that the bunker was a secret place, so it was already a good hiding place, therefore, there was no need for other hiding places,' said Jing Yang.

'Yes, Jing Yang is right,' said Mr Wang. 'It confounds me why they built this secret passage.'

Turning to Jing Yang, Mr Wang asked, 'How did you get this map?'

'It was hidden behind a sink in one of the rooms,' said Jing Yang. 'Colonel Cooper told us about it.'

'Colonel Cooper?' said Mr Wang. 'One of the spirits?'

'Yes,' said Jing Yang. 'He said he was the one who designed the secret passage.'

'He's also the one who designed the bunker,' Angelina

chipped in.

'I see. I see,' said Mr Wang. 'So I am right. This chap Cooper is an engineer.'

'What's this thing?' asked Tim, pointing at a wheel on the drawing. The teenagers had gotten up from their seats and were now crowding around Mr Wang.

'This appears to be some kind of contraption,' said Mr Wang. 'See this arrow descending onto some dotted lines in the corridor, next to the end of the Fortress Commander's Office?'

'Dotted lines meaning a tunnel under the corridor?' asked Tim.

'Yes, this symbol over here indicates a drain tunnel,' said Mr Wang. He was fingering a pictogram where the dotted lines originated from. 'So the dotted lines represent the drainage tunnel running along the length of the corridor over here and then turning into the other corridor over there.'

'This wheel in the tunnel under the corridor has a pair of long thin lines going into the Fortress Commander's Office,' said Jing Yang. 'Is that a secret door?' Jing Yang was now fingering a rectangular outline on a wall.

'How do you know?' asked Mr Wang.

'Colonel Cooper told us,' answered Jing Yang. 'He spoke of a secret door at one end of the wall in the room.'

'We saw an outline of a door on the wall yesterday,' said Tim. 'It must be true.'

'Very likely. Very likely,' said Mr Wang. 'This chap Colonel Cooper hid the wheel mechanism under the bunker so that nobody would be able to find the secret door. Clever chap he is.'

'But why this elaborate setup when the bunker was already a secret place?' Mr Wang wondered aloud. He reached for a mug behind him on the desk and motioned the teenagers to help themselves to the packets of drinks he had placed on a side table next to their seats.

'Did you ask Colonel Cooper what they kept in the

secret tunnel?' Mr Wang asked Jing Yang.

'No, we didn't. We didn't think of it,' said Jing Yang.

'We didn't have enough time yesterday,' Angelina said. 'They were worried my mother would scold me so we left in a hurry.'

'This map looks like a draft that Colonel Cooper prepared for his own use,' said Mr Wang. 'See? There are no references to the functions of the various rooms in the bunker. Colonel Cooper knew what they were used for, and since this map was his own copy, he did not feel the need to label the rooms.'

'Is it safe to go into the secret tunnel?' asked Jing Yang. He had been eager to pose this question to Mr Wang since they entered his house.

'Safe? Of course, it is,' said Mr Wang. 'You guys went into the bunker, didn't you?'

'Yes,' they chorused.

'Did you feel it was dangerous in there?' asked Mr Wang.

'No,' they chorused.

'It's a perfect example of British technology at its best,' said Mr Wang. 'These guys thought of everything. They even studied the soil to make sure it could support a bunker before they went ahead to build it. It's no wonder it has stood the test of time.'

'But, the secret passage runs under the reservoir,' said Angelina. 'What if it collapses?'

'Ha!' exclaimed Mr Wang. 'That would never happen – not in a million years.'

'That long?' Tim exclaimed in surprise.

'It's just a saying, just a saying, young man,' retorted Mr Wang. 'So are you planning to explore the secret tunnel soon?'

'Are you coming along with us?' asked Tim.

'Me?' said Mr Wang in surprise. 'Oh no, not me. I'm too old for such things. So it is you guys who want to go on an adventure, right?'

'Yes,' said Jing Yang and Angelina.

'Of course,' said Tim.

'Does your aunt, and your mother know?' Mr Wang asked Jing Yang and Tim. There was silence in the room. Jing Yang was afraid that Mr Wang would tell his aunt about their plan if he found out they had not told Aunt Dorothy their plan.

'I take your silence to mean that she does not know anything about this,' said Mr Wang. 'No need to look so worried. I won't snitch on you.' The boys heaved a sigh of relief. Mr Wang could be counted on to keep their little secret after all.

'Don't you feel excited about the possibility of finding treasure in the secret tunnel?' asked Angelina.

'My dear girl, I am a historian, an academic,' said Mr Wang. 'I lust for knowledge – but never for gold bars or jewellery.'

'Last?' said Angelina. 'What's that?'

'It's lust – l-u-s-t,' said Jing Yang. 'It means eager desire.'

'Oh I see,' said Angelina.

'If you guys manage to find treasure, I will be very happy for you,' said Mr Wang. 'You will be rich! But, remember, treasures such as these which were looted belong to humanity. We don't own them, so don't forget to do the right thing.'

'What right thing are you talking about?' asked Tim. He was clueless. From the expression on her face, it was clear Angelina was equally clueless too.

'When I mentioned doing the right thing, I was suggesting you donate it to a charitable foundation, for projects that benefit the poor, the underprivileged, and the old,' said Mr Wang. 'But, don't take it to heart, it's only a suggestion. After all, if you find any treasure, it's yours.'

'Of course, we will not keep the treasure for ourselves,' said Jing Yang.

'No, we won't,' agreed Angelina.

'We are doing it for thrills,' said Tim.

'One more thing, be careful down there,' said Mr Wang. 'You won't know what you will find there. It's likely nobody has been in the tunnel since the war ended. That's nearly seventy years ago.'

'Don't worry. We'll be very careful,' said Jing Yang.

'And Mr Savage,' said Mr Wang. 'This guy is treasure-crazy. Don't give him a chance to hurt you again.'

'We won't,' said Jing Yang.

'Be off now, and good luck in your search for treasure,' said Mr Wang. He got up and showed the teenagers to the door. As they were walking along Hai Sing Close towards the boys' house, they talked about exploring the secret passage.

'When are we going into the bunker?' asked Angelina. 'I've got to cook up some excuse to give to my mother.'

'We just went there yesterday and your mother wasn't too happy when we got home,' said Jing Yang. 'Let's give it a rest for one or two days, shall we?'

'But she wasn't really angry,' said Angelina, 'just annoyed.'

'Still, it is not too nice to do such things to annoy your mother,' said Jing Yang.

'Oh, alright, you win,' said Angelina.

'So we aren't going after all?' asked Tim. 'Then I can do my own things for a change.'

Tim went into the house, while Jing Yang accompanied Angelina home. It was already half past five when they waved goodbye to each other outside Angelina's flat.

Jing Yang hurriedly returned home. He had to tell Tim his plans for the night. It was unlikely for Angelina to talk to Tim for the rest of the day, so it was safe for Tim to know the plan now.

Tim was with his mother in the kitchen. She was preparing dinner and it was usual practice for mother and son to chat about the things that had happened at school that day. It was their way of bonding with each other.

Mother and son were close. Tim would confide in his mother for she always lent a listening ear whenever he met with problems at school.

Jing Yang waited till the family-bonding session was over before he poked his head into the kitchen. He beckoned Tim to follow him up to his room.

There, with the door closed behind them, they talked about their impending visit to the bunker.

'I thought we are not going there so soon,' said Tim. 'Why the sudden change in mind?'

'I don't want Angelina to tag along. It's bound to be dangerous,' said Jing Yang. 'I don't want her around.'

'What if she finds out?' asked Tim.

'She won't,' said Jing Yang. 'Between now and tonight, both of us won't be talking to her.'

'What will happen when she finds out after the whole thing is over?' asked Tim.

'Let me worry about it, then,' said Jing Yang. 'Remember, we set out at half past eight.'

'Sure thing,' said Tim. 'What shall we bring along?'

'Let me see – torch, matches, biscuits, water bottle, pen knife, and bandage,' said Jing Yang, flicking his fingers up one by one as he read out the list. 'And don't forget the Godell prism and the map.'

After dinner, the two boys packed their bags and bided their time waiting for Tim's mother to finish with the washing up in the kitchen. They tried hard not to arouse her suspicion that evening. Tim had helped his mother dry the crockery and the cutlery – something he did regularly. Jing Yang had disappeared into his bedroom as usual. At half past eight, when the boys were sure that Tim's mother had retired into her bedroom for the night, they strapped their backpacks behind them, slipped out into the balcony, and climbed down the pipe into the garden. Then they climbed over the gate into the lane in front of the house.

The boys were about to turn into Lorong Low Koon when they heard footsteps coming from the carpark on their right. They craned their necks. It was Angelina running towards them, with her ponytail bobbing along behind her as she ran up to them. She had been standing at the bollards, next to the carpark, waiting for them to come out of the house. Though Jing Yang had tried to hide from Angelina his plan to explore the secret passage that night, this girl had seen through his pretence almost effortlessly.

'Aw! What are you doing here?' asked Jing Yang. He was annoyed. In his mind, he was trying to figure out how she had found out about their trip. He was so sure he had not given the game away. Did this girl have sixth sense or some kind of power he did not know about?

'Hi Tim,' said Angelina. She was panting as she pulled up the straps of the backpack on her back.

'How did you find out?' asked Tim.

'Let's get out of here before your mother hears us,' said Jing Yang. The teenagers had been too surprised at Angelina's appearance to notice they were attracting attention.

Farther up Lorong Low Koon, when the group was out of earshot of Jing Yang's house, they stopped.

'You can't come along with us, Angelina,' said Jing Yang.

'Why not?' asked Angelina.

'Because it's too dangerous!' said Jing Yang. 'We don't know what can happen to us. We might be caught.'

'I don't care,' said Angelina. 'I just want to be with you,' said Angelina.

'Why don't you listen to me just this one time?' Jing Yang pleaded with her. But Angelina was adamant in going along with them.

'You certainly are a stubborn girl,' said Tim. 'Let her come along if she wants to,' said Tim. 'It's getting late. We don't have all night to argue with her.'

Jing Yang glanced at his watch. It was now a quarter to nine. He looked up into the air for a few seconds and then pronounced reluctantly, 'Oh, alright. You can come along.'

'Hurray! All for one and one for all,' said Angelina to the chagrin of Jing Yang. She was glad to be part of the adventure tonight.

16 *CAUGHT AGAIN!*

It took a while for Jing Yang to accept Angelina's unexpected presence. It was only when they reached Dhoby Ghaut MRT station that he spoke. He updated her on their plan; he did not want her to spoil their plan for the night. Now, he had an additional load on his mind – her safety. If Mr Savage caught him or Tim, he could accept the situation, but what if Mr Savage also caught Angelina. He was in a dilemma now; he did not know how to protect her if they were caught together. This man was too strong for them to handle. Angelina was now ahead of the two boys, sauntering along the footpath outside the MRT station. This girl did not realise the danger they were heading into, Jing Yang thought to himself. Indeed, she did not; she merely thought they were having an adventure. Her idea of adventure was having fun and being with the person she liked. It was a simple idea for a simple-minded girl like Angelina.

'Did you remember to bring the Godell prism?' asked Jing Yang. He suddenly remembered the all-important crystal. It would be of great help to them tonight.

'Yes, I did,' said Tim. 'But, it wasn't easy getting it out of Mum's room. She was in there for ages.'

It was now half past nine. In the moonlight, they could see the sky above them. But the open space around them was a different matter. The smattering of lamp-posts around the park did not help to lift the outlines of the structures in it out of the darkness. But, it was the ideal setting for the three teenagers. It would help them greatly in their stealth mission while they stole about that night. It was not a weekend so the park was almost deserted. The last they had seen of the guard, he was still at the guard post. He did not seem to have off-days. He was always on duty whenever they were on the hill. There was no one else loitering around, except the three of them. The night was still − there was not even a breeze to sway the branches of the trees around them.

They crept to the concrete structure in single file. But, alas, they had forgotten to dress in dark clothes, their light-coloured attire reflected whatever light was available around them. They could not blend into the dark background.

In the dead of the night, anything that moved could be heard. Their footsteps were hardly silent as they stepped on the crisp dry leaves strewn on the ground.

At the concrete structure, they leaned against the wall next to the metal door. Tim inserted a key into the keyhole and it clicked into position. The lock had not been changed. He opened the door and the three of them stepped onto the landing in the stairwell. The skylight above them offered some light into the stairwell. But they needed their torches to light up the cat ladder. One by one, they grabbed the rungs of the ladder and made their way down to the bottom of the stairwell, landing by landing. At the bottom of the stairwell, they took a breather before filing past the escape route passageway into the corridor where the mini-gallery was located. The bunker was eerily silent and dark, except for the areas where the light from their torches fell on. Though they were sure there was no one in the bunker, they were hesitant about speaking to one another, so Jing Yang gesticulated whenever he needed to give instructions to the two behind him. They could see the LED light from an emergency exit sign on top of the doorway into the Signals Control Room at the end of the corridor ahead of them. There was a right-angle bend in the corridor at this point; they were near the Fortress Commander's Office. Jing Yang was the first to step on the metal drain cover beneath his feet in the corridor. The metal grating vibrated under the weight of his feet. He paused for a moment, and then resumed his pace; there was nobody in the bunker at this late hour. They turned the bend in the corridor – the two boys in front and Angelina a few steps behind. Suddenly in front of the two boys was a large dark figure. As the light from their torches fell onto the figure, they realised, albeit too late, that it was Mr Savage standing in front of them. The boys had walked straight into the arms of Mr Savage. He had been lying in wait for them at the bend in the corridor. He grabbed the two boys and held them tightly. His arms were now full. They had no room for Angelina who had just come up in front of him. Jing Yang and Tim shouted for Angelina to run. But she was too shocked to move. And she could not leave them behind. Jing Yang kept yelling and shouting for her to run as the boys struggled to free themselves of the guide's grip on them. Alas, he was too strong for them. Their struggles were futile against his brute strength.

'Go, Angelina, go,' Jing Yang shouted again. 'Go get help!'

It was then that Angelina realised she was their only hope. She turned around and dashed for the cat ladder at the end of the passage. She was crying, but she could not stop running, she told herself. Her friends' freedom depended on her getting help. She scaled the cat ladder onto the first landing. She stumbled onto the landing. Then she picked herself up and climbed up the next set of ladders. She dared not look down. She was afraid Mr

Savage would be down below her. Her tears were getting in the way of her vision. She wiped them with a hand. By the time she was on the final set of ladders, her fingers kept slipping off the rungs of the ladder. Finally she climbed onto the landing next to the door. She turned the knob and dashed out. There was nobody around. She had to seek help but her mind was in a frenzy. Her thoughts flashed to the guard post and the guard there. He could help her, she thought. She ran to the steps in front of the Fort Canning Centre, clambered down the flight of steps, almost missing one, and made for the guard post. The guard had heard her footsteps pounding along the lane. He was now walking up the lane towards her. She stopped in front of him and stammered some words. They were unintelligible to him; she was uttering gibberish. She caught her breath and tried again.

Pointing up the slope, she said to him, 'My friends – a bad man has caught them. Help them.'

'Where are they?' asked the guard.

'Up there,' said Angelina. 'Come quick. Follow me.' She did not wait for his answer. She grabbed him by the arms as she turned around to run back up the lane. He followed her. When she got to the top of the steps, she stopped to wait for the guard to catch up with her. There were lives at stake and he was moving too leisurely, she thought. When they reached the concrete structure, she stopped and looked at him pleadingly. The door was ajar. The guard opened the door and walked onto the landing in the stairwell. He took out a torch and shone it down the stairwell. Then he grabbed the top rung of the cat ladder and swung onto the ladder. He beckoned her to follow him down the ladder. She did not hesitate. She was too worried about Jing Yang and Tim to think clearly. She climbed down the ladder after him. Once they were at the bottom of the stairwell, the guard led the way up the passageway into the corridor. He was not using his torch now. Could it be because having been on night duty for years, he had become accustomed to dark places and so did not need the use of a torch to guide him around a place? But it was as if he was familiar with the surroundings. But it could not be so, for the bunker was not under his charge.

The unlikely pair negotiated the bend in the corridor, walked past the Fortress Commander's Office where the corridor forked, and headed for the other rooms in the bunker. The guard peeped into the rooms as he passed them. Suddenly, behind them came a booming voice. It was familiar to Angelina. It belonged to Mr Savage. Angelina shuddered in her thoughts.

'Look at what we have got here!' Mr Savage exclaimed.

Angelina and the guard turned around. There in front of them was Mr Savage. He was alone. He had quietly come up behind them. Angelina hid behind the guard, clutching his shirt as she stood peering at the burly figure.

'Well! What a catch we have today! First, two young boys and now a little girl,' Mr Savage continued.

'Yes, it's quite a nice catch, if I may say so myself,' said the guard. He dragged Angelina out from behind him. She was too shocked for words; she had walked into a trap. These two men were in cahoots with each other. There was no way to save Jing Yang and Tim. She could not even save herself now. Angelina burst into tears.

'Now, don't be teary eyed, young lady,' said Mr Savage. 'I will let you join your friends shortly.'

Mr Savage turned to the guard. 'Seah, these youngsters are spoiling our plans. We have to figure out what to do with them. We can't have them meddling around in the bunker.'

'Where are the other two?' asked Seah.

'In the gun operations room,' said Mr Savage. 'Put her in there with them.' He handed to the guard a set of keys and walked off in the direction he had come from.

'Come with me, girl,' said Seah. He grasped her arm firmly and dragged her to the next fork in the corridor. He made a left turn and stopped in front of the locked room. 'Your friends are in here. You need not be worried anymore. You will all be together again.' He unlocked the door and pushed her into the dark room. There were two figures heaped together on the floor at the far end of the room. They were wriggling. The guard pulled her alongside the figures and sat her down next to them. He then tied her hands behind her and gagged her. Then he left the room.

The figure next to Angelina leaned onto her. It had to be Jing Yang, she thought. In the darkness, all she could see was a silhouette, but the outline it made against the white wall was unmistakable. She collapsed onto the figure, sobbing. The two figures made muffled sounds; they were trying to talk to her. Soon her eyes became accustomed to the dark room and she could see more details in the room. The light-coloured T-shirts that the two figures were wearing were reflecting the light from the underside of the door. Angelina was sure it was Jing Yang she was leaning on, and it was Tim next to him.

There was little activity in the room the next fifteen minutes. Jing Yang was busy thinking of a solution to their predicament. He had got them into the mess and he had to get them out of it now. The only way out was to enlist the help of the spirits in the room. They were around alright; Jing Yang could feel them in the chilly breeze that seemed to move around the room in spurts here and there. It was just that they could not talk to him. Jing Yang asked himself why this was so. It had to do with the spirits having no material object they could hook onto, he told himself. There had to be a way to make contact with these two spirits and he was determined to find it, even if it took him all night. The crystal bracelet he was wearing on his wrist seemed to be of no help at all. No matter how he concentrated on the bracelet, there was no response from the spirits in the room.

Then he remembered they had brought along the

Godell prism. It was in Tim's pocket. He tried to recall what Aunt Dorothy had said about the power of the Godell prism. His mind floated to the day they first laid eyes on the Godell prism. Aunt Dorothy had said something about its ability to cause magnetic waves to vibrate simultaneously in different spectrums, transferring electrical energy and enhancing contact between spectrums. He recalled that she had said it could communicate with another dimension. That meant it could communicate with the spirits directly, without the spirits entering another object. Just what else did she say? Yes, she did mention something about an eclipse of the sun giving immense power to the prism. What was the date she had said that the eclipse would take place? He remembered now what she had said to him that day – the eclipse would take place at about seven o'clock on 22nd July 2009. Today was the 21st July 2009. In a few hours it would be the fateful day, he told himself. But it would be too long a wait. He had to do something now.

Did the Godell prism have enough power to summon the spirits? He had to try something. He could not wait any longer. Jing Yang elbowed Tim. His mouth was gagged, so he could not tell Tim what he wanted him to do. It was too dark for Jing Yang to see him; he could not gesticulate to Tim. There was one thing left to do. The prism was in Tim's pocket. If he and Tim were really related by blood, then Tim could sense what he was trying to tell him. Jing Yang pushed himself over, falling onto Tim's lap. Then he used his head to nudge Tim on his hip, near the pocket where the Godell prism was in. Tim seemed to be looking at him. Jing Yang hoped Tim would understand what he was trying to tell him. Somehow, they had to use the Godell prism to make contact with the spirits in the room. Tim was responding now; he was wriggling his hips, apparently trying to empty the pocket. Jing Yang used his chin to nudge the prism out of Tim's pocket. It was tediously slow work; he had to move his chin to and fro continually. The constant rubbing was hurting his cheeks.

Finally, the pouch which the prism was in was beginning to appear at the opening of the pocket. Just a bit more work and the prism would fall out of the pocket, they thought in unison. Finally, there was a soft thud on the floor; the Godell prism had landed on the floor. Jing Yang pushed himself over Tim's body to get to the other side where the prism lay. He could not see the prism as his hands were tied behind his back. He could only feel it with his hands. He groped around behind him and grasped the object. He squeezed the prism out of the pouch and clutched the prism tightly in his hands.

Now, the prism was in his hands. He only had to concentrate on communicating with the spirits in the room. He was sweating profusely now but he did not let it bother him. He just could not give up. It was their only hope. Five minutes into the activity, he felt the knots on the rope behind him begin to loosen. Goose pimples were popping all over his arms. The spirits were behind him now, helping to untie his hands, he thought. He had to do his part. He struggled to free his hands. It seemed to be working; he could almost squeeze his left palm through an opening in the knot. Then he wriggled his hands free of the knot.

Hurray! The rope was now unravelling from his wrists. He had freed himself. Jing Yang got up and unmuzzled his mouth. He heaved a sigh of relief. Now he had to free the other two quickly, before those wretched men came back. He untied the knot behind Tim's hands first and then turned his attention to Angelina's hands. When her hands became unbound, she grabbed hold of Jing Yang and cried. This girl was so emotional, Jing Yang thought to himself. Tim had removed the gag himself and was now standing next to them. He had retrieved his mother's precious crystal from the floor and was now looking around the dark room. He went to the door and tried turning the knob but it would not budge. The door was locked. In his confused state of mind, he had forgotten he held the key to the door in his pocket. Jing Yang reminded him when he and Angelina walked to him.

As Tim searched his pocket for the keys, Jing Yang suddenly remembered the spirits. In his anxiety to release the others, he had forgotten it was the spirits who had helped them. He told the other two about what had happened. It was strange; they had heard no voices in the room. Evidently, the spirits could not speak to them at all. The Godell prism could not let that happen, but it had enough power to help the spirits unravel the knot on Jing Yang's bound wrists.

'Thank you, Colonel Cooper. Thank you Major Todds,' the teenagers said at once as they bowed. The air in the room around them suddenly felt icy cold. It had to be the spirits responding to their grateful gesture.

When Tim opened the door, the three teenagers walked out into the corridor. They were careful not to make a sound, just in case the two men were still in the bunker. Jing Yang motioned Tim to shut the door and lock it. This way, the men would think that they were still in the locked room. They moved stealthily around the bunker, taking pains not to utter a single word though they were excited at being free at last. It had certainly not been an enjoyable experience for them – being bound, gagged and locked up. They had to be extra careful from now onwards, to avoid a repeat of that unpleasant experience.

'I don't think those men are around,' said Jing Yang.

'Shall we go home then?' asked Angelina.

'No, not yet. We haven't explored the secret passage yet,' said Jing Yang.

'Yes, we haven't found the treasure yet,' said Tim in agreement.

'But, what if they catch us again?' asked Angelina. 'We will be doomed!'

'We have checked out all the rooms here. They don't

seem to be around. I think they have gone off and won't be back till tomorrow,' said Jing Yang.

'But I'm sure the guard is still in the park,' said Angelina. 'He's on duty you know.'

'All the more why he won't be coming into the bunker tonight,' said Jing Yang.

'Let's not waste time arguing,' said Tim. 'Let's go into the secret passage.'

'Yes, we should, but first of all we need to talk to the spirits. Thank them properly, you know,' said Jing Yang, pointing to the Fortress Commander's Office.

The three friends trooped into the room where the two wax models were seated. They stood in front of the wax models.

'Put the Godell prism on the desk, Tim,' said Jing Yang. Tim took out the crystal from his pocket and placed it in the centre of the table, in front of General Percival. 'Now join me in concentrating on the Godell prism.'

'What's that thing on my desk?' asked General Percival's look-alike.

'Colonel Cooper, you are here!' said Jing Yang.

'Thank you, sir,' said all three teenagers at once.

'Now what was that for?' asked General Percival's look-alike. 'What did I do?'

'Thank you for rescuing us just now, sir,' said Jing Yang.

'Oh, that little thing,' said General Percival's look-alike. 'It was nothing at all, nothing at all. Todds and I were merely doing our part as gentlemen. We just can't stand bullies.'

'Sir, is Major Todds here?' asked Tim. He was curious that General Simmons' look-alike was silent.

'Well, that old chap. I believe he has gone to visit the lavatory,' said General Percival's look-alike. 'Having the runs, you know.'

'You have to pass motion too?' asked Tim in disbelief.

'Of course, young lad,' said General Percival's look-alike. 'Don't you?'

'Sir, can you thank Major Todds for us?' asked Angelina.

'Why, sure of course, young lass,' said General Percival's look-alike.

'Now, why are you here again?' asked General Percival's look-alike. 'It's dangerous in here with those two men on the prowl.'

'Sir, do you know what they are looking for?' asked Jing Yang.

'Young lad, you haven't answered my question yet,' said General Percival's look-alike.

'Sorry, sir. We intend to explore the secret passage tonight,' said Jing Yang.

'What? With those men around?' exclaimed General Percival's look-alike.

'They are not in the bunker, sir,' said Jing Yang. 'We intend to do a quick check and then run off before they get back.'

'So you know when they will be back?' asked General Percival's look-alike.

'We are taking our chances, sir,' said Jing Yang. 'Are these men looking for treasure, sir?'

'Seems to be so,' said General Percival's look-alike. 'I've heard them talking about some gold bars buried under the bunker.'

'But you didn't tell us there were two of them when we were here last,' Tim protested.

'Young lad, you didn't ask me,' said General Percival's look-alike.

'Sir, have you seen any gold in the bunker?' asked Jing Yang.

'No, never did,' said General Percival's look-alike. 'I've been here for nearly seventy years and have yet to come across any gold in the bunker.'

'Oh!' Tim exclaimed in disappointment.

'But, then I haven't gone down into the secret passage

since – since 1942, I believe,' said General Percival's look-alike.

'You haven't?' said Tim. 'But I thought you could fly all over the place.'

'Fly all over the place?' said General Percival's look-alike. 'Goodness me, I can't do that. I can only move around on this level. In fact, I can't even get out of this bunker, even if I want to.'

'Why, sir?' asked Angelina.

'Yes, why indeed, young lass,' said General Percival's look-alike. After a short pause, he continued, 'I was killed in this bunker.'

'You were?' said Angelina.

'Who killed you, sir?' asked Tim.

'How did you die, sir?' asked Jing Yang.

'One question at a time, please,' said General Percival's look-alike, flabbergasted. 'I didn't know that my death was such interesting news.'

'Sorry, sir,' they said at once.

'Sir, tell us how you died, please,' Jing Yang pleaded with him.

'I...I was tortured...and then killed here in the Gun Operations Room,' said General Percival's look-alike. His voice choked with emotion as he spoke. The three teenagers stood glued to the spot. They were shocked. So that was why the Gun Operations Room always felt icy cold when they were in it. Colonel Cooper had been killed there. He was haunting the room. They waited patiently for him to continue his story. 'Those damned Japs – they wanted to know everything about the bunker...so they tortured me, day and night, day and night, for days on end. At first I tried to endure. I really did. But I was no hero. Finally, I just could not take the pain anymore. I caved in and told them about the secret passage.' His voice had fallen to a murmur.

There was an eerie silence in the room. The teenagers felt a cold shiver run through their body. It was a sad story and their hearts went out to Colonel Cooper. He was a victim of a terrible tragedy. He might be no hero to himself, but the three teenagers deemed him to be a hero of the war, for he had served his country selflessly and sacrificed himself.

It took a while before the three friends regained their composure. The voice from General Percival's look-alike had fallen silent, but they were sure he was there. He was merely wallowing in his sorrow. It was Jing Yang who broke the silence.

'Sir, we have to go down into the secret passage now,' said Jing Yang.

'Wish us luck, sir,' said Tim. There was a moment of silence in the room.

'Oh, yes indeed. God speed!' said General Percival's look-alike. He had collected himself by now.

'Thank you, sir,' said Angelina. 'See you later.'

'Bye, sir,' the boys said together.

17 *THE SECRET TUNNEL*

The three teenagers went out into the corridor, to the drain cover next to the lavatory. Jing Yang lifted the cover, praying as he did so. He was hoping the drain tunnel would not be flooded. What luck! There was no water! He would not be drowned after all. But the floor in the tunnel was wet, so were the walls. The tunnel was only big enough for one person to crawl through. Jing Yang told Tim and Angelina to wait for him in the corridor while he went down. He cautioned them to place the cover back into position and then hide themselves if they heard any noise. He placed his hands flat on the sides of the opening, jumped into the tunnel and bent down. He was now on his knees and he would have to crawl on bended knees all the way to the wheel. He tried hard not to touch the sides of the tunnel for they were damp. He did not bring out the map, for he had memorised the map by heart.

Jing Yang took out the torch from a pouch on his waist and pointed it in front of him. The light travelled a long way; it appeared that the tunnel ran parallel to the corridor. He guessed that the end of the tunnel was where the escape route passageway started. He was not going that far tonight. He pointed the torch onto the right wall as he crawled along the tunnel. It was a concrete wall. He had to look out for any openings on this wall. The wheel had to be somewhere along this wall. It was hot and smelly in the tunnel, but he did not mind.

Jing Yang had just moved some twelve feet into the tunnel when his torch shone onto a recess on the wall. It was a square-shaped recess about one-and-a-half-feet wide. He crawled up to the recess and shone the torch into it. There it was – the wheel that was drawn on the map. It was a metal wheel with eight spokes, just like in the drawing. It was about one feet in diameter and the spokes extended beyond the rim of the wheel. Jing Yang tried to sit up in the tunnel, but he could not sit upright. He had to bend slightly. It was an awkward position but it was the best he could do under the circumstances.

Now he had to turn the wheel to open the door in Fortress Commander's Office. He placed a hand on a spoke at the eleven o'clock position and the other hand on a spoke at the five o'clock position and pushed the wheel in a clockwise position. The wheel would not budge. It could be rust that was preventing the wheels from rotating. Then he pushed with all his might. It would not budge either. Jing Yang leaned against the wall for a breather. He needed to think. Did wheels and knobs work the same way? He thought of the tap in his bathroom. He had to turn the knob anti-clockwise to turn on the tap and clockwise to turn off the tap. Yes, perhaps, the wheel worked this way too.

He leaned forward again and grabbed the spokes on the wheel. He turned the spokes in an anti-clockwise movement. There was a slight click in the wheel. He tried again. The wheel could move slightly only. The wheel had not been worked in nearly seventy years so it would take some effort to get it turning again, he thought. Now he had to muster all his strength. He leaned back and rested for a minute. Tim and Angelina were likely to be restless now; they had waited too long. He was tired but he could not give up. They had already gone so far in their quest for adventure.

Jing Yang leaned towards the wheel again. He opened and closed his hands repeatedly. Then he grasped the spokes and gave his all. The wheel was moving! He grabbed a spoke with both hands and pulled it downwards with all his might. The wheel rotated on its axis. There was the sound of something moving in the small gap beyond the recess. He continued turning the wheel in an anti-clockwise direction until it would not move at all. The sound had stopped now. Perhaps, the secret door had opened. He had to find out. Jing Yang turned to face the direction of the drain cover and crawled towards it. Soon he was just below the opening. Tim and Angelina were peering at him. They too had heard the strange sound. Jing Yang placed his palms onto the sides of the opening and lifted himself out of the tunnel. He put the drain cover back in its place. Now they had to check out the Fortress Commander's Office to see if the secret door had really opened.

The three teenagers walked into the Fortress Commander's Office. They bowed to the generals at the desk before moving to the back of the room where the secret door was, behind the wooden cabinet at the right end of the wall. The two wax models were silent. The spirits could be somewhere else in the bunker, they thought. Angelina stood watch at the doorway while the two boys first removed a wooden box blocking the way before dragging the wooden cabinet out from its position at the end of the wall. The boys had to use all their might as the wooden cabinet was heavy. Suddenly, Angelina let out a cry; she had seen the secret opening. The boys stopped their work and craned their necks to look behind the wooden cabinet. It was the secret opening alright. The concrete door had slid down so that the top of the door was flush with the floor surface. It was dark in there. Jing Yang shone his torch into the opening. It was a shaft with walls all round the sides. He directed the light downwards. There was no floor beneath. It was a hole in the floor leading to a tunnel. There was a cat ladder set against the right wall of the tunnel. So this was how they could get down into the tunnel, Jing Yang thought.

'Come, let's pull the cabinet farther away from the opening so that we can get into it,' said Jing Yang. The boys heaved and pulled till the cabinet was about three feet away from the secret opening. It was now just behind the wax model of General Percival. 'Sorry, sir,' muttered Jing Yang.

The three teenagers shone their torches into the secret opening. It was time for them to explore the secret passage. They were visibly excited; they had forgotten it was late and they should be home now. Jing Yang was the first to climb down the cat ladder. He put away his torch. The illumination from the other two teenagers' torches was sufficient for him to see his way down. He found himself on a landing. He took out his torch and shone it around him. There was a wheel, similar to the one in the drain tunnel, on one side of the cat ladder. It had to be for opening and closing the concrete door from within the secret tunnel. Here, the air was stale; it had not moved in ages.

Opposite the cat ladder was a flight of four steps leading down from the landing onto the floor of the tunnel. He waved the other two to come down to join him below. When they were all standing on the landing, Jing Yang led the way down the steps in single file, for the width of the passage was only about three feet wide. They bent their heads here as the ceiling of the passage below them was only about five feet from the floor of the landing. At the bottom of the steps, the passage widened; it was now about six feet wide. They no longer needed to bend their heads as the passage was about ten feet high. There was one more step about three feet in front of them.

The light from their torches revealed a long passage. It

was concrete all around them on the walls and the floor. The ceiling was also concrete, unlike that in the bunker which was of steel beams placed horizontally and slotted neatly between one another. As they traversed the passage, the light from their torches picked up the end wall about eighty feet ahead of them. Jing Yang shone his torch at the end of the tunnel. There was an opening on the right; the tunnel bent at right angle there. They walked down the tunnel and negotiated the turn.

In front of them was a big rectangular room, which was much bigger than a classroom. The big room looked like an underground shelter. Their torches picked out the layout of the room. Directly in front of them was a row of three adjoining metal cages – each about five feet wide and deep, and constructed of iron bars embedded vertically from ceiling to floor. Each cage had a metal grill door. The doors were all open. There was nothing in the cells. A wooden crate sat next to the cage nearest them. There was a table at the far left end of the room. Scattered around the room were four chairs; two hurricane lamps; and three tins of what smelt like kerosene – very old kerosene. Could the hurricane lamps work still? They had to try, for the batteries in their torches were draining all too quickly.

'Did you remember to bring the matches?' Jing Yang asked Tim.

'Yes, I did,' said Tim and he unstrapped his backpack. He put his hand into the bag and groped around. Then he retrieved a box of matches.

Jing Yang picked up a hurricane lamp and filled it with some kerosene from a tin on the floor. Then he placed the lamp onto the table. 'Here! Help me light this lamp,' said Jing Yang to Tim. 'Hope it works.' When lit, the hurricane lamp burst into life, illuminating the room and warming it as well.

'Switch off the torches,' ordered Jing Yang. 'We may need them later. No point in draining the batteries in them.'

The teenagers looked around the room. They were likely to be under the reservoir now, for the walls and the ceiling in the room were moist. There were water marks, in big and small patches, all over the ceiling. There were streaks of water on the walls.

But, the three teenagers were disappointed. Their dismay showed in their faces. There was no treasure to be found – no gold bars, no golden statues, nothing but old furniture and fittings scattered around the room.

'So much work for nothing,' yelled Tim.

Jing Yang and Angelina were silent. They were introverts, preferring to hide their despondency.

'No worries,' said Jing Yang. He was trying to cheer up the other two. 'All is not lost. After all, we did have an adventure in the bunker. That's good enough.' But he was not convincing the others – why, he was not even convincing himself with that remark. Inside, he told himself he had to soldier on. There had to be some truth to the treasure story! He approached the wall near him and placed his fingers over its surface. Perhaps, just perhaps, there was a secret door here somewhere. There had to be one, he told himself. He just could not give up. But, really, would there be another secret door in an already secret tunnel nestled under a secret bunker or was he merely deluding himself?

But, it was in his nature – not giving up despite the odds piled up against him. He had inherited this spirit of perseverance from his scientist parents. Then he recalled Colonel Cooper talking about the secret tunnel. Yes! The map, the map! In his excitement, he had forgotten about the map in his pocket. He dug into his pocket and retrieved the parchment.

'Place it on that table so all of us can see it,' said Tim, pointing at the table at the far end of the room. Jing Yang, Tim and Angelina crowded around the table and Jing Yang unfolded the parchment to reveal Colonel Cooper's map. Jing Yang ran his fingers along the outline of the room they were in. The three cells were shown in the map as rectangular boxes in a corner of the room opposite the passageway they had come in from. At the opposite end of the room were two thick parallel lines drawn some distance apart, running from one wall to the other. Jing Yang was wondering what they represented. He had no idea how to read a plan let alone decipher what the lines meant. He wished Colonel Cooper was down there with them.

'Look, the first parallel line has got two perpendicular dotted lines some distance apart from each other cutting across the parallel line near its centre,' said Tim. 'What are these supposed to represent?'

'Search me,' said Jing Yang, tapping his fingers on the table. He was in deep thought. 'The first parallel line looks like a wall,' Jing Yang continued. 'But what are these dotted lines?' He was now looking at the wall in front of him. 'This parallel line could be this wall here,' he said, tapping the wall in front of the table they were standing at.

'If that is the case, why is there another parallel line behind this line?' asked Tim. 'There's only one wall here.'

'Remember – Mr Wang said something about dotted lines representing something hidden underneath something else?'

'Oh, Angelina, you are not making sense at all,' said Tim. 'Don't speak gibberish.'

'I am not,' said Angelina. 'Tell him I am not speaking nonsense, Jing Yang.'

'Alright, alright,' said Jing Yang. 'Let's have some peace here so that I can think.' Then he paused to collect his thoughts. 'It's just possible that there is a room behind this wall.'

'How can that be?' said Tim in disbelief. 'The distance between the two parallel lines is so small. Even if there is a room, it would be too narrow for any useful purpose. You can't even put this table in there. Why would people make such a small room?'

'Assuming there is such a room,' said Jing Yang, 'then the dotted lines represent a doorway. But, there is no door here. It's just plain wall.'

'Could there be a secret door here too?' asked Angelina.

'A secret door?' asked Tim. He ran his fingers along the surface of the wall in front of him. 'If there is a doorway, and they sealed the doorway and then painted over it, the doorway will show a difference in tone from the rest of the wall. But the colour of the wall is uniform.'

'You are right, Tim,' said Jing Yang. 'But, if they want to hide the doorway on purpose, it is likely they will paint over the entire wall so that the doorway blends in with the wall. Notice the wall here and the other walls are of slightly different tones.'

'Yes, that could be it,' said Angelina. 'You are so smart, Jing Yang.'

'Why are you always fawning over Jing Yang?' said Tim unhappily.

'Gosh! Both of you quit this nonsense,' said Jing Yang. 'We have work to do; we can't be distracted. Come help me move this table away from the wall.' The three teenagers together dragged the table out and left it in the centre of the room.

'We need more light here,' said Jing Yang to Tim. Tim grabbed the other hurricane lamp from the floor, filled it up with kerosene and, after lighting it, brought it to the wall they were examining. He placed it on the floor next to the wall.

'See? On the map, the dotted lines in the first parallel line lie in the centre of the wall,' said Jing Yang, spreading the map onto the surface of the wall. 'That should be right about here. So the doorway, if there is such a doorway, should be here too.' Then he removed the map and stretched both arms in front of him to indicate the rough position of the doorway on the wall in front of him.

'Let's pore over this area with a fine-toothed comb,'

suggested Angelina.

'You guys examine the bottom part of the wall,' said Tim, 'and I will check the top.' They started work on the wall immediately, looking for crevices or gaps – anything that looked suspicious. Tim even knocked on the wall.

'Tim, if there is a brick wall blocking the doorway, all that knocking or tapping isn't going to do any good,' said Jing Yang.

'What do you suggest we do, then?' asked Tim. His fingers were getting sore from all that knocking.

'Let me think,' said Jing Yang. He looked around the room. There were hurricane lamps and chairs; these were of no use to them. There was a wooden crate next to the metal cages. Jing Yang walked over to the crate and lifted the cover. In it were some axes, spades, wrenches and pliers. There was even a bayonet in its sheath. Tim and Angelina also went over to look at the stuff in the crate.

'Wow! A soldier's bayonet!' said Tim, picking up the bayonet and unsheathing it. He was elated. He had never seen a bayonet before, let alone handle one.

'Let me hold this in my hands,' said Angelina to Tim.

'Be careful!' said Jing Yang. 'It's sharp!'

'Don't worry! It's safe to hold,' said Tim. He handed the bayonet to Angelina. 'It's heavy,' she remarked.

'Give me the bayonet,' said Jing Yang to Angelina. He took the bayonet from Angelina and walked to the wall where they suspected the doorway was located. He unsheathed the bayonet and poked the surface of the wall with it, first horizontally, then vertically.

'What are you doing?' asked Angelina.

'Looking for gaps in the wall,' said Jing Yang. 'If they blocked the doorway with a brick wall, there should be gaps around the outline of the doorway.'

'Let me try,' said Tim. He took the bayonet from Jing Yang and worked on the wall with it. He stabbed parts of the wall at random. Then he stopped. The tip of the bayonet had become stuck in one part of the wall; it had penetrated about an inch into the wall. 'Look!' said Tim to the other two. 'There seems to be a gap in this part of the wall.'

With Jing Yang's help, Tim managed to pry the bayonet out of the wall. He stabbed the surface below where the bayonet had been stuck. He chipped away little bits of the wall until the gap widened. Then he worked the bayonet downwards to the lower part of the wall. The gap in the wall was now running vertically down this part of the wall; the outline of a doorway was now taking shape. It could be the left side of the doorway, Tim thought.

'Let's focus on this part here,' said Jing Yang, placing a hand on the wall next to the gap. 'See if we can remove this portion to reveal the room behind the wall. I don't think it's concrete. They wouldn't have poured concrete to cover the doorway. It's more likely to be brick and mortar.'

'Do you need more light?' asked Angelina. She had picked up the hurricane lamp next to the wall and was holding it in her hands.

'Yes, please, Angelina,' said Jing Yang. 'Place it here, next to Tim, on the left.'

'We need something stronger to break the wall,' said Tim. 'Can you get me an axe from the crate over there?' Jing Yang crossed to the other end of the room and took out an axe from the crate. He handed it to Tim.

'Here!' Jing Yang said to Tim. 'Use the sharp edge to penetrate the gap and then turn the axe around; use the back of the axe to strike this portion of the wall to see if we can dislodge the bricks from the wall. The mortar is very old so the bricks should dislodge easily.'

'Be careful!' said Angelina. 'The axe is rusty.'

'Stand away, Angelina,' said Jing Yang. 'Stand on Tim's left. The head of the axe could fly. I don't want you in the way.' He pushed Angelina to the left of Tim and stood in front of her.

Tim swung the axe behind him and chopped into the gap he had made on the wall. He managed to widen the gap and then turned the axe around so that the back of the axe faced the wall. He proceeded to pound the wall with the back of the axe. Finally, there was some progress. The part of the wall on the receiving end of the axe was now receding. The brick was giving way; it was moving out of its lodged position.

'Let me take over,' said Jing Yang. 'Take a rest.' He took the axe from Tim and swung it at the recess in the wall.

'It's working,' said Angelina excitedly. 'The brick is almost dislodged.'

Jing Yang glanced at his watch. It was showing half past eleven. It was way past their bedtime. He wondered whether Aunt Dorothy was asleep or had found out they were not in bed or at home. Then his thoughts turned to Angelina's mother. She would be worried sick by now as her daughter had not returned home. But, they were too near a very important discovery. He just could not give up now, not when news of the treasure was so near.

'Yipee! It's through!' yelled Tim. 'It's through.' He had dislodged the first brick in the wall in front of him. With a thud, the brick landed on the floor on the other side of the wall. He dropped the axe onto the floor and used his hands to push the bits and pieces of brick around the hole through it. He coughed; the dust was getting into his nose and mouth. He peered into the room. It was dark inside and he could not see a single thing. He grabbed his torch and shone it into the hole. He could see the opposite end of the wall – the room was only about five feet wide.

'Let me take a look,' Jing Yang said to Tim.

'Me, too,' said Angelina. Jing Yang let Angelina poke her face into the hole as he shone his torch into it.

'See anything?' Jing Yang asked Angelina. 'See anything?' He was clearly excited.

'The hole's too small,' exclaimed Angelina.

'Let me have a look,' said Jing Yang. Angelina stepped aside to let Jing Yang peep into the hole. The light from his torch illuminated the interior of the room behind the sealed doorway. He could not see the sides of the room.

'Do you have a mirror with you, Angelina?' Jing Yang said to her.

'Yes,' said Angelina. She dug into her pocket for her mirror and passed it to Jing Yang. 'Here!'

Jing Yang took the small round mirror from her and inserted it into the hole using his left hand. Then he trained the light from his torch into the right side of the sealed room. From the reflection in the mirror he could make out two small wooden crates on the floor. One was open. There appeared to be some kind of sticks in the crate. He could not see what these objects were.

Then he switched the things in his hands so that the torch was in his left hand and the mirror in the other hand. The light from the torch was now falling onto the left side of the sealed room. He peered into the reflection in the mirror. There was a warm glow in the corner of the room. Actually, the whole wall was glittering. Jing Yang could not believe his eyes. Was it gold that he saw in the mirror? A big mass of gold glittering away? His jaws dropped! His hands were quivering. He could not contain his excitement.

'Tim, Tim!' he shouted. 'Angelina! The gold; it's here.'

Tim and Angelina felt the excitement in his voice. Jing Yang had to have seen treasure in the sealed room, they figured.

'Let me look!' cried Tim.

'I want to see too,' squealed Angelina.

Jing Yang moved away from the hole and Tim and Angelina pushed their faces into each other as they huddled together in front of the hole. Tim held the mirror in front of him and illuminated the left side of the room with his torch.

'I can see it. It looks like gold,' Tim exclaimed.

'For goodness' sake, don't keep shaking the mirror. I am getting dizzy,' said Angelina. She grabbed his arm and held it tight. 'That's better. *Wah*! So much gold!'

'Is that so?' boomed a voice from behind them, startling them. Tim dropped the mirror he was holding. When they turned around, who did they see but Mr Savage looming in front of them. The guard was standing behind him.

'Seah, look at what we have here – these two little boys and this little girl – again. They are supposed to be upstairs in one of the rooms. They seem to have lost their way. What a pity! Tsk! Tsk!' Mr Savage exclaimed.

'Run!' yelled Jing Yang to Tim and Angelina. 'Quick! Run for your lives!'

'Catch them!' said Mr Savage to the guard. 'Don't let any of them get away.'

Though the three teenagers tried to outrun the two men, they failed to escape their clutches. Mr Savage caught hold of Jing Yang by the collar and dragged him onto the floor. Angelina, who was behind Jing Yang, stopped in her tracks. She was shocked to see Jing Yang being fallen by the burly man. She ran to his side instead of making for the passageway. This gave Mr Savage a chance to grab her by her arm. Tim tried to run past the guard but tripped and fell onto the floor. The guard pounced onto him, catching him by his neck and pinning him onto the ground.

'Quick! Push them into this cage, the one nearest me,' said Mr Savage to the guard. Mr Savage bundled Jing Yang and Angelina into the cage and stood at the doorway. The guard got to his feet and pulled Tim up from the floor. Then he pushed him into the cage the other two teenagers were in.

'There, simple task completed successfully,' said Mr Savage. He was pleased with his catch. 'Go upstairs and get a chain and a padlock. I'll wait here.'

Mr Savage closed the grill gate and stood watch outside the cage. The three teenagers huddled together in the middle of the cage. They could not decide the next course of action. They dared not charge at the grill gate; it was pointless anyway for they were no match for the big man and his strong arms. Besides, the boys feared he would hurt Angelina. All three merely stared at the man looking at them menacingly from outside the cage.

'I don't know how you guys got out of the room upstairs, but you certainly aren't going to get out of this cage,' said Mr Savage, slapping the iron bars of the cage with his hands. 'By the way, thanks very much for finding this secret place for me. I've been looking for it for many, many years. It surprises me that it has been right under my nose the last four years.'

'You monster!' exclaimed Tim. 'You won't get away with it.'

'I won't?' said Mr Savage. 'You mean you won't get away, not this time – not ever. So there is gold behind that wall, after all.' Mr Savage clasped his hands and appeared to be in prayer. 'Thank you for answering my prayers,' he murmured.

'Mr Wang was right! You really are crazy!' said Angelina.

'Mr Wang? Who the heck are you talking about, young girl?' asked Mr Savage.

'Mr Jonathan Wang, your classmate at university,' said Angelina. 'He said you were crazy.'

'Jonathan Wang?' said Mr Savage. He was searching his mind for a match to the name. 'Ah! That busybody Jonathan Wang. Always poking his nose into my affairs. He said I was wrong. Said there was no treasure. Now I have proven him wrong. There IS treasure here after all. Ha! Ha! Ha!' His laughter was sinister and haughty. They had no doubt he was being arrogant, but now he held the upper hand, for they were his prisoners. There was no way he would let them off, they told themselves. Would he kill them to silence them? The thought sent shivers across their bodies.

'My mother is waiting for me to come home,' sobbed Angelina. She was scared and clung onto Jing Yang's side.

Jing Yang put his arms around her. He told himself to be strong. He could not break down; he could not let Angelina see his weak side. Angelina needed him most now. He fought hard to keep the tears from welling up in his eyes. Then he stifled a sigh. He had been silent for the most part of the last ten minutes. He had been trying to think of a way to escape from the two men, but he was now in too confused a state to think clearly. Tim was cursing Mr Savage under his breath. That was all he could do. How he wished he was as strong as Mr Savage. Then he could give Mr Savage a fight for his money.

'Ah! Seah, you are back at last,' said Mr Savage to the guard. He stood watch while the guard wrapped a chain around the grill door and the iron bars of the cage and then padlocked the chain. The guard then pocketed the key.

The two men walked across the room to the wall with a hole in it. They took turns to peep inside.

'Seah, there must be gold in there,' said Mr Savage. 'These kids were screaming that they saw gold; it must be true.'

'We've got to get in there,' said the guard. He picked up the axe the boys had been using and handled it.

'This won't do,' said Mr Savage. 'It's not strong enough to break the wall.'

'I've got a power hammer in the guard post,' said the guard.

'No use!' said Mr Savage. 'There's no electricity in here.'

'Sorry! I forgot,' said the guard. 'What about a sledgehammer? I can borrow one from the contractor's shed in the main building.'

'How are you going to get in?' asked Mr Savage. 'It's past midnight already.'

'You forgot that I am a guard,' said the guard. 'I have the keys to every room on this hill.'

'Ha! Ha! Ha!' said Mr Savage. 'I nearly forgot. Go now.

I'll wait for you here.'

The guard went off and did not return till a half-hour later. When he came back into the room, he was holding a large hammer with a very long wooden handle. The head of the hammer weighed as much as twenty pounds and the stick was about three feet long.

'That's just right!' said Mr Savage as he took the hammer off the guard's hands. He took off his shirt and threw it onto a chair. Then he flexed his muscles and went to work on the wall with a hole in it. The brick-and-mortar wall sealing the doorway was no match for Mr Savage's brute strength. He hammered away the brick wall almost effortlessly. Soon it was crumbling before him. Within minutes the brick wall had been reduced to rubble and a large hole stood in front of him. He chipped away the jagged edges until the doorway was restored.

By the time the demolition work was finished, the big room was filled with dust and the three teenagers were coughing away. Mr Savage threw down the axe and stepped into the dark room. The guard went in after him, carrying a hurricane lamp. There on the left of the room were row upon row of gold bars – three bars deep – each stacked neatly on top of the other. The gold stash was almost six feet high. The gold bars stacked up in the corner glowed warmly. The glitter of gold was simply irresistible to the two men. Their jaws dropped as they stared at their loot for almost a minute, not saying a single word in between.

'Give me the hurricane lamp,' Mr Savage said to the guard. He surveyed the gold bars in front of him. 'Wow! Let's see. Ten bars times three rows times ten columns times one hundred pounds each. Why, there must be about three hundred bars here totalling thirty thousand pounds of gold. What a treasure horde!'

'*Wah*! Is there really that much gold here?' asked the guard.

'Yes, really, Seah,' said Mr Savage. 'At today's price, this gold is worth more than $700 million dollars.'

'*Wah*! That much?' exclaimed the guard. 'We are rich! We are filthy rich.'

The two men spent the next few minutes fingering the gold bars and carrying some in their hands. Mr Savage took two bars out of the room and placed them on the table in the room. Then he sat back in a chair to examine them.

'The gold belongs to all people, and must be returned to the people,' said Jing Yang. 'Leave them alone.'

'Yeah! Don't lay your filthy hands on them,' said Tim.

'Hah!' retorted Mr Savage menacingly. 'That's right! We are the people; the gold belongs to us.'

'What shall we do with these nosy kids?' asked the guard. He had just stepped out of the treasure room, and was carrying a gold bar in his hands.

'Leave them here, of course,' said Mr Savage. 'No one will ever find them here – long after we are gone from here.' Then he laughed sinisterly.

'You are evil!' screamed Angelina, wiping away her tears. She had been crying and had now almost run out of tears. Jing Yang squeezed her back again.

'No point shouting at these men, Angelina,' said Jing Yang. 'They are incorrigible.'

'Yeah! Scum of the earth – they are,' agreed Tim.

'Go ahead!' said Mr Savage. 'Call me all the names you want to. Make yourselves happy – for the last time.'

'How are we going to get the gold out of here?' the guard asked Mr Savage.

'We?' said Mr Savage. 'You mean I.' With that remark, Mr Savage took the gold bar he had been handling in his hands and knocked the guard's head with it. The guard was taken unawares and fell off the chair. He lay dazed on the floor with blood oozing from his head.

'Look! They are fighting,' shouted Tim. 'They are fighting over the gold.'

'Let them kill themselves,' said Jing Yang.

Before the guard could gather himself together, Mr Savage walked over to him and lugged him by the collar to the wall. He knocked the man's head against the wall repeatedly. Screaming in pain, the guard searched his pockets frantically for something. Soon, he held in a hand a large paper cutter which he dug into Mr Savage's side. Mr Savage released his grip on the man, clutching his side and yelling in pain. He fell onto the floor and rolled over, writhing in pain. He was now bleeding in the abdomen. The guard took this chance to lift himself off the floor.

Then he lunged at Mr Savage with the paper cutter, piercing his chest with the paper cutter. Mr Savage screamed in pain as the blade penetrated his body. The guard tried to jab Mr Savage with the cutter again but this time the burly man managed to deflect the attack with his strong arms. The blade sliced into Mr Savage's arm and Mr Savage recoiled in pain. The injuries inflicted on Mr Savage were serious but this man was like a gorilla.

Mr Savage shrugged off the pain and attacked the guard who was only half his size. He punched the daylights out of the guard, sending him crushing to the ground. The paper cutter flew out of the guard's hands. The guard was now defenceless against the big man with strong arms. As Mr Savage was about to get near him, the guard grabbed hold of the hurricane lamp next to him and threw it at Mr Savage. Mr Savage warded off the projectile by hitting the lamp with his arm, sending the lamp flying into the room where the gold was.

The lit lamp landed onto the wooden crates in the room and suddenly there was a huge explosion. The flame from the hurricane lamp had ignited the old explosives in the crates. There were more explosions as the surrounding explosives ignited in succession, rocking the walls of the room, and sending concrete pieces flying all over the place. The teenagers were lucky, for the iron bars deflected the bigger concrete pieces. But, Mr Savage and the guard were not so lucky. Mr Savage took a direct hit from the explosions as he had been standing in front of the doorway when they went off. He was thrown against the other wall in the big room. He hit the wall and slid down onto the floor, lifeless. His back had been ripped apart. He had been decapitated; but his head was nowhere to be seen.

18 *CLINGING ON TO DEAR LIFE*

Water was now gushing into the two rooms. The explosions had ripped open the ceiling in the treasure room and water from the reservoir above it was now flooding into the room and flowing out into the big room. The three teenagers could not see where the guard was. The accompanying dust had blinded them momentarily and they had taken their attention off him. They had to look for him; he was holding the key to the metal cage they were in.

The strong walls in the big room had absorbed much of the impact of the explosion. The three teenagers were only grazed by flying pieces of concrete. They were not seriously hurt. But they were doomed. The water level in the big room was rising fast and there was no way out of the cage; they were sitting ducks in the cage waiting for death.

'Are you alright, Angelina?' asked Jing Yang. 'Tim?'

'Never better!' exclaimed his cousin. He was glad the man he nicknamed Monster had perished from the face of the earth. 'But the water is coming into the cage fast.'

'I know, I know,' said Jing Yang. 'I am thinking of a way.' Turning to Angelina, he asked again, 'Are you hurt?'

'Just a scratch on my leg,' said Angelina. Jing Yang had shielded her with his arms but in the confusion, he had forgotten about her legs. Still, she was better off than he was. He was hurt in both arms and legs. He was bleeding as he had been hit by some splinters.

'Look out for the guard,' said Jing Yang. 'He's our only hope out of here. He has the key to the padlock.' The three teenagers kept a keen eye on their surroundings. The murky water prevented them from seeing what lay on the floor. By now, the water level had reached their knees. The guard, if he had indeed died, could not be seen. There was nothing, except wooden remains of crates and chairs, floating on the water. Mr Savage's body or head was also not visible.

'If the water level goes up to our heads, we have to climb onto the horizontal iron bars to keep above water,' said Jing Yang. 'I think the guard is dead or he would have come back for the gold. We have to hope his body comes up to the surface soon.'

'How long do you reckon it will be before the water reaches the ceiling?' Tim asked.

'It took half-an-hour for it to come up to our knees. I would say three hours at most,' said Jing Yang.

'We have only got three hours to live?' said Tim in astonishment. 'But, I haven't enjoyed life yet. I don't want to die yet. I am only thirteen! I have a full life ahead.'

'Don't go making Angelina upset again,' said Jing Yang. 'For goodness' sake, she just stopped crying.'

'Where is all the water coming from?' cried Angelina.

'The explosions must have blown a hole in the ceiling,' said Jing Yang.

Jing Yang looked at his watch. It was now four o'clock. They had been in the bunker for more than six hours. It would be school time in four hours. They might not make it to school today. They just might not be able to attend school again. How he wished he had not dragged them into the mess they were in. At that moment, Jing Yang hated himself for letting his heart control his head. It was unwise of him to have poked his nose into this treasure thing. Now he regretted his actions. But, alas, it was too late for regrets. They were waiting for death – slowly but surely.

Tim was now fiddling with the padlock. Jing Yang waded to him to lend a hand. It was a heavy-duty padlock and they did not have the tools to break it open. The bayonet and the axe were somewhere in the room, submerged in water. They were helpless using just their bare hands. Tim shook the iron bars. Though the iron bars were seventy years old, they were as strong as they were the day they were installed. The British certainly did not stint on quality when they built the place.

There was nothing else they could do but wait, and hope against hope that somehow help would arrive. Perhaps, Angelina's mother had got tired of waiting for her to come home and had contacted Jing Yang's aunt. Just perhaps, they had figured out that Jing Yang, Tim and Angelina were in the bunker and were on their way over to search for them. And hopefully the secret door had been left open so their rescuers would come dashing down into the tunnel to save them from imminent death. Alas, it was wishful thinking.

At five o'clock, the water level was just above Angelina's waist.

When Jing Yang next glanced at his watch, it was now showing half past five. He looked at Angelina. The water level was reaching her chin. Jing Yang and Tim were about a head taller than her so they could stand where they were. But Angelina had to waddle in the water to keep her balance.

'Go to the iron bars. Cling on to them,' said Jing Yang to Angelina and Tim as he helped Angelina reach for the iron bars.

Now and again Jing Yang would duck underwater for a look, but he could not see beyond his hands in the muddy water.

Suddenly Tim was shouting excitedly. He was pointing at someone floating in the water near him. It was a body. It was not Mr Savage's, he was sure, for its head was attached to it. It was floating on its back.

'Quick! Go to that end of the cage and wait for it to come near,' said Jing Yang to Tim. Tim climbed along the iron bars to the corner of the cage. Jing Yang left Angelina's side to join Tim. The corpse was bobbing in the water, coming close to the two boys.

'Get ready to grab it,' said Jing Yang to Tim. Both boys stretched their hands out of the cage.

Jing Yang was queasy about touching the corpse, but he had no choice. Their lives depended on him being able to retrieve the key to the padlock. He closed his eyes and reached out to grab the body as it floated past him. He almost caught the body, but it bobbed in the water and turned away, moving towards the treasure room. Jing Yang kicked the iron bars. He blamed himself for being a coward. If he had kept his eyes peeled open when the body floated past him, he would have grabbed hold of it. Tim was shouting. He was angry at himself and Jing Yang for letting the opportunity slip. The corpse was now moving farther away from the cage, towards the far corner of the big room.

It was now quarter past six. The water in the room had risen to a depth of seven feet. Time was running out for the three teenagers. Soon, they would have to say goodbye to school, their friends, parents and all things that meant so much to them. If only they were given another chance, they would have done things differently.

Angelina was getting tired. She had been standing too long on an iron bar which ran horizontally across the length and width of the cage to give support to the cage. She needed to come down for a rest. But she could not. It was a watery grave that awaited her if she gave up. Fortunately, Jing Yang was always by her side, propping her up whenever she slipped off the iron bars into the water. Jing Yang had almost given up thinking of ways and means to get out of the desperate situation that they were in. He was now almost resigned to his fate, but he tried to keep a straight face so as not to alarm Angelina and Tim. It was now that they needed him most. It was also now that they would look to him for hope, for inspiration, he told himself. He had better not let his emotions get the better of him.

His watch gave the time as quarter to seven. It would have been time to go to school about now. At this time, they would probably be on the bus to Punggol. How he wished it was all a dream, that he would wake up to find himself, Angelina and Tim on the bus heading for school. But, he was awake now, and they were still in the secret room under the bunker.

Tim had grown tired of looking out for the guard's body and was resting his head against the iron bars of the cage. Jing Yang kept an eye on the corpse which had come to rest in the far corner of the wall. There was practically no chance of the corpse coming past them again.

Jing Yang held on to Angelina. The water level was now only one foot from the ceiling. In a matter of minutes they would drown. But they could not lose hope. Angelina was shivering from the cold and he was hugging her to share the warmth of his body with her. He wanted to rub her hands but he had no free hands to do so. His left hand was holding on to her and the other hand was gripping an iron bar so that he would not fall into the water. What made things worse was Angelina could not swim. Jing Yang was exhausted. So were Angelina and Tim. The adventure had drained them – physically and mentally.

Jing Yang thought of the spirits in the Fortress Commander's Office. He wondered what they were doing now. Soon, he, Angelina and Tim would be like Colonel Cooper and Major Todds, haunting the bunker, he told himself. But he didn't realise just how wrong he was, for that very moment an eclipse of the sun was taking place outside – in the open skies. The moon had almost blanketed the sun across the Asia Pacific region. The entire area suddenly plunged into darkness.

At the appointed time, the heavens opened and a bolt of light swooped down onto the earth, through the skylight of the escape stairwell, into the passageways of the bunker and entered Fortress Commander's Office. It penetrated the Godell prism, causing the crystal to glow with such force that it illuminated the entire room with its intense brilliance. The energy released from the Godell prism radiated into the two wax models which the spirits were in and warmed them. It gave them extraordinary power. They were suddenly alive – able to move their arms and legs. And for the first time when they talked, their mouths could move in sync with their speech. They could also blink! It was just awesome, but alas it was only temporary. Some six minutes later, when the eclipse of the sun had done its work, their internal strength would leave them and the wax models would become lifeless again.

It seemed they were alive again for a single purpose – to save the three teenagers. Was it fate that made this event happen? Or was it merely a coincidence that the eclipse of the sun and the impending death of the teenagers would take place almost simultaneously. Whatever it was, heaven was kind to the three teenagers, for the wax models which had taken on a life of their own would come to their rescue.

'By George, I can move. I can really move,' said General Percival's look-alike, standing up and stretching himself.

'Yikes! I can move too!' said General Simmons' look-alike. He looked around the room and then at the desk. 'Player's cigarettes – just my brand of cigarettes. Gosh! I haven't smoked for ages, I do declare.' He picked up the cigarette tin and opened it. 'Why, it's empty!' he exclaimed in surprise. He brought the tin to eye level and peered inside. 'It's really empty.'

'And my stubble's grown too long,' exclaimed General Percival's look-alike. He stood in front of the sink behind the desk and ran his fingers across the stubble on his chin. 'Now, where's the razor? Where's the mirror?' Then he opened the drawers of the desk, looking for a razor. 'We British officers must shave every morning, you know.'

The precious minutes ticked by. Did they not know they had been entrusted with a mission to save three youngsters from their impending doom?

'The crystal on the desk is glowing,' said General Simmons' look-alike. 'It wasn't like this last night.' Then he remembered the three teenagers. 'Sir, the three youngsters have not returned from the secret tunnel.'

'They haven't?' said General Percival's look-alike. 'Could they be in trouble? I saw those two men going into the secret tunnel too.'

General Simmons' look-alike walked to the opening behind him and looked down. 'Gosh! It's flooded in the tunnel, sir.'

'Is it now?' said General Percival's look-alike. He went over to take a look. 'You sure are right, Todds. The tunnel's overflowing with water. It's almost reaching the ceiling. It will come into this room soon. We'll get wet for sure.'

'Sir, the kids are still in the secret tunnel,' said General Simmons' look-alike. 'Has something happened to them? Should we take a look down there?'

'Oh yes, Todds,' said General Percival's look-alike. 'We had better take a look. Their parents would be worried sick if they don't return home soon. Let me go in first.' General Percival's look-alike sat on the floor next to the opening and removed his socks and shoes. Then he got ready to climb down the cat ladder.

'Oops! I forgot, I can't swim,' said General Percival's look-alike.

'Really?' said General Simmons' look-alike. He had

removed his peaked cap, socks and shoes, and was now waiting for his turn to enter the water. 'Haven't you forgotten we are no longer mortals on this good earth? It doesn't matter now whether we could swim or not when we were alive. Now, we can do practically anything we want to. We are – in a word, superhuman,' said General Simmons' look-alike. 'Go on, jump in. We have no time to waste, sir.'

General Percival's look-alike climbed down the cat ladder and stepped onto the landing. The water came up to his knees. General Simmons' look-alike followed closely behind.

'Are you ready, sir?' General Simmons' look-alike asked him.

'As ready as I can be,' General Percival's look-alike said.

'Let me go into the water first, sir,' said General Simmons' look-alike.

'No, let me take the lead,' said General Percival's look-alike.

The steps down into the tunnel were totally submerged in water. The two men waded down the steps and treaded in the water. They were taking too long; time was not on their side. In minutes they would lose possession of the wax body they were in and the three teenagers would drown.

'Sir, this is not the way to go into a rescue mission,' said General Simmons' look-alike. 'It's just too slow. Follow me. Do what I do, and quickly, sir.'

'Oh, alright, Todds, anything you say,' said General Percival's look-alike.

With General Simmons' look-alike in the lead, they dived into the murky water and sped through the passage into the big room within seconds. They had realised they were endowed with supernatural powers and were putting these powers to good use at last.

'There they are, sir,' said General Simmons' look-alike.

It was simply amazing. They were talking in the water.

The three teenagers were hanging on to life by a thread. The water had come up to their chins though they had climbed up to the top of the room and they could not go any farther – their heads were already touching the ceiling. They were having problems breathing as water kept getting into their mouths and noses. Angelina had already swallowed some mouthfuls of water and she was feeling sickly.

'Let me break open this padlock,' said General Percival's look-alike. 'You help the kids keep above water.' He took the padlock in his hands and pulled the shackle out of its body almost effortlessly. Then he opened the grill door and swam up towards the teenagers.

'Colonel Coopers will take you kids out of the cage,' said General Simmons' look-alike as he appeared above the water next to the teenagers. 'First, take a few deep breaths before you go underwater.' General Simmons' look-alike who was on the other side of the cage then released his grip on the three teenagers. They breathed deeply a few times, and at the word go, ducked into the water, accompanied by General Percival's look-alike. He guided them down to the opening in the cage and then up to the surface of the water. When they broke the water surface, they choked on water. They were too tired to focus on what they were doing.

'We need to do this one more time,' General Percival's look-alike said to the three teenagers. 'We need to go down again, swim through the doorway into the passageway outside. Are you ready?' The three teenagers nodded. Jing Yang held on to Angelina's side. He had to help her as she could not swim.

'Ready! Let's go!' said General Percival's look-alike. They all ducked into the water again, swam down to the doorway leading to the passageway, and resurfaced on the other side of the doorway. Jing Yang, Angelina and Tim gulped some water in the process. They were choking again when their heads emerged from the water.

'We made it! Time to swim back to the secret door,' said General Percival's look-alike. 'Todds, you lead the way, please.'

'Yes, sir,' said General Simmons' look-alike. 'Glad to do so, sir.'

The two soldiers and the three teenagers swam along the passageway towards the beginning of the tunnel where the secret door was located. Once or twice, Angelina and Jing Yang went underwater as they were too tired and the two soldiers had to push them up to keep their heads from submerging in the water.

'We are almost there,' said General Percival's look-alike. They were now about five feet away from the opening where the cat ladder stood. The two soldiers pushed the three teenagers towards the opening, holding them by their arms.

'Watch for the steps under the water. Stand on them and walk up to the cat ladder,' said General Simmons' look-alike. 'Go on, you can….' Suddenly life left the two generals' look-alikes. Jing Yang, Angelina and Tim were wadding up onto the steps next to the cat ladder when the two soldiers collapsed into the water and then bobbed up onto the surface of the water. They were now nothing more than rigid wax models. The two spirits had left their shells, for the eclipse of the sun had come and passed. It was now daylight again across the Asia Pacific region. The two spirits had left for another world – another dimension. Their mission on earth had come to an end.

The three teenagers had made it to safety, thanks to the spirits of Englishman Colonel Cooper and Australian Major Todds. Jing Yang, Angelina and Tim sat in waist-deep water on the steps, staring at the lifeless wax models. They owed their lives to these two chaps from another time – and another dimension. They were totally exhausted, but they could not stop thinking about these jovial and selfless spirits who had come to their rescue just when they thought they had come to the end of life itself.

'Colonel Cooper and Major Todds, thank you very much,' cried Angelina. 'We love you!'

'Colonel Cooper and Major Todds, we owe our lives to both of you,' yelled Jing Yang.

'Colonel Cooper and Major Todds, thank you from the bottom of our hearts,' said Tim.

It was a fitting sendoff for the ones whom the teenagers had met by chance here in the bunker, and whom they had befriended. Jing Yang, Angelina and Tim were in tears as they made a final pronouncement.

'Colonel Cooper and Major Todds – godspeed,' they shouted at once into the flooded passageway.

From the secret door opening above the three teenagers came some shouts. Someone or some people were calling their names. The voices were unfamiliar to them. Suddenly, some heads popped down from the door opening.

'Are you kids alright?' asked one of them.

'Come, let me help you up,' said another.

When they got out of the secret tunnel, they realised that two of these men were policemen and the third was the manager of the underground bunker. The men accompanied the three teenagers out of the front entrance into the lane outside where Tim's mother, Angelina's mother and brothers, and Mr Wang were waiting. Tim and Angelina rushed into their mothers' arms while Jing Yang recounted their adventure to Mr Wang.

The thirty-thousand-pound gold stash was turned over to the state, which in turn apportioned a sum of $200 million as compensation to the Far East Prisoners-of-War for their suffering and internment in POW camps in South-east Asia, and a sum of $20 million for the restoration of the Battle Box attraction. Jing Yang, Angelina and Tim were not left out. For their role in helping to discover the treasure, they were each awarded a certificate of appreciation and an all-expenses-paid scholarship tenable at a university of their choice, which they could activate when they entered university.

At a press conference to announce the grants, a government representative told the gathering, which included Jing Yang, Angelina, Tim, Aunt Dorothy and Mr Jonathan Wang, that the $20 million grant for a complete makeover of the Battle Box would be used for installing a spanking new air-conditioning system and the hardware and software for a complete museum guided tour system. There would be interactive display devices running on a broadband network which would remotely monitor and control all video presentations. Visitors would be able to manually playback different media on screens installed in the rooms of the bunker. Scheduling and automated powering up and down of displays could be done at the touch of a button. A spectacular mini-museum display with audio-visual content would also await visitors to the museum.

The entire system would include mannequins that could move and talk using animatronics, synchronised lights, voiced overs in headsets and speakers around the bunker and a state-of-the-art computerised system to integrate everything for a complete experience. But the locked room – the original Gun Operations Room – would remain locked and unused out of deference to the two soldiers who were killed in the room.

Jing Yang, Angelina and Tim were elated to hear the news that the Battle Box would be restored as a world-class museum, befitting the historical importance of the bunker. The bunker was closed now for repairs but when it reopened next year, the three teenagers would surely be the first in line to visit the Battle Box Museum as it would be known after the makeover. Colonel Cooper and Major Todds certainly did not sacrifice themselves in vain.

USE OF SINGLISH IN THE NOVEL

The author has used only a smattering of commonly used Singlish terms such as *wah*, *lah*, *aiyah, heng-ah* and *alamak* in the novel.

Angmoh	:	Caucasian
Aiyah	:	a moaning sound uttered to express regret
Alamak	:	similar in meaning to 'alas'
Heng-ah	:	similar in meaning to 'luckily'
Lah	:	added to the end of a sentence for positive emphasis
Pasar malam	:	Malay for night street market
Wah	:	similar in meaning to 'wow'

Some of the places mentioned in the novel do exist.

Montfort Secondary School and Greendale Secondary School are schools located in Hougang and Punggol respectively. The author taught English Language to upper and lower secondary students in Montfort Secondary School (2000-2004) and Greendale Secondary School (2008).

Punggol Plaza and Hougang Mall are shopping centres which serve HDB housing estates in the heartland. VivoCity is a shopping centre located next to Singapore Cruise Centre in Telok Blangah Road.

The Battle Box museum is a World War Two historical site which is visited daily by hordes of tourists and classes of students. It has a loyal fan base consisting of World War Two veterans and their families who make regular return visits to honour those soldiers who died fighting the war in Singapore and the region.

Also, an eclipse of the sun did take place across the skies in the Asia-pacific region in the early morning of 22nd July 2009.

Cover illustration by Raymond Han

(Model: Angelina Goh)